LOVE ON THE RANGE

Suddenly, he took her wrist in an iron grip and pulled her down to him. His breath on her face was heated, but not bad. He used the other hand to pull her close after he removed his hat. He looked so deeply into her eyes that she felt as naked as he was, as exposed. Then he captured her mouth with a kiss so fierce, so deep, that she nearly collapsed on top of him. A slow burn started deep in her belly, then, suddenly, she was free and she had to move quickly to get to her feet.

Best Man for the Job

Best Man
for
the Job

Susan C. Yarina

Long Meadow Romance

Best Man for the Job by Susan C. Yarina

© 2006 Susan C. Yarina
Published by Long Meadow Romance

For information on Long Meadow Romance, call 615/514-0173.

ISBN 1-933725-09-5

Design by Armour&Armour
armour-armour.com

First Edition 2006
1 2 3 4 5 6 7 8 9 10

1
The Challenge

CLAY CARTER WAS DOWN on his luck. Again. He spread out the precinct's copy of the *Arizona Republic* newspaper and rolled his shoulders to alleviate the pain from the old bullet wounds sprinkled down his back on either side of his spine. Tension always made them ache worse, and he was tense.

This damned desk job, he thought, *is going to kill me.* He had been put here ever since the shooting, the one that nearly took him out for good. The one that haunted him day and night and gave him cold sweats when he wasn't awake enough to put up his guard.

He didn't usually gamble, but since he had been shot, he just didn't seem to have good sense sometimes. The gambling and drinking had cost him big: his savings, his fiancée, his antique car, and worst of all, his self-respect.

Well, he had screwed up major-league this time. He owed his former partner over six thousand dollars. And he had just paid off rookie Ron Casey the four thousand dollars he had lost to him. He had to have a change, a place to heal, so he could get his head lined up again to where his emotions couldn't rule him. He spread out the paper and glanced at the classifieds. That's when he saw the ad.

"Wanted. Ranch foreman. Must have experience with rugged rangeland. Room and board and wages."

He knew the wages couldn't be much, because he knew ranching Arizona desert range land didn't return much, but at least he would be away from temptation, away from the drinking he couldn't seem to control anymore, away from the gambling that was getting a grip on him.

He dialed the number, listened to the message, and wrote the directions, time, and date down on a card that he carefully slipped into his wallet. He took a second to sip his hot, black coffee and smiled for the first time in a long, long time. He had hope. He was determined the job would be his even before he had dialed the number.

"IF I HAVE TO MAKE another blasted doughnut,

I might just die!" Lee Ann Waters muttered as she sprinkled yet another batch of doughnuts with powdered sugar. Doughnut baker was the latest in her string of minimum-wage jobs, and she was fed up with it already. She had to be up at four every morning and have the first batch in by five to satisfy the early morning customers. With care, she arranged the frosted confections in the front case, alternating them with the chocolate iced she had done earlier. With a flick of her thumb, she turned on the two massive, gleaming steel percolators that would provide the gallons of coffee her customers would require that day. The aroma of the rich, dark brew nicely cut the sickly, sweet smell that permeated the shop. The gleaming mound of off-white dough on the stainless steel worktable had risen and was ready to be punched down for one last kneading. This, she enjoyed! This, she could do. All of her frustration poured into the punch she delivered to the quivering mound. Was it just six months ago that her life had been right on track and she had been a busy, happy woman, traveling back and forth between her family ranch and her work with Pro Horseman Clinics exhibiting her training methods with horses?

Now, all of that was over. Pro Horseman Clinics had closed, because of financial and less-complicated reasons, bringing her training exhibitions to a halt. Her father and their ranch were gone. The Double H brand was theirs no longer, and the Two-Horse Ranch, situated in the High Sierra desert of Arizona, was a thing of the past. A large tear slid to the tip of an eyelash and hung there, quivering, in her peripheral vision. The light overhead was caught in it and sent a tiny, glistening rainbow to remind her of happier times before her father had died and she'd sold the ranch to pay off its debts.

Rainbows were Duke Waters's favorite sight, and Lee Ann had caught him many times, staring off in wonder at one arched over the high desert ranch on which she was born and raised. He would always say the same thing. "Lordy, honey, just look at that. If that isn't the prettiest of God's creation, I don't know what is." He had been her hero, and she hadn't found anyone who had even begun to measure up to him in her thirty years on this Earth. She started to wipe the tear away and was stopped by the gloves she wore to handle the food. The back of her wrist worked, though, to wipe away the evidence of her sorrow, just as the bell at the front door signaled someone coming in.

Her first customer breezed in, bringing the fuel-laden air of the city with him, and requested a glazed, with a large Java. He settled down to read to-day's copy of *The Arizona Republic*. Lee Ann rolled out dough and began cutting round shapes with a hole in the middle for the next batch of cake dough-nuts. These would be topped with white frosting and covered with little multi-colored sprinkles. She blew the errant wisp of blonde hair out of her eyes and slid the commercial-sized baking sheet into the massive maw of the stainless fronted oven, just in time to pull out another covered with risen dough-nuts that required glazing while hot. The hot pad slipped a fraction, causing her glove to melt to her skin in a tiny spot, which hurt like the very devil. As soon as she could set it down, she plunged her hand into the large ice bowl she kept on hand for just such occasions. No blister seemed to be forming. Not yet, anyway. It was definitely a hazard of the job, and her hands bore many such little purple marks in various stages of healing. Still, the job wouldn't be all that bad if it just paid the bills, but it barely paid the rent to her tiny studio apartment and put food on the table, much less the board and feed for the three mares she used in her training exhibitions. She had used the last of the ranch sale money to pay their board up through next week, and then she just didn't know what she was going to do.

SUSAN C. YARINA

After the doughnuts were glazed, she stepped to the counter to remove the paper, which she noticed was open to the want ads. She took off her gloves, wiped her hands on her apron, and held the ads up for a closer look. What could it hurt? She already had two jobs, counting the cosmetics she sold; why not three? Nothing interested her in the first three columns, but about halfway down the fourth column, her eyes lit on an ad that captured her imagination with its possibilities.

"Wanted. Ranch foreman. Must have experience with rugged rangeland. Room, board and wages." A phone number followed. From the area code, Lee Ann surmised it was in the Phoenix area, which surprised her. She wondered momentarily if it were one of those ranch/farm hybrid places with fenced pasture and irrigation, but decided that didn't fit the description of "rugged range land."

Curiosity got the better of her, and she dialed. By the end of the message that played, she was determined the position would be hers.

With the job of foreman, she hoped she could keep her horses there free, arguing that they would earn their keep, and, even with minimum wage, she could actually save money, if room and board were included as the ad said.

Lee Ann knew it would take good luck and a lot of grit to convince the owner that she was "man enough" for the job. So far, luck was with her. All the message had said was that anyone applying for the job should go out to where the forest road leading to the ranch came off Highway 60, on Saturday at six a.m., to meet with the owner.

2

See the Man

THE SUN SENT FINGERS of glowing pink, peach, and blue ahead of itself, reaching above the rugged frontage range of the Superstition Mountains, turning them from a forbidding gray mass in the pre-dawn to the purple mountain majesty of first light. Lee Ann took in the sight, along with a deep breath of the chilly air that flowed in through the side vent of her pickup truck's window, and sighed with pleasure. The drive had been long in miles, but not in time, because most of it had been freeway. She counted off the mileposts and soon came to the one before the forest road she should turn on. In the distance she could spot a tan, one-ton pickup. Her pulse danced a little jig as she reminded herself of her introduction speech. She recited it in her mind, a mantra to control the surge of adrenaline that even now threatened to make her nauseated. It was no good—as she drew nearer and began to be able to make out the features of the ranch owner, a surge of bile crawled up the back of her throat, threatening to gag her. So much rode on these next few minutes. If she couldn't get him to approve her for the job, she might have to send the mares to auction. She simply couldn't afford to keep them. Without this job, the future would look mighty black for sure, with all she had put into her training going with the mares off to auction, to some stranger who would do God-only-knew-what with them. She couldn't accept such a thing. She shook her head to clear it, straightened her spine, and stiffened her jaw as she pulled her truck off the road next to his. The first thing she saw as she stepped out of the truck were his eyebrows under his light tan cowboy hat as they flew to hide under the brim. She stuck out her hand in what she hoped was a firm gesture, and introduced herself.

"Hi!" She pumped the large, brown work-worn hand vigorously. "I'm here to see you about that foreman position."

The slight smile on the weather-beaten face of the six-foot-tall rancher disappeared. "Your husband couldn't come for himself?"

Lee Ann could feel her own smile drop as she enlightened him. "No, sir. No husband. Just me. I was born and raised on Duke Waters's spread, and I can rope, ride, and shoot with the best of them. I am not averse to shooting varmints of any kind and will protect your place with my life. I know how to inoculate, brand, and castrate with no help, if you have a squeeze chute, and can even preg-test cows."

A wry smile lifted one side of the man's mouth as he turned away to rub his hand over his clean-shaven jaw. At the last minute, she realized he was trying to hide a full-blown smile, and her heart surged with hope. At least he didn't dismiss her with no thought.

He shrugged out of his denim jacket and threw it onto his pickup's front seat. The sun was beginning to warm the air. He took so long to reply, she was tempted to add more to her list of accomplishments. "I train ..."

His upheld hand stopped her sentence. "And do you have a name, Miss ... ?"

It was her turn to grin as she looked down at her dusty boots and jammed her hands into her pockets to keep them from shaking. "Yes, sir. Lee Ann Waters, sir." Heat crept up her neck into her face, and she knew she was flushed with embarrassment. With a swallow, she lifted her eyes to his warm brown ones and assured him, "And I am the best man for the job."

"Looks to me," he said as he swiveled on his boot heel as he did a spin and took in the nearby traffic, "like you might be the only *man* for the job."

Her hands firmly knuckled on her hips, she elaborated. "Even if I wasn't the only one, I would be the best one. I could outwork any of Dad's hands from the time I was fourteen."

Again, he rubbed his hand over his mouth, wiping away a grin. "You don't remember me, do you, young'un?"

It registered on her fear-clouded mind that she hadn't really looked at him, hadn't even asked his name, really. She blinked to clear her vision and tried to place him. She tried to picture his wiry form as it might have been years ago when the silver hair could have been brown and maybe the bifocals had been missing. The image came to her. "Oh, my gosh. You're Charles Bruce. Charlie?"

This time the smile remained on the work-worn face. "You bet. How's your dad, Lee Ann?"

It still hit her like a sledgehammer, even though her dad had passed away six months ago. "He, uh, you hadn't heard?"

"Heard what?" He put out a hand to her shoulder to steady her as she swayed. "Hmmm?"

"Dad passed away over six months ago." She blinked furiously to keep the ever-present tears at bay. Now was not the time to cry. Suddenly, she found herself pulled into arms that reminded her so much of her father's that she could cry. And did.

"Oh, honey, I'm so sorry. I must have gotten further out of touch with Duke than I thought. I had been about to call him, too. I had heard at the auction last month that some Two Horse cattle had come through. Some good cows. Should have known Duke would never have sold off fertile four-year-olds if everything had been okay." He continued to hold her and pat her, as if she were one of his own daughters.

Lee Ann made a massive effort to control her muffled sobs and managed to quiet, but the tears continued to track down her cheeks one after the other like drops of water from a glass filled too full. She pulled back and nodded, lifting her head and taking a deep steadying breath. "Yeah. It all had to go. In his will, he instructed that I sell the Two Horse, to pay its debts."

"Oh, no. Most people might not understand how that cost you, but I do. That place had been in your family for generations, hadn't it?'

She nodded, wiping the tears dry. "Grandpa and Grandma Waters had homesteaded it. Back when good money could be made from beef."

"Those were the days." Charlie put his arm around her shoulders and swung them both around to face the Superstition Mountain range. "My spread is back there, about eight miles in. Forty deeded acres and about fifteen sections under graze lease. Do you really think you could handle it?"

"Hire me and let me prove it." The two stood companionably, looking at the rugged range ahead of them. "I've got three good mares I will need to have here to help me with the job, though."

"Good. Hope they are rock horses."

"They'll do whatever I ask of them, Charlie. They've got some special training on them." Just then a large green pickup pulled up in a cloud of dust and exhaust fumes.

GOOD, THOUGHT CLAY Carter, *he's still here. Looks like he's got his wife with him*. He swung his lanky legs over the edge of the bench seat and dropped to the ground. Holding out his hand, he hurried over to introduce himself.

"Howdy. I'm Clay Carter. I'm answering the ad,"

he said. "You the folks needing a foreman for your spread?"

The woman before him stood absolutely still and looked up into the older man's face with intensity. The man rubbed his jaw, then dropped his hand forward for a shake. "That's what I'm here for. Lee Ann and I were about to cash it in and head back to headquarters. I'm Charlie Bruce and I put the ad in the *Republic*. Back there is the Silver Rock Ranch," he hooked a large thumb over his shoulder, "some of the roughest range land that the good Lord ever made." He stepped over to the tan pickup and opened the door to the seat in the back of the extended cab. "Suppose you mount up, and we'll head back to headquarters."

"Sure thing." Clay made short work of locking up his truck and doing as the man he already called "Boss" in his head had asked. Somehow he levered his long legs in without making a fool of himself in front of the pretty green-eyed blonde who neatly negotiated the step-up on the running board and settled onto the high seat.

The forest road to the ranch was full of potholes, washboard, and barely submerged boulders. It snaked around hills and arroyos and drove through creek beds full of river rock big enough to break horse and cattle legs alike. Clay tried to imagine what it would be like to negotiate a fast-moving cutting horse up some of the rocky crags that loomed all around the lower flats, if you could call the hills and arroyos flats.

He focused on some of the slopes and realized he could see cattle and game trails along most of them. A pretty fragrance wafted back to him, and he wondered if it was from the pink blossoms on some of the stunted desert trees that he saw scattered here and there. Seemed like all the trees were in bloom. One kind of tree had green bark and yellow blossoms dripping off its fern-like branches. He would have to find out the names for the different trees and all. Didn't look to him like much could even live on this land, let alone thrive, yet here and there, scattered into small groups, he saw cattle, fat cattle. The bulls looked good, heavy with muscle and ripples of fat. Their black or red hides shone in the bright sun, and calves scampered around mothers whose bags were heavy with milk.

He noticed Charlie's wife looking around with the same open curiosity evident on her face. He thought that a little odd. Just then a huge white and tan speckled bull leaped down off a rise to the right of the truck. Charlie braked hard and yanked the truck to the left. As the cloud of dust settled, the huge shape loomed closer. It lowered its massive head, decked out with some of the longest sharpest horns Clay had ever seen, and shook them threateningly. To his surprise, Charlie opened his truck door and ejected himself toward the monster.

"Dang you, Trouble! One of these days I'm not going to be able to stop in time. Now git!"

Clay watched in awe as the man faced the beast, took off his hat, and started swatting the big speckled face with it. The bull's response was to moan and step closer to Charlie. Lee Ann let out an explosive breath as Charlie reached over and patted the bull between the eyes, then followed up with a scratch or two under its jaw, which seemed to put the bull right into slobbering ecstasy.

"Oh, Lordy," she breathed, "I thought Charlie was a goner for a minute there." Turning to face Clay in the seat, she went on, "Must be a hand-raised bull. I heard they do that with Longhorns sometimes, to make them tractable." Abruptly, she giggled. "Looks like they might have overdone it with that one."

Charlie took to swatting the massive brute again with his hat, and this time, though complaining in a mournful bawl, it moved off into the brush on the low side of the road. Charlie hopped up onto the seat muttering, "Spoiled, spoiled rotten."

Lee Ann laughed. "I'll say. Was he bottle raised?"

"Just a mite too long, if you ask me." He turned in his seat, "You okay back there?"

Clay nodded and forced himself to relax. He wasn't sure if he was tense because of the bull, or because when the woman in the front seat smiled at him, his heart had plum dropped to his toes, then shot like a rocket to his throat. Her smile did something incredible to her face, and he knew right then and there that he would do all he could to see it again. He knew it wasn't right—she was another man's wife—but he would do it just the same. The rest of the way to headquarters, he studied her profile when she turned to Charlie in conversation. He became aware somewhere along the way that the perfume he smelled wasn't the trees's, it was Lee Ann's. If she were single, he would have asked her what it was.

Several cattle gates later, headquarters of the Silver Rock Ranch came into view. A long, low, adobe ranch house sat at the center of the whole operation. A frame bunk house sat to the west of and behind it. A stone pump house nestled near a creek densely shaded with cottonwood trees along both sides.

Between the house and the pump house a low red barn with hitching posts sprawled, with the corrals and cattle chutes attached to it. Just the other side of the creek and trees loomed ragged tall crags that Clay swore could rival some he'd seen in his home state of Colorado. Of course, there, it would be pine trees sprinkled up and down the slopes, not saguaro cactus. Come to think of it, there were *lots* of cactus. All kinds. As he climbed out of the back seat of the pickup, he noticed, when he got a branch in the face, that even the trees had thorns on them.

He followed suit when the boss stamped his feet on the mat in front of the door. Dust obligingly fell off in a puff. Charlie motioned Lee Ann in first. Clay got an image in his mind's eye of the older man carrying her over the threshold, and it really got his goat. So many of these older cowboys had young chicks, he'd noticed. He just shook his head as he swept off his own cap and hung it on a peg just inside the door. Not for him. He liked women his own age, preferably someone he could have an intelligent conversation with. And no matter how pretty she was, the woman who seated herself at the oak kitchen table in the great room had shown no signs of great intelligence, so far.

"What did you think of the place, what you

could see of it, as we came in?" Clay realized the question was aimed at him.

"Oh, uh. It looks rugged. That's certain. Looks like most everything can poke, pinch, and stick ya." When Charlie nodded, Clay went on, "And barren. What is it your stock eats?"

With a deep chuckle, Charlie settled himself into a chair. He poured them each a cup of coffee from the pot he'd taken off the back of the stove. "It's still warm. Anyone need anything to doctor it with? No? Okay then. Aw, well, there's plenty out there this year. A little farther in off the road, you'd find grass under the trees and scrub. These are range cattle, half-wild, and they can exist on what's there and thrive on what might kill pasture beef. So, if it's out there, and it's green, they eat it. All this explainin' makes me wonder, boy, where you're from and why you think you can run this place?"

"I was born and raised on my granddad's place up outside of Silverton, Colorado. This land might take getting used to, but I think cattle are about the same everywhere." He slid a glance and a smile to Lee Ann. "Except for that speckled bull maybe. He's a mite different."

"I keep him here for a friend of mine. Isn't anything but a big ol' pet. Why, Jack paid a million dollars for that bull. Used to give me heartburn when I thought about anything happening to him. But Jack told me to just forget he was here, that he'd be no trouble at all. But he's nothing but. Eats clothes off the line, fights with every bull I own, makes speckled calves with my good Angus-Saler crosses. Well," he seemed to catch himself, "so we have two ranch-raised youngsters here then."

Clay looked around. "Two? Who would be the other one?"

"Why, Lee Ann here."

"You mean, your wife was raised on a ranch, too?"

"Lee Ann? She's not my wife." Charlie chuckled and shook his head.

"You're not? Then, who . . . ?"

Lee Ann stood and held out her hand. "Lee Ann Waters. I'm your competition!"

3

Let the Race Begin . . .

"BUT, BUT YOU'RE A woman!" Clay sputtered.

With a smile full of sass, Lee Ann countered, "I'm so glad you noticed." And she was glad, she realized, 'cause he was one heck of a good-looking cowboy.

He stood up partway as if he were hobbled or something, and his forehead creased with worry. She wanted to brush the little lock of wavy black hair off his forehead and smooth away his worries. *Get a grip*, she told herself. *He's the competition.*

"Are you going to allow this?" He aimed his question right at Charlie, who sat looking as if this conversation had nothing to do with him.

"I just might. Now, sit back down. You look like a new calf seeing the branding iron for the first time."

Lee Ann thought the look that swept over

Clay's face at that remark was darn cute, but she wasn't about to dwell on that. "*Allow* this?" Sarcasm dripped off her words.

"Well, I mean ..." Hiding his confusion, Clay took a brisk sip of coffee and promptly choked on it, nearly spraying himself and everyone else. Somehow, he managed to yank a red bandanna out of his jeans pocket and catch the result. His face turned a dull, dark red and sort of stayed that way.

Lee Ann noticed Charlie took the opportunity to continue the interviews, which had taken such a twisted turn.

"I know pretty much why Lee Ann here can run this place. We had a pretty good talk before you got here. Which reminds me, why were you late? I can't abide with lateness, just a personal pet peeve of mine."

"Oh. I'd like to apologize for that." Clay's gaze held the older man's. Lee Ann had to give him credit for that.

"Apology accepted. Now, why did it happen?" Seems Charlie wasn't going to be put off the trail.

"I uh, well, I hate to admit it, but I got lost. I, um, overshot the milepost and went quite a ways before I realized."

Mercilessly, Lee Ann pounced on the detail she

had noticed. "But you came in from the town side. You don't mean to say you missed it twice?" She couldn't believe it, but he *could* turn a darker red. This time his gaze fell to his hands, clasped on the table.

"Oh, oh. And I just bet you never did stop for directions." She chortled, "Just like a man!" His clasped hands gripped tighter, and his knuckles turned white. She did notice that he had nice solid working hands and swallowed a little when she saw how white the knuckles were. She sank to her chair then, wondering if she had gone too far with the gray-eyed stranger. Who knew? Maybe he had a violent temper and was about to go postal on her. She checked to see Charlie's reaction to her words.

"That's enough, Lee Ann. I'm the one doing the interview here."

She about spouted off something about men and their macho refusal to ask for directions when she caught the jut of Charlie's jaw and decided he meant business. Mortified, she sat still. After all, the man had a right to conduct business his way. "Yes, sir."

"Now. Suppose you tell me what it is that you have done up 'til now with your life, son?" Elbows on the table, he steepled his fingers and focused on the younger man.

"Like I said, I was raised on Granddad's ranch, and I learned everything I needed to know to run it, 'cause that was Granddad's plan, you know, that I take over for Pa and him. But when I turned eighteen, I decided I'd had enough of the great outdoors. I wanted something more exciting."

"Life dull on your spread then?" Charlie seemed to take mild exception to this.

"Seemed so to me, sir. At the time." Clay forced his hands to open and flexed them a bit.

"And just what did you take up in the big city, then?"

She wasn't sure, but Lee Ann thought maybe there was a little derision in Charlie's voice. *Good.* She focused on Clay to see if he could redeem himself.

"I went to the Academy of Police Sciences and graduated at the top of my class, sir."

It seemed he could. Lee Ann sat back, deflated. *So much for him being an incompetent,* she thought. She cracked her knuckles as she always did when she was vexed. And she was vexed.

Both men turned toward her and stared at her hands. "Doesn't that hurt?" Clay seemed concerned.

"Nope." Didn't take much to distract these two, she noted.

"Like police work, do you?" Charlie persisted.

"Yes, sir. It was a great life."

"Lee Ann, why don't you take a look down to the barn and see where you might keep those mares of yours?" Lee Ann jumped up, smiled, and "Yes sirred" her way out the door. Outside, she paused and sucked in the early spring air until it hit her that she had just been dismissed. Shrugging, she headed for the low red barn. She didn't know quite what to think now. The first thing she'd thought when Charlie had told her to see where she wanted to put her horses was that the job was hers, that he had made his choice. Then she remembered he had said, "*might* keep her horses." Her brisk walk slowed to a dispirited shuffle.

"Shoot," she said to no one in particular. "I don't have the job any more than he does." A few steps outside the barn, she was met with a silent snarl pasted onto the face of one of the ugliest, biggest mutts she had ever seen. Years of experience around animals brought her to a stop. She squatted so as to not seem threatening and held her hand out like she didn't really care if he sniffed it or not. Sure enough, he relaxed and his stiff gray fur fell back to its usual disarray. The stub of his tail wagged just once, and she knew she was in.

She stood and wandered into the barn followed by the big dog with "Bum" etched onto his leather collar. Her hand fell to scratch behind the upright ears as she looked around. The main aisle was wide, long, and had at least forty stall doors, twenty to each side. Most of them stood empty, she noted as she strolled along. A few had some good-looking Quarter horses in them, and a few had some older horses that had clearly worked hard for a lot of years. Midway down, she found the tack room and supply room. At the end of the aisle, hay was stacked floor to ceiling. She pulled a stem and was pleased with the crisp way it broke when she bent it; that meant it had been dried properly. Nice green dry leaf fell off the stem, but not too readily, which meant it was this year's cutting. She couldn't see much blueweed, so the cutting was probably the crop's second. Well, if this were what her mares would get, it would make her a happy girl.

"No use counting your chicks before they're hatched," she cautioned herself. Lifting a huge bin lid, she found the bran and in a second the oats to round out a working horse's diet. Still accompanied by Bum, she stepped out the back barn door into the bright sunlight. Her cowboy hat shaded her from the worst of the glare. She stepped through the pole pen's front gate, careful to close and latch it after her, and took stock of the layout. A number of various sized pens all came, one way or the other, off a main aisle that ran straight to a huge holding pen with loading shoots at one end. Each pen had concrete waterers built to hold up to the rough traffic of a herd of cattle and horses.

Above, a windmill screech-screeched, setting a rhythm with the wind that belonged to this place just like traffic noise belonged to the city. Except for that and the occasional lowing of the cattle nearby, it was absolutely quiet. Ah, how she had missed the quiet these past few months. Could this place be her salvation? She shivered with nerves when she thought of the fact that the cowboy inside Charlie's house could be convincing him that he was the best man for the job.

"Over my dead body," she shouted as she sped back through the gates and the barn aisle, with Bum gleefully bouncing along behind her. Just outside the front door she caught her breath and quietly stepped in. Apparently, she made no noise, because neither of the men looked up. Charlie was nodding as Clay finished his sentence.

"... so, you see, I need this job, badly." The rugged strong features of the profile of the younger man before her struck Lee Ann. Her heart did a queer little leap in her chest, and her pulse sped up. She told herself that her reaction was just her nerves, because so much was at stake.

"I have to ask this then . . ." Charlie probed. "How long would you be willing to stay? I mean, until you get over the shooting and then you're done with me and my place?"

"Shooting?" she gasped. "I mean, never mind. I'm interrupting. I'll just step right back outside." Her right hand flew to a spot at the base of her throat where she could feel her pulse jump against her skin like a trapped bird while her other hand found the door knob.

Rising, Clay tipped his head as if he had a hat on. "I don't mind if you stay." He pulled back a chair close to him and indicated with a smile that she sit there.

If he were a killer, he was a friendly killer. She seated herself, ready to fly if he acted oddly at all. He reached forward to grab her coffee cup, and she nearly jumped out of her skin. Solemnly, he placed it before her and poured the cooling coffee from the pot.

"You always such a flighty little filly?" The corners of his steel-gray eyes crinkled in amusement. Whatever they had talked about had helped him regain his footing, she noticed. He seemed very sure of himself now. As his slightly woodsy-spicy fragrance overrode the coffee's to waft up her nose, goose bumps sprinkled themselves up and back down her arms. If he were a killer, he was a very attractive killer. He didn't take his eyes from hers, and she seemed powerless to drop hers. A long moment passed, and then Charlie broke it.

"I have a proposal." The blonde and dark heads both swiveled his way.

"I want to hire both of you."

"What?" Lee Ann could tell Clay was as stunned as she was.

"Just for a while." Fingers still steepled, the boss man's gaze rested on the rough-hewn beams above. "I can afford you both, for a while. Seems to me you are equally qualified."

"A woman foreman?" Disbelief dripped off Clay's question.

Charlie's front chair legs previewed his thoughts as they hit the ground, and he fixed them both with a stare. "You *both* have to prove yourselves. No quarter given. At the end of the month, I'll make my decision, granting that both of you still want the job."

Lee Ann was first to her feet, hand out. "Thank you, sir. You won't be sorry, boss. No, sirree."

Clay followed a little more slowly. "You can count on me, sir. I give you my promise."

For a moment, Charlie paused, eyeing the younger man thoughtfully. "Yes, you did. Let's see that you stick to it." Unspoken communication passed between the two, and, for the second time that day, Lee Ann wondered what had been talked about.

"You'll sleep here with me, Clay, and Lee Ann will have the privacy of the bunkhouse. That suit you both?" He stood and pushed in his chair, ending the interview.

"Suits me. How 'bout you, Blondie?"

"The name is Lee Ann, buster. And I guess it will have to do." She didn't like it. She didn't like it one bit. He would have more time to talk to Charlie, to influence him. Drat! She would just have to find time, make time. One way or the other, she would make equal time. No time like the present to start. "Meals?" She looked around for evidence of a cook.

"I've had to learn to be a fair hand at chow since Florence died three years ago. If you think you can stand it, I'll cook breakfast at five a.m. and dinner at six p.m. Otherwise, you're welcome to fix your own. All I ask is, when you see we're getting low on supplies you write it down on that notepad by the door."

"Sounds good to me, but my Dad thought I was a good cook, and I sure could spell you now and then." Lee Ann swiveled on her boot heel to face Clay, body language shouting, "One for me."

Clay offered, "I do all I can to boil water and heat TV dinners, so I'll be plum happy to take you up on your offer, both of you." He fixed her with a stare and finished spitefully, "Even if it means I have to finish up your work on the outside."

She knew her lower lip pouted out as she thought, *One for Clay.*

As for Charlie Bruce, he rocked back and forth on his heels and chuckled. "I can see this month is going to be an interesting one here on the Silver Rock. How soon can you both start?"

Clay's voice joined hers in unison as she nearly shouted, "Monday!"

"Well, then, I guess the next order of business is to get you each a set of keys." Keys jangled as Charlie took them off the peg by the door and walked over to a large oak roll-top desk, where he inserted one into a locked drawer. Like a hound on a trail, he hunted until he found the two bunches he needed, then handed them over. "Don't go losing those; I don't have any more spares. You oughta be able to tell which key goes where by eyeing the locks. Rule is, leave everything the way you found it. If it's locked, leave it locked; if it's unlocked, leave it . . . well, you catch my drift. Lee Ann here has stock horses. You?"

Lee Ann watched while Clay took a moment, as if he couldn't quite remember if he had these thousand-pound animals laid around somewhere or not. It made her grin.

"Can't remember where you laid your ponies, cowboy?" He looked up as if he had been stung. His gray eyes took on a green hue, like a tornado sky.

"'Course I remember. I was just tryin' to think how I could get 'em down here."

"By horse trailer?" she offered just to get him.

"Whoa, there, you two. Another proposition. You don't need to bring down any stock. I've got a slew of two-, three-, and four-year-olds out there that need trainin' up. You two willing?"

Lee Ann rubbed her hands together. "Just happens to be right up my aisle, Boss. I'll be glad to."

"Want us to start with the four-year-olds?" Clay stepped forward.

"Sure. They'll hold up to hard work right away. Good idea."

Charlie led the way back out to the truck, and

Clay whispered near her ear, "I'll be sure to show you which ones the four-year-olds are."

God, if she could help herself. Lee Ann stuck her tongue out at him and chuckled as the branch of the thorn tree smacked him for the second time that day.

4

... And May the Best Man Win

ALL DAY SUNDAY, CLAY worried and mulled, mulled and worried over how he was going to explain to the Chief that he couldn't come in Monday, that he'd taken another job. And here it was Monday, he was about two minutes from the station, and still he didn't have a clue what he could say. Further, he knew if it went badly and the Chief ordered him to stay, he would. He had developed the habit long ago of not burning his bridges. What could he have been thinking? You don't just walk out on a job without notice, and worse, he didn't even have the ranch foreman position yet, not really. He parked the patrol car and walked in to his desk. He was still shaking his head when Chief Brogan walked by. He got up to follow, and in the next two steps he knew what his strategy would be. He always had worked best under pressure.

"Chief Brogan, I need to speak to you."

The tall man in blue paused as he inserted the key to the door of his office. "Yes, Carter? What is it?"

"I'm sure you know I've been having trouble adjusting to the shooting."

The chief sucked in a deep breath and sat. "I got the report from our psychiatrist yesterday. It's good you came in . . ."

"Well, good. 'Cause I think I have a solution. In fact, I'm sure of it, sir."

"Why don't you let me tell *you* what the department has come up with first?" The grin on the chief's face was downright unusual, in Clay's experience. But there was no doubt; it *was* a grin plastered on his ugly mug.

"Ooo-kay." No telling what was coming next.

"You're a good cop, Carter, but I know you're having some personal problems. However, in this precinct, we don't back out on an officer in need of assistance."

Damn, this is getting spooky. Clay just listened, afraid of what came next.

"We took a vote and decided. We're sending you on an all-expenses-paid week in Cancun."

"To—to where?" Clay's mind reeled.

"Cancun. Mexico. Surely, you've heard of it? Sand, sun, bikinis, good food, fishing, parasailing?"

For a long moment Clay wrestled with temptation, until a certain face loomed in his mind's eye. A face with a tongue stuck out at him. Lee Ann Waters's face.

"Naw, Chief. Sounds good. Too good. How can the department afford it?"

"The guys all pitched in. Can you believe it?"

"Yeah. Trouble is, I can." He twirled the pen on the desk between the two of them. "But I can't take it. Truth is, I'm already committed somewhere else."

"What?"

"And I have to leave in just a few minutes to get there on time."

"What?" This time the word seemed a lot less friendly.

"A ranch, sir. I took the position of foreman." Well, he *had,* in a way. "And I start this morning."

All traces of the smile had fled his superior's incredulous face. "You had better explain."

For the next few moments Clay bared his soul to the man before him, and being accustomed, as he was, to keeping everything to himself, it left him shaken and vulnerable.

Chief Brogan got up and walked the length of

his office back and forth. He paused with his hands resting on the back of his chair, as if he needed something solid to hang onto. "Hard work. You up to it?"

"Yeah, I am."

"Done this before?"

"Yep."

"Be able to handle it?"

"Yes, sir. I was raised on my granddad's spread in Colorado."

"So this might be a time for you to, uh, sort of, get back to basics then."

"I believe so, sir."

The next thing Clay knew, the chief had walked out from behind the desk and offered him his hand. "All right, Carter. If this doesn't work out for you, I want you back here. Got it?"

Stunned, Clay accepted the handshake. "You're saying I still have a job here, sir?"

"That I am, Carter. Even with your problems, you're still one of my best men, and don't you forget it."

"I'M THE HAPPIEST girl, in the whole USA!" sang Lee Ann as the wind whipped her hair into a tangled mess through the open truck window. She leaned forward to better see around the snowbird, or "winter visitor," as the chamber of commerce liked to call them. This one was going about thirty in the fifty-five mile an hour speed zone. Even that couldn't get under her skin today. She waved cheerily at the gray-haired driver as she pulled the truck and trailer around the slower vehicle with a speed that belied the weight of truck and the four-horse trailer that it pulled. She checked quickly in the side mirrors of her pickup to see if the trailer was staying stable. It was. And she could still see two heads through the frosted windows in the front of the stock trailer. That meant that two out of her three mares were still standing. Good enough for her. She stepped on the accelerator, and the last few miles to the ranch road flew by as she continued her song, the first one she had sung in the past six months, she realized. "It's a zippity do dah day. I'm the happiest girl . . ."

The song died on her lips as she spied a green truck already high-tailing it down the forest road ahead to the Silver Rock spread. Here she was, a good hour early, and he had gotten here before her. Drat and damn. And there was no way she could beat him now, because she couldn't haul her horses down that rough road with any speed at all, or it could break their legs. She took a deep breath and lifted her foot off the accelerator as she braked and turned onto the forest road. Clay's truck was a mere speck in the distance. She banged her hand on the dashboard. "Shoot!"

By the time she pulled into the headquarters yard and over to the barn, Clay's truck was parked and empty. Lee Ann pulled the truck and trailer in a U and proceeded to back into the barn. Her heart nearly leapt out of her chest when a wail rose that could wake the dead. For one god awful moment she thought she had hit something or someone. She was out of the cab in a flash, only to see Bum come stalking forward with a snarl, grumbling and griping in dog fashion, all the way.

"Good gravy, hound. You scared ten years off me easy." She turned to get back into her truck and almost ran into Clay Carter.

"I figure that makes you about eighteen, then." His grin was infuriating this early in the morning.

"Not even on a good day, cowboy," she snarled, her good humor gone. She got up into her cab and continued to pull back.

"My, my. Had your coffee yet?" He motioned her back.

"'Nother foot or so. There. That's it. Stop." He held up his hand.

She jumped out to check the position of the trailer and saw red. The trailer was right up to the hitching post. She couldn't unload the horses if she tried.

"Little too close, Lee Ann," Charlie walked up with a piece of note paper in his hand.

She felt the slow burn creep up her neck that signaled her face would be beet red. Without so much as a good morning she stomped back to her cab and crawled in, pulling the three-feet-plus forward that unloading would require. After she got out she acknowledged her superior. "Good morning, sir." She paused to check the time. "I'm here a little early."

"It's okay. This character already got me out of bed."

Lee Ann knew better. The boss was up, shaved, and fed, she was sure of it. Already there seemed to be an easy camaraderie between the two she hated to see. "I see. Where would you like my mares?"

"Makes no never-mind to me, Lee Ann. Put 'em where you see fit. Though for our piece of mind, not next to Booger, the stallion on the far end. He'd just as soon go through a wall for a mare as go round it."

Never trusting a stallion had kept Lee Ann in

one piece more than once. Hormones did strange things to horses sometimes. A mare in heat was another thing to watch. "I'd just as soon as have them up on this end if you don't mind, then."

"Sure thing. Here's the list for today. I'll try to have one for you each morning. I kept it light today. Maybe you'll have some time to settle in later." With a wave he crossed over the dusty yard to his pickup. "I'm going into town for some supplies. I'll be back in about four hours."

She glanced at the list and felt Clay at her back, peering over her shoulder to read it. Suddenly, she was aware that they were alone, in the middle of a ranch, in the middle of a huge wilderness. The sheer size of the man behind her was not lost on her. Her hand shook slightly as she read aloud. "One: Clean out stock tank in the upper corral. Two: Mend front gate. Three: Feed stock in back pens. Four: Take inventory of barn equipment and note repairs. Five: Ride flats and bring in any unpaired calves. Six: Castrate young bulls." She finished. "I guess that this means we've got about two minutes to settle in." She turned to face him and handed him the list.

Clay grinned at her and tipped his cowboy hat back on his head. "You're wastin' daylight, darlin'. Need help unloading those mares?"

The gate on the trailer required its usual pounding with the heel of her hand before it swung open with a screech. Her mare Star swung her nicely muscled rear away and angled so she could blink at the two of them with her big brown Bambi eyes. Lee Ann stepped in with her, crooning, "No, we don't need any help from the big, strong man, do we, sweetheart?"

The mare bobbed her head as if in perfect understanding and followed her out, stepping down regally as if she owned the place. She trumpeted a greeting to any that could hear and was rewarded with a shrill scream and thump from the direction of the barn, the stallion end.

"What have you got here?" Clay's hand stroked the silky buckskin hide. "She looks like a Colorado Quarter horse."

Lee Ann couldn't keep the pride out of her voice. "She is. Bred for the mountains. She was a present from my father when I turned twenty. Her hooves are iron, and she has legs to match. She's my oldest." Giving a tug on the lead, she headed for the barn. With a quick look around in the dim light, to be sure the stall had no unwanted inhabitants, she opened the half-door and unbuckled the halter. The good mare stepped on inside, like Lee Ann knew she would.

Clay came up and leaned on the door with her to watch while the mare circled her surroundings with nostrils flared, until finally she sighed and took a deep drink out of the waterer. "Breeding?"

"You can't tell?"

"Kiger Mustang a-ways back, I'd guess." He took his hat off and ran his hand over his head, making the shiny black hair more unruly, not less. A lock fell forward, causing Lee Ann to reach to smooth it. Before he could guess what she was up to, she redirected her hand to her own hat, which she took off.

"Yeah, that part's easy. What else?" Over the hay smell, she scented him. Her stomach clenched as excitement hit her. Unnerved, she stepped away to get the other mares. He stayed right behind her.

"Maybe some Poco Bueno? Doc?" He reached up to release the outside latch to the inner gate of the stock trailer for her.

"Thanks." She stepped up and swung the inner gate open, then latched it there. She patted the larger gray on the rear. "Move over, Mickey. Let me get your lead." The quick release on the tie bar stubbornly refused to yield, so she took a deep breath and tried again. She sneezed, the quick release worked, and Mickey jerked back, all in rapid succession. Only by scrambling and hanging shamelessly onto the halter for leverage did she keep from falling on her keister. Mickey objected to the weight with a head toss and a snort. That was what put her down.

"Need a hand, buckerette?" A large brown hand hovered in front of the pair of hooves and boots in her immediate line of vision from where she sat in the dirt.

She grabbed that hand and yanked unnecessarily hard to gain her feet. "Buckerette? What the heck . . . ?"

"Don't know. The word just came to me as I watched you dangle for a minute off that mare's head then drop to the dust. Just came to me." His grin was evil.

Lee Ann came as close to flouncing that day as she ever had in her life. With mare in tow, she quickly set her up in the stall next to Star.

"Do I get to guess about this one too?"

She whirled to face him with hands on hips. "Why not, buckaroo?" She waved her hand in the air as if to dismiss his question. "Don't know, just came to me . . ."

"I'd say Gray Badger."

"You would?" She cocked her head to get a better look at him. "Why does everyone assume a gray horse comes out of the Badger?"

He peered over her shoulder to get a better look into the stall, it seemed. Lee Ann noticed his hard chest pressed against her back, and his hands sort of accidentally settled on her hips. She shoved back with her rear, not thinking of where she might hit him.

He did step away, with a strange look on his face. "I'm wrong?"

"On both counts, mister. She's not out of Badger, and I'm not easy."

"Hey. *I* didn't say you were easy."

"No. But your wanderin' hands sure did." She stomped back out to the trailer where the last mare stood shifting restlessly back and forth in the trailer. The lead released easily, and the mare backed out quickly. "Easy, Sugar." The sun sparkled off the golden mare with such brilliance that she had to turn her head away to get her eyes to adjust before she stepped back into the barn. He was there where she left him, still with a silly look on his face.

"Wow!" He ran his hand over the mare's golden arched neck and lifted a strand of the silver mane. "What a lovely lady you are."

Smacking his hand down, she passed him and whisked her prettiest mare into the stall across from the other two. "She doesn't like being handled by strangers, either."

"Hoo-oo. Snobby ladies, both." He backed away, hands held in the air. As he left toward the stallion end of the barn, she could barely hear his last remark. "And she is a Sugar Bars baby, or I have lost it entirely."

The halter buckle opened easily, and Lee Ann patted the pretty mare a second before she headed for the feed manger. "Well, maybe he hasn't lost it entirely, has he, sweetheart? Your great-great-grandfather *was* Sugar Bars." Stepping back into the breezeway, she carefully latched the half-door to the stall. She could just barely hear the conversation Clay was having with the big stallion at the end of the lane.

"They may be snobs, Booger, but I think they might be worth the trouble, old boy."

She already suspected his feelings weren't hurt easily. Now she was sure of it. And arrogant? Most definitely, which could, just maybe could, be used against him. How did that old saying go? Pride goes before a fall?

CLAY WATCHED AS LEE ANN pulled her truck to line up with the others in the ranch yard. She did a good job of it, leaving the trailer in one row, then parking the truck in another. He noticed she hadn't blocked any of the other vehicles and had left everyone plenty of room.

The easy, feline grace with which she jumped down from the truck and strode toward him sent his libido up an awareness notch. Her glistening blonde hair seemed alive as it floated about her in the morning's errant breezes. Even from here, he could see the spiky black lashes that framed her emerald-green eyes, clear under the brim of her tan cowboy hat. He admired the neat way her light green shirt tucked into her jeans, which fit her like a second skin. A brown belt and boots matched the leather holster on her left hip, which housed what looked like it might be a three-fifty-seven magnum. She wore the gun with the grip pointed toward her right hand, backward of the usual style.

As she neared, her gaze caught his, and he whistled low. He knew it was the wrong thing to do, and the wrong thing to say, but he couldn't help himself. "You look like you might just be able to use that thing." Her rapid intake of breath swelled her shirtfront until the buttons strained. He couldn't help but stare.

"You could say that. My dad taught me when I was six years old." Her eyes flashed in a way that he knew meant she would take a challenge.

"Care to try a shooting match?" His stomach actually knotted with the challenge. What was with him? They had matches every day on the force. He was supposed to be getting more stable out here, not less.

"Any time, hot shot." Suddenly, her hand flew to her throat and she backed up a step. "Er, that is . . ."

"What?" He could have sworn a flicker of fear crossed her face. But before he could comment, she was in his face, all bravado.

"Not two out of three, either. One match, six shots." She looked around. "There ought to be some stuff we can set up against the butte over there."

He bent and picked up a piece of dead tree root at his feet. "This do?"

"Yeah, and anything else about that size."

Soon they had twelve objects lined up about fifteen yards away on the butte. He fingered his own pistol at his right hip and unnotched the trigger band on his holster. He usually wore the standard patrolman-issue Glock, but for some reason he had strapped on the old forty-five his granddad had given him when he turned thirteen. Just seemed like the thing to wear on a ranch. Still, he hadn't shot the thing in ages, hadn't cleaned it either.

He opened the cylinder and spun it, giving a

quick blast of breath down the barrel. It didn't look dirty enough to cause a problem. He looked up in time to see Lee Ann reach over and undo her trigger band.

"Rapid fire, starting at the left, straight over. The first six are mine." She wasn't going to make this easy.

"Absolutely. Ladies first." He stood back and waved her forward.

She drew a line in the dirt. "From here."

"From there." He straightened up. "On your mark, get set, go."

In movement so fast it was a blur, her hand sought, found, and aimed the gun. In rapid successive explosions, each object disappeared in flying shards. The root, the can, the paper cup, the bottle, the piece of metal, the cactus pad. And even though she had a curious way of letting her hand flow with the kick, she snapped it back so quickly only a fraction of second passed before she was back on target.

"You can only tie me now." Her chin jutted and her breath came fast. The flush of victory stained her cheeks.

"True enough." He stepped over to the line, but couldn't resist one last look at her. It was probably that look that botched it. *Lord, all this and she can shoot.*

He drew the gun and hammered away at the targets. He barely nicked the first and missed the second entirely. He finished the row and came back to get the one he had missed.

"That wasn't necessary, you know." Her mouth was close enough to his ear that he felt as well as heard her triumphant whisper. "I win, buckaroo. Too bad the boss wasn't around to see." With that she snatched away the list and danced off to the tool shed.

5

Chores First

LEE ANN LOOKED AROUND the interior of the tool shed and whistled. The basic equipment was there, but covered with grime and cobwebs. She would need a shovel for the stock tank. This time of year, algae overgrowth threatened to fill them, combined with whatever dribbled out of the mouths of the livestock. She hefted a good solid square-cut shovel over one shoulder and a coil of rope over the other and headed for her truck. Just outside the door, she slammed into six feet of solid muscle.

"Whoa, there, little filly." Two strong hands steadied her and hitched the rope back up to where it belonged.

"Watch out! You knew I had gone in there." She shoved past him, burning from the impact. It was as if every single spot that had touched him was on

SUSAN C. YARINA

fire. The faster she got away from him, the better. She jumped into her truck after throwing the gear in the back and started the engine. Only, it dawned on her, she didn't have the faintest idea where the upper corral was.

"Want to give me a hand with this?"

A quick glance showed him straining over a large piece of equipment on the ground. She hopped out and grabbed the bar handle on her side of what appeared to be a gas-driven generator. With effort they got it to the open tailgate and with another shove, he got it farther in. The interplay of muscle, visible through his shirt, made her breath catch in her throat. She coughed to cover the strangled sound, slammed the tailgate closed, and whisked back to her seat. The passenger door opened, and Clay jumped in with a grin. In his hands he held some protective gear.

"So, let's get going. I've got the generator and welder so we can mend the front gate. I think a good weld will do the job."

Lee Ann turned in the direction of the front gate. At least she knew where that was. The truck rumbled and groaned as they made their way over the flats. Clay happily counted cow calf pairs. "I count twenty-four." He stuck his head out the window to see better. "Nope. Make that twenty-six. And, hoo'ey, there must be four unpaired calves over there and two more under that palo verde." He pulled back into the cab and turned the full force of his smile her way. "Wanna do the calves last?" He seemed like a fish just finding its way back to water, happy and in his element and way too cute.

"We may have to, but we don't want to wait too long or they might scatter. I don't know how far they can roam from here." Lee Ann gave her attention back to the road.

"I see the top line fence over to the top of that ridge, see?" He had his finger just below her nose. She glanced quickly to where he pointed and caught a glimpse of it. He managed somehow to settle much closer to her. "And not too far ahead, there's the cattle guard. We know that behind us is the fence to the main yard, so that just leaves the fence to the north." As he gazed steadily to his right, she noticed he didn't *move* to his right. Darned if she couldn't feel the heat coming off his body. "I can't spot it."

At the front gate, she jumped out of the cab like a scalded cat, just barely remembering to look where she jumped. It shook her up. Usually, nothing interfered with her sense of caution. She had to be more careful. There were snakes, rocks, and any number of things to jab, scratch, injure, and lame a person in the desert. She bent to retrieve some pipe from the ground, which seemed to be left over from the original construction and, with luck, might just be long enough to fix the broken top bar. "What do you think? Will this do the trick?" She held the pipe out longways to him.

"I think we might be better off without the little fella inside." With a mischievous grin, he applied his mouth to his end of the pipe and puffed. Out popped a huge, fuzzy, orange and black spider to hit Lee Ann square in the chest.

She squeaked and jerked back in reflex, her boot caught on a buried rock, and she sat down on her rump, hard. The spider tumbled away and ran. "Why you dirty . . ." She let the rock her hand found finish the sentence for her. It hit Clay in the chest with a nice satisfying thump that made him blow air out.

"Hey, rocks. No fair." He reached out a hand to help her up.

"I wouldn't call a poisonous critter *fair* either." The proffered hand got a slap as she scrambled up unaided. "Don't touch me."

He shrugged as he offered his reasoning. "Yeah, but at least the tarantula was soft."

"Why don't you be useful and get the generator

going and the welder plugged in." The toolbox in her truck yielded a rasp that she usually used to file horse hooves when shoeing. "I guess this will take off the rough end of this pipe enough so we can weld it to that one."

Clay settled a welder's hat and mask on his head, laid out the generator, and pulled the starter. Then he plugged in the welder and started it while snapping his head forward, causing the mask to slip into place. A spark flew, then the bright arc formed. "You hold the pipe on this end, and I'll weld." He grounded the pipe. "Okay by you?"

Gloves already pulled on, Lee Ann settled her hat and mask into place and nodded. "Sure. Well? What are you waiting for?"

He flicked the torch off, laid it down, and slowly began unbuttoning his shirt. Meantime he seemed to be looking everywhere but at her. Her heart sped up, and a lump formed in her throat as she saw the firm planes of his chest begin to make their tanned appearance. The shirt gaped wider and wider until it finally fell open. She couldn't move and just stared. "What the heck do you think you're doing?"

"Well," his words broke the spell and she looked up in time to see him grin again, "unless I missed something, this is the only thing we have to put out any sparks that might take hold of all this dry grass here."

Oh, God. She had forgotten all about spotting for fire. What was happening to her mind? One look at his trim torso supplied the answer.

"Unless," he raised his eyebrows suggestively, "you'd rather use yours?" The shirt dangled from his fingertip.

She grabbed at it and spat, "In your dreams." With determined concentration, she slammed the pipe to the break and held the weld rod. "Weld."

He had a nice bead forming when she noticed the scars scattered down his back on either side of his spine. She jerked when she realized that they were probably bullet holes and undoubtedly the shooting he had mentioned.

"Hey. Hold it. You almost ruined my bead."

She tried not to look as the sweat ran in rivulets down his bare back, making little detours around the ridged flesh of the scars. She counted them. Six holes. Good God, he had taken six bullets. Could a man do that and survive? No, it had to have been buckshot. Still, her hands started to shake as she imagined the grueling pain he must have endured, might still be enduring.

"Can't you hold it?" He glanced up at her from

where he knelt to attach the lower end to the bar below.

She bit her lip and held tough. She looked away to a calf making its way up the hillside to the topline and concentrated on it.

"That's better, just a minute longer." A crackling sound behind them made her look away from the calf.

"Clay, quick. Stand up." The flame was almost to his leg. She whipped the shirt over her head and into the fire that had already spread to the size of a basketball. Panic dried her mouth and made her pulse race. She slapped at it three or four more times until it was out.

And she thought she had been shaking before. "It's really dry out here, big time."

"Well," he shrugged. "We're almost done."

"Just the same," she tried a smile, "I'd rather not burn down the boss's spread the first day, anyway."

A small smile curled his lips as he drew a bead again. "Maybe the second or third day."

This time, she kept her mind on her work and her hand steady as she glanced around periodically to watch for sparks. With a flourish, he finally whipped the flame away from the last weld.

"That should do it."

Lee Ann stomped out a spark trying to be a flame and turned to inspect the weld. "Looks good. You know, as opposed to your shirt." The charred denim hung from her fingers, a ghost of its previous self.

He plucked the garment from her hand and smelled it. "Phew! Won't be wearing that any time soon. Guess it just retired to mechanic clothes."

Tossing it into the bed of the truck, he lowered the tailgate and, with her help, lifted the generator and welder in. His flesh gleamed brown and white, ridged with hard muscle.

She dragged her glance away then reached over to push the generator forward. She couldn't budge it. She started to comment on it, when she realized she had better not. It was best if he didn't know. Instead, she busied herself finding the rasp and replacing it to her toolbox.

"There's no way you could move that generator by yourself, you know." He slipped into the passenger side of the truck.

He'd noticed. "So?" She started the truck and turned it around to head back to the yard.

"So, how would you have done that job?"

"I'd . . ."

"What? Have the boss put it in your truck for you? Shoot, that's not getting the job done."

He hadn't even let her finish her sentence. She was sure steam was shooting out of her ears. "I'd get my own, Mr. Rude One, and make sure I had an extension cord and just leave it in the truck bed all the time. So there!" She noticed he had no comment, just sat there shaking his head and whistling some dumb little tune over and over.

In no time they were back at the yard. As she jumped out of the truck and yanked the tools out to put back in the tool shed, she challenged. "So! I guess you know where the upper corral is?"

The generator plunked down in the shed next to her boot, followed by the welder. "I guess that's one we'll have to work out together. There's gotta be a map of this place somewhere." She thought she could hear a touch of humility in his voice.

They looked in the barn, in the tack room, in the out buildings, and finally headed to the main house.

"This is probably where we shoulda looked in the first place," Lee Ann fumed.

Carefully pulling aside the thorny branch outside the front door, Clay followed her in. "Yep."

Inside was no different. Nothing to be found. Clay plopped down in the desk chair and opened a drawer.

"You can't look in there!" Lee Ann clamped her hand around his wrist.

"Do you have a better suggestion?" His jaw jutted with determination.

"Well, have you looked up here? Really well?" Just then, she spied a tip of parchment peaking out from under the blotter. Lifting the pad, she whistled. "Pay dirt!"

Clay slipped the sheet out while she replaced the ancient ink-stained square. "Bingo."

With his boot, he angled another chair over to the desk and indicated that she should sit. "Here." He pointed to the near-center of the map. "Here's the yard and these are the buildings." Looking closer, they squinted to make out the printing.

"This thing is ancient. Looks like it's written in an old fountain pen." Lee Ann grabbed a clean piece of paper and traced out a replica quickly.

"Hey. You're pretty good. What did you say you do for a living?"

"Ranch foreman." She quipped back. "You?"

"You're fast. I'll give you that." He pointed. "There's the upper corral, back out the road behind the barn. Looks like it might be a mile or three out." He turned to look her in the eye, bringing them nose to nose. "I meant before this."

68

"Horse trainer." Guilt nagged her even as she noted how nicely his mouth was shaped. "Well, not just before this. Doughnut baker and cosmetics saleswoman."

"No kidding?" A deep chuckle accompanied his reply.

"No kidding." She stood to get some space between them. "You?"

"Cop." He stood, closing the space again. She would have stepped back if she could. "But, just recently, desk cop."

"So, you jail the bad desks, do you?" *Lame, Waters, lame.* There seemed to be no end to his sense of humor. He laughed and grabbed her upper arms.

"Get your map." He set her back so he could head for the door. "We have work to do." Or, maybe there *was* an end to his sense of humor.

6

Chores Last

CLAY INHALED THE CLEAN scent of the head bowed below him. She had all the right ingredients for a first-class female, that was sure. She smelled great, was built better than most and, man, could she sass. Something about that brought out the tease in him, that and something else. Something he couldn't name, but along with it, a desire to dominate her. No, that wasn't quite it, but it would do for now. He was going to prove to her over and over that he was the best man for this job, or die trying.

"Here it is!" Her shell-pink nail tapped the map. "The upper corral."

Clay glanced at the map and could see the inscription in the corner clearly. "We can probably take the truck in there, according to the legend. Looks like one of the few kept-up roads on the place."

Lee Ann folded her copy of the map into eighths and tucked it into her back pocket after making a few more scribbles on it. "Let's head out, then."

"Do I get to put on a shirt, or work on my tan?"

Not even glancing up, she chuckled and replied with one of the boss's phrases. "Makes no never-mind to me."

He moved closer to her and tried to capture her gaze. She wouldn't look at him. Maybe she found him repulsive. Her cheeks reddened. Maybe she didn't. Finally, he was so close she was forced to look up or bury her nose in his chest. He noticed her breath had quickened. When she looked into his eyes, he thought he could see a flicker of interest.

"If you want to work half-naked, it's up to you. But don't ask me to put aloe vera on your sunburn later."

This wasn't working out the way he had in mind, because suddenly he could envision himself putting the clear soothing gel all over her body, *all* over her body. He sucked air like a drowning man, and turned away abruptly to get his shirt from his room. He thought he could hear a small satisfied chuckle as he bent to retrieve it from the drawer, but when he came back in the room, she was just looking at him, all wide-eyed innocence. "Ready?"

"Am now." He held the door open for her. *Where had that come from?*

"I don't need you to hold doors for me, cowboy." Nevertheless, she slipped through it. "If we're going to be working together, I can't have you fallin' all over yourself with the niceties." *There it was again, that sass.*

"Don't tell me who I can and can't hold doors open for. It's part of what a man is expected to do." He stepped up into the passenger side of her truck.

She faced him from behind the wheel. "Then get around here and close my door for me." Her laugh tinkled like wind chimes in the desert breezes as she cocked her head at him then waited face forward, clearly not willing to close her own door now.

Shoot, now what was he going to do? Still, she waited.

"All right, all right." He trotted around and started to reach for the door when he changed his mind. With a deft grab, he had her levered out of the cab and stood her beside him on the ground. "Men do the driving." Before she could do more than stutter with surprise he had her upper arms pinned and walked her before him to the other side of the truck. With a grunt, he hefted her into the passenger side. "Women ride along." There, that felt better. She was curiously quiet as he strode back to his place. He found out why when he reached for the keys.

"Give 'em here." Her sleek mane of hair shimmered as she shook her head and jutted her jaw stubbornly in a way he was beginning to recognize as hers.

"Nope. My truck. I drive it."

"We're wasting a lot of time here."

"I agree."

He held his hand out. Surprisingly, she held out the keys. As he moved to take them, she snaked her rear over and did a bump and grind that shifted him right out of the truck onto his behind in the dirt.

"It's not far. You can walk." Her wind-chime laughter floated out of the truck as she took off, truck tires spitting grit into his open mouth.

And so he did, not exactly cussing her the whole way, but close. It wasn't far to the upper corral, but it was all uphill and his boots were made a whole lot better for riding than walking. As he swung open the gate and stepped down into the corral, he saw something that made him go cold, then hot all over.

Lee Ann was churning out green water and slime with every scoop of the square-head shovel. The water splashing from the watering trough molded her sage-green shirt to her body like a second skin, and the cold had made clear tipped points of interest at the center of each pocket. He swallowed the lump in his throat and hollered over the noise of the water. "Want me to tie up that float so you don't have to fight the water so much?"

"Good idea." She faced him squarely with a frank smile of pleasure that lit her whole face up, causing her green eyes to slant just like a wild cat. He would do well to remember that she *was* like a wild cat in more than one way. She had claws, and she was as independent as the day was long. Furthermore, it seemed she was a mercenary little thing and would take whatever she could get from him, just like most cats he had known. He couldn't help the grin he knew was sliding onto his face as he bent to grab an old piece of baling wire and wrapped it first around the float, then the pipe above it. The gush of incoming water slowed to a small stream and the dirt, rocks and slime at the bottom of the trough became more evident by the moment.

He looked around and realized they had brought only one shovel. Not for the first time that day did he feel like six kinds of fool. He wasn't about to let her know it, though. He stood and gazed around the corral. There, under the rusting tin shade at one corner, he thought he spied a handle. He ambled over and picked up a rusty, broken-handled spade-head shovel that must have been used about a million times for this job. Shrugging, he allowed it would probably do. Still, he pulled his muleskin gloves out from under his belt and put them on against the splinters that poked out up and down the length of what was left of the handle.

He joined Lee Ann's efforts and soon they had the trough clear. They stood together stretching out their backs and absorbing the sun's rays onto their water-cooled shirts. Clay let his gaze wander over Lee Ann's trim strong body. *Big mistake, Carter.* Suddenly, he busied himself untying the float as the all-too-frequent tightening in his groin started. It seemed to happen every time he looked at the woman. How was he going to work with her if this happened every time he looked at her?

He glanced up at her face just in time to see a sly smile cover it. "What's the matter, cowboy? Can't keep your mind on your work?"

There was no help for it. He had to do it, if he was going to call himself a man. Yep, unless he wanted to be like those little bullies they were going to castrate, it was time to take a stand. He didn't remember closing the distance between them, but suddenly she was in his arms all warm and wet. He slammed her into his chest and closed her wide-open mouth with his own. He had invaded her mouth before she could even resist and, when he molded himself to her pliant body, he thought he might just have died and gone to heaven.

THE QUIVERING STARTED from deep in Lee Ann's womb and spread outward like a flame following a tracery of gunpowder that seemed to have replaced her veins. She remembered to breathe and had to pull hard to get a draught of air. She was sure it was lack of air that was causing her knees to weaken and her head to spin. The shirt that just seconds before froze her, seemed to boil where he touched her. For just a moment, she allowed herself to melt into his solid hardness. She had been so alone lately and, in thinking of that aloneness and the plight she found herself currently in, she found the power to stiffen her spine and rear back from his attack. He was fighting dirty, all right. Well, two could play at this game. Suddenly she was on him like hell won't have it. She nibbled his ear until he groaned. She caught his lip in her teeth and took him to a point just before pain, then ground her upper torso mercilessly into his as she plunged her tongue into his mouth to twine with his. Just when he started to lean her back and take her to the ground, she danced away, delivering a stinging slap on her way.

"Don't think I don't know what you are up to, mister." She spat. "Now, let's get those bulls castrated." She hoped her tone implied that it was more than just the bulls that she would like to do the dirty deed to. She desperately hoped Clay couldn't see the wobble in her knees as she threw her shovel in the bed of the truck and hopped in. Just a second later he was there beside her, frowning but still clearly aroused.

"What the hell was that?" His gray eyes turned before her gaze into a stormy green accented by dark brows drawn to a scowl above them.

"You tell me." She rammed the truck into reverse and tromped it. She had to lay her arm behind him and look over her shoulder to see where she was going. His heat shimmered against her arm and the smell of wet, aroused male hit her in the face. Lord. She wanted him. For just a second, she entertained the idea of using him, just as he'd planned to use her. She paused and looked into his eyes, considering. His lip curled just a bit, and he smiled, sure of himself—too sure. She decided that he might be a fire she couldn't play with without getting burned, so with massive effort she feigned repulsion as she lifted her own lip. "Why would I want ground beef, when I have filet mignon waiting in town?" *Oh, God, where had that come from?*

"Filet min-what?" He pulled himself away and straightened up. "You don't mean to tell me there's a Mister Waters?"

She nodded rapidly, unable to stop the lie. She glanced over to see what effect the news had on him.

"No sh—I mean, no kidding. Married? Really?" His words had softened, and he sounded a little upset. He was good; she had to admit it. But then he was a cop. He had to be good with people.

"N-no. Not married, not yet." She let her words imply engagement.

"I don't see a rock on that left hand." His eyes turned almost black as his brows cast them into deep shadows in a scowl.

"I just haven't picked it out yet, that's all." She edged the truck up to the outbuilding they had seen the castration tools in.

He had her door opened before he stopped her on the seat with a hand planted firmly on her chest. "You don't get out 'til I hear his name." The look on his face said he didn't believe her for a minute.

"Will Duquette." Her mild love interest from Pro Horseman put a name to her lie.

"Will, huh?" He dropped his hand and allowed her out. "Will he yes, or will he no?" He stepped along behind her into the shed. "Will he stay? Or will he go?"

If that didn't described Will to a tee. How right he was. She pasted on a smile. "Oh. He'll stay all right. And I'm sure he wouldn't have any trouble coming here if he had known what you pulled back there."

He stood close behind her, blocking out the light to the entrance of the shed. His voice deepened impossibly. "And I'm sure he would have gotten real steamed if he had seen the way you cozied up to me, too, huh?"

Hurriedly, she grabbed the crimps and blade, antiseptic and forceps and shoved past him, so he couldn't see the flame in her face. She strode out to the bull pens as fast as her legs could carry her, hoping the breeze could cool her. Fiercely, she concentrated on finding the bulls. Finally, she saw them in the pen nearest to the pump house. They were a hardy, stout little group, and she would need the squeeze chute for some of them. She pointed to the pull gate that led to the chute. "Do you think you could be of some help here and open that?"

He flipped loose the knot that held the rope onto the fence, then gave a good hard tug that sent the bar gate rising to the top. She handed the tools off to him and stepped into the pen and found her way to the back of it. The half-wild range babies scattered before her like leaves before a wind. It didn't take much clapping to make them rush to the opening and head down the runway to the gate at the end. They lined up bawling and carrying on, head to tail until the runway was full, at which point Clay dropped the gate, holding about ten in.

Lee Ann found her way to the squeeze chute and worked the apparatus until she was sure she understood the levers that worked the sides and the yoke. The sides would squeeze the animal until it was immobilized, and the yoke would trap its head. Then, by moving yet another lever, the calf could be swiveled onto its side, allowing shots, castration, ear notching, and any other kind of treatment needed. Everything seemed to be in smooth working order, so she motioned to Clay to let the first calf in. With a jump the two-hundred-pound beast landed in the chute. The familiar beat came to Lee Ann as if she had done it yesterday. One, head in the yoke, lever down. Two, squeeze bars, crank down. Three, back gate dropped, to stop the next animal in line. With the beef immobilized, she turned to get her tools. Clay came up with them in hand.

"Lookin' for these?"

"Yeah. Do you think these guys need shots, too?"

"Boss didn't say anything about shots."

"But I'd say they need blackleg at the least."

The sound of a large truck began to overshadow their conversation, and they both looked up to see the boss pull in.

Lee Ann slapped her hand and pointed at the castration tool, which Clay handed her. With her other hand, she swiveled the calf up so she could get to his scrotum. Clay reached over and obligingly pulled up the top hind leg so she could gain access. Charlie's voice caught her attention, and she looked up.

"Lee Ann, I sure wish you wouldn't do that."

Swinging the castration clamps in her hand, she held his gaze. "Do what?"

"Castrate that heifer there."

In horror, she glanced down to see four pert little teats gleaming pinkly between the calf's hind legs.

7

And Chores Always

CLAY TURNED TO CHARLIE. "It seems she has trouble telling the difference between a heifer and a bull. Not sure I'd trust her with the position of foreman, boss."

With a grin, the boss took off his hat and wiped inside the brim with his bandanna. "That's a fact, Clay. Why, could be, she'd run off all my good heifers to market for meat."

The fact that his eyes twinkled didn't stop the burn of mortification from steaming up Lee Ann's face. With a groan, she slammed down the crimper and ran to the second calf in the chute. A glance down told her what she should have seen before. None of these little critters had the proper plumbing. "Well, shoot!" She couldn't help it, so she took her ire out on the lowest bar of the chute with a well-placed kick. The calf on the inside bawled with fright and leaped madly against the restraints of the metal run.

"And to top it off, she scares the little dudes, too?" Clay's face was pure concern. A cowman protecting his herd. *Yeah, right!*

She spun on her heel and faced him, hands on hips. She had been about to tell that he had helped her haze the heifers into the chute, when her code brought her up short. She had been raised to be better than a common tattletale. With a sneer, she stomped past the two men. "You'll get yours, Carter." Disgust firing her movements, she flipped open the gate to the main corral and let the heifers loose. Slamming it closed, she strode back by him. "You gonna stand there all day, or help me find the bullies?"

Charlie stopped her with a hand on her arm. "I should have told you, they are back behind the pump house there." He motioned with his arm, and sure enough, there stood a likely group, all with the proper fixtures.

"You all have any other questions? I did take off kind of quick."

"No, sir." Just like a man. He wouldn't ask.

"Yes. We do. These need shots?"

Charlie brightened. "Matter of fact, they do. Didn't I write that down?"

"No, sir. If you'll just tell me what you want and where to get it, we'll consider it done." Lee Ann stood before him, ready and willing, while Clay shuffled his feet and looked down at the ground. She hoped he felt silly for not asking about the shots.

"Vaccines for blackleg are back to the house."

Two hours later, Lee Ann's hands ached from reaching up into the scrotum of the bull calves, pulling down the large vessels of the cremaster muscle, and scraping them down to prevent bleeding. If the job wasn't done right, the steer could exsanguinate. Here was where mettle had to be proved. She flexed her fingers in her work gloves and willed circulation back into them, then went back at it again. She and Clay were starting to get the feel of each other, to develop a system and a rhythm. She hazed the calf into the chute, he swiveled it up and released one side of the chute to lift a leg away, so she could crimp, cut, and scrape. Bum greedily grabbed each set of "Rocky Mountain Oysters" as she tossed them to the ground. By then, she had the shots into the calves. Clay fixed a numbered tag to the left ear with a punch and she notched the right ear with the little V that was the mark of the Silver Rock, so from a distance the animals could be identified by their ear marks long before a brand or a number could be seen. Clay then released them, where they went bawling into the main pen, back to their mommas for the comfort they were still young enough to need.

"Hope the boss wasn't planning on a meal of ranch oysters for dinner." Clay replaced the vaccines into the cooler they had come in.

"Well, if he was, I guess he should have said something." She toed the belly of the huge canine lolling at their feet. "But I know someone's who's glad Charlie didn't mention it." With a sloppy grin, Bum licked the boot poking his ribs now, while he squirmed on his back and moaned in doggy ecstasy.

Just then, Lee Ann's belly did a little griping of its own, loud enough to be audible. At which point Clay's answered, which set them both to chuckling.

"I guess we better clean up some and head in for some chow." In agreement for a change, the two gathered up everything, checked the gates to be sure all were closed, and headed back for the main house.

The door opened to a nice display of sandwiches, fresh fruit, tall cold iced teas, and an assortment of chips. "Don't you two go expecting this every day. I just got inspired by the new groceries I brought back." With a wave, the boss indicated he wanted them to sit. Since they had washed up when they cleaned the equipment, they did just that.

"Why, this is real nice, boss."

"It is. Thanks." Lee Ann closely inspected her hands for residual mud, blood, or goo, then picked up a thick sandwich and lit into it. She didn't think the finest filet could taste any better at the moment, and she could hardly get it down quick enough to get to the tea. She took a long, long draw and then leaned back her head in enjoyment, letting the last swallow trickle down her parched throat. Castrating was hard, thirsty work.

Nearly choking on his own bite of food, Clay noticed the ivory column of her long neck and fought the desire to put his hands behind it, then lay down hot kisses one after the other. . . .

"I said," Charlie shook his head, "youngsters, did everything go all right?"

"Just perfect, boss." Lee Ann shifted a little in her seat. "That is, after I got the difference between the heifers and the bulls down right."

When the boss's face split into a huge grin, Clay knew that she had taken the blunder and turned it around with a cute look and a laugh at herself. If that didn't beat all.

"What do you have left?"

"Inventory of repairs in the barn equipment and bringin' in the cow calf pairs." Clay helped himself to a large red apple.

"Best bring those calves in first. Seems like you have plenty of daylight, but once you get to tinkerin' on things in that barn, time can go pretty darn quick."

"We talked about that, sir. And we had planned on doing that next."

Not ask questions? He would show her. "Just how far does that north fence go up out of the flats?"

"Oh, it ambles some, that's for sure." Charlie replaced the tomato in his sandwich, which had slipped out onto his plate. "I'd say no farther than a quarter of a mile. But you want to keep them from heading up that way. Helluva cholla forest can make things mighty interesting."

He wasn't about to ask what kind of a forest a "cholla forest" was. "Well, I can bring calves out of just about any kind of ground. You can count on me, sir."

CLAY REGRETTED THOSE words about two hours later, when he got his first sight of the maze of teddy bear and chain cholla that comprised the northern edge of the "forest" Charlie had mentioned. He couldn't see a way into the mass of thorny three-foot-tall cactus that clung to everything it touched with almost diabolical tenacity. He'd had to stop four times now to pick it out of the little green filly he had chosen for the ride. She complicated things greatly by slamming one particularly vicious clump right into his hand as he tried to dislodge it from her front fetlock joint. It seemed to like him better, so when he stood with rein in one hand and clump in the other, Lee Ann took pity and handed him her comb. "What do I do with this?" *Women. Was she really worried about how he looked out here in the middle of nowhere?*

She leaned forward in the saddle to rest her forearms across her palomino's withers and answered with a sigh. "Put the tines between your hand and the clump. Then flick it outward. Be careful where you send it."

"Well . . ." He hated the way his hands shook, but the pain from the toxic thorns was pretty bad. "Hey! It worked." Only a few of the thorns were left, but the relief was so great, he hardly noticed the pain as he plucked the last few. He handed the comb back to her, sucking one thumb of the hurt hand. "Sthanksth."

"Keep it, you'll need it again." With that, she simply disappeared before his wondering eyes into the maze of murderous plants. He mounted up, still nursing the hand until he had to get both back on the reins. There was no way the filly was going to go into the narrow passage he finally spied woven between the hostile cacti. He took a rein in each hand and held them out off the sides of her neck, effectively "framing" her head and giving her no choice but to go forward into the trail the cattle had cut and Lee Ann had followed. The filly was being very stubborn about it. Well, she would just have to do it, so he gigged her a bit with his spurs. She leapt forward. Boogered now, she snorted, eyed the closest cactus, and backed away at high speed.

Clay reached down and unbuckled his spurs, put them into his saddlebags, and tried again, with heavy leg pressure, to move her forward. He had gained a little progress so he pushed it. He really slammed his legs home, right behind her girth. She jumped forward, hit the cactus with her shoulder, and started spinning in mindless anger, picking up several more clumps as she went. Clay's world turned into grabbing leather and spinning lights as he fought wildly to hang on.

He was staying pretty well glued until she

reached for the sky, in the biggest buck he could remember having sat. For a moment he had that giddy sensation he always had at the top of a roller coaster hill, just before going down, and then he did go down. The filly hit the ground with the force of a jackhammer, now convinced she was trying to dislodge a wild cat that clawed at her every spin.

In a sickening second of clarity, Clay saw the direction he was going to land in—pure granite and cactus. At the last minute, he let loose, determined not to land face first in the mess. Pain exploded as he landed full straddle on a fine specimen of teddy bear cholla. He whooped all the curse words he knew in one explosive shout, then lay on his back where he'd rolled, legs pinned one to the other by his own forest of spiny clumps. Not far from where he lay, the red filly grazed, unconcerned with the few pads of spines clinging to one shoulder, other than the occasional flicker of hide that indicated that she knew they were there.

He knew he was going to have to get up somehow and cover the distance of thirty feet or so between them, but damned if he could think how. He was reaching for the comb he had put in his back pocket when into his line of vision, an angel hovered. Thank the good Lord, he had been saved! The angel spoke with Lee Ann Waters's voice.

"Don't you know you can't *force* a thousand-pound animal to do what you want?"

He answered with something that sounded like, "Fffubar, mfft, damhorse, hellbithch." The poison racing through him was seriously addling his ability to speak.

"Poor animal, must have thought you lost your mind." She came at him with murder in her eye, he was sure. He held his hand out in front as, impossibly, he levered himself to a sitting position and scooted away.

"See? You don't like the idea of getting poked any more than she does, do you?"

"D-d-don't! Yow! Stop it!" At least he could speak clearly now. "Quit that!" Her answer was to reach around behind him and hand him the other comb.

"Come on, you need to help. We have to get these out of here fast. I think you're reacting to the toxins." First she pulled off his boots, then she yanked on him like she wanted him to stand. She couldn't be serious. "Get up!" She was.

"Why?" She was strong for a little thing. She had him on his feet, so he made a serious effort to part his legs. As the clumps holding them together let go, he thought he might know what living Velcro felt like. "Yow!"

She let go of his arms to fumble at his belt buckle. Now she was getting amorous? Well, some chicks had strange triggers. She had it undone in no time and yanked open the top of his jeans. Just a second before he realized what she was up to, she yanked down hard.

"Mary, mother of God, spare me," he screamed at the top of his lungs as hundreds of needles lost their grip on his flesh. He grabbed onto her to keep from toppling over onto loosed clumps of cholla that sprayed every which way off him. With her boot, Lee Ann swept a spot in the sand clear.

"Sit." He did.

Now, moving slowly, she pulled the jeans off and carefully turned them right side out again. Amazingly, most of the cactus had fallen away. When she was satisfied they were clean, she carefully laid them across a jojoba bush and turned to stare at him.

"My good Lord. Aren't you a sight?"

He glanced down at his legs and higher and saw what she meant. He was covered in speckles of blood and needles—even, he realized, in his crotch, which was bare, as his briefs had come away with his jeans. He stared in absolute horror at where some of the largest spines had lodged.

"Oh, no. You're not touching me there, no way."

If he had thought of Lee Ann Waters viewing what usually could make him proud, he had never envisioned this. And the picture he had in his mind involved a whole different sensation than he felt now. She came at him with a shiny instrument that she produced from somewhere. "What are those?" he nearly shrieked.

"Kelly clamps. You should have a pair. Man, you don't know much. I thought you knew the desert?"

Through clenched teeth, he admitted, "No. I pretty much stayed in—ouch—the city since—ouch—I—ouch—came here—ouch—to work." It was better when he closed his eyes.

"Wow! That one caused a real gusher," she said. He shouldn't have looked. A wound at the very top of his thigh was spouting up like a little red fountain.

Normally, he was good with blood; maybe it was the toxins, maybe it was the heat, maybe. . . .

"Good, you're out cold. Makes what I gotta do next a little easier." Lee Ann surveyed the mess before her. It was some kind of ugly, too. Everywhere she looked there were needles poking out of him.

She had come out of the cholla forest just in time to see him straddle a cholla like a rider taking on a bronc. She knew then what a mess he was in for and now, for the first time, she felt a little sorry for Clay Carter.

She drew back her hand as she reached for his slack scrotum. She couldn't quite touch it, not until she looked at his face, which was getting whiter under his tan every minute. Then she knew she had to get the ones out of his scrotum and his crotch and the insides of his thighs so he could sit a horse, because she couldn't just leave him here.

The sun was at its hottest and, even now in the early spring, it could be deadly.

I won't think of what I'm handling, I'll just concentrate on one square inch at a time. First, she got up, found his hat, and shaded his face with it. Then, she began. She got really fast before she was through. It was toward the end that he woke. She was moving him to see if she had gotten all the thorns out of his penis when she noticed a change in his breathing. There were still several really nasty-looking ones on the underside. "How long have you been awake?"

Sucking air, he replied, "Just a few minutes. It seemed easier on us both if I pretended."

"Could be." The next one was more difficult to get, and she had to manipulate and poke with the clamps.

Low groans slipped through his clenched teeth. "How many more?"

Lee Ann found she had to clear her throat before she could speak. "Just one." She cleared it again. "But it has to come out, or when you sit the horse . . ."

"Sit the horse?" he managed through gritted teeth.

"It'll go so far in, no one will be able to get it out." With a deft jab, she yanked.

Suddenly, he had her wrist in an iron grip and pulled her down to him. His breath on her face was heated, but not bad. He used the other hand to pull her close after he removed his hat. He looked so deeply into her eyes that she felt as naked as he was, as exposed. Then he captured her mouth with a kiss so fierce, so deep, that she nearly collapsed on top of him. A slow burn started deep in her belly, then, suddenly, she was free and she had to move quickly to get to her feet.

"Thanks," he managed before he roared with pain as he stood. He swayed woozily, and she propped him up with an arm.

"Do you always say thanks that way?" She reached to get his jeans and briefs. "Here."

He shook his head as if to clear his vision. "Only to lovely ladies saving my manhood."

She had the grace to chuckle and then took his arm away. "Can you stand? I'll get my mare." Promptly she had the mare back and sidled up to him. "Stand, girl. She'll stand there for you as long as you like. Use her to hang on to and get your jeans and boots back on."

"Boots?" He grabbed the good mare's saddle skirting to hang on and worked a leg into the jeans.

"Sure, you know, boots? Those things that protect your feet?" Maybe he was a little worse off than she thought.

She turned to find his mount and murmured to the little red filly as she sidled away. "Come on, sweetheart. I only want to help." The filly's eyes showed plenty of white as she rolled them fearfully. "It's okay." Smoothly, she dipped to pick up the reins and brought her forward until she could reach her neck and stroke it. "There, there. Let me just get these off." Expertly she flicked the cactus clumps off, one after the other. To her credit, the little filly stood her ground, seeming to know that she was being helped.

Clay had his jeans and boots back on when she got back to him. "You still dizzy?"

"Yeah. What causes this?" He grabbed his head as if to stop it spinning.

"The toxins in the cactus, I think. Can you sit a horse?"

"Heh, maybe not comfortably. But I can almost ride in my sleep."

"Then you take Sugar. She won't try to get out from under you, if you should get off balance." She mounted the younger red mare to finalize the swap.

"I'd be fine on the filly, you know." His scowl showed the injury to his pride.

"Sure, sure. Just humor me. I don't want to go cactus picking again today."

Funny how quickly he got into the saddle at the mention of that.

8

Hazards of the Job

SUGAR WAS AS GOOD as usual and kept Clay in the saddle with careful steps and an easy gait. Lee Ann watched closely and slowed the pace when she needed to. It didn't take long to get back to the ranch house, but by then Clay's skin had taken on an ugly purplish color and his fingers had swollen up. His eyes were open but not focusing for long on any one thing. She didn't stop until they reached the front door of the ranch house. She hailed the house. "Charlie!"

A second later the door opened. By then she was down and ready to catch Clay. He just sort of tilted her way and let go. She staggered under the burden and would have fallen but for Charlie's quick help.

"What happened?" His deep voice was rough with concern.

"Near as I could tell, boss, he tried to ride a clump of cholla out in the flats." She shifted so the weight of him could be shared.

A harsh groan of denial issued forth from the hot burden they carried. "Not!"

"He decided to take that little red filly to the flats and, last thing I knew, he was trying to follow me into the cholla forest on her. When I turned to see what was taking him so long, I swear he was flying off her, legs apart, right onto a big teddy bear cholla."

A shudder went through her as she saw the whole thing in her mind's eye again.

"Let's get him to his bed. I'll strip him down, you run the bath tub." No doubt about it, Lee Ann thought, Charlie Bruce was used to running the show.

"I got most of them out of him, but now he's re-acting to the cactus, I think." With a heave, they got him onto his bed. Charlie wasted no time stripping him. "Lee Ann, there's some Benadryl and Advil in there. Bring two of each."

She grabbed a glass of water on her way back. Clay was down to his briefs and pulled up a little on the stacked pillows. "Hey. I can do this. I'll be all right. Really."

"Umgh." Charlie took the pills and held them out. "Allergic to anything, youngster?"

"No." Clay shook his head. "I probably don't even need . . ."

"Take them." Charlie brooked no argument.

"Yes, sir." Obediently, he swallowed them and finished the water when Charlie motioned him to.

Lee Ann didn't realize she had been holding her breath until she spoke and it whooshed out. "Water's ready."

"You say you're ready?" Clay leered.

"Smart alec. For you to get into the tub. You need to soak."

He stood and swayed, his face suddenly slack with dizziness. Charlie grabbed him and guided him forward. "Not that you need it, Cholla Buster, but I'll give you a hand to the tub."

Lee Ann hurried forward to help and grimaced when she saw the amount of blood on his briefs. "Those need to come off."

"Why, Lee Ann Waters, what would your pa say?" Charlie teased.

His teasing helped some. "I had to pull a slew of needles out of him, uh, there, so he could, uh, ride." She glanced up at him, knowing she was blushing now.

"Figure it'll be better to leave them for now, just the same. Soaking 'em off might be kinder."

"This water is icy!" Clay eased first his left foot in, then the right, as a powerful shivering gripped him. He shot a glare at Lee Ann as if it were all her fault. "And this one doesn't know the first thing about being kind."

"Coulda left you there." She turned on the hot water and swished it around. "I'm not gonna make this much warmer. It has to be cool to take down the swelling."

"Yep, then you would have needed Air-Evac for sure. Might still." Charlie mused. "So you might thank the lady."

Clay's jaw sagged open. "Seriously? It's her fault, you know. She headed into the cholla forest."

"Did she ask you to follow?"

"Well, no. Not with words."

"And you say you were on the little red filly? The one with no markings?"

"Yeah, but she was fine . . ."

"Never had been ridden."

"She what?" Again Clay's jaw sagged. "You must have the wrong horse. I coulda swore she had. She took the saddle and bridle like she was used to it, stood . . ."

"Imprinted."

"Stood while I mounted her. What's that you

say?" Clay screwed up his face, which Lee Ann noted was regaining some natural color.

"Don't you know the technique?" Lee Ann couldn't believe that he didn't know about the de-sensitization program that a veterinarian had developed to help young horses accept new sensations. It was done at birth and brought about amazing advances in what a young horse would accept. "You imprint 'em all, Charlie?"

"Most. I may have missed one or two." He shrugged a denim-clad shoulder. "But I figure those will show the difference." He knelt down and grabbed the band of Clay's briefs. "You ready to give these up?"

Scowling, he shot, "You look away now, hear?"

Lee Ann rocked back on her heels. "Why should I? You don't have anything I haven't . . ." She screeched as he planed a handful of water her way. "All right, all right, don't soak the boss's floor here."

Charlie motioned her out of the bathroom ahead of him. "I think he's going to be okay; we'll just leave him to soak for a while."

"Okay, boss." She headed for the kitchen chair and started to sit when she remembered the horses. "Oops. I need to get the horses and put them up," she said.

"I'll meet you down to the barn in about thirty minutes."

With a nod, she was out the door. Needless to say, the untied horses were nowhere in sight. She looked around as she headed for the barn to get another horse to go after them. Luck was with her, though, as they had both gone into the large corral and were munching some leftover hay, with the only mishap being one of Sugar's reins broken. Alone, she thought about the happenings of the past hour, and sagged with relief when she thought of how really bad things could have been. Bones could have been broken, heads cracked, anything really. Well, just hazards of the job. She would have to deal with it. She straightened back up and reached for Sugar's saddle. In no time she had her mare untacked and returned to her stall. The little red filly, really a mare at four, stood quietly while Lee Ann untangled her tack and methodically, quietly took it off. She made sure to rub her down and was just feeding her some oats when something made her aware that she wasn't alone. The hair on the back of her neck stood, and she reached for a pitchfork that leaned against the wall nearby. She nearly jumped out of her skin when he spoke.

"Now is that any way to act toward a man whose

life you just saved?" He turned her to face him. "I've had enough holes poked in me for one day." Gently, he pulled the tool from her hand and laid it against the wall.

"You shouldn't be up." He tipped her head up and looked into her eyes. She swore her bones were turned to jelly. She should be mad at him. He had been no end of trouble this day.

"I had to thank you." He was going to do it again. Her veins seemed to turn to liquid fire as he slanted a warm, hungry kiss over her lips, which she swore took minutes to complete, and totally robbed her of all good sense.

"You're going to get sick . . ." That his second kiss was a little too warm registered somewhere in her addled mind. Next, he had her pinned up against the stall door and held her there with pressure from the waist down. He plundered her lips mercilessly as evidence of his desire filled out his jeans to fit her neatly where nature intended. She squirmed and gasped. "You can't. You're hurt." She glanced down and saw to her horror that blood now spotted her jeans and his. He looked too, then paled and for the second time that day, passed out, just as Charlie Bruce strode into the barn.

He surveyed his help lying on the ground and

swore softly. "That must have been one dynamite kiss."

"I'd like to say it was me, but truth is, I think he's really sick. We'd better get him to the hospital."

"Looks like it." If Charlie noticed the blood on Lee Ann's jeans, thankfully he didn't say anything. The two managed to wrestle two hundred pounds of limp cowboy onto a bale of hay.

"Can you hold him there?" Lee Ann nodded and stood with legs apart to get enough leverage to keep him upright on the bale. Charlie got the truck there lightning-quick. They decided to lay him in the back seat when all was said and done, knowing that they would have more help to get him up at the emergency room.

CLAY WOKE TO WARM pressure on his hand and someone murmuring his name over and over. But what really helped him open his eyes was the command: "Clay Carter, you cuss! I said open your eyes."

Simplest thing in the world. Why couldn't he do it? It seemed he had to put every ounce of will into getting his eyes open. Ridiculous. Finally, he could see bright light and a lot of white. Blinking hard, he focused. To his right, he saw an IV pole, above it a white, sound-proofed ceiling, and to his left Lee Ann Waters.

"Hi, there." His voice sounded froggy, even to him.

Her head jerked up, and she dashed tears out of her eyes. "About time you listened to me."

"How long have I been out?" Some of the grit was leaving his voice. "Water?"

"Sure." He heard water tinkle as it was poured. Next thing he knew it was at his lips. "About twenty-four hours." Gratefully he swallowed and let it trickle down his parched throat. So he had lost a whole day. Suddenly, full-blown, memories of his hospital stay after he had been shot came back to him and set his skin crawling.

"I hate hospitals, you know."

"No. I didn't know, but then not many people love them. You're not so different."

Her attempt at sass didn't fool him. He had seen the tears. "Were you crying?"

"Absolutely not." The cup was taken away. He opened his eyes wide for a better look at her. There was no doubt about it. Her face was swollen, and her eyes puffy. He couldn't recall his ex-fiancée crying over him once after the shooting. It was one of the things that made him wonder, not for the first time, if she had really loved him. He felt a curious sensation in his stomach, or his heart, he couldn't really tell which, when he realized that though she had known him just a couple of days, Lee Ann had cried for him. He smiled and reached out to rub a wet spot on her cheek.

"What's this, then?"

She backed out of his reach and wiped furiously at her face. "My eyes always water when I'm tired."

He decided he needed to let her save face, so he left it alone. "They say what happened?"

She nodded as she smoothed her rumpled shirt into place and took a swipe at her hair. "It seems something really nasty was on those thorns and, let's see—how did they put it?—'inoculated you with *E. coli.*'"

"What? Did you ask for a translation?"

She nodded vigorously. "Yeah. Means that one of the cactus needles had bacteria from animal waste on it and the needle injected it directly into your bloodstream."

"Weird." He shook his head and struggled to sit more upright. He felt her shoving something into his hand and realized it was the bed control. With it he raised the head of the bed and sat up to see her better.

"They said that it wasn't all that rare, just that they had never seen it happen with a cactus needle and never uh ... there." She stared out the window, and her cheeks blazed red.

"Figures." Abruptly, he thought of what Charlie must think. "I suppose I'm off the list for foreman." Here was her chance to gloat. Her pretty green eyes widened before she answered.

"Hey, don't worry about that." She actually smiled and patted his arm. "Boss said he's just glad we got you here in time. That accidents happen. Said he or I could have done the exact same thing." Her humility touched him.

"But you wouldn't have."

"Oh yeah? Why not?" She seated herself close by his side again, her smile belying her sass.

"'Cause you would have maybe known the mare was imprinted and been more careful with her."

The assessing look she threw at him made him even more aware of how careful she was being with him. Damn, he must have been really sick.

"Maybe. Maybe not. I use the technique, but ... no. I think I would have thought someone had done most of the work on her already, you know, at least ridden her a couple of times. Even imprinted babies will fight the saddling up a little. I didn't see any of that."

"No, but still when she fought me, and I forced her into the cholla forest—you would have known better then."

She grinned and ducked her head, caught. "I know from experience how painful cholla can be. I may have respected it a little more." She tilted her head at him, pure mischief. "And I certainly would have *never* tried to ride one."

"I didn't . . ." He held his hand out in protest. She grabbed it with both of hers. He could have sworn an electric shock ran up his arm, but he let her hold it.

"Oh, yes, cowboy. You did. You even had one hand up in the air, to keep from grabbing leather." Her giggle undid him.

The chuckle came from deep in his belly. "It must have looked like that, huh?" He shook his head side to side and withdrew his hand to pass it over her tangled hair. "That what Charlie meant when he called me a 'Cholla Buster'?"

She nodded vigorously, then did the darndest thing. She crossed her arms and laid them and her head on the bed beside his lap and fell instantly and deeply asleep. That her concern for him could keep her from succumbing to such profound fatigue touched him as few things had in his life, and in his police work he had seen plenty. He stroked her hair until he felt himself drifting off, thinking he might just have found something precious.

9

A Matter of Style

LEE ANN HAD JUST about caught up to Charlie's never-ending list over the past several days, so she had some time to do what she loved best. Through careful observation, she had figured out which young horses in the Silver Rock's herd weren't imprinted. She had never tried imprinting with a horse as old as the two-year-old bay gelding that now stood quivering in front of her. But a quick look at her book by Dr. Miller the night before had mentioned that it still did a lot of good, even some time after the birth, to do the imprinting process.

She chuckled as she ran her hands over the shiny, well-built Quarter horse, pleased by his calm, friendly response to her touch. She looked him over as she methodically went to tapping him fifty times or more on each sensitive area of his body. She poked fingers in his ears, his eyes, his mouth, and his rectum, and now was prodding all the other touchy spots. As she reached for his underside near the rear, his natural good nature took a turn and his hind leg whipped up to glance off her hat, knocking it askew.

Taking a quick peek underneath, she found the reason. A slightly inflamed incision line could be seen right behind the folds of his sheath. He had been gelded recently and remained very touchy. It would take some more time, but she persisted and after about try fifty, was patting it very lightly with no flicking of his hide, no evasion of her hand.

His expression remained hooded, and one ear flicked back, so she moved to the other side and began the whole experience over. Just as she had expected, the hoof on that side flew toward her as well. All horses had to be taught on both sides because the two sides of a horse's brain work independently, as if they were two brains, unlike human brains, which have a crossover. So all of the imprinting had to be done from both sides.

If she did her job right, and the gelding was receptive enough still, she would make the job of the veterinarian as well as the farrier and anyone else who might handle this animal a little easier. Dr. Miller had documented this well in his book on imprinting and, for Lee Ann's money, there was no better time spent on an animal.

On the common-sense side, it just seemed right to show a horse what it might expect from a human. From the time she was big enough to do it, Lee Ann had instinctively done a lot of handling that closely resembled imprinting on all the foals of her father's ranch. But now there was a system to it, and a name, thanks to Dr. Miller.

After she gave the bottom of his last hoof a final pat, she set it down and stood, hands on hips, to view the results. She stepped away, and the little horse snorted and reached to sniff her hand, seeming loath to stop the contact, which he was beginning to find enjoyable.

She was undecided whether to leave the lesson there on a good note, or to pick up a rope that was near at hand and begin rope training. Lazily, she picked up the soft cotton rope she used for training and looped it over the end of the little bay's rump. Other than his eyes opening wide as he turned to look back at his rump, and his nostrils flaring for a second, he did nothing.

She walked toward him and rewarded him with a pat and a rub on his neck. "Good boy, Little Joe." Carefully, she lifted the rope off him and flicked it at his head. He blinked at her, then snuffled at the rope as it curled on his shoulder. Inching it up his neck, she flipped it over his head and let it settle low. Gradually, she tightened it, then looped a section around his nose. Little by little she put a persuasive pressure on it and pulled forward. Before he even knew it, he was giving in to the pressure of the rope, which was the foundation of training a horse to work with a saddle and bridle.

"That's it, little fella. There you go." This time when she patted him, she felt a fine sheen of sweat on the neck and noted that the muscles had tensed under the hide. She eased the rope off and gave him a final pat before pushing him back to the main group in the large corral. "That's it for you today." As always, when she trained, her concentration was total, so she hadn't heard a thing to warn her that she had company.

"Yep. In about four years, at that speed, you might have a mount."

"Clay, you're home." She was embarrassed by how happy she sounded.

"Good thing, too. Looks like you have about half the herd spoiled rotten." His clear gray gaze swiveled from her face to behind her.

She turned to see about half the herd at her back, demanding some time from her. She laughed and shrugged her shoulder. "Well, at least I don't have to run them down to catch a ride."

"Neither do I." With a swift motion he brought his lariat up and stepped up to the top rung of the corral separating them. As he whirled the stiff lasso above him, she figured out what he intended to do.

"Clay, don't you dare!" His throw never faltered as his loop settled over Little Joe's neck and he cinched it down tight by snubbing the other end on a post. Squealing with fright, the little bay lunged away to the end of the slack. He leaped for the sky in an effort to dislodge the thing that threatened to choke off his air. His eyes rolled at Lee Ann as if registering that she had betrayed him. She knew he couldn't understand that the rope had not come from her. Her hand found her knife; she had it out and opened in a flash. "You let him go now, or you'll lose your rope." Somehow, she was through the fence and in his face, eyeball to eyeball. Her breath whistled through clenched teeth.

He shrugged and released the rope, leaving it to trail behind the now frightened and running gelding. "You're sure not very happy to see me, are you?"

"How dare you interfere with my training?" She took her hat off her head and swatted him with it until he backed up a step or two.

"Hey, couldn't you at least treat me as well as you do him?" His eyes sparkled with amusement, which only made her madder.

"You probably just undid what I spent the last hour doing, you creep." Returning her hat to her head, she promptly knocked it off again, climbed back through the corral bars, and headed toward the trailing rope.

"Hey! No harm meant. Here's your hat!"

"No harm meant, yeah, right." It took her another ten minutes to get the bay to even let her near enough to get the rope. He made good use of the rest of the herd in evading her, and by the time she had her hand on it, the rope was covered in mud and worse things. She had a few tense moments as she got close enough to ease the lasso off his well-formed head. He made as if to race away, but she held him with one hand on his mane and another on his nose.

"Whoa, there. It's okay, Little Joe. It's okay. I won't let him near you, don't worry." The intelligent deep-brown eyes looked at her, then at the offending human on corral fence. He sighed and began to lick his lips and chew on a forgotten bit of hay in his mouth. After he stood a little more quietly she rubbed him on the face and neck until she could let him go and walk quietly away from him. She stalked over to Clay and threw the lariat at him. "Touch any horse I've started, and you're a dead man." For the first time, she noticed Charlie in the shadows, watching.

"That's not hardly fair, young'un. He has to work these cayuses too."

For a moment, she stood, undecided. She was sure the boss trained his horses the old cowboy way and that she was up against the old methods of breaking a horse, which included breaking his mind, his spirit, and sometimes, unfortunately, his body.

She climbed the corral fence to give herself time to think. She realized that her job might hang on her reply. She swung around and faced both of them. "Give me two and him two, and at the end of the month, you ride them and tell me which one you'd rather have under you in a storm." Everything in her body dared Clay to take up the challenge.

"You're on, lady," came Clay's cocky reply. "And I'll just bet while you're pussyfootin' around with your hand-fed babies, my picks will be putting in a good day's work." His jaw jutted in her direction, and his eyes glittered with the challenge.

If she hadn't felt so strongly about how he intended to treat the horses in his cowboy-training plan, she might have just given in to the urge to slap him . . . or to kiss him. "Aarrgghh. I can't believe this. Are you going to let him cowboy train your good youngsters, Charlie?" Frustration shimmered in her words.

Wiping his jaw, Charlie took his usual good time to answer. "Well, now, Lee Ann, it's been done for years thataway. I don't see much wrong with it."

"Of all the . . ." She stared at him in disbelief. "But you imprinted them. . . . I thought . . ."

"Your way takes a lot of time, Lee Ann. I got thirty horses there as needs trainin.'"

"My way takes no more time. I've made adaptations." She looked back and forth between the two. "Oh, God. I see it's hopeless. You're both members of the Cowboy Club. Why should I even bother? You've both made up your minds."

Charlie moved out into the sunshine and stood nearer to her. He tilted his hat up at her and proceeded to surprise the heck out of her. "I've seen lots of changes since I started this place with my pa, Lee Ann. If I hadn't kept up with those changes, I woulda lost this place. No, ma'am. I haven't decided. I want to see what you can do. I recall an uncle of mine by marriage, Indian, Apache. He used some mighty peculiar methods that put me in mind of yours a bit. So, no, ma'am. I'm honored to have you try. If yours is the best way, it'll show." He turned to Clay. "But, sir. *I'll* do the pickin'. That's only fair. Agreed?"

"Yes, boss." Clay grinned at Lee Ann, even though she could see that he wasn't expecting what Charlie had just put forth.

"Seems fair," she agreed.

"So, you still want to work that bay you called Little Joe?" Lee Ann couldn't believe her luck. He was a good, honest colt.

"Yes, sir."

"Then Clay should have a two-year-old too. Take that little sorrel with the white off-hind leg."

Charlie knew the herd well. That one would have been Lee Ann's second choice.

"And then, Lee Ann, take that flea-bitten gray. She's a four-year-old. Little Arab blood in her, so she might do things a little different than the natives." He grinned. "Sometimes those foreigners tolerate the heat a little better."

"Sir?" Clay wasn't getting it, Lee Ann could tell.

"Arabs. They ran full out in the hottest deserts in the world. That comes in handy here when those temperatures climb above a hundred and eighteen. I brought in a full blood stallion for a couple of years here, so most my stock has some Arabian blood.

They don't tie up or founder in the heat, like some do. Now, let's find something for you."

Charlie swung his rope above his head a time or two and the dominant mare obediently moved the herd about a bit. "There you go. That dun with the star. Four-year-old. Bandito, we call him. He's got a little mustang. Think you can handle him?"

"No doubt, sir. We have mustangs in Colorado. They're all horses. As long as they've got four legs, I can break 'em to ride, sir."

"Guess it's time to break out the hip boots. It's gettin' deep here." That was about the oldest cowboy brag there was, thought Lee Ann. She wondered what he would do with, say, a camel. "A camel has four legs. Could you break one?" Then she noticed it. "What's that on your arm?"

"This?" Clay pointed to a little plastic-and-tape apparatus on his forearm. "Oh, that's nothing. I still have a couple of rounds of antibiotics to get through, and they hook in there."

"Why couldn't they just give you pills?"

"Oh, I have some of them, too."

"He's still supposed to take it easy for the next day or two. I probably shouldn't have let him down here, but short of hog-tying him . . ." Charlie stood with hands spread helplessly.

"Don't you worry your pretty head. I'll be down to help first thing tomorrow."

He had the most infuriating way of implying that she couldn't get anything done without him. She all but spit the words, "I'll have you know I can do just fine without you." Jumping down from her perch on the fence, she added guiltily, "But I'm glad you're okay." The grin he sent her way tingled to her toes.

CLAY WAS UP THE next morning with the first peeps from the quail outside his open window. For the first time since he had gotten the infection, he felt like his old self. He bounded out of bed and landed on the cold floor. He still needed to infuse the last dose and take out the heparin lock. He got it over with then and poured himself a cup of coffee.

As he sat drinking it, he flexed his arm to relieve the slight ache still in it from the IV. Charlie came in and, with a nod at him, went about the business of breakfast. They ate in companionable silence and were actually out the door before either of them spoke a word. Movement in the corral caught their attention at the same time, and of one accord they moseyed that way.

The sight that met Clay's eyes was something he was sure he'd remember all his born days. Lee Ann had a saddle and bridle on Little Joe and seemed to be in deep communion with him. She stood slightly off to one side of him and was speaking to him in words too soft to carry. The little bay's ears flicked back and forth, and his whole body showed that he was totally intent on Lee Ann's every word. The sun gleamed off her golden mane, and every line in her body said that she was focused on the task at hand. Quietly, she stepped to the youngster's side and climbed up as if it were nothing, as if nearly a ton of unpredictable horseflesh wasn't beneath her.

Clay started forward, certain that she would be on the ground in the next second. Charlie's hand stopped him. "Leave off."

He glanced at the older man, who just pointed back at the corral. Still speaking softly, she raised her voice a bit until he could hear. "Walk." The pretty little gelding took a tentative step forward. At her rewarding pat, he took another, the whole while listening to the flow of words coming from his rider. As the pair began a slow walk among the herd, with the bay staying focused the whole time, Clay stood dumbfounded.

"I'll be darned." He took in the fact that Charlie was standing with arms crossed, leaning back and apparently completely enjoying what he saw. "You think that's the way to break a horse?"

Tipping his hat back, the older man's grin grew even wider. "It's a matter of style, my friend. And I guaran-dam-tee you, hers is prettier than yours."

He almost didn't catch the boss's second comment as he hurried off to get his rope. "The proof will be in the puddin'."

"That's for sure." Clay grumbled as he lifted his rope out of the tangle of gear he'd dumped on the tack barn floor. "Her little pampered pet is bound to come undone when a two-thousand-pound bull comes at him on the fight. That horse won't be able to hear her pretty words, and it won't know what to do." The mental image of what his own words painted made him scared and then angry. "She'll get herself killed."

Pleased with the progress made, Lee Ann was just easing down off Little Joe when she spotted Clay coming out of the tack barn, rope in hand, looking like a summer monsoon brewing in the western sky. His words were clipped, harsh. "You *will* get yourself killed." He didn't stop until he was nearly nose to nose with her, his height making him stoop.

Holding her ground, she spoke, deliberately using the soft language she usually reserved for wild animals. After all, she mused to herself, in his present state he wasn't really so different from one. "Excuse me?"

"Do you think when things go bad, that animal will work for you?" He slapped the rope on his thigh loudly. The bay at her side backed a step. "He needs to be more afraid of you than of whatever's out there." He swept one arm in a wide arc.

It took every ounce of her strength to stay quiet. "I don't think so."

He raised the rope and made to bring it down on Little Joe. Before she could even think, she grabbed his arm and threw her weight behind it. Her venom-filled words struck him in the face. "Don't even try it." She was angrier than she had ever been. "You are *so* sure you're right. But you agreed to the terms, buster. Now leave me and my horses alone if you know what's good for you." Surprise showed in his widened eyes, his startled stance.

"I just don't want you to get hurt. I'm only thinking of you."

Her glance back at him told her that he looked sincere, but she couldn't believe it because she thought he might do about anything to win the job. She firmed her hold on Little Joe's lead and took the jigging horse to the tack barn with her. There, she tied him to the hitch and untacked him with gentle hands that soothed away the nervous dance Clay's behavior had started. She hadn't really decided whether to put him out with the rest of the herd or put him up in a stall, when she heard the commotion that decided for her.

An angry squeal of a horse followed by a crash let her know that Clay had begun his training. She wasn't going to let Little Joe be traumatized any further by allowing him to see the brutality. She led him into a stall with thick bedding. If not for the noises coming from outside, she would have stayed and watch him settle in on the soft bedding. As it was, she slid the door clip in place and patted him quickly before she raced out the door to the round pen.

Her gut gripped as she watched Clay pop the whip behind the terrified sorrel, making it move at an even greater pace in the small confines of the round pen. It stumbled slightly, crashing an already skinned shoulder into the bars, before it regained its balance and, with eyes wildly rolling, whites showing, lunged forward again.

She looked around searching wildly for Charlie, hoping he would put an end to the spectacle. He stood in an adjoining pen, calmly nailing down a loose plank on a chute. His indifference just fanned the flames of Lee Ann's fury. She focused on the man with the whip and later couldn't even recall getting to him, but suddenly, she was there and wrenched the long black whip from him in a vicious twist. "What the hell do you think you are doing?"

"My job." His mouth tight, his gray eyes glinting, he rounded on her. "And just what the hell do you think you're doing?"

"Making you quit hurting Charlie's valuable livestock. You have no right." Her chest heaved with effort to breathe as she fought the urge to hit him.

"I have every right." He towered above her, and the wind whipped his hat off his head, making his black hair stick out in angry spikes. She could feel his anger now, and her instincts told her to back down, but her heart drove her onward.

"You have a right to *train*, not to *injure*." Tears threatened to fill her eyes, making her even madder.

He raised his voice. "Charlie? You got a problem with this?"

"Nope." His answer struck her hard, and the tears trickled down her face. She began to shake, and the whip dropped from nerveless fingers to thud in the sand at her feet. With one last look at the shaking sorrel, she turned and ran. It was just too much. How could she hope to fight it?

Her flight took her to the barn, where she buried her face in Star's mane and sobbed for all the injustice and pain in the world, for all the mute animals and small children who were senselessly brutalized. With shaky hands, she slipped a bit into the willing mouth of her oldest friend, Star, and sprang onto her back. Guiding her out the back of the barn with squeezes of her knees, she galloped off, ignoring the men's voices calling her name. She pushed Star and let her out, thundering over the flats and up one of the steep hillsides, then down the other side to another flat, which she sped over without thought. Finally, when she sensed her mount's fatigue, she reined her in and they walked for an hour more, coming to a stop beneath a stand of cottonwoods. A stream bubbled under the twisted roots along the stand of trees, and birds chirped and tweeted in the branches interlaced overhead. She wiped away the tears that still slowly trickled down her face, dripping off her chin. She knew as she sat there, in the idyllic oasis, on the wide, muscled, warm back of the mare her father had given her, that she cried for all the hurts. She cried not just for the pain of the sorrel, but for her own pain, her own injustice. Her father should have never died. She should have never had to sell the ranch she loved, leave the work she loved, where she had been understood, even sought out, for her methods. Taking a deep breath, she drew in the fragrant, moisture-laden air and let nature heal her, as she had done many times before. A noise in the underbrush startled her, and she realized with a shudder that she had left her pistol back at the barn. A large gray head materialized, a very ugly large gray head. "Bum," she whispered, "How did you find me?" She swung her leg over and slid to the ground to pat his rough head in greeting. A smooth granite rock hung over the trickling water from the underground springhead. She seated herself on it, and Bum happily laid his head in her lap, arranging himself in a curl around her. Her mare hung her head above her, and Lee Ann found comfort in their embrace.

10

Simply Lost

HOW LONG SHE'D SAT, she didn't know, but suddenly the breezes changed direction and the shadows lengthened. Bum stood up and stretched nervously and whined. Lee Ann cast an eye heavenward and shivered. The clouds piled up high behind the frontage range, and the first slash of lightning split the midday calm. Just seconds later the crash of thunder shook the ground beneath her feet. Usually, the monsoon storms hit in late afternoon, but once in a while they started earlier, and she guessed that this was one of those days.

The lightning was all but on top of her. She had to make a choice, and quick. Bum walked a few steps, whined, and came back to her. Her hand fell to his rough head with a reassuring pat. "It's okay. We'll ride while we can." With a hop, she gained Star's back and reined her back the way they had come. It wasn't hard to keep the mare in the relative protection of the trees and shrubbery, because even the horse could sense the danger of being in the open. They ate up the ground in an easy lope, weaving and dodging under tree branches and around desert scrub, managing to stay beneath it most of the time.

It seemed as if the storm were holding off when Lee Ann came to the last flats she had to cross to get back. There was no cover, with the trees undershot by fencing here. Branches whipped in earnest now, and the sky had darkened to an ominous hue of slate gray. The top of the mountain range was socked in with tumbling purple clouds. Rain spattered here and there, chaotic winds pushing it every which way.

She held the dancing mare in, contemplating the wide-open space while common sense battled within her. She should just get down and walk around the edges of the flats. It would take her another hour to get back that way. But in one dash, she could be across the flats in minutes and back to the warm dry barn in another fifteen. She took another look around and noted that even the giant saguaros were swaying in the wind. The mare decided it, by taking two leaps forward. Why Lee Ann let her go, she never knew. The last thing she remembered was a blinding flash of blue light and the smell of sulfur.

WHEN THE MARE and the dog raced by Clay as he came out of the barn, his skin crawled. An hour earlier Charlie had saddled up and headed out to find Lee Ann, telling Clay to stay put in case she came back, so he was alone. His heart crawled up his throat and stayed there as he took the bridle with its torn reins off Star and put her up.

He turned to the whining dog and pointed back outside. "Go, boy. Find her. Find Lee Ann." Bum whined. "Go get Lee Ann." With a wag of his tail the gray mutt circled and lay down in the hay with his paws over his nose. Disgustedly, Clay pushed past him. "Worthless animal." His guts were twisting inside like something alive as he voiced his fears. "She could be hurt, and you just lie there."

He gathered his tack and headed for one of the older horses in the end stalls. In no time, he was saddled and headed out. Maybe he could find some tracks. The spattering rain had already wiped out some of them, but here and there he spotted some at the edge of the corral. As long as the raindrops remained wide apart, he might still be able to track her.

He shook out the reins and let the big range horse move out. He found he couldn't go too fast or he would lose the trail, and he backtracked several times before he found the right speed. The trail was easy as long as it was in the flats, but once it headed over a rocky hill, he lost it. The best he could do was ride in the direction she had started and try to pick the trail up on the other side. The rain was beginning to fall in earnest, with fat wet drops, and he knew it was only a matter of time before he would have no trail.

Clay pushed his mount a little harder and, in doing so, nearly missed the turn she had taken toward an even bigger hill. Even though she had taken two hills, her general direction was downward. He spent nearly an hour zigzagging back and forth, casting about each time he lost the trail. Still, each time he would be about to give up, he would see a glint on a rock caused by a metal shoe, or see a couple of dents in a row that on a closer look turned out to be the toe of a horseshoe. Fear for her caused a weird sensation to jitter up and down his spine.

Star had a tendency to dig in with her toes, he noticed, a tendency that he was becoming happy about, for without it, he doubted he could have held the trail. He had about decided Lee Ann might have headed for some cottonwoods he could see in the distance when the skies opened up and nearly drowned him.

Panic seized him, and he squeezed the big horse tight, speeding him up as he realized the implications. He prayed she was on high ground because he could see the low areas already filling with run-off. Even though he had stuck to the city since he came to Arizona, he had rescued enough motorists from flooding low spots in the roads to know the killing potential of the run-off perpetrated by these summer storms.

Just then a large gray beast sped by him, and an anxious bark pierced the racket made by the rain, wind, whipping trees, and rushing water. Recovering nicely from the leap his horse had taken when spooked by the dog, he dug down deep in the saddle and called for speed. The big horse poured it on, and in a couple of leaps was close on the dog's flagging tail.

At the top of the next small rise, he saw it: a dark bundle on the ground that had to be Lee Ann. He tried to call her name and found he couldn't get anything past the lump in his throat. He jumped off the horse as soon as he got near her and dropped the reins. He took a precious second to see that the horse would stay put when ground-tied.

His legs shook uncontrollably as he knelt beside the still form. Her arms and legs were in a sprawl that told the story. She had either hit the ground unconscious or became that way as she hit. He straightened her slowly, trying not to take her head out of alignment with her body. It was possible she had broken her neck. He shuddered at the thought of her beautiful young life reduced to immobility. He had turned her to her side when he whispered the words, "Come on, Lee Ann. I'd simply be lost without you."

Water pooled around her form, beginning to run to the downside. He looked around frantically. He found her hat a couple of yards away, shook it out and placed it over her face to shield it from the rain. He stood again, wondering what he could do next. He couldn't just leave her alone. He stomped his foot in frustration. "Damn." He had decided the best he could do was to make a travois out of the tarp he always carried with his bedroll on his saddle, when he heard it.

"I heard what you said." No. He must have imagined it. Still he stooped and lifted her hat. A slight smile curved her pretty lips, which he noticed were pinked up a little.

"What?" he whispered, daring to hope. "What did you hear?"

With a groan, she rolled to one side and pulled herself up, making use of his arm and nearly pulling him over in the process. "Lost." Her face was in his now. She was kneeling in front of him, her breath soft on him. His heart constricted and his loins tightened into a pool of desire as he pulled her to him, holding her close.

"No." He kissed her sandy wet cheek and pulled them both upright, where she felt so right molded to him. "You were out, you know. You probably imagined it."

She shook her head slightly, making him grin. "Nope. Simply lost without me, cowboy. You said it."

He leaned her back, studying her face. She had sand plastered in her rain-darkened hair, all over her face, down her soaking wet shirt. He sucked in his breath as he saw the bold outline of her upthrust breasts, nipples plainly hard and upright. He was sure someone had just kicked him in the belly—and lower—and his breath exploded out of him. He flashed a quick look at her face.

The face that looked back was pure woman, knowing what effect she was having on a man. He wanted to kiss her, take her, turn that look into pure need. In a flash in his mind's eye, he saw what she would look like begging him for release, and his whole body flushed hot. With massive effort he translated that need into a tender kiss, taken only after he carefully supported the back of her head with his shaking hand. If it were possible, she molded herself more deeply into him, and he felt his control slip.

Firmly he took her shoulders and pushed her back a step. No one had ever taken him that near to the edge, never. He didn't like for a minute that she could. He drew in a deep draft of the icy wet wind that now blew steadily from the northeast. "Do you think you can sit behind me on my horse?"

She nodded and tried a couple of steps. She was beginning to be able to work out what had happened and where she had hit. "Yeah." The deep need she had felt just seconds before fled, leaving her shaking and wondering if she had imagined it. "I think I managed to tuck and roll. My shoulder is pretty sore." She rolled her head around in a tentative circle, causing Clay to suck air. She could swear he was holding his breath. "My head and neck are fine."

The air whooshed out of him. "So . . . everything but the shoulder's working?"

She stretched and waited to hear from the sore spots. "Just the shoulder and collarbone." Rolling her shoulder and rubbing her collarbone, she finished. "And they're okay. Just be sore a couple of days."

His face shone with relief. "Sure?"

"Yep. You gonna stand here in the rain all day or give me a ride back?"

He stood staring for a second more, then shook like a big wet dog. In a bound he was up on his horse and reaching down for her. She had a bit of a hard time getting to him for a hand up, because once she had shown signs of life, Bum had begun dancing enthusiastically around them both.

"Down, mutt." She patted him on the head and reached for Clay's large, warm hand. The ranch horse responded with only one crow hop before stepping out with his double burden. They had no sooner crested the first rise when Charlie hailed them from one slightly to the south.

"Clay, Lee Ann." He waved his hat, making it easier to spot him in the cactus and desert trees.

"I'm fine, Charlie." And she *was* fine, she realized. With a sudden stab of fear, she knew how close she had come to death's ugly face that day.

"Lee Ann?" She could feel as well as hear Clay's deep voice as she laid her head on his back.

"Hmmm?" She pulled herself as close as she could get to his comforting bulk and wrapped her arms around his waist. The smell of wet leather, horseflesh, and cowboy invaded her senses.

"What made you fall?"

"Lightning." She felt him stiffen in her arms.

"How close?"

"The air turned blue, and I could smell sulfur." His answering shudder somehow made her feel better, because now someone knew. Knew and cared.

"Thank God you're okay."

She could see the worry wrinkles on Charlie's face long before he reached them and was unprepared for his hard words.

"Pull another stunt like that one and you're off my place. I don't care if you are Duke Waters's daughter."

For one of the few times in her life, she was at a loss for words. She felt tears sting her eyes, but knew the rain hid them.

"Take it easy, boss. Lightning unseated her, and she had a bad fall."

"She'd a sat it, if she'd not let her anger get the better of her. She'd a put a saddle on, and by darn she'd a sat it."

From somewhere, she found the courage to speak. "I'm sorry. You're right. It won't happen again."

"Damn straight it won't." With a fierce grimace, he wheeled his mount and took off at a gallop toward the ranch.

"That's the maddest I've ever seen him." She shivered with shame.

"Well. He was just worried. We both were. Doggone it, Lee Ann. You can't fight the whole world. And, if you're gonna, don't be so hurt when people fight back."

"Hmmph." What could she say to that? Well, he had a point. She had come at him pretty hard. Maybe she could just talk to him when he was doing something she didn't like. "I can't stand to see animals abused, Clay Carter, and the sooner you realize that, the sooner we'll get along."

"Aw, there you go again. I wasn't abusing that horse. Just rufflin' his feathers some. I'm just training the way my pa and his pa before him taught me." As suddenly as the clouds had come up, they parted, and sunlight lit everything up. The air stilled, and birds began to sing their joy over a clean, new world.

"Stop by that fence corner over there." She pointed to some heavy posts that formed a corner and then a gate.

"You all right?" He strained to get a look at her.

"I'm fine. I just think we need to talk." She put a foot on the crossbeam, and Clay heeled the gelding a little closer to it. "Thanks."

She walked over to a smooth granite boulder

that was in the partial shade of a lacy mesquite tree and sat. He dismounted and headed toward her. She studied the loose-hipped way he walked and knew in that moment that he had ridden all his life. His muscular legs and the way he carried himself told her.

"Don't you think it might be time for a change?" She patted the rock beside her.

"Why fix what ain't broken?" He sat with one long blue-jean clad leg stretched out for support. "Least, that's what my granddad always said."

"How can I put this?" She struggled to keep control of the anger that always surfaced when she was faced with this kind of resistance. "Do we still build houses the same way? I mean, look." She pointed to the remains of a crude adobe building that lay across the meadow. "I'm sure it worked. It kept the rain off, the cold out. But it was dirty and the rain melted it. It wasn't exactly broken, but when wood frame houses came along, my grandpa and yours went for them. It was a better method. Cleaner, held up better in the elements. They took to the new houses and never looked back."

Clay's scowl caused the wayward lock of hair to fall forward on his forehead. She resisted the urge to put it back. "Still. The old one worked."

She just stared at him until he moved restlessly. "Really?"

"Aw, hell. I see what you're saying, but I still want to do the test."

"What test?"

"You know, at the end of the month."

Jaws clenched, she persisted. "I suppose you sack out, tie up feet, throw them over, the whole thing."

"I break horses."

He was immovable. She could see that now. "Yes. You do. I *train* horses."

"Your way might be better." She almost fell over. Struggling, she righted and turned to him. "What?"

He looked her in the eye, straight in the eye. "But you gotta prove it. It's all I ask. If I'm going to change something I been doing one way all my life, I gotta have proof."

Hope unfurled in her heart like a new blossom opening to the sun. "Really?"

"We have to have some kind of scoring system, though." His brows drew together in concentration as he focused on something she couldn't see. "A scorecard."

"Oh, I get it. Like a point for each thing a broke horse can do. It will have to be realistic. We can't turn out finished horses in three more weeks."

He rubbed the five o'clock shadow on his jaw and screwed his face up, thinking hard. He was adorable. She felt as if maybe she could work with him.

"Yeah, you know. Walk, trot, canter. Stop. Rein without fighting the bit or hackamore or whatever. Back up . . ."

Nothing much. She had Little Joe halfway there already. She'd start the Arab in the morning. Piece of cake. "Okay."

"Move that big black bull from one end of the corral to the other, away from the herd."

She gulped. "Okay."

"'Cause, I think that's where your method will fail you." No staring off into space at an imaginary score card now. He was looking right at her with challenge glinting in his clear, gray eyes. "I think if times get tough, your babies will cave in."

"Bet me." She stiffened her spine and stood hand out, waiting.

"You're on." He shook on it. "Twenty bucks?"

"You got it!" Babies. Babies! She'd bet her babies any day. Somewhere in the back of her mind, though, she wished she'd raised these herself. She just hoped that Charlie's imprinting methods didn't have any holes in them.

11

Not on the Job

CLAY STOOD IN THE center of the round pen with the little sorrel trotting at a steady pace in a circle about him. Lee Ann walked by the pen and looked Clay's way. He smiled and waved. The little sorrel lagged to watch her and got a pop of the whip on his hip for his mistake. She stopped to watch him leap forward, fear showing in the white of his eye. If he came in toward the man at all, he also got stung for that, and Clay wasn't allowing the most minor of infractions this morning. Further, when the horse didn't stop the minute Clay spoke the word "Whoa," he endured yet another sting accompanied by a harsh tug on the lead line. She could see that the horse understood the words *walk, trot* and *canter* and performed them well, again to avoid the sting of the whip.

Lee Ann used a similar technique but rarely touched the young horses. She found that just the sound of the popping whip was more than adequate to move out healthy young horses, and while on stubborn cases she sometimes touched them with the whip, stings were totally unnecessary. She winced as the little red got mixed up on a reverse and the whip popped a welt on his shoulder. The confusion and pain in his big brown eyes caused an angry tear to come to her own.

"Disgusting," she sneered as she passed to collect her whip. Clay winced. It encouraged her to see that he wasn't totally oblivious to her feelings on the subject. Maybe if she objected long and loudly enough, he would consent to learning a better way.

She realized that she knew him well enough already to know he would stick to his methods to the end of the competition. Still, she thought she could see him taking it a little easier with the whip. She wasn't sure if she wanted that or not, because she wanted him to use his method so she could prove him wrong. She smacked the dirt with her whip and headed to the barn for the Arabian gray.

The barn was cool in the morning with drafts of air pulling the scents of horses, cattle, hay, and desert through its breezeway. She breathed in what she thought of as one of nature's best perfumes and paused outside the gray's stall. She noted the large intelligent eye and the finely chiseled head set on a nicely arched neck that bespoke power and youth. The mare circled the stall and noisily blew air out of large, dilated nostrils. She reacted with a start when she heard the pop of a whip outside.

Lee Ann eased inside the stall, taking care to latch the door. "It's all right, girl. That's not what will happen to you." She ran an appreciative hand down the silky hide the color of sweatshirt gray. "You're so soft." Gradually, under her firm strokes, the muscles relaxed. The tiny pointed ears swiveled toward her, signaling attention. "Fleece. We'll call you Fleece. How does that sound?"

Lee Ann stroked the mare all over and began the patting and poking that was part of the imprinting method. Although alert and busy, the mare responded nicely, never moving away from prodding hands. She moved her dainty hooves around Lee Ann's boots with consideration and lack of fear and lifted them easily when asked. After a few minutes, Lee Ann was satisfied that the imprinting program had been completed.

She smiled and reached for the halter, and slipping it easily over the ears, buckled it into place.

Calmly, the pretty mare waited for what was next. Lee Ann led her out into the sunlight. The gate on the round pen stood ajar and Clay was nowhere to be seen, so she took the little mare over and tied her to the stout bars, then returned to the barn and came back with Sugar. Leading the mare in, she latched the gate. Shaking out the lunge line she had attached to the halter, she moved the gold mare out with a word: "Walk."

Sun glinted off the palomino's hide as she quietly moved to the bars of the pen and swung into a long, ground-eating walk, one ear attentively cocked at Lee Ann. At each gait, cadence and pace were perfect and commands executed well. Every so often Lee Ann murmured, "Good girl, work on." The feeling of supreme happiness seeped into her; it was always present when she was tuned in with one of her mounts. She turned a bit to see that the gray mare was attending to what was going on. She was. Out of the corner of her eye, she saw Clay standing in the shade of the barn. He was leaned up against it, with a look on his face that could only be described as disdainful.

"You expect her to learn just by watching?" Sarcasm laced his question.

"Not *just* by. No." Impatience laced hers.

When she was finished, she called Sugar to her and rubbed her forehead. The mare gave a happy sigh and licked her lips, chewing on some imaginary piece of hay. Opening the gate, she switched the short tie for the long one on the gray and pulled her in, leaving the palomino outside.

"C'mon, Fleece," she whispered in her ear. "I know you've got it in you, and you *were* paying attention." Standing in the center of the round pen, she shoved her away into the direction she wanted. "Walk." The mare stamped restlessly in place. Lee Ann bent and picked up the whip. She touched the rear of the mare. "Walk." The mare turned and touched the whip with her nose.

A dry chuckle preceded his comment. "*No habla Inglés, Senorita.*"

"I'll thank you to keep your comments to yourself. If you can't stay quiet, go away." She jiggled the lead line and firmly repeated the command. The light came on. She could see it. The little mare dipped her head and moved out at a springy walk. "Goooood girl," she crooned, shooting a triumphant look over her shoulder at Clay.

The mare turned and reversed with a light shove on her shoulder after she came to a stop, then walked on command in the other direction. Once in a while Lee Ann noticed that distractions caused confusion, but by and large, she held her gaits and did incredibly well.

Lee Ann made her repeat all the steps for each gait, and even though she had to pop the whip the first few times to change the mare's gait, she never did have to touch her. She ended the session on a good note with a stop that lacked precision but was correct. As she led Fleece out, Clay commented, "You took longer than I did."

She stopped by a patch of bermuda grass and let the mare eat. Clay nearly bumped into her. Clean soap and aftershave wafted by her. Emotions warred within her. One second she wanted to smack him. The next she wanted to kiss him. Instead she faced him.

"In the long run, I *will* save time." She tucked a long strand of bermuda into her mouth and savored the spicy grass taste of the tender end.

"How's that?" He joined her and chewed on one, too.

"The other end." She pulled the grass out of his mouth and showed him the light-green tender tip that pulled out of the joint. "It's sweet." Whether consciously or not, she had gotten much closer to him.

"I know something sweeter." He reached around

behind her and pulled her to him. His lips were mere inches from hers.

"While you are chasing after your horse, who just ran off 'cause he's afraid of you, I'll be getting about my work, with my horse standing right behind me." His lips landed on her saucy grin.

"Never happen," he challenged, never taking his lips away.

"Will too. And you're kissing my teeth, you know."

"Yeah, I know." It was his turn to grin. Their teeth knocked as the gray mare tugged on the line, trying to get to a better patch of grass.

Lee Ann leaned away as she spotted Charlie's truck coming toward them. "We're not being paid for this."

"Hmm. Okay, I'll stop." He dropped his hand and reached for Sugar's lead. Just as they got to the barn Charlie met them.

He held the little sheet of paper aloft. "Who gets it today?"

"My turn." Lee Ann took the list and checked it quickly to make sure she could read it all. As always, it was an ambitious list and far more than they could get done in one day. Deep down, she suspected Charlie was trying to get everything caught up around the place while he had the two of them working for him. She couldn't blame him, really, but the task was enormous. The place was really in need of a lot of TLC.

"We'll take care of it, sir." Clay rumbled.

"Hold on a minute, you two." Charlie took his hat off and wiped out the brim. "Now I know that you are both healthy youngsters. But if you are going to court, do it on your own time."

Lee Ann felt heat climb her neck. He had obviously seen them kissing. "We're not courting."

"Yes, we are." Clay held their boss's gaze. "But you're absolutely right, sir. We'll do it on our own time."

"Good." He replaced his hat and took measure of them both. "Not that I disapprove, you understand."

What could she say? She had been kissing him. But court? Not for the first time she marveled at how old-fashioned Charles Bruce was. Court? "Clay Comes a-Courtin'"? She giggled and skipped past them both, humming a little tune to go with the phrase.

Fleece settled into her stall, and Lee Ann leaned over the half-door to watch her for a minute. The even breathing and barely damp hide told her that the mare had been pushed, but only a little. The clip-clop of hooves in the dirt told her that Clay was coming with Sugar, so she opened the stall door and waited.

He led her past and closed the door with a click. "Mighty pretty mare."

"Thanks." He moved closer to her. Lots closer. "None of that now." Her heart sped up as he leaned closer, but all he was doing was adjusting the hay net that hung just inside the door.

"Little too loose. She could get hung up." He left his arm there, suspended just above her left shoulder, and leaned on the frame. He let his gaze drift to her mouth.

Suddenly shy, she glanced away and then back, wanting to know what he planned to do. His eyes took on a stormy quality that took her breath away. She felt just like a mouse in a trap. "Not on the job," she whispered.

"Oh," he sighed. "I'm not going to touch you now, but maybe tonight, after hours, I'll find you in the moonlight by the upper corral."

His closeness unnerved her. The fact that he was off-limits frustrated her. His sexy growl undid her. Her knees buckled, and he caught her. She hoped he would break the rules. He stepped away. She should have known better. A cop, break the rules?

* * * * *

THE DAY'S WORK had been grueling, hard, sweaty, and frustrating. Working with Lee Ann and not being able to touch her was hell. There she would be cranking on the "come along," tightening the fence they were repairing while he twisted the next splice. She would be pouring sweat and popping muscles. She never complained and could work like two men. Never for a moment did he think she was masculine, though—far from it.

Every minute of every hour he longed to hold her, kiss her, and taste her salt. Now he was washing his own sweat and salt off and fervently hoping she would show up tonight at the upper corral. The cool water sluiced over his tired muscles and worked its magic, restoring him. Clay flexed his fingers and eyed the deep cut on the inside of the first joint. It would take a long time to heal and play hell with his card game. He realized with a start that this was the first time in days that he had thought of gambling. He pictured himself with a deck of cards. Usually, the excitement that came with the thought of a good game, a good hand, got him going. He was really doing all right, but he knew it was thoughts of kissing a certain blonde in the moonlight that was helping him do it.

* * * * *

THE WATER SHEETED over her, easing her aching muscles. The moonlight lit the small room with a blue-silver pearly light. She didn't need to turn on the light to shower because it was so bright. That made her think it would be easy to find Clay in the night by the upper corral. The thought put her pulse into overtime and caused warmth to pool deep in her belly.

She shouldn't get involved with him. Even though he was a cop, he was a cowboy, and he stood for an awful lot she didn't like. Her father had asked her not to marry some no-account cowboy. He had said he wanted more for her. Her shoulders drooped at the thought of her hard-working father, his earnest face lined with years of hard labor.

At the time, she fancied herself in love with Andy Silvercreek, and she was all of sixteen. He was almost a pro rodeo rider by that time and could sit even the meanest bronc as if he were on a Sunday ride. He could also drink like there was no tomorrow and had a reputation for being rough with the ladies, though he treated her like she was delicate glass. Her father said he would never amount to anything, and he had been right.

On a drunken ride one night, Andy had plunged through a railing with his Jeep and gone to his death in the rushing waters of Cibecue Canyon. She thought she might die for the love of him and for the loss, but she hadn't, and she hadn't ever dated a cowboy again. Still, she dried off, and still she dressed, and still she walked the Jeep trail to the corral. She told herself that he wouldn't come or that she would leave before he got there or. . . .

Suddenly he was there. She knew because she scented him on the night's breezes. She stood to run, to leave. Two strong arms captured her and held her close. If he had pushed then, she would have slapped him and left. If he had not just held her close for twenty long minutes, as if she were a lifeline and he might drown if he let her go. If he wasn't so tall, so perfect; if only he didn't feel like her other half.

Finally, he kissed her senseless and kept it up until she had to lean on one of the rough poles of the corral for support. She felt drugged. When she looked into his eyes, she could see that he was drugged, too. With a moan of need, she wrapped her arms around his neck and drew him closer. He touched her everywhere until once again her veins felt like a tracery of gunpowder fired by the pulse of her desire. She burned, and only he could douse the flames.

Her hands found the Mexican blanket draped over one of his shoulders only seconds before he shook it out and spread it on the ground. A moment later, when he lowered her to it, she realized his intent. She shoved at him and, while he hesitated, he didn't stop.

He looked deep into her eyes and began unbuttoning her blouse, one slow button after the other. The cool breeze brushed across her nipples, already hard, and peaked them to the point of pain. His fingers made short work of her front-opening bra, and then he began to worship her with his hands and his tongue. The whole while he rubbed himself on her in a sinuous rhythm that destroyed her caution, devastated her mind.

Her hands moved to his hips to stop him. It only made him increase his leverage and push harder. One hand slipped, and she brushed the length of his desire. It stopped the breath in her throat. He groaned and leaned away, and somehow her hand found his top snap. With a twist that should have required practice, she opened the top of his jeans. In the next motion, she had unzipped his pants.

It was as if she were two people. There was this sensible one standing back and advising, "Now don't do this. You'll only get hurt." And then there was this other one, saying, "More, oh more. I don't care about anything but this awful need for him." A whiff of beer on his breath stopped her, reminded her of that other cowboy, that other night, so much like this one in so many ways. She should tell him.

"You won't be the first."

His tongue met hers and teased it. Now she could taste the beer as well as smell it. "I didn't expect that you had been wrapped up and saved for me." His words were slightly slurred.

Lust or lush? "Have you been drinking?" What did she know about him, really? Other than he cowboy-trained horses.

"Yeah, why?" The slight defensiveness of his tone was not lost on her. His heated thrusts had stopped. She was aware of an embarrassing dampness at her crotch.

"I can't do this." He held her pinned half a minute more, then sat up, never taking his eyes from hers for a second.

"I brought protection." He ran his hand through his hair, making it stick out in every direction. Lord, she wanted to push back that one lock that slanted over his eyes. "But it's not that, is it?"

"No. It's not that." Her blouse hung open, her bra undone, and suddenly she felt horribly vulnerable. Seeming to sense it, he quickly fastened her bra and buttoned a couple of buttons. "I don't know you.

Not really." Her heart hurt with all she wanted to tell him. And yet, what could he do? Could he change what he was, who he was? "Why are you here?"

A quick rub of his jaw telegraphed the confusion he felt. "I thought you wanted this. As badly as I did—do."

"No, I mean the ranch. You're a cop. Why are you here?" To still her panting breath, she pulled her knees up and wrapped her arms around them, then shooed away a mosquito trying to feast on her wrist.

"Oh, that." He seemed to take slow measure of her and decide something. "I guess I can tell you." His heart pounded so hard, it shook his shirt.

"I got shot. In the line of duty." He sat back and let his legs sprawl as he looked up at the full blue moon. "I lost something."

Lee Ann laid her hand on his knee. "Go on."

"My nerve." He faced her, his face lined with shame. "Not in the usual way. I could still do my beat, but they wouldn't let me for a while yet. There are rules, you know."

"Well, in what way then?"

He drew his gaze back to her and sat up straight with his look penetrating deep.

She couldn't hide from him at all, like this. She hoped she could stand what he had to say.

"I drink and I gamble. I've had big losses."

It turned out she couldn't. The fear slammed into her hard. In a flash, she pictured Clay careering out of control in his truck, over the edge of a riverbank, plunging to his death. She tore her gaze from his and fisted the back of her hand into her mouth to keep in the scream that exploded in her mind. She jumped up and sped down the trail back toward the ranch as if devils were on her trail. Maybe they were.

12

A Fine Fiddler

"NEXT WEEK WILL BE roundup." Charlie faced Lee Ann and Clay across the table in the kitchen. A pot of chili simmered on the stove, and its fragrance spiced the air. Lee Ann had made her own special recipe of cornbread, using the cornmeal she got up in the little town of Snowflake, Arizona. She had just taken it out before seating herself opposite the two men.

Clay noticed that these days she always managed to keep plenty of space between the two of them. He felt like a low-bellied scum-sucker every time he remembered the look of terror his words had put on her face that night a week ago. What he had said had been bad, but it didn't warrant the look she'd given him. Besides, the cure was working. He didn't want to drink or gamble anymore. The ranch was taking it out of him. Question was, if he went back to work, could he stay out of it? His attention drifted back to Charlie's drone.

"Things are different since the old days. We don't have as many seasoned hands around. I'll have two. But, besides them, we just have to make do with whoever shows up to help. Now, we get some good riders in, and then we get some yahoos. It's a trick to get the yahoos to calm down and not run the weight off the cattle. Then we'll also get some help from the neighboring spreads and some old friends from farther away. Lee Ann, it might interest you to know that the Lockharts are coming down."

A pretty smile crossed her face. "Really? Bob and Josie?"

"Yep."

"Folks you know?" Clay found himself hoping the smile would stay.

"Yeah. Neighbors of the Two-Horse. It'll be good to see them." She did smile, but turned quickly and got up to fetch chili and cornbread. "They might be getting up there in years, but they *are* good hands." At least she was talking to him. He watched her set the steaming bowls on the table for dinner.

"Generally, folks come in on Wednesday and Thursday, and we start Friday. Some will stay in the bunkhouse, some here in the main house, and some bring their own places along. Most of them know how it's done, but if not, send them my way and we can get it straightened out." Charlie buttered his cornbread with a slab of thick, fresh butter and smiled beatifically after the first bite. "Lee Ann, this cornbread just might give you an edge."

Her tongue came out at Clay, and she grinned before she thought about it. He couldn't help but chuckle at her sassy expression. "Don't count your chickens before they're hatched." Then he took a bite of the cornbread. He couldn't remember ever having tasted any so good. "Why can't we just hire her as a cook?"

She stood up so fast, her chili nearly spilled. "Because I left that job and a bunch of others just like it behind. I am *much* more than a cook, brother, and don't you forget it!" Her napkin tented over her food where she had thrown it, and she stalked off out the front door, presumably to the bunkhouse.

Charlie's eyebrows had scaled up his forehead, but not for a minute did he stop eating. He slowly and thoroughly demolished every bit of the food in front of him.

Though it now tasted like cardboard to him, Clay did the same thing.

"I thought you two were courtin'?" A toothpick appeared from his shirt pocket.

"Yeah, I thought so too."

"She acts like a scalded cat every time you get near. Something I need to do to you for old Duke's sake?"

"No. Nothing happened. Not that I wouldn't want it to." Clay kicked back and rocked on the chair legs.

"That chair has four legs, son. Want to talk to me about it?"

Clay let the chair back down with a thunk. "Just maybe I do. I don't know how to go about it, so I'll just say it." Heat climbed to his face at the thought of what he was about to share. Gentlemen don't kiss and tell, but he was sick and tired of stewing about it. "We were out by the upper corral."

"Pretty place." Charlie steepled his fingers and gazed at them with a knowing smile.

"Yeah, it is. And things were going along pretty well. And then the damndest thing happened."

"Go on."

"She asked if I drank. You know, if I had been drinkin'?" He shook his head. "Well, I'd had a beer or two. I sure wasn't stoned. Well, that seemed to bother her some, but nothing major. Then she asked me why I didn't work as a cop and, damn it all, I shouldn't have told her, 'cause that's what set her off." His guts roiled at the memory.

"You mean you'd lie to her?" The older man's face looked troubled.

"No, sir. Just shouldn't have said." He rocked back on the chair legs again.

Charlie reached forward and pulled him down. "Clay, I'm going to talk to you like your dad, if it's okay."

"Yes, sir. You sure remind me of him." He indicated the chair.

Charlie chuckled drily. "Yep, well, first off, don't think you can keep things from a gal as smart as Lee Ann. Second, I think I can clear up the mystery for you, but God help you if you ever tell her I told you."

"But you just said . . ."

"I know, I know. Here's how it went." He took a few minutes to tell Clay about Andy Silvercreek's drunken death.

"How did you know about that?" Clay couldn't see now how he could ever regain Lee Ann's trust or interest even.

"The ranching community isn't a big one, and a loss like that, is hurtful. He was a fine hand with horses and would have enjoyed a good future with his skills. He also had a knack of bringing in beef and horses that had been lost for years. Could sniff 'em out and bring in the wildest ones. He saved many a year for many a rancher, and he made good money because of it."

"So, he would have made a good life for him and Lee Ann." An unexpected stab of jealousy speared him at the thought.

"No. He wouldn't have." This time it was Charlie who leaned back on two legs.

"Why?"

"Because he gambled away everything he made at the casinos. Duke used to beg her not to marry some no-account cowboy. He was always on her about it. Like all dads, he just wanted her to have a good life."

The truth hit Clay like a sledgehammer. He was like history repeating itself for Lee Ann. "My Lord. I didn't know."

"Well." Chair legs resounded heavily on the plank floor. "Now you do. What are you going to do about it?"

"I'll just tell her . . ."

A large brown finger waved just below his nose. "And get us both killed? Ah, ah, ah. Not a word."

Clay sat for a long moment, spinning his spoon

in his empty bowl. "She is just going to have to see that I'm a changed man. That's all."

With a nod of satisfaction, Charlie rose and went to his big, battle-scarred oak desk. He ran a few sheets through his fax machine and handed them over. "Take these out to her. These are the cow/calf lists. I want every one of them accounted for before this week ends. Here is the bull list."

Clay gathered up her chili bowl and tucked the lists under his arm. He had to start now. He had to get back on some kind of footing with her. A sparkle of apprehension skittered down his back when he realized how important it was that she think well of him. He was just going to have to prove to her that he wasn't Andy Silvercreek. And that meant staying sane and staying sober.

LEE ANN THOUGHT SHE had cried all her tears out the other day, when she realized how close she had come to loving Clay Carter and how he could never be hers. But she sat there on her bunk in the dark and they flowed again like a silent river down her face, over her chin, and onto her shirt. How dare he suggest that she be hired as a cook? Who did she think he was?

Just then a scratch on the bunkhouse door raised hairs on the back of her neck. Had she latched the door? *It could be most anything.* She knew that lots of animals roamed these parts: bear, mountain lions. Then it came. A long, drawn-out howl ending with a yip-yip-yip. *A coyote! Maybe a rabid coyote. Rabies sometimes runs rampant in these mountains, carried by bats and skunks.* A deep shivering grabbed hold of her.

She edged over to where she hung her holster on the back of the chair and eased her three-fifty-seven out of it. On cat feet, she slipped over to the window and pulled back the gingham curtain. What she saw there made her smile. She tossed her gun onto her bed. Standing with his head thrown back stood Clay Carter, howling like some demented thing, holding her chili in front of him. She couldn't hide her smile as she opened the door and held out her hands for the chili.

"Do you open your door to just any old coyote, lady?" He thrust the bowl into her hands. "I could be rabid, you know." He leered at her, looking more like a crazy hyena than anything remotely rabid.

"You deliver to all ranches, or is this the only one?" Taking the bowl, she plunged the spoon into the still-warm chili. "Mmmm." She cocked her head to one side and looked at him so charmingly, it took his breath away.

"Lee Ann. About the other night . . ."

"Don't ruin it." Another bite disappeared. "For tonight you're just the chili delivery boy—er, coyote." She grinned, clearly liking his lunacy as well as the chili.

"And the list server." He held out the papers with a flourish. "The secrets to the Silver Rock ranch."

Wiping a bit of chili off her lip with her thumb, she licked off the red spot. "Otherwise known as the livestock tally sheet?"

"Indeed. Sir Charles says they must, absolutely must, be all in and accounted for by Sunday eve at the latest, my lady." He used his best court manners to no avail.

She squinted at the sheet in the dim light. A low whistle escaped her lips. "Wow. Who would have guessed this range held so many." With a plunk, she sat in a chair near a battle-scarred table. "I sure hope we get plenty of help. Did we ever happen to notice just how far this herd can spread out?"

"Looks like we may need to take a look at that map again." He took a chair and settled it near her. "And if we have any hope of bringing them all in, we will have to ask Charlie where their favorite haunts are." He held out his hand toward the door. "Shall we?"

With a shrug, she polished off the last of the chili. "This has to go back anyway. We might as well pow-wow." When she got up and headed out the door, he considered it a major victory.

Lee Ann's head spun with all that had to be done in the next week just to get ready for roundup. As she walked the last few feet to the main house with Clay behind her, she knew they had to get down to business, and fast. The last of the equipment repairs had to be done, the vaccines and supplies ordered, and, oh Lord, who would cook for the crew that was coming?

When they arrived, Charlie had three stacks of paper piled in a neat row on the desk. He smiled, handed one to each of them and took one of his own.

"Just read. If you have any questions, I'll answer them when you're through."

She took hers to the leather chair under the elk horns, and Clay sat at the table. In the soft light of the lamp, she made out the information. It was all there. A brief outline of what would be accomplished each day, followed by assignments for everyone. She was relieved to see that a couple of Charlie's female friends were bringing the food and would take care of that end of things.

At the end of all the information was a clever invitation with a lariat around the wording, "Y'all come. After the work is done, there is fun to be had. Freddie Fine and his fiddle will bring those tired feet back to life, and we'll all dance in the moonlight."

Before she could stop it, a picture of her and Clay dudded up for a dance, twined together in a perfectly fitting match and swaying under the moonlight, flashed in her mind's eye. Ducking her head to hide the heat she knew colored her face, she ambled over to the desk.

"Boss, we need to see where these little critters of yours like to hang out."

"That I can help you with. They're creatures of habit. It's the newer ones that usually give us the trouble, and Lord help us if they find the breaks in the fence, 'cause they could be anywhere. One year, we found one clear over to Apache Lake." He pulled out the old parchment and began pointing.

"Whoa, wait a minute there." Clay got closer. "Do you have any maps we might write on?"

"Yep." Charlie pulled out the lower drawer on the desk, reached into files, and came up with several pages stapled together. "Here." A skeleton drawing of the canyons and creeks and fences made things clearer.

Lee Ann grabbed a pencil and scribbled in the ear tag numbers, as Charlie indicated where they would find which cattle. It was a tedious process, but they both oriented themselves to the canyons, fence lines, and waterways as well as learned where they might find the herd.

"Guess that about does it. Now the next couple of days would be a good time for the two of you to finish riding fence. Particularly work those sections on the west side. It takes the most pressure from hunters, hikers, and riders."

"They cut it?" Lee Ann remembered that on the Two Horse, they'd had very little of the problem because of the relative isolation of the place.

"Cut it, knock it down, drive over it. You name it, and the public does it."

"Why do you have so much trouble here?" Clay wondered.

"Well, I lease state land to graze. Most folks think state land means it's theirs as much as anyone's. And that they have a right to be on it."

Clay shook his head. "If that doesn't beat all. We'll stay right on top of it, sir."

"Good deal. I'll have bob-wire tied out at most of the corner posts on the outside, so you don't have to carry it. Just be sure to loop and tie whatever's left

BEST MAN FOR THE JOB

so some fool animal doesn't walk through it and cut themselves to pieces."

Out of the corner of her eye, Lee Ann could see Clay stretch. His shirt nearly popped at the seams when he took a deep breath. She realized she had stopped breathing and forced herself to take a deep draft of air, all the while chanting to herself that he was bad for her. He caught her looking and flashed a wink and a smile her way. Mortified, she made a big deal out of folding up the map.

"Tomorrow's gonna come mighty early." Her accent thickened and she dropped her consonants when she was embarrassed. Maybe he hadn't noticed. It wasn't until she had gone to college that she noticed how lax her dad had been in language. He talked like most westerners, with a decided twang and lots of colloquialisms and lost or abbreviated endings. In college, she rapidly corrected herself, but here she was, back on a ranch just a few short weeks and sounding just like a little cowgirl again. "So, I'll just be heading back to the bunkhouse."

THE RINGING OF the dinner bell woke her, and though it seemed she had just closed her eyes, daylight filtered through the gingham curtains. With a groan, she dressed as fast as she could and ran a brush through her tangled hair. Vague memories of a dream where she and Clay danced in the moonlight nagged her as she struggled into her boots. Turmoil lashed her as she fled from her thoughts by running to the main house for breakfast.

Clay opened the door as she reached for the knob. He stood before her, clear-eyed, dressed, shaved, and ready for the day. By comparison, she felt shoddy as she stuffed her shirttail in the back of her jeans and scooted by him to the table.

"I was about to go looking for you." His pearly whites were a little hard to take this morning.

"I know the way to breakfast," she snapped.

"Be nice, youngsters." Charlie grinned as he dished out potato and egg hash, which was his specialty. It was fried in bacon grease, awful for you and the best thing this side of the Pecos, Lee Ann had decided. She wrapped her hands around a big mug of steaming cowboy coffee and sipped. It was hot and rich and the perfect way to get a jump-start on the day.

"I thought I might take out Miser to ride fence. You got anyone up to it yet?"

Challenge gleamed in Clay's eyes.

"Miser?" Lee Ann forked in a mouthful of hash and chewed reflectively. "Who's that?"

"The little sorrel. I named him that 'cause he is so stingy." Charlie brought over the last of the toast and seated himself.

"Stingy?"

"Yep. He won't let me rub him or pet him at all. Just snubs me."

Lee Ann chuckled derisively. "Do you blame him?" She slathered some apple butter onto her toast. "I mean, he'd hafta be a psycho to want to snuggle up to someone who beats him with a whip. I say he shows good sense."

Charlie seemed really intent on his food, but a twitch appeared at the corner of his mouth.

A scowl darkened Clay's face for a second. "Never thought of it that way ... Hey, I don't *beat* him with the whip."

"Okay, okay. I exaggerated."

"You're avoiding the question, buckarette. Got a mount ready?"

"Matter of fact, I do, buckaroo." She jabbed a potato and popped it in her mouth. "Wanna take bets on who walks home and who rides?"

"No!" His face sobered. "I'm not a gambling man anymore."

She nearly choked on the hash. "You're what?" The words were whispered.

"You heard me. And I won't touch another drop of liquor, either."

Suspicion crept into her voice. "You two been talking about me?" She studied each in turn.

Charlie's head swung to and fro as he continued to work the figures on the pad he held. Clay just held her gaze, clearly and calmly.

"Will this be enough feed to get the cattle through while we work them?"

"You're asking me?" Now Lee Ann knew they had talked. Charlie Bruce knew exactly how much feed he would need, having done this at least a hundred times in his life. "Did you tell him about Andy?" Her voice had climbed about two decibels.

"Don't go blamin' Charlie. I asked." Clay stood and put his hand on her arm. She shook it off, like a horse shaking a horsefly.

"Damn. I could shoot you both just as soon as look at you. You, " she pointed a shaky finger at Charlie, "had no right. And you, you, you shouldn't have asked." Her breakfast heaved in her belly, so she ran for the door.

As soon as she was outside, she took a deep breath and tried to rein in her galloping emotions. When she felt she had a little control, she stomped toward the barn, grumbling all the while. Bum trotted up and positioned himself so that one of her swinging hands thumped his head. Petting him seemed to help. By the time she had Little Joe tied to tack him up, she felt a semblance of her normal self. Clay had come out and tacked up Miser without a word or a look her way. As she turned to get her fence tool, she nearly ran right over Charlie.

"I want to apologize, Lee Ann. You're right. I had no right. And I'm sorry. I just tried to think what Duke might have said to the boy if he was courtin' you back then."

A mouse of shame crept up her. She raised her eyes to his. "Why would you tell him?"

"I think you're givin' him a bum steer. That's all. He should at least know the rules you play by." The older man's gaze didn't waver. "Besides, I think he'll keep his promise."

She searched his face closely and saw he believed what he'd just said. "You said before that you approved of us courtin'. You must like him."

"Yes, ma'am. I do."

A tear came to her eye because he cared and because he cared enough to interfere. She knew for a fact that it wasn't his way. She gave him a quick hug and a smile, and his lined face lit up. "You know, Charlie Bruce, you're still a handsome man yourself."

She stepped up and mounted Little Joe. "So will *you* make a bet with me?"

His deep laugh and answer reassured her that they were fine again. "No, no. I'm smart enough to know when a young stallion is on the range."

She almost missed his second comment as she rode out. "And smart enough to know when it's the right stallion."

So, Charlie believed Clay's promise. Problem was, she had heard plenty of promises before and had been around to see them shattered, time after time.

13

Ridin' the Line

THE NORTH SECTIONS OF fence turned out to be mean territory to cover. Clay had ridden rough ground plenty, but this beat it all—and him on a green horse. *I must be nuts*, he thought, *certifiable*.

Three or four times already the little red gelding had taken missteps that nearly carried them both to the bottom of drops in excess of two hundred feet. He knew the sweat that covered his body wasn't all caused by the bright spring sunshine. He lifted his shoulders and rolled them while easing his head around in a circle. It helped the muscles loosen to where he wasn't wound as tight as steel strings on a Spanish guitar. Before him, riding pretty as you please, Lee Ann sat easily on her little bay. It was a lot to ask that the youngsters travel ground this rough, as they were just getting used to balancing themselves with a rider. Little Joe seemed to have cat feet and an unerring sense of balance. Of course, Miser carried by far the bigger load with Clay's weighing easily fifty-five to sixty pounds more than she did.

Clay watched Lee Ann get down at another break, and slip on her work gloves to repair the fence. Her mount stayed glued to her side. He liked the way she had of tucking the reins in at her hip, and darned if that little horse ever tugged at all.

He looked around for a place to tie his horse and found a likely-looking ironwood. Miser jerked back with wild eyes when Clay pulled the reins over his head. The signs were unmistakable: The horse would bolt, given half a chance. Well, he would just have to be sure to tie him snug. Darned if he would give Lee Ann the satisfaction of seeing him walk back. He had to admit to a stab of envy at the quiet way the other two worked. She had already located a loop of wire and was splicing it onto the break. With a few deft twists, she held out the end for him to attach to the other side. Other than a fine sheen of perspiration covering her upper lip, she looked fresh as a daisy. With a growl, he took it and worked it onto the post.

"My, my. Aren't we testy?" She bent and grabbed

the middle wire, spliced new wire on, and handed it to him. "Hot, cowboy?"

"Not really." He had to be truthful. "It's still under a hundred."

"Tense, cowboy?" She handed him the bottom wire.

He growled again. He couldn't lie to her, but damned if he was going to answer her. He looped the wire around the post and stood to tighten it with the fence tool. She was right in his face, all fresh-smelling and golden. His pulse did double time, and he took a deep breath and a step back all at once. His boot hit something, and he tried to step around it but failed. Doing a fancy dance, he managed to remain upright but crashed into Miser's hip. The horse leaped away with a squeal, and the sickening sound of breaking branches rent the air. With a wild leap, the gelding found the freedom he sought and took off in a blur of red.

Anger flashed through Clay like heat lightning flashes through the summer evening sky. "Now look what you caused." He pointed an accusing gloved finger at her.

Calmly, she slid the reins over her horse's head and mounted up. "I'll try and catch him for you." Little Joe bounded into a smooth lope at a spoken command and a touch of her heel. She turned and called over her shoulder. "Seein' how it's *my* fault."

It wasn't hard to see where the red had gone. Broken brush and chewed-up ground marked his progress. Lee Ann shivered with delight. Things were working out just the way she had imagined. If this didn't show Clay Carter the error of his ways, nothing could. She slowed Little Joe to a walk and concentrated on the trail as it now wound over some dells of granite. To the untrained eye, the trail would seem gone, but Lee Ann had been tracking things for fun ever since she was a kid.

One fine endless summer day, she had spent the whole day tracking the progress of their big red rooster, who had a missing toe. Her father had said she reminded him of a speckled hound dog pup on a trail as she crawled along with her blonde hair trailing in the dust. And her mother always had a fit when she came in that dirty.

Her mom. She tried not to think too much about her. It had happened when she was only seven, and yet even now, it hurt like a fresh wound. One day she was there and the next, she was gone. Delia had a heart defect that no one knew about and, well into her eighth month of her second pregnancy, her heart gave out, killing both her and the baby.

A sudden stop brought her out of her memories. Little Joe shivered, he whinnied so hard. An excited answer came rippling back from just beyond the granite dell. Sidestepping in excitement, Little Joe asked to be let out, but Lee Ann held him. If they started running, the other horse would bolt. As it was, Miser came high-stepping out of the brush, ears pointed so hard they nearly touched.

She let Little Joe go forward at a prancing jog-trot. She asked him for something calmer, with a soothing, "Walk," but he was too young and too excited, and she figured the jig was his best at this point.

Miser came boldly forward and met them, nose to nose, his large nostrils blowing loudly, his neck arched. "Here, boy. Here, Miser." He jerked away with her first try at his reins, but the second time let her have them—what was left of them. Little Joe had calmed the minute the two touched noses and responded nicely when she turned them both back toward Clay. She almost felt sorry when she spotted him picking his way along the trail, his attention on the ground. The slight wind she was riding into kept the noise of their approach from him, but not his muttering from her.

"Rotten . . . blast his hide . . . I shoulda known . . . he's gonna pay . . ."

"No," she enunciated clearly and loudly. "He's *not* going to pay, or I won't bring him one step closer. Not one."

He stood on the rise, hands on hips. Mad male. All six foot of dark and dangerous cowboy. "Bring him here. I'll decide how he's to be treated. Do you understand me?"

Everything feminine within her called her to obey. He was so masterful, so dominant, so. . . .

"Oh, I understand, darlin'. I understand perfectly." With that she turned abruptly and headed back to headquarters.

SHE HAD PUT UP both horses, showered, and just settled herself at the dinner table with Charlie when the door banged open. Without even looking up she knew the dark figure silhouetted in the doorway. "See, Charlie?" She calmly reached over and took a roll to butter. "Told you he'd make it back before dark."

Charlie seemed to be inordinately involved in buttering his own roll, but he managed a grunt. "Uh-huh."

"So, as I was saying, this is the response of the fear-trained horse. I never was in any danger of *my* horse leaving me. But really," she leaned forward as if speaking in confidence only to him, "Little Joe surprised even me by staying calm when Miser took off. So I was able to . . ."

"Lady!" The door slammed closed like a clap of thunder. "You're enough to drive anyone to drink." Clay strode to his room and continued to bang around, spouting muffled epithets that she was sure she didn't want to hear. Had she pushed him too far?

"Looks footsore to me." Charlie gazed toward the racket. "That shower he's taking oughta help."

"Mmm-huh." She would feel horrible if he drank. She chewed methodically on her piece of fried chicken. When he came out a few minutes later, tucking his white T-shirt into clean jeans, she watched him closely for any signs of drinking.

"Knock it off, Lee Ann." His face was still clouded with anger.

"What? Knock what off?"

He gripped her wrist and jerked her toward him. "I don't care if you had me hog-tied, pried my mouth open, and poured it in. It still wouldn't be your fault if I swallowed. You can't *make* me drink. Got it?"

Relief plastered a silly grin on her face. She knew it. "We only have to get the south and east fence lines tomorrow. I rode the rest of the west line coming back, and there was only one break where a saguaro had fallen over. I fixed it."

He still had her wrist. He held it so tightly her fingers had started to turn blue. He loosened his hold, then lifted her hand to his face and placed a perfect warm dry kiss on the back of her hand. "Why, thank you, ma'am."

His blue eyes traveled up her arm to hers and lit there. The grin undid her. The most perfect white teeth, in the most sensuous lips, in the most bronzed face, framed by the most raven hair she had ever seen.... Never thinking that they weren't alone, she leaned forward and kissed him. She allowed her tongue to slide to the perfect teeth and run along them.

"You're kissing my teeth, you know." His chuckle sent her reeling backwards, and heat swarmed from her lips clear to her scalp and then down through her whole body. He'd done it again. Made her forget totally where she was and what she was trying to accomplish, used her own words on her. She had to laugh.

"Yep, that's tough on him, Lee Ann. You said you were going to be tough on him, and by darn, that's hard." Charlie joined in the laughing.

* * * * *

THE NEXT MORNING dawned, spitting rain and blustering winds. The curtains flapped in the open window, bringing in the outdoors. Clay loved the smell of the rain on the desert. He didn't know quite what it was that caused the particular cucumber and cinnamon scent, but he knew he'd remember it all his life. Remember it and look for it.

He stretched, hearing from his sore feet. Dismissing a flash of irritation with a smile, he wondered if Lee Ann liked the rain. An elusive picture ran round in his brain, and he tried to corral it, get it to settle down so he could get a better look at it. The alarm hadn't gone off, so he dozed.

Not far away in a high valley, two riders trotted along side by side—he on a white stallion, she on a black one. The two rode like a matched pair, changing paces to accommodate the ground, in perfect unison. They rode through a pole gate that had an arch over it proclaiming, "Welcome to the Double C Ranch." On they rode to a beautiful ranch house that looked vaguely familiar, spread long and low in a valley with hardwood trees scattering shade here and there. Red flowers brightened window boxes that fronted all the windows the length of the house, under the porch that shaded the whole front. The double doors swung wide open as the two dismounted and tied their horses to the hitching posts that stood either side of the entrance. Three children ran out of the house followed by an elderly-looking woman flapping her apron, trying to keep a floppy-eared hound pup from dashing inside. "Mommy, Daddy," the three children, two girls and a boy, cried.

He wondered who the riders and children were. Why did they seem so familiar? The couple grabbed up the little ones and swung them in a circle. He could almost see their faces. He bolted upright, suddenly and clearly awake. "Good God Almighty." The parents were himself and Lee Ann.

The alarm went off, jerking him into action. He jumped off the bed and smashed down the off button to still it. His hand shook. He wiped his face to clear it of sleep and found it cold and covered with sweat. Anxiety rippled through him. He needed a shower, a good hot shower. Marriage? Children? With that little hellcat? He searched his memory for the dream. Yep. Two of them had been girls. Hell, this was no dream. It was a nightmare. He would have no part of creating more little Lee Anns for the world.

The hot points of water worked their magic on him, and by the time he was shaved and dressed, the dream was a mere memory—until he opened the door and saw her give him a heart-melting smile with her "Good Morning."

He felt it like a punch in his gut. He wanted her. Not just to have her: to take her. He wanted the whole enchilada, marriage, even rugrats. Even little girl rugrats. He shook just a little as he poured his coffee and settled next to Charlie and her. He even managed to smile politely as she dished out biscuits and gravy for him. He lit into his meal like a starving wolf and finished it in record time. He had to get away. This couldn't be real. It was just working in close proximity with her. It was just sex, lust. He watched her as she settled herself and finished off her breakfast. She was something to look at, that was for sure. He stood to leave and got stopped by Charlie.

"What's your rush, son?" He motioned to the chair. "Set a spell. We need to talk." In Clay's odd state of mind, Charlie sounded ominous. Now what?

"Lee Ann said you should be back early afternoon from ridin' the south and east fence lines. That how you figure it?"

He sat with a grunt. "Yep."

"Good. I think the earliest of the help will be driftin' in, and I'll be in town getting the last of the supplies. Here's the list she gave me. Do you need to add anything?" Charlie grinned. "Like blister patches for your feet?"

"No, sir." Clay hitched up his britches. "Don't figure I'll be walking too much more."

"How do you figure you'll correct that little problem with the red?"

"I'll get it out of him. Don't you worry, sir." He sure didn't like the look the boss was leveling at him. "Maybe some beer."

"Oh, there'll be plenty of that."

Lee Ann grabbed the list, added several things, and flashed them both a smile. "I want to make a couple of batches of brownies." She stood waving her pencil around. "You two like walnuts?"

Both nodded in unison.

"Black walnuts or English?"

Before he could help himself, Clay blurted out, "My mom, rest her soul, made the best black walnut brownies in six counties." He hadn't thought of them in a long time.

"You haven't tasted mine, buckaroo." The playful punch she sent to his midsection made him suck it in and kept him from identifying the tugging in the region of his heart. Somehow, he hoped Lee Ann's brownies tasted like sawdust. She had already crept under his skin too far for comfort.

"Thank you, Lee Ann, for breakfast." Charlie rose and took his dishes to the sink. "You cooked; I'll do clean up."

Sending a condemning look his way, Lee Ann hopped up and took her dishes to the sink. What could he do but follow? He knew what he offered sounded grudging. "I'll help you, boss."

Smiling like a fox in a chicken house, she offered, "I'll get your mount out for you and hitch it to the post. Which one will it be?"

He thought the challenge had been thrown.

"I'll be riding the gray," she added.

He knew she'd had no time to work the horse. "Are you nuts?"

She stood before him, hands on hips, waiting for an answer.

Sullenly, he wiped out the skillet and lowered it into the suds. He had to pick an equally challenging horse or the day wouldn't be fair. "Pull out Bandito for me."

"You don't sound too happy. You sure you want him? If you ask me, Miser needs more work."

He gritted his teeth as he ground out, "I said Bandito."

"Okay, whatever you say. You got a list for us, Charlie?"

"Not really. If you get the lines done and help folks settle in, that will be plenty for today." He dried the cast-iron skillet Clay handed him and settled it back on the stove.

Lee Ann headed out the door whistling to herself, happy to be alive and happy to be doing her favorite thing in life, training horses. She patted Bum on the head as he greeted her with a slobbery kiss on her knee. Fleece was head down in her stall, her face buried in the hay she had pulled out of the net, munching contentedly. Lee Ann didn't let that fool her. The mare was skittish and flighty, and she couldn't let her guard down a minute today or Lee Ann might be the one walking back. This filly would definitely keep her on her toes.

Fleece accepted the halter gracefully enough and showed only a little resentment at being pulled away from her food. When Bum came up behind them, she danced forward and skinned the back of Lee Ann's heel through the boot. A firm elbow to the chest reminded the mare of the distance she was supposed to keep, and she dropped back to the proper place and stayed there. Tying the lead to the hitching post with a firm, quick release knot, she secured her and turned to get Bandito, who came along much more easily.

As she stepped out of the barn two things happened at once: The bright sunlight blinded her momentarily, and a gray blur whizzed by that sent her flying into the gelding behind her. It took her only a second to realize what that gray blur was. Fleece ran up and down the breezeway, trumpeting to all that she was loose and she was hot. Her neck arched, and her tail flagged up behind her. A resounding crash at the end of the barn told Lee Ann that Booger, the stallion, was ready to answer the call.

"Oh, no," she groaned as Bandito nearly jerked her arm out of the socket, trying to keep an eye on the racing mare.

From behind her a deep chuckle sounded. "I'll just take my horse now. Guess yours needs some attention."

Handing him the rope, she tried to avoid looking at him. "I-I'll just go get her. I think she might be in heat." Booger's slinging his front feet over his stall door confirmed her impression. She kicked it into high gear and sped down the breezeway, anxious to get the mare away from him before he came over the door. "Please, God," she whispered, "Don't let the door give way."

She got there just as the stallion levered himself high enough to nip Fleece on the arch of her neck. "No, no, you two. No time for this." Somehow she managed to slam the upper iron-bar window into place and grab Fleece's halter at the same time. The walls of the stall shivered with the impact of the heated stallion's body behind it. Hurriedly she dragged the mare back down the breezeway. Only when she had her tied with a solid knot did she breathe a sigh of relief.

"You shouldn't really tie a green horse with a knot you can't quick release, you know."

"*I know.*" She hadn't actually shouted, but anger fired her answer. "I'll have to find a quick-release clip. She obviously knows how to undo quick-release knots."

"Hmmm." His broad back faced her as he worked to secure the saddle he'd just placed on the red dun's back.

She soothed the mare with stroking motions of the grooming brush while she watched out of the corner of her eye. She could feel the mare calming under her, even as she watched the little dun tighten up.

"You should probably take a little more time . . ."

With a snap, Clay tightened the cinch down hard. The little dun went straight up, making Lee Ann happy she had tied the mare a good distance from him. He screamed and went up again as soon as his hard black hooves hit the ground. He fought it for a good five minutes, until he panted and shivered.

"Now, he'll always resent the saddle and the cinching. You may have just ruined a good horse, mister."

Clay shook his head. "No. And I might add I'm just about to head out. You?"

In spite of wanting to hurry, she took her time and saddled her mount up slowly. By the time she was ready to step up, Fleece had regained her composure and was nicely in tune. Humming, she went to get the fence tools. She was still inside when she heard the scream of rage. Nearly dropping her tools, she sped back outside in time to see Clay sailing high into the air. She had to hand it to him: He never let go of the reins. As a result, he was dragged a good twenty-five feet before Bandito stopped backing wildly away.

Though Fleece was dancing a bit, she got up without a problem and rode past where Clay struggled to get to his feet. "C'mon, cowboy, we have work to do." A small chuckle slipped by her lips.

She had gotten to the east fence line when she heard pounding hooves behind her. The gray mare danced in a circle with the excitement of being joined. Throwing his weight every which way, the little red dun came at a dead run, with the stop being more like a set of crow-hops than a real stop.

"'Bout time." She tried to ignore the warmth swirling in her belly as she looked the hard-put cowboy up and down. His hat was gone, his bandanna strangling him, his holster askew, but six foot of pure working muscle held the thousand-pound belligerent beast in check. She shook her head at the battle of wills she witnessed. The raw power Clay's method took hit her in the face, and she wondered if that was the real reason she had developed her methods. She simply didn't have the strength that the cowboy displayed now. But as she sat and watched the spectacle continue, the real reasons for her methods flooded back.

The dun grabbed the bit in his teeth and reared, trying to dislodge the hateful burden on his back. The cowboy stuck like he was glued and leaned forward and forcefully ripped the bit sideways, dislodging it from the foam-flecked mouth. He gigged the horse in its heaving sides, and it responded with a bellow and three huge bucks, coming down each time on iron-hard legs with the force of a jackhammer. It would have dislodged a lesser rider and, though moved, Clay stuck.

Lee Ann soothed her mare with soft hands and a calm voice. The mare would not be moved from the battle, so they stayed, forced to watch. "It's all right." She spoke the words over and over. The mare kept reaching back, touching her nose to the toe of Lee Ann's boot for reassurance as she switched her weight around nervously.

Finally, Clay gigged his horse, and the sweat-drenched beast took a normal step forward. He was quick to praise, a pat to the lathered neck and words softly spoken. "Good boy." The horse froze for a second then took another step. Each forward motion was rewarded with a pat. Before long, he walked in a circle with little resistance.

Lee Ann stepped off her horse, tucked her reins in at her hip, and found the end of the break in the wire. She winced as Clay strode up, peacock-proud of his dominance.

"Well?" He made sure she faced him. "What do you think of that?"

She rolled her head to ease the tension in her back and answered him sadly. "I think you ought to look into his eyes. Then take a look at my mare." She faced him fully. "If you can't see the difference, then you *are* hopeless." Her insides hurt with the contradictory feelings that roiled there. There was so much to like about this man, and there was so much to hate.

BY THE TIME the entire fence was repaired and the sun had already begun its descent in the western sky, the help started drifting into the ranch yard. The commotion of vehicles circling and rearranging, accompanied by the cacophony of whinnying and mooing livestock, unnerved the green mounts that Lee Ann and Clay sat. Determined to make them move through it, they rode them both hard. Finally, they had their mounts to the hitching post, where they dismounted and unsaddled. When they put their horses in their stalls, they faced the whirl of dust and humanity in the ranch yard together.

"Why, Lee Ann Waters, is that you?" A wrinkled gray woman in a plaid shirt and denim overalls rushed forward to hug her.

"Josie! Charlie said you'd be here. I'm so glad." She hugged tightly to her old friend. The graying man behind her held out his hand to Clay.

"And who might you be, young man?"

"Clay Carter. Foreman of the Silver Rock, sir." He took off his hat and shook hands. "And I'll bet you're Bob, uh, Lockhart, right?"

"*One* of the foremen, Bob." Lee Ann glared at Clay. "We're both in the running for the permanent position." *How dare he say he was foreman?*

Bob chuckled and tipped his cowboy hat back on his head. "Both in the running, eh? Well, I'll be darned." Slowly, the older man looked from one to the other of the sweat-stained competitors. "She's a well-trained filly, man. You'll have a tough time beating her."

Josie Lockhart slapped her knee. "My money's on Lee Ann, Bob. You act like it's a foregone conclusion that he's going to win, just because he's a man." It was her turn to glare. "I say Lee Ann's as good as they come." She patted Lee Ann reassuringly.

"Thanks for your vote of confidence, Josie." She had an uncomfortable thought. "But I'd appreciate it if you all didn't say anything about this to the others. We don't want roundup turned into a betting match. Wouldn't be, uh, good for, uh, morale." There. That was a decent-sounding reason.

"Whose morale?" Bob looked her up and down. "Ours is just fine. And a few little bets won't hurt anyone."

Lee Ann groaned and took Josie's arm. She had a bad feeling about the week to come.

14

Spring Roundup

CHILLY AIR SWEPT PAST Lee Ann's face when she opened the front door to see what all the commotion was about. She stepped out onto the porch and squinted her eyes, gazing toward the main yard in the dim pre-dawn light. A large truck seemed to be discharging a number of bulky stock horses already saddled. As they each leapt to the ground, one of a group of young cowboys would grab a lead and haul a mount over to the hitching rails under the tack barn roof. She counted about fifteen in all. Charlie came out behind her, stuffing his work gloves into the strap that buckled his chaps closed.

"Yep, these are the yahoos. They're good boys, but they are used to arena work only, or just about. Some are pretty wise, but some just as soon run every ounce of meat off the stock as look at 'em. Trick is to get them to calm down and do the work without ruf-flin' their feathers much. They're workin' free, just for the experience, and I'll expect you two to teach 'em right." Clay had silently joined them. He whistled low.

"Cocksure and full of piss 'n' vinegar." Lee Ann glared at him.

"That so?" She watched him while he appraised the help.

"My granddad used to say it when I was young. Guess I can see what he meant. Now."

Charlie chuckled and snugged his hat down straight, as he was wont to do. Lee Ann fell in nat-urally behind him as he headed for the melee. She felt Clay right behind her. Just as they got close, the truck let out a blast and pulled in a large circle be-fore settling in beside the other vehicles parked in the yard. She turned to watch and was caught from behind by young, strong hands.

"What do we have here?" The tall thin fellow whistled his appreciation as he turned her to face to-ward him. "Pretty as the day is long." At a long look from Clay he took away his hands as if she were hot to the touch. "Pardon me." Then he swept his hat off and bowed. "Pleased to meet the lady." When he stood, his face was red. Lee Ann decided to take him out of his misery.

"*Who* you have here is the foreman of the Silver Rock." She swept off her hat and executed a similar bow.

The gangly hand's eyebrows shot up his forehead as he turned to Charlie. "That so, boss?"

"Truth is, Russ, I got myself two foremen this year." Charlie looked back and forth between Clay and Lee Ann. "Just lucky, I guess."

Russ whooped and headed for the others who were busy tying on ropes and gear, checking cinches, and tightening girths. "Hey fellas, guess what the boss has gone and done?"

Lee Ann cringed at the howl of laughter and turned away from the pointing fingers. Her chin inched up a notch, and she faced them again. She strode forward, all of five foot eight inches tall, and slapped her chaps with her rope. In a low, strong voice that she had learned carried a long ways, she spoke. "The boss will be ready in about five minutes, and all of you are expected to be mounted and ready to go. First man caught causing a beef to run off weight unnecessarily will be sent back to head-quarters on foot. Anyone causing a wreck is put off the place for good. Anyone not agreeing to this, leave now."

Quiet reigned. A scowl showed here and there,

but before long, some good-natured teasing began. "You hear that, Josh? This ain't no ropin' arena. This here's the real thing."

"Hey, Chance. Can't wait to see if you walk back." Josh yanked hard on Chance's chaps, causing them to fall around his ankles. "Got no butt, that's why they won't stay up."

"Oh my, if he looks like that now . . ." Lee Ann said with a wry look at Clay.

"What?" He adjusted his gear.

"Well, don't you know old cowboys don't die?" She looked sideways from under her hat at him.

"Really? Why's that?" Clay cocked his head at her.

"They just get a little behind."

"Aw shiiiit, Lee Ann, I didn't even see it coming. It's too early in the mornin' for that." Still, a gorgeous grin lit his face, making the morning a little brighter.

By the time Lee Ann got back with Mickey, most of the men were mounted and things had quieted considerably. Charlie sat mounted under the tack roof on a battle-scarred red roan. Clay sat on a raw-boned sorrel range horse out of Charlie's older string. She was glad he didn't try to show her up with one of the youngsters, because with this many untried riders, there would be situations. It was just the nature of roundup, and she knew having a solid mount could mean the difference between life and death.

"This is modern ranching, so I have a cheat sheet." Charlie held up a sheaf of white papers and handed them to Clay, who started passing them out. "You'll find the ear tag numbers of the cows and the cow/calf pairs listed along with descriptions. Try to bring 'em in with the right mamas. We don't need orphans of our own creation."

Lee Ann circulated among the riders, pairing up old-timers who had done this ride many times with youngsters who may or may not have. By the time Charlie was done with his instructions, everyone knew where they were to ride and had at least one point man who knew the place.

"I don't expect you'll be staying and helping with the cooking?" The sparkle in Josie Lockhart's eyes belied the question.

Lee Ann's heart, warmed by the sweet woman's smile, answered. "You know better than that." She squeezed the hand offered. "But I'll be back at noon to help eat it."

"Well, honey, it's not a road I would have chosen, but I'm real proud that you have." Josie rummaged around in a canvas bag she held sling-style across her front. "Here, take this and eat it. You'll need the calories."

Lee Ann took the jerky she knew Josie had made herself and smelled it. "Heavenly. Your soy-garlic?"

"Yep. I'll just hand out some to the boys. Can you see Bob up there?"

Pointing to the east end of the barn where the older hand was mounting his cow pony, Lee Ann heeled her horse toward Clay while she stuffed her jerky into her saddle bags. "Thanks, Josie. You're a doll."

"You ready?" She trotted by him.

"As I'll ever be." He bit his words off hard. "Any instructions for me?" She knew in that moment that the way she had taken hold of the morning had made him feel left out, overshadowed. *Men's egos sure can be touchy*, she thought.

"Sure." She couldn't resist a wink as she glanced back over her shoulder at him. "Stay away from the cholla." He ducked his head, shrugged with hands held out, topping it with a big old "Aw, shucks" grin.

SHE'S TAKEN OVER *all morning,* he thought. Right then Lee Ann was facing a lead cow determined to go up the slope of the mountain to the west of the group they'd found. She was a large cow, and horned. Suddenly, she threatened the woman on the horse who blocked her way. Never faltering, horse and rider pivoted off the rear end to block her each time she jumped first one way and then the other. The whole rest of the herd waited to see what the old brindle cow would do. A little brindle look-a-like stood a short way off, watching with big eyes. It was an unworked calf that looked to be a couple of weeks old at the most.

Then it happened. Lee Ann got a little too close to the calf, and the mother went wild with a bellow of rage. A lunge forward and a wild upward swing of the wicked horns came close to her horse's heaving chest. She didn't give, not an inch, merely held tough, talking her horse into sticking it out, with low words, tight legs, and body language that shouted, "I'm not moving."

The bellow went up a notch, and the cow leapt forward again. This time her swinging horn caught on the breast strap of Lee Ann's horse, which reared and squealed with fright.

Clay hadn't realized he was moving forward, driving the small group he'd found, until all of sudden, he was there in the midst of the screaming, bellowing, and dust. The horn was pressed deeply into the mare's neck, wedged there by the breast strap. He couldn't see blood yet but with the lunging of the beasts he knew it would be just seconds before he would. His hand found his buck knife and had it open and at the breast strap in a split second. Just as it seemed the struggling cow would thrust her horn deep, he sliced the breast strap apart, freeing her.

Lee Ann and Mickey fell over backward, so great was the strength of her pull. Gasping, she shouted as she held on to her stumbling mount, "That was my good breast strap!"

Her face was red with fury, and, if his relief hadn't been so great, he might have shouted something about an ungrateful whelp, but all that came out was a relieved "Whew!" He glanced at the mama cow, who had regained her feet and was mooing solicitously to her babe, who grabbed a teat and sucked with all its strength.

"Here." He got down, sliced off a length of the cotton rope he always carried and reached for her dangling breast strap. "This will do, until I can replace it." Quietly, he worked until it was attached to her D-ring with a good solid square knot in the middle. He finished cutting off the damaged part, rolled it, and handed it up to her. The herd was beginning to get restive, so he quickly remounted in a smooth motion and replaced his Buck knife in its sheaf.

"I guess I shoulda thought of my knife. Stupid, huh?" She reached forward to rearrange Mickey's mane and pat the mare on the neck. The good mare stood ready to do whatever was asked of her next, gentled under a loving hand.

"I think you were too focused on the cow." He carefully kept his face neutral. His heart resumed its normal, slow rhythm.

"Felt like if I lost my concentration for a second she would scatter the whole herd. And I definitely didn't want to be between her and that baby . . ."

He took a deep breath, realizing that for now, everything was going to be all right. "Gets that way sometimes." Sweat trickled down his shirtfront, so he took his bandanna and wiped.

"Where did you come from, anyway?"

He guessed that was as close to thanks as she was gonna get.

"The ridge behind us. They heard that old cow of yours holler and, boy howdy, they scampered over that ridge like a herd of deer."

"How many?"

"Oh, um, think I counted twenty-two. Sixteen of those are cow/calf pairs."

Just then, Charlie came over the ridge, concern lining his leather face. "Thought I heard a wreck."

"No, sir." Clay noted they had answered in perfect unison.

With a lifted brow, all Charlie said was "Um-huh." He looked them both up and down, and his eyes lit on Lee Ann's makeshift breast strap. "Your gear giving out on you already?"

"I stressed it some, boss." Her chin was notched up a way, which Clay was beginning to find way too sexy. "But it'll hold until we get this group to the corrals."

"I have two good foremen, and I find them together with one group of beef? Where is everyone else? Shouldn't you two be spreadin' out your talents?"

Clay decided the air was definitely turning frosty. Just then Bob Lockhart came over the same ridge with a good-sized group ahead of him. Doing drag was Josh, and Chance was on flank.

"I'll head up that little canyon there." Clay pointed to the north and east. "When we topped the ridge, I saw a big group and what looked to be only two riders." He caught Lee Ann's eye and her nearly imperceptible nod, then tipped his hat to his boss and took off in a swinging lope.

All the way up that slope, he thought of what had just happened. All the way up the slope, the scene replayed itself in his mind's eye. All the way up the slope, he considered that even of the women in the force, there were not many who could have come through that wreck as well as Lee Ann Waters had. And she thought she had been stupid. He said the thought aloud.

"Lee Ann Waters, you might be tough on folks, but you're much tougher on yourself." Since he understood such a thing, he smiled and started whistling a tune he remembered about someone lighting up his day.

The group in the canyon had progressed little, and the two hands were having a hard time holding them. They counted out at sixty-two, and one other hand came out from an arroyo with a cantankerous bull, ear tag number one. The bull was old and mean, and clearly wanted to be left alone for his early siesta. Clay wondered if he really was Charlie's first bull, as the number would make it seem, and decided against it. The Silver Rock was too old for that. So maybe he was number one in the second round of bulls. That might be. At any rate he sure was giving the red-faced hand on the grulla gelding a tough time. He suspected the wrangler hadn't seen many this size, and his lack of confidence was show-ing. Clay knew that by simply adding himself to the equation, the bull would turn. And he did. He held out his hand.

"You were doin' fine." The youngster took his hand and shook it hard.

"Name's Harley Dubson. How'd you know he'd turn?"

"Aw, he's too old to be dumb. When the odds doubled, he knew it was time to leave." Clay took a swig on his canteen. The water was warm, but it was wet and he was grateful. Harley followed suit. "I'm the foreman, Clay Carter."

The kid took on a kind of dumb adoration look. It embarrassed Clay.

"How long you been foreman here?" Slowly but surely, the bull was catching up with the main group.

"Three weeks." He slapped his rope to his leg and whistled to hurry the bull along. The pace picked up a little.

"What? No way!" Harley's jaw dropped open. "You ride like you was born there."

"Way, kid." He gigged his horse and cut off a lone young heifer trying to break away. As soon as she settled back into the main group, he resumed his place by the kid. "Grew up on my granddad's place, the Double Cee, and he still hopes I'll run it one day."

"Why aren't you doin' that now?" Harley pushed his leggy grulla forward confidently when the bull lagged. The bull shook its head and sped up.

"Nice." He coughed to clear the trail dust and decided to tell it straight. "I thought I had to get away to the big city. Ranch was dull to me. It was all I'd ever known. So I came here, where it was warm enough for me for a change and became a cop."

"No way!" *Oh Lord*, he thought, *bet this kid waits hand and foot on me from here out.*

"Way, kid." He decided not to elaborate on what brought him here. Might knock some of the polish of the kid's idol. *On second thought.* "Got shot. Stupid, really. Needed to get away to get back on my feet."

"Shot. Way?" The kid wasn't even watching where he was going, and he was headed for the cholla.

"Watch out, kid. You don't want to tangle with those."

"Jeez, man." He hauled on his poor horse's mouth until it gaped open-jawed to a stop. Then he thumped it hard in the ribs and yanked it to the right. "Thanks."

"Later, Harley." Clay decided he'd had enough hero worship for the day, tipped his hat, and took off to the other side of the herd, where some heifers and young steers were making passes at an arroyo leading away from the main canyon.

LEE ANN WAS among the first back for lunch, not brought there by hunger but by the need, no matter how unliberated, to help Josie with chow. She unsaddled Mickey and let her go for a good roll in the horse corral. She watched for a moment until she was satisfied that none among the strange horses there would bother her good mare. She turned away to find Josie. The temporary cook shack was where she found her, slicing smoked turkey and laying out a serving platter.

"Hi, Josie. I'll just wash these paws quick and give you a hand."

"Sure you can, sweetie?" Josie didn't miss a beat and had the turkey carved in minutes.

"Sure. Wow, roast turkey?" Lee Ann remembered that the older woman was famous for her spreads at cookouts. The icy cold water pumped from the creek felt good on her hands.

"Yes, ma'am. It holds up real well for sandwiches. Could you ladle up a couple bowls of the gravy?"

The big gleaming steel cook pot on the grill emanated delicious smelling steam. Inside was about a gallon of ivory turkey gravy. She marveled at its lumpless state as she ladled it into the ironstone bowls it would be served from. Carefully, she spread clean dishtowels over the bowls to keep out the ever-present flies that accompany even the cleanest cow operations.

The big doors of the outdoor baking oven banged open, and golden brown biscuits sent forth their mouth-watering aroma. Suddenly Lee Ann was hungry, very hungry. She hustled to grab some pot-holders to get the second shelf's bounty and follow Josie to where they laid them out. Again, she covered everything with clean towels.

They turned as one to the sound of incoming cattle when Clay and his group headed the huge bunch into the main holding pen. Dust billowed and rolled down toward the creek, thankfully away from the cook shack.

The cattle milled about, setting up an incessant bawling and mooing as the press of the herd separated mothers and babies. She knew that in an hour or two, they would naturally find each other. The

hands worked with their cow ponies and gate ten-
ders to separate out the cow/calf pairs into "to be
worked" pens—for the calves that hadn't been inoculated, ear-tagged, branded, or castrated—and the
"already worked" older calves that Charlie had been
bringing in and working piecemeal as he found
them in the early spring.

The first group was larger by far, as most of the
cows would have been receptive about the same
time, the last couple of months of summer when
food was plentiful and days were long. Enough con-
ceived early, though, to cause a good rancher to go
out and gather them in for a check-up and to brand
them as his.

Lee Ann never tired of watching the calves: new
life, innocence incarnate. Roundup was such a melee, so she kept a sharp eye out for injury. She jerked
her attention to a shout. One of the hands misunderstood Charlie and had inadvertently turned a
bunch of sorted young steers into the cow/calf pen.
She hurried to get where she belonged, instructing
the help, but Clay beat her to it.

In a series of shouts and hand waving, he had
everything running smoothly again. Her neck
burned as it always did when she fell short of doing her job. She hated feeling stretched this way,

between women's work and her job, but then remembered that Charlie had said that he had the cooking chores taken care of, those many days ago when they had discussed the arrangements. So her place was clear.

The rusty rebar served as her highway to get to Charlie. "Lunch is laid out."

"Five more minutes. Just as soon as the last of these paired cow/calves are put up, you can ring it." His eyes never strayed from the herd.

When he gave the signal, she would tell Josie who would ring the dinner triangle. She didn't worry that the young hungry hands wouldn't know what it meant. Didn't worry at all. She sat atop the highest rung of rebar and pulled her list out of her hip pocket.

From what she could see, they had about a third of the cows in and, of those, most had reproduced. No doubt about it, the Silver Rock had a fine herd. The cows mostly looked to be black and red Angus, crossed with Brahma, Corriente, and maybe some Simmental and Saler. That meant that they were largely brown, red, and black with a low ear on them and good stretch on the frame bringing in high weights at butchering time. The cross was also highly heat- and drought-tolerant, thrifty and disease-resistant. It had taken quite a few years, she was sure, to come up with this type.

She swept her gaze over the entire operation and held her breath for a moment when someone left the main gate open a tad too long. One bull ambled toward it like he might take a notion to hightail it back to the flats. Clay must have had antennae because, suddenly, he was just there, shouldering the gate closed and, if she could read lips properly, cussing out whoever had done it. She leaned forward to hold the cow/calf pen closed when Charlie swung it toward her and dropped down to secure it with a chain.

As she made her way back to the cook shack, she waved her hat over her head to Josie to clang the triangle. The sound cut through the cacophony with amber notes, pure and warm, and, slowly but surely, the hands drifted in and began tying their ponies, some taking them for water, some loosing cinches here and there. Satisfied that all were finding their way and that Clay was bringing up the rear, she washed her hands one more time and started directing traffic.

Josie had laid out huge bowls of fresh fruit on ice as well as homemade pies and cookies. Huge coolers dispensed lemonade, water, and sodas.

Charlie served beer only at night. Two pretty young gals that seemed attached to a couple of the hands stepped forward to help Josie, and Lee Ann relaxed enough to fill a plate of her own. She had just swung her leg over the low branch of an ancient ironwood when Clay pulled up a lawn chair beside her.

"You say Josie and Bob lived next door when you were little?"

Nodding, she bit into the warm gravy and turkey over biscuit and let the juices trail down her parched throat. "Mmmmm." She chewed and washed it down with lemonade. "In a manner of speaking. Their headquarters were about three miles from ours."

He chuckled. "Nothing a good horse couldn't cover pretty easy, should a kid get real hungry." He took his hat off and settled his blue-gray gaze on her. Amazing how clear the whites of his eyes were, considering all the dust and wind.

She snapped her fingers. "Like that. You better believe it. And wait until you taste her prickly pear-blackberry pie."

"Oh yeah?" His eyes sparkled. "That good?" At her nod, he continued. "Any brothers or sisters?"

"Almost."

One of the hands ambled by. "Can I get you anything, Ms. Waters?"

She shook her head. "Thanks, no, I'm fine. You tank up now, cowboy. 'Cause next time we quit, it'll be dark."

"Yes, ma'am. Sir." He tipped his hat to them both. Good manners, it seemed, were alive and well in the West.

"Wasn't that nice?" She watched the wrangler join a group sitting on the logs laid around the unlit fire pit and took a bite out of a crisp red apple.

"He's a bit young for you, don't you think?"

She nearly choked. "You think I'm a cradle robber?" Her eyes watered as she fought to swallow the bite of apple.

"I'll just have to see if I can keep your mind on someone a little more your age, won't I?" He waggled his eyebrows at her.

The ice in her glass seemed to have a mind of its own and somehow just happened to make its way down the front of his shirt. He rose to get her back.

"Ah, ah, ah. Watch it! Can't have the hands see us acting like a couple of kids. We have a rep to maintain."

"Why, you little rat. Don't think you won't pay for this. Don't think for a minute . . ."

His eyes twinkled, and she decided again that she loved the fact that he had a good sense of humor.

Excitement rippled up her back as she entertained the idea of what the payback might be.

LATE THAT NIGHT, as the firelight rippled over everyone while they relaxed around the firepit, Clay wondered why Lee Ann had changed the subject when he'd asked about brothers or sisters.

Josie Lockhart came by for the third time with a big pot of coffee and offered him some. "We've switched to decaf," she chuckled, "as if anything could keep you guys up tonight."

He touched her arm to quietly get her attention. He didn't think Lee Ann, who was clear on the other side of the firepit talking to one of the wrangler's girlfriends, could hear.

"Josie. I asked Lee Ann if she had any brothers or sisters and she said 'almost.' I don't want to pry, but she sounded so sad . . ."

"I like you, boy. So I might just tell you." She glanced over at Lee Ann and sat down next to him. "Her momma died when she was seven, trying to bring her little brother into the world."

Clay sucked in a breath but kept his head down. He knew if he looked up, Lee Ann could see the pain and shock in his face. "Oh, no."

Josie picked up a stick and drew in the dirt. "It's a real treat to be here with her tonight. Bob and I helped raise the little scamp. Her Daddy tried, bless his heart, but Lee Ann grew up all tomboy. Still," she dropped the stick and rose up to top off his cup, "don't let the little stinker tell you she can't cook. I taught her right well."

Clay chuckled and allowed, "She tells me that you bake the only and the best prickly pear-blackberry pie in the Southwest."

"If you want to find out, you better get over there and try it out yourself, before it's all gone." She shooed him with the faded apron she held the big coffeepot with.

"I'll just do that, ma'am. And thanks." He lifted his cup in her direction. "For everything."

Starlight through the branches of the palo verde and ironwood rimming the ranch yard lit his way as he walked to the trench table holding the desserts. It was good that he hadn't delayed. There was already a slice taken out of the last pie. He was pretty sure Lee Ann hadn't had any, so he took two slices and made his way over to her.

"Can't imagine you missing out on this." He held out the extra plate and pie. She looked up at him, and damn it all if he could breathe. Her hair was coated with dust, she had tear streaks where her eyes had watered and made tracks on her face from the dust, but the way the moon lit her face and her hair glowed all pearly paralyzed him.

"Are you going to give it to me, or just stand there?"

That snapped him out of it. He was able to hand it to her. "Room for me?" There wasn't. But he didn't care. He knew the help would move, would let him sit. The red-headed gal at her side made to get up.

"No. Don't, Dixie." She glared at him. "We were talking here."

He recognized a snub when he heard one. Funny how it got to him.

"Well, all right." He jerked away and sat back where he'd been. He started to get up and get himself a beer, like so many of the others were, when he remembered the promise he'd made. "For all the good it will do me with her," he grumbled to himself.

15

A Curious Thing

THE HOT STINGING NEEDLES of the shower did a lot to help work out the kinks that the previous day's work had put all over her aching body. No matter what shape she was in, it went this way with roundup. But she knew as soon as she was on the trail, with the morning sun warming her back and a good horse underneath her, she would somehow lose the aches and pains. The water pressure had been good, so she knew that she'd beat most everyone up. Good thing, because she wanted to get out and saddle Fleece up. Little Joe was the more stable of the two youngsters, so she picked Fleece for now, while she was fresh. Later this afternoon, she would work Joe.

By the time she had Fleece saddled and clipped securely to the hitching post under the tack barn,

Clay and Charlie were seated at the trestle table along with some of the early rising hands. They were tucked into the biscuits and gravy pretty well already, and Josie was topping their mugs with steaming hot coffee from her big splatter-blue coffeepot.

"Good mornin'," both said in unison. Charlie tipped his hat, and Clay and a number of the hands removed theirs. She wasn't sure if she liked being acknowledged as a woman or not. Would it undermine her authority?

"No need to remove your hats, gentlemen." Hats were neatly replaced.

"You already got a mad on, Lee Ann?" Clay looked positively evil in the early morning light. She hoped it didn't mark the trail for the day.

As she passed behind him, she grabbed his bandanna and snugged it up tight around his neck.

"Nope. And I wouldn't do anything to help one along, if I were you, cowboy."

For a second, she could feel as well as hear his good-natured chuckle, and it gave her goose bumps. What would it feel like to hear that chuckle if she had her head on his bare chest while they were snuggled up together somewhere? That thought had her nearly jumping out of her skin. She shook herself slightly before she picked up her tin plate and cup, just to get her skin back on right.

Charlie had a map spread out on the table by the time she got back. He quickly pointed out some of the trouble spots where the terrain was tough going and where certain animals were known to hide. He would tap a spot, and then Clay would point to one of the lead men. Everyone seemed to know that this was his assignment for the day.

Lee Ann was in agreement until it came to one man. Durb Gleeson troubled her. She had seen him handle his mount in the rankest way and knew that it was just a cover up for lack of expertise. She shook her head and, with a tap and point, changed his assignment to an easier canyon. Clay glanced her way and raised an eyebrow, but didn't dispute her. She wished she could say the same for Durb. He sent a murderous look her way and muttered something unintelligible.

"What's that, Durb?" She stood straight and held his feral gaze. "You have a problem with that canyon?"

"No. Why'd you change it?" He wiped his greasy mouth with the back of his hand and straightened up belligerently.

She deliberately softened her voice. "Because, last time I looked, I was foreman of this crew."

"You? I thought he was." He hooked a thumb in Clay's direction.

"You thought wrong, mister." Clay's eyes deepened to a stormy hue. "We share that responsibility, and whatever either of us says goes."

For a second it looked like the large man was going to do what was asked. Then his lips lifted in a snarl. "If you ask me, Charlie, I think you're gettin' soft in the head, lettin' a woman have a say."

Charlie's hand stopped on the map. Slowly, he stood up from the table and faced Durb. "I didn't ask you, Durb. I'm not in the habit of askin' you, Durb. About anything. Now, would you like to apologize to the lady?"

Lee Ann felt a tug at her heartstrings as she watched Charlie take her side. She knew that ranchers were reluctant to make enemies of anyone who might come back later and sabotage their operation. She felt bad to be the cause of a possible problem.

"No." He spat tobacco at Lee Ann's feet. "It's a sad day when a woman is allowed to run an operation, that's all I'm sayin'." A drop of tobacco juice dripped from his stubbly chin, turning Lee Ann's stomach.

"Take your gear and get out, Durb." Charlie turned toward Clay. "Would you be a gentleman and see Durb off the place, Clay?"

Durb stood staring back and forth between the three of them. "I'll be damned. You're gonna do it, aren't ya? The last place a man can be a man, and you're gonna let a woman get her fingers in. You're not the man I thought you were, Charlie Bruce."

Clay gave the man a good shove. "Get goin'. Don't give me a reason to hurt you."

Durb managed to poke a finger in the middle of Lee Ann's chest. "You and me, little lady. Sometime when all these big men aren't around to protect you. You and me."

The sentence had hardly left his mouth when a crack from a hard fist shut it. The big man hit the ground hard, sending up a swirl of powder-fine dust. Clay stood over him, chest heaving. "Give me another reason, man."

Lee Ann leapt forward. "No, Clay, he's not worth it. Don't." The crowd that surrounded them parted to let Durb past. She longed to throw herself into Clay's arms for the comfort that might shake the feeling of dread that had been born in her chest with Durb's threat, but the eyes of the hands were all on her. She stiffened her spine and stepped away from him.

"It's all over now. Everyone, please just finish your breakfast." She hoped no one could see the fine tremor in her legs as she settled herself at the table, determined to choke down the meal that suddenly tasted like sawdust.

CLAY WAS GLAD to see Durb go. The man even smelled bad. How he had gotten a place on the Silver Rock roundup, he couldn't figure. By the time he had escorted the beat-up old Jeep with its scroungy single-horse trailer off the place, breakfast was long over and everyone had taken off to bring in the beef. He found Charlie down by the sorting pens, taking notes and watching the herd.

"How are we doing?" He settled himself beside the boss man on a top rail.

"Oh, I'd say we have about three-quarters of them. Hands did a good job yesterday." He finished counting and closed the note pad, which he shoved into his shirt pocket. "Got something to show you that they found this morning, a bit of a puzzle."

Charlie headed back out behind the barn, walked behind a little rise, and pointed to a dark red mound covered with blood and mud and flies.

The faint odor told Clay that it hadn't been dead long. "My God. What could have done that?" The long slices in the calf's hide laid the flesh open down to bone. The hide was nearly all hanging in strips.

"No animal would do that." Disgust made Charlie's voice harsh. "Whoever did this was less than an animal. Enjoyed killing."

Suddenly, a picture flashed in Clay's mind's eye of a woman's body this had been done to. The cuts were eerily the same. Strips in even vertical slices from top to bottom. The consensus had been the same: Whoever had done it had enjoyed killing. The monster who had done it was arrested and imprisoned and became known as the "Pink Ribbon Killer." That had been several years ago. He was sure he would never forget it.

"Looks like it happened last night. Carcass is too fresh for it to have been yesterday." Clay took out his Buck knife and poked around, lifting flesh here and there. "There's the ear tag."

Charlie's eyebrows rose to his hairline. "Hmmphh. Must've been one I worked a couple of weeks ago." An incessant hoarse bawling could be heard coming from the holding pens. "If that's mama caterwauling like that, then it happened about four this morning. Woke me, she was in such a fit."

The two made their way to the pens and spotted the mother. Charlie pulled his list. "Yep. They're a pair." He lifted his eyes to Clay. "Or were."

Clay remembered there were no drag marks

where they'd found the calf. He went back to satisfy himself that he'd missed nothing. That close to the barn, there were many tracks, human, horse, cow, calf and even some deer. Then he found what he was straining to see. A boot heel track that went much deeper than the others. A big boot heel. "Cripes," he whispered mostly to himself. "One helluva big man."

"What's that?"

He nearly jumped out of his boots at the voice close behind him. He didn't realize Charlie had come back with him. "I think whoever did this carried that calf." He faced him squarely. He needed some answers. "How big do you figure that calf was?"

"Well, you can see, sort of. He wasn't real big. Born early, I reckon. Maybe hundred and fifty, two hundred at the most."

"Out of the folks that came to help, which ones don't you know?"

"Know 'em all. Some better than others, why?" Charlie held his hands up in front of him. "Oh, no. None of them would do a thing like this."

"The front gate locked at night?" He was hoping for a lot.

"Not during roundup. We have people driftin' in and out the whole duration."

"How about Durb Gleeson? He's a big man. He coulda carried this calf."

Charlie shook his head surely. "No, sir. He may be rough, but Durb's lived near here for fifteen years or more, over in one of our line shacks. Why, it's been because of him that we've caught rustlers a time or two. He's one reason no one much bothers the Silver Rock."

Still, Clay could see the glimmer of doubt in the older man's eyes. "Okay then, why wouldn't you just hire him for foreman? Tell me that."

"He takes spells. Where he just lays and drinks. Hard stuff. Enough it should kill him. More than once, I've ridden out to the line shack 'cause I've seen buzzards circlin'. But he's always been breathin'. So I just prop him up and feed him coffee 'til he comes around. Then, he's good for another six months or so. Drinks, but not like when a spell takes him."

Clay decided as soon as he could he'd put in a call to his partner and have him run a background check on Gleeson. Maybe he had a record. What could he be living on now? "Know what he did before he came here?"

"He has owned up to a couple of things, mostly when he's braggin', drunk and on the town. Says he's a retired cop, a sailor, a feed and tack store owner, and a farmer from way back. You take your pick."

"Have any friends?"

"No. Not really."

"Now, when someone says 'not really' to me, I always listen a little longer, because it usually means there's more."

"Well, on the rare occasion, he's in the company of the town drunk, Crazy Jake. Think they just know each other from being locked in the same cell." Charlie dropped a rope on one of the calf's extended legs and snugged it up tight. "Look, we could go on about this all day. You're not a cop right now; you're a foreman. Mount up and pull this calf up that side canyon and up a slope. Coyotes might as well have dinner."

"How can you just blow this off?" Clay couldn't believe it. "There's a nut runnin' around out here somewhere."

Charlie stopped just short of the barn. "Clay. There's lots of nuts runnin' around out here in these mountains. All of Arizona knows it. Hell, maybe even the entire West knows it. Most of 'em are lookin' for gold, and most of 'em are harmless. But this is far from the first time we've had an animal turn up dead that looked like it was killed abnormally. Now, I've got a ranch to run. You with me?"

The whole time Clay saddled up Bandito, his thoughts returned to the gruesome killing. Lee Ann's pure, sweet, smiling face kept intruding on his thoughts, and he knew fear for her. He was certain she could handle a lot, but somehow, deep down, he knew she was incapable of handling this alone.

Bandito liked to have killed him before he got the calf dragged up the slope. He skittered every which way and bucked full out a time or two and about the time he would travel straight ahead, he would snort loud, trying to clear his nostrils of the dead smell, and look backwards while going forward. But it sure had taken the edge off him by the time Clay had him back to the corrals.

Clay heard a shout from above the corral. The group from one of the higher, closer canyons came spilling over the rise at a trot, with a bunch of around twenty-five cattle in front of them. The point man had his hands full with an old cow, which obviously didn't feel like being driven this day.

Clay pulled open the gate with surprisingly little trouble from Bandito. The horse danced under him as the herd plodded by. He pulled the gate closed and strained to reach the chain guard. Just when he thought his saddle was going to take a slide under the little mustang's belly, he sidestepped into the gate, pretty as you please, enabling Clay to drop the chain into its slot. His hand found the wet neck and patted it to reward the good move.

By afternoon, they were really good at it, because they got to do it over and over. In between gate keeping, he pushed the little horse into the sorting corral and drove cow/calf pairs to the sorted pens. Bandito no longer seemed to mind the crush of crowding bovines, nor the unending demands Clay placed on him and, though he would occasionally wring his tail when asked for a lope, moved out willingly enough.

Lunch had been a strung-out affair, each group of wranglers coming in when they got their bunch corralled. It bothered him that he hadn't seen hide nor hair of Lee Ann.

Finally, though, Harley came in with the largest group yet, pushing another very large, very grumpy bull with red in his eye. Lee Ann brought up the rear riding the pretty youngster Fleece, now stained with sweat and dust. He watched for a moment as the two moved like one and admired the skill it took with a green horse.

His attention was abruptly dragged back to the pen when the enraged bellow of a bull sounded directly behind him. Harley moved forward confidently, slapping his rope on his leg, hissing "Shoo, bull. You just get back. Shoo." The leggy grulla bulked up and stepped forward nicely when Harley asked. Bandito didn't even seem bothered when Clay asked him to help. Then Lee Ann surged forward on Fleece to close the only remaining gap between the bull and freedom.

The bull made as if to stop, but then Harley did the unthinkable—he rounded as the bull passed and went behind him. The bull plunged forward, bellowing and pawing. Harley had pulled back, but it was unnoticed by the bull. Clay waved his arms trying to gain the animal's attention in the split-second he had. The big brindled beast rushed Lee Ann. Even though she dug her heels in and commanded the mare forward, it was too much. The mare gave way and leaped backward to avoid the bull. He sideswiped her like a massive locomotive that sent both mare and rider flying. In the end, the mare was down with Lee Ann's right leg pinned tight beneath her.

Clay never knew how he got to her side, but he was there, levering the saddle horn up so he could drag her out from under. He pulled her out and had her slung up on Bandito in one second, and in the next he leapt upon the gray's back as she rose. The whole herd tried for the gate, but someone had managed to close it, so the job at hand was to get them both out of the crush. The swirling dust choked him and, for a moment, he couldn't see. Then, the herd moved and he could spy a clear space to the back gate. Looking back to be sure Lee Ann was hanging on, he led them both to safety.

He reached up to pull her down from the saddle. It seemed his heart was in his throat.

"She would have gotten up." She hadn't lost her hat, and her face was hidden. Maybe he hadn't heard right. Surely, there was a thank-you in there somewhere. "What?"

"I was just waiting for her to get up."

"Lee Ann, there was a whole herd coming right for you. You didn't have time to wait."

"It would have only taken her a second more. She was listening, and she was responding."

He tipped her chin up to him, so grateful she was alive, and grabbed her by both shoulders to shake her. "Damn it, girl. This is just what I was talking about. That horse should have been more afraid of you than the bull." His teeth ground aloud, he was so furious.

A shudder ran clear through her; he could feel as well as see it. Her jaw jutted and she pierced him with a steely glare. "A second more, and she would have been up, I tell you." She ripped out of his hands and grabbed the mare's reins. Through slitted lips, she hissed, "Thanks. I'll do the same for you."

For a second, he just stood there, then decided that if she put herself in danger like that again, and lived through it, he might just kill her himself.

LEE ANN MANAGED TO get out of the corral before her legs started to shake. She managed to get to the barn before a single betraying tear stole its way down her dusty cheek. She dashed it away and considered, for the first time in her life, that her training style might need an adjustment or two. She had asked that mare with everything she had to hold tough and, in the end, the mare had caved in. Just the way Clay had said she would. That's when the tears came, hot and heavy. She hid herself behind a pile of hay and allowed them to clean her of the day's tension. Then she slipped to the nearest horse trough and dashed them away with the clear, cold water from the sluice. She had just wiped her face with the back of her sleeve when Charlie came around the corner.

"Heard you took a fall." His lined face creased

even more as he stopped in front of her. "Lee Ann, they say the mare backed down."

Mortification put a slow burn that began in her belly and climbed to heat her face. "If I'd had a second more, she would have responded."

Charlie took his hat off and wiped out the rim with his bandanna. "The hands seem to think you didn't have that minute. I can't have that with my riding stock, Lee Ann. They have to come through in a pinch. This may make the difference in who I hire." Fixing her with a hard look, he replaced his hat and then turned to go.

"I'll wear spurs." She hated to say it. Spurs were harsh and inflicted pain.

"What?" He turned, incredulity heavy in his voice. "You don't already have them on?" He peered at her boots. "Darn straight you will, and if you don't, you can't stay. I won't have the death of Duke Waters's only child on my hands, you hear?" He grabbed his hat and angrily swatted the barn door on his way out. "Damn."

Out of the shadows, just inside the door, stepped the person she wanted to see least in the world. From what she could see of it, his face was filled with compassion, yet she couldn't help her next words.

"That must have been music to your ears, eh, cowboy?"

He held out a hand in supplication. "No. Nothing like that."

"Right." She turned angrily and grabbed the stall door. Fleece stood just inside, still saddled, head hanging, just as if she knew she'd failed. What it meant was that Lee Ann had failed in her training, and it was a bitter pill to swallow. It was all right to be kind to animals, but when that kindness endangered you both, it was wrong, could have been dead wrong.

From behind came two strong arms that wrapped firmly around her and a chin that tucked her head under it. A deep warm voice murmured, "We all make mistakes from time to time. What I like about you is that you learn from them. Makes you a cut above."

His spice and leather enveloped her, along with the arms that warmed her and the comfort that folded about her like a down quilt. She felt weak for letting him hold her, but shame shackled her where she stood. "Guess I'll learn to wear spurs again."

"They can be used kindly." He turned her to face him and tipped her face up to his. "I know you will."

For a long minute, she stared into his eyes.

There was no laughter there, no smug look of superiority. What was there was loving kindness framed by dark handsome cowboy, and he took her breath away. "We have to get back." It came out in a whisper, though she could have sworn she'd intended to say it strongly. "There are calves to work."

"Yep." He set her back from him and smiled. "Just as soon as I unsaddle your horse, boss."

A shaky laugh somehow passed her lips as she unbuckled the cheek strap and took the wet headstall off the horse. "Boss. That's real funny."

He set the heavy roping saddle on the rack outside the door. "I don't mean it to be funny. You held your own out there, and I know you'll do it again." He strode out of the barn.

Lee Ann thought she heard him whistling, "You Light Up My Life." There was so much to love about that cowboy. He had risked his life for her again and never once cussed her for being a fool, even though she was sure he thought it.

16

When the Work is Done

I SHOULD BE HAPPY about this, Clay thought. Charlie had all but told him the foreman position would be his. Last night as they were going in to bed, he'd said, "I didn't like the way Lee Ann trained up that gray, Clay. It looks like you may be the new foreman of the Silver Rock." He thought he wanted that worse than anything. Then why had the boss's words made him feel so grim?

"Yowch!" He yanked the razor away from the bleeding angle of his jaw. "That's what I get for not concentrating." And what was it he'd said back? That the boss should just keep an eye out. That Lee Ann had real talent with people and animals alike. That she seemed to bring the best out in everyone, and how could a foreman be any better than that? Then Charlie had looked at him as if he had two heads and gone to bed.

One thing about all this, he thought as he rubbed his jaw to find the spots he'd missed. He sure didn't miss gambling and drinking. How could he? He had to be on his toes every blasted minute with her around. He yanked on his jeans and socks, then reached for his shirt. If she wasn't something. If he lived to be a hundred, he would never completely understand her, but he did respect her. And he did like her; hell, more than like.

He pulled hard on his second boot and got it on. His left foot was a little swollen, making it difficult. He tried to remember why that might be, then it came to him. Fleece's front hoof had banged it when he was trying to lever the saddle up to get Lee Ann. When he pictured her there, pinned, white-faced and working hard to get her horse to respond, knowing the cattle were coming too close and getting pushed from behind, he shuddered. In another second they would have trampled her and Fleece both.

The pull on his heartstrings was evident even to him. Criminy, he might just love her. Love? Was this what love did? Made you feel like your insides had become raw with pain when you see someone else suffer? He buttoned his shirt up wrong and had to do it again. He yanked open the door and hit himself in the knee. He'd never felt that way about Linda. Not even on a good day. And when she'd calmly announced she had found someone else and handed him back the solitaire ring, it had barely touched him. But all Lee Ann had to do was look a mite troubled, and he found himself troubling right along with her.

Out in the main room, he reached for his hat and pulled it on slowly while he got used to the idea. He shook his head as he walked out the door. He didn't even flinch when the palo verde tree with its nasty thorns smacked into his back and stuck him as he passed by. He remembered Lee Ann's high laugh when it had happened on the first day they were here, and even that made him smile.

Well, now that he knew he loved her, he just had to tell her. She should know. Suddenly, he felt like bursting into song. Except he was in front of about thirty-odd folks he barely knew. Someone handed him a coffee mug, and someone filled it. He remembered to smile and thank them, but the only thing he was hungry for was the sight of one tall, slim, blonde woman—Lee Ann Waters.

Her laugh beckoned him to the cook shack and, somehow, he was there. Josie almost ran him over, coming out with a full platter of hot cakes and bacon. Quickly, he steadied both her and the platter.

"What's the matter, can't see?" Josie drew back as he fixed his gaze on Lee Ann. "My, my," she whispered loud enough for him to hear, "aren't we looking particularly twitterpated this morning?" Her cheery, hoarse laugh filled the air. "Someone here for you, Lee Ann."

Her hat was off, and a sheen of sweat covered her heat-pinked face. The light behind her caused a small halo to form in her hair as it tried to fly out of the braid she had so carefully created.

"Lee Ann, I want to tell you something."

"I know, I know. We need more eggs. I'm frying them as fast as I can. It's been a while since I did short order, you know. I'm a little out of practice, and the guys are a whole lot hungrier than they were yesterday. They didn't eat near this much . . . mfffttpptt."

He'd shut her up the only way he knew how. Her mouth felt warm and tasted slightly of bacon. He slid his hands up her supple back and marveled at how good she felt, all soft, but sinewy, too, like some big tigress. And Lord, she tasted good and smelled better. He felt liquid fire pool below his belt and groaned. When she collapsed against him and melted into him, he thought he might lose his mind. Then without warning she shoved him. Hard. He nearly fell on his butt. "What was that for?" Couldn't she tell how he felt about her?

"Just because I'm in the kitchen, don't you go thinking I've gone all soft and you can take advantage." She turned away and grabbed something on the plank table. When she faced him she had a knife, and her eyes glittered with anger. "Try that again and you may come up with something missing."

He held out a hand. If only she would. . . .

"Yowch!" He yelled for the second time that morning. She had hit his hand hard with the knife. For a second, he expected to see blood, thought she'd lost her mind. Then he realized she had hit him with the back of the knife, flipped it so fast he hadn't seen.

Josie bustled past him. "Lee Ann, you got those eggs?"

"Yes, I do. I'll just serve the boys out of the skillet. They'll stay warmer that way." She shoved past him with a glare, threw down the knife, and hustled out to serve whichever plates were being held out.

His stomach rumbled, and Josie shoved a plate at him. "Whatever you had to say can wait. Fill your belly, boy. It's going to be a long day." Her tone softened. "And at the end of it, there'll be a dance. A square dance. And Lee Ann likes a man who can dance, she surely does."

Hope filled him. He would tell her then. Holding her close, under the moonlight. He'd show her something about dancing. He would sweep her off her feet and. . . .

"Clay Carter, you going to stand there all day?" Charlie's deep voice filled the area. "You're a mite slow, son. I'm about to give out assignments, and you haven't even et yet."

He shoveled the pancakes and bacon in as fast as he could and washed them down with a cup of coffee on his way to the barn. Today, he'd ride Miser. And unless he missed his guess, Lee Ann would ride Little Joe.

THE WIND LIFTED her hat a bit and made Lee Ann reach up to remove it. The slight exertion of saddling up Little Joe had made the top of her head damp under the hat. Mounted and moving, the cool air eddied about and dried her hair quickly. Little Joe had a long, reaching walk that was surprising for his size and build, and she knew by the end of the day, her back would still be supple because of it. She knew some otherwise good horses that could nearly jar your teeth loose by the end of the day and cause your back to tighten and get sore. It was just one more reason to appreciate the smooth two-year-old gelding.

There were only a few more cattle to bring in this morning, then the rest of the day would be spent working the herd. Three reliable men trailed her. They were headed for one long canyon that had a side chute everyone had missed, it seemed. No one could remember going up it when the map had been reviewed. The chute would quite easily hold the number of cattle missing, though in truth, it probably didn't have them all. So the other riders were spreading out and combing all the canyons and flats one more time.

As they neared the entrance to the side canyon, Little Joe suddenly put on the brakes. His ears pointed to the left slope of the second hill in. Lee Ann took her binoculars out of her saddlebags and trained them where he looked. She whistled low. The other three riders had caught up.

"What do you see?" They crowded close, causing Little Joe's ears to flatten and his rump to tuck.

"Here. None of that. You mind your manners." She straightened him and heeled him about. "Near as I can see, the whole rest of the herd. There must be really good graze and water back there." Each took a look through the binoculars.

"Dave? Head up that hill and call any hands you might be able to see from up there. Gary, Sam, and I will head in and begin bunching them up."

He tipped his hat and swung away to do what she'd asked of him. She and the other two walked in slowly to the deepest part of the canyon and began to put a little pressure on the ambling, grazing cattle. The wind had lessened to a slight cool breeze, and the animals were full and happy so they moved forward easily, nearly wearing little cow smiles. The calves were full of themselves and still felt secure enough to scamper about, though they settled down to stick to their mamas once the pace picked up a bit.

Her gelding pivoted well on his hind legs when asked for a quick turn. It had to have been bred into him, because she certainly had not had time to teach him. She liked the way his head dipped and his ears flattened when he had to go after a beef. Among ranchers it was known as "cow sense," this ability to spot, drive, and outguess cattle. Little Joe seemed to have a large helping of it. If she had her own place, she'd make a good offer to Charlie for him. For a minute a pang near her heart reminded her that she no longer had such a place, but on this sun-filled morning, doing one of the things she loved most in the world, it dissipated quickly.

The small bunch she had, joined one Sam had, then Gary's, and pretty soon nearly all the beef she had seen through the binoculars were ahead of them. In time, Dave returned with three more riders, and they situated themselves nicely around the herd.

A young heifer exploded from behind a scrub bush and leaped up the slope nearest Lee Ann. The grade was steep, but it seemed to slow her only slightly. Little Joe was already asking to follow, so when she touched her spurs to his sides he lunged to follow. Her throat closed slightly when he fell backward a step or two. He had never had to handle a hill with the weight of a rider on his back. He did it right, though. He squatted all the way around and dug in. With a powerful surge of his hindquarters he continued upward.

Lee Ann did all she could by levering her weight forward over his heaving shoulders. In just four leaps he was behind the heifer, and in one more above her. He swung his head low and nipped her in the side, and she responded by turning and heading back for the safety of the herd. He slid and skittered and rolled his eyes. His ears flattened, and he popped a sweat over the steep downgrade. For a heart-stopping moment, Lee Ann thought he was going head over heels. She pulled him up and turned him back up the slope to a less-acute angle. He caught on quickly and finished out the slope in a series of switchbacks. At the bottom of the slope he stopped and shook himself like a big dog. She laughed and reached out to pat him. His good nature and easy recovery made her smile. By the time they had the herd back to the gathering corrals, he had perfected his newly acquired skill as well as a little jog trot that made it easy to keep the herd going.

She couldn't seem to spot Clay anywhere. She watched until the herd was all in the main corral, thanked the hands, and rode on past the squeeze chutes. A strident yell made her focus on the man behind the mature cow in the chute. He had a protective plastic sleeve on and had been up to his armpit in cow, checking to see if she was pregnant and if so, how far along. Lee Ann knew from experience that it was hard work—the cow had strong muscles that worked to expel the invading hand and arm of the examiner. Someone was pointing behind and below him and hollered something Lee Ann strained to hear. It was Clay in the chute, she realized. Finally, she heard it. But she had to be wrong. She heeled Little Joe a bit closer and cupped her hand behind her ear. About the same time Clay's face whited out and he jumped to the top bar of the chute, she could tell what the excitement was about.

"Rattler!" Almost too quick to see, a slender, long, mottled brown snake struck straight up and barely missed Clay's boot. He managed to gain the very top rebar of the chute, at which time the rattler redirected itself to the fat rump of the cow in the squeeze.

"Open the squeeze and let that cow out before she gets struck," Lee Ann ordered. One of the hands had the lever up in a flash. The bellowing bovine needed no urging to escape the confines of the chute. Once out, she wheeled to face the danger, head low, horns swinging, pawing the ground in anger. No longer confined to the small space, the diamondback rattler dropped down and slithered out in the general direction of the cow, which took a swing at it with her hooked horns before lumbering off to join the others.

Clay climbed back down and faced her with a glare. "Don't you have something better to do than just sit on your pretty horse and watch?" Quiet suddenly reigned. Even the cattle were quiet. He was embarrassed and taking it out on her.

"Don't you have anything better to do than pregtest rattlesnakes, cowboy?" For a split second there was silence, then laughter swelled and guffaws drew a smile to his face.

"Yep. I'd say that rattler was in her first trimester, for sure." That brought even more laughter, and Clay eased down off the chute, removing the filthy sleeve as he came. He stood at her side looking up. The work began again, with a vet-tech taking his place.

His warm hand lay on her thigh, and he looked up to her face. Under the brim of his hat his eyes sparkled true-blue. She did like the looks of this man and the way his eyes mirrored his moods.

"I hear there's a dance tonight."

"Usually. Yep. Today's Saturday, so I guess so." Her heart did a little jog trot in her chest.

"Will you be there?" His scowl confused her.

"Be there?"

"I didn't mean that." He plaited a section of Little Joe's mane.

"Well, handsome, what did you mean?" That seemed to encourage him.

"I mean, will you, er, um, go with me? Be my date?"

He'd said it. All kinds of emotions rumbled around inside her, but what won out was something warm, low in her belly. "Your date?" She sidled Little Joe slightly out of his reach.

"Hey, that was almost a side-pass." Admiration was evident in his tone.

"I can't take any credit. This horse is one in a million. He seems to have come with everything built right in. If I had a place, I'd offer Charlie most anything for him." She hated the near whine that sounded in her voice.

"Hey, I guess I understand that." He stepped in close again. This time he swiftly grabbed the saddle horn and was up behind her before she could take a breath. The one-in-a-million horse took a leap for the air and nearly unseated them both. If he'd had just a little more size on him, he might have managed to dump them both.

Lee Ann felt a giggle bubbling up. She clamped her free hand over her mouth and with the other reined the horse to a stop. He stood hump-backed, but he stood.

"I'm not getting down 'til I have an answer," he said. His hands were firmly clamped about her waist. They were large and warm and nearly spanned it.

"Do I have to only dance with you?" Shoot, he had made her breathless again, and her question had barely come out audibly.

"What's that?" He leaned closer. People were

beginning to notice, and the work in the chutes was slowing. She tried harder.

"I say, with only four or five women here, it would make some folks mad if I only danced with you!" This time it came out loudly, real loudly. Heads swung her way and, as the meaning of her words sunk in, frowns showed up here and there.

"Don't you even try to hog all the fun tonight, Carter." The burly man smiled a tooth-gapped grin at her as he notched a calf's ear and blood sprayed like a guttering candle.

"We'll hog-tie you and throw you out for the coyotes, you try that." Skinny Harley looked as if he meant every word.

Clay seemed momentarily off balance, and he loosened one hand from her waist to hold it out to plead. "Aw c'mon. Give a guy a hand." He laughed and played to the crowd.

Lee Ann took the moment to shove back hard. He slid right off Little Joe's rump, who threatened him with a tucked butt. He swung out of the way and fixed her with a heart-breaking grin, which she was sure had served him well many times in the past.

"Have a heart." His hand clutched at his chest.

"I do have." She heeled Little Joe into a lope

toward the hitching rail by the tack barn and threw back over her shoulder, "That's why I'm dancing with everyone!"

17

May I Have This Dance?

"WHY, ISN'T SHE JUST the prettiest thing you ever did see?" Josie Lockhart arranged another bowl of potatoes on the trestle table right next to the fried chicken. Clay popped an olive into his mouth before he looked up. He nearly shot the thing out of his mouth, then choked on it as he caught sight of the vision before him. Somehow, the white puffy blouse and denim skirt had turned Lee Ann the athletic horsewoman into Lee Ann the woman with all the curves. No one had a right to look that good. In fact, he was getting a little irritated with her. The cotton gauze of the blouse showed a little too much of those curves off, and even the ones that were covered up were too, too. . . .

"What's the matter, buckaroo? You seem all choked up." She batted her eyes in an exaggerated fashion. She drifted past him as he finally managed to swallow. Her sweet perfume reminded him of orange blossoms.

The yard had been transformed into a dance floor with the help of many hands sweeping away the dirt and putting down fine sawdust. Along the edge of the tack barn, Chinese lanterns glowed, sending soft lights of varying hues into wide multicolored circles. Oil lanterns sat atop the trestle tables groaning with food and drink, bathing it all with a warm golden light. He watched while she wandered here and there picking at the fruit and vegetable trays. Just when he thought she'd forgotten him altogether, she sent a look over her shoulder at him that turned his blood to fire. He sucked breath to cool it.

The band consisted of a fiddler, a guitar player, and a bass player. They tuned their instruments with exuberance, and a caller was warbling his voice like a sick rooster. Already, several of the riders had seen Lee Ann and were making their way to her. A sharp shove from behind him shook him from the deadening inertia that seemed to have gripped him.

"You're the one she wants. Get right in there and fight, cowboy, 'cause unless I miss my guess, it *will* be a fight." Josie's brown eyes sparkled with mischief, and her grin seconded the motion. "Go on now. Git."

But he wasn't in time. Seemed Charlie got the first dance. Now, he knew that Charlie thought of Lee Ann as a daughter, but that didn't do a whole lot to salve the slow burn in his craw that started the second he saw her in another man's arms. He turned away so he wouldn't have to watch and grabbed a glass of lemonade off a table. He swung back because he couldn't bear not seeing her. She moved with the grace of a gazelle and seemed to be able to read the older man's mind, because she never took a misstep. The song went on forever.

He downed the lemonade in a couple of swigs and slammed down the glass just as the slow tune stopped. Charlie executed a mannerly bow and lifted her hand to the next dancer. The next dancer? Clay nearly bowled over a woman coming toward him as he tried to reach Lee Ann. He reached forward to steady her. It was Lee Ann's red-headed friend.

"Dance?" Her green eyes twinkled. Before him Harley bowed low and kissed the back of Lee Ann's hand. If that wasn't so old it hurt. He saw her nod, and Harley wrapped his long, scrawny arms around her. She looked enchanted. Clay forcibly relaxed his scowling face and drew his lips up in what he hoped passed for a grin.

"Why sure, ma'am," he told the redhead, "I'd be delighted." Well, two could play this game, that was sure. He twirled his partner away to the rhythms of an energetic square dance caller.

"Swing yer partner down real low, get along now and do-si-do . . ."

Problem was, at the end of that dance, Lee Ann had another partner and then another. He had danced with the only other four women until he was blue in the face, and the redhead was beginning to think he was stuck on her. Well, this could go on all night long, and he might not even get to talk to Lee Ann, let alone dance with her. It called for an aggressive maneuver. That was better. He was thinking like a cop now, not like some love-struck cowpoke. What was it Josie had said? Twitterpated? If he remembered correctly, her reference was when Bambi had fallen for Felina. In a maneuver that would have done a seasoned ball dancer proud, he swirled the redhead close and pulled Lee Ann's hand off her partner's shoulder. He didn't look too quarrelsome, and Clay was pretty sure he could take him, if things went wrong.

"The little lady's with me. She, uh, promised this dance to me. Did you forget, darlin'?" He stared into her eyes and willed her to play along.

"No." She grinned and replaced her hand. "I'm sure you're mistaken."

"No, darlin', *you're* mistaken." He dared her to dispute him.

"Miss Waters, I'll take care of him, if he's botherin' you." The brown-haired, medium-built dancer sized him up.

Clay didn't even spare the guy a glance as he fixed a glare on his "darlin.'"

Lee Ann slowly drew a card out of her skirt pocket and squinted at it. She replaced it and sent the guy a melt-in-your-mouth grin. "I'm sorry. He's right. I *did* promise him this dance."

It took Clay a second to realize that she held her arms out for him. He nearly stumbled as he stepped forward and took her in his arms. The tune was a slow one, and he gathered her close. They swung away in a slow beat that seemed to rhyme with the tattoo of his pulse. He finally had her where he wanted her. She melted into his curves just as if she had been made to fit there. The slow tune seemed to go on and on. Nothing had ever felt so good, so right....

"I said the music has stopped." He looked up, dazed. Sure enough, the musicians were laying down their instruments and heading for the beer kegs.

He drew her away, holding her gaze with his. She seemed mesmerized. Now was the time. He pulled her to a corner where the lanterns came through the ironwood leaves in a dappling that made everything look lacy, romantic, and perfect, it seemed to him. It was now or never. "I found out something today."

She lifted her eyes to his, and he swore he could see to his very soul. Her eyes dilated slightly and held his. His breath seemed to lock up in his lungs. "I, uh, I . . ."

She squinted and cocked her head to one side.

"You okay?"

He nodded and gaped like a fish out of water. Finally he gasped in a harsh breath. God, he was scared. "I think, no, I *know* that I love you . . ."

"You do?" She seemed a wide-eyed innocent, so fresh, so young.

"Yeah. And I've been trying to tell you all day."

She put her fingertip to her mouth, like a little girl expecting a surprise. "Really?" She reached up and twined her arms around his neck.

"Really." She actually looked a little goofy, now that he concentrated. What was she doing with his neck?

"If you think I'm falling for that, you must think

I'm a pretty big fool, Clay Carter." Now she looked like the Lee Ann he knew, all sass and spite.

"Yep. I love you, and I want to marry you." Her arms dropped from behind his neck.

"Well, you can't." She didn't stick her tongue out. She didn't have to. "'Cause you're all tied up."

What the hell did she mean now? And where was she going?

"Lee Ann?" He stepped to follow her until he gagged on the sudden pull on his neck from the bandanna tied to the ironwood. "I'm going to take a switch to you, you little wildcat . . ."

By the time he made it back to the dance floor, she was already dancing with yet another eager partner.

LEE ANN DANCED UNTIL she couldn't any more. She was so mad she could spit. What kind of fool did he think she was? Did he think she couldn't figure out what he was up to? He was just going to marry the competition and get the job done that way? Just get the little lady breedin' and she'd be no problem. Put a ring on her finger and make her forget her career? That kind of thinking was archaic. But then, she suspected Clay Carter was an archaic kind of guy. He was kind of old-fashioned.

She lowered her chin to her partner's shoulder and watched Clay settle under the tree he'd managed to escape. He leaned back with a drink in his hand, which he lifted to her. He seemed belligerent, almost. When he smiled and slugged down the glassful, she jerked away from her surprised partner and ran to him.

"Clay Carter, give me that." She reached down and ripped the glass away, sniffing it briefly before setting it down. It smelled like . . . tea?

Before she knew what was happening, he'd jerked her down to the ground beside him. The power of his embrace stunned her. He pulled her close. His eyes were black with fury, and his lips pulled back over his teeth in a snarl. His voice was a low rumble but very, very clear. "I may pull a trick on you once in while, like this." He lifted the glass. "But I never, never lie. Got it?"

Her heart fluttered, and she nodded. "Yes." She tried to pull away.

He was having none of it. His lips descended, warm and wet and slightly lemon. He molded them to her and invaded her senses. He seemed to wrap himself around her until she trembled, and yet only his hands touched her wrists and his lips, her lips. It was some kind of trick. She felt absolutely overtaken.

She wanted to pull back. She fought to think. He said what? That he absolutely never lied. Did she know that to be true?

She couldn't think. His scent was spice and leather and warm, wild male. So if he didn't lie and he said he loved her. . . . So if he didn't lie and he said he wanted to marry her. . . . Her body wanted to believe; her body wanted . . . him.

His tongue touched her lips, warm, wanting in, and, God forgive her, she let him in. His taste touched hers and became known, oddly familiar, forever imprinted in her mind. That scared her. She had to remember all that was at stake here. She had to remember all the cowboys who at one time or another had tried to take her body, without regard for her and what she wanted out of life. She had to remember . . . what?

In the moonlight, her fears seemed groundless, what she wanted, frivolous. What could be more important than love? Her head swirled, and she used his support at her wrists to keep her balance. The kiss went on, deepening until she thought she would drown. Her breasts suddenly felt tight in the confines of her bra and blouse, and a need built low in her belly that almost made her want to cry. A moan escaped her lips.

He finally released her, and she nearly fell against him. With a look that nearly resembled pity, he gathered her in his lap and wrapped his arms around her. Tears streamed down her face, and she hid it in his wide shoulder. She didn't ever want to love again, to feel this pain. She had lost the two other men she had loved so much, and she had never wanted to hurt that bad again. It would seem she had no choice.

When she finally thought to look up, she was surprised to see that the dance was still going on. Seeming to understand, he pulled her to her feet. He bowed low. The band picked up strains of the song "May I Have This Dance for the Rest of my Life" and played.

"Well, Lee Ann, what's it to be?" He twirled her and pulled her close and swayed to the rhythm.

"This one dance, and then," she sighed, "and then we'll see."

18

An Unusual Choice

THE NEXT DAY BROKE blustery and wet. Lee Ann could smell the rain long before she actually could see it. Of course, she couldn't actually see much of anything. She was in the cave her flannel sheets and comforter made, and for a moment she entertained thoughts of staying there. She poked a tentative finger out as a temperature tester and pulled it back in after just a couple of seconds. There might have been a fire in the main room of the bunkhouse, but there sure wasn't in the foreman's room.

A delicious, satisfied lassitude filled her, broken only by a banty rooster crowing its fool head off somewhere. Wait a minute, they didn't have any roosters. The coyotes ate them all. What the heck was going on? Lee Ann jumped out of bed and went to the door. The blasted thing sounded as if it were right on the other side of the door. She yanked it open.

Clay stood with his legs wide, holding an old-fashioned portable tape player in front of him, looking back over his shoulder at the wranglers sleeping in the main bunkroom. Guffaws of laughter let her know that they were all in on it. She grabbed the player, yanked it into the room, and closed the door on him. Finally, she jabbed the right button to kill the rooster. Through the cracks in the old door she heard laughter and his voice.

"C'mon, lady. Daylight's burnin.'"

What a joke. There wasn't even a hint of light out the window. She stalked over and drew back the curtain peering toward the east. The cold of the floor seeped up through the socks she had worn to bed, and she shivered. Okay, so maybe there was a touch of some faint light in the east.

"Go away. I'll get up when I darn well please." She gazed longingly at the warm blankets and was going to dive right back in when he said exactly the wrong thing.

"We're hungry, woman. We need breakfast."

The door swung wide in her hand. How she got there so fast, she didn't know. She was so angry, she thought she might explode into tiny little shards of something. She wanted to bite him, claw him. How dare he?

"Then, *man*," she nearly shrieked the word, "*You* better go help Josie, 'cause I did it yesterday, and it's your turn!" She slammed the door so hard she felt it through the floor. Flinging her pajama top off, she ripped a sweatshirt out of the ancient set of drawers and pulled it over her head. Stepping out of her bottoms, she yanked on her jeans.

"Ow!" Her thumbnail ripped on a jean rivet. It didn't make putting on her boots any easier. Ugh, what a way to start a day.

Suddenly, she stopped. Just moments ago, she had felt so good, all warm and cozy and satisfied. *Satisfied? Where had that come from?* Then she remembered. She had dreamed of him, and they had made mad, passionate love, and he was amazing. She had just climaxed when that stinking rooster woke her.

Zipping her jeans, she tiptoed over to the door and opened it. She just wanted a peek at him. He was nowhere in sight. She opened it wider and stuck her head through. The men all slept in their clothes, and most were up and pulling on their boots and hats. A few were adding jackets today.

"He went to help Josie," one gnarled older fellow allowed.

"No sh—I mean, no kidding?" A giggle bubbled up inside her and spilled over.

"No shkidding," he grinned. "Said something about doing what the boss wanted."

"What did you say?" She knew she was pushing it.

"I said abso-darn-tootin-lutely!" He clapped on his hat and opened the door, which he just remembered to hold open for her. Proudly, she grabbed her hat and coat and stepped out.

"Darn tootin." She threw back her head and laughed, glad to be alive. The wind gusts nearly tore her hat away, but she got to the cook shack in record time, hat intact.

Without a qualm, she seated herself and pigged out on the spread before them. She got great satisfaction from being served her coffee, just like she'd served it yesterday. Josie seemed to like her new help, too.

"Hey, sweetie pie, I've got some great buns in the kitchen." Josie's eyebrows lifted and lowered suggestively. "If ya catch my drift . . ."

"Why Josie Lockhart, I never." Lee Ann tried for prim and proper.

"Well, if you haven't, honey, you probably should."

"Again with the eyebrows! You should be ashamed." But she couldn't help it; she laughed.

Clay was quite a sight. He had a white apron on, had tied a bandanna over his hair, and was shoveling out eggs like he was moving dirt. However, most of them were ending up on plates. He hovered over her left shoulder. In a falsetto voice he inquired, "Eggs, ma'am?" Then, he lowered it to an alto. "Mmm, I mean boss?"

"Yes, little lady, er, fella." Merriment rippled through her. She loved the way he could poke fun, even at his own expense.

Charlie walked by, and his brows shot to his hairline. Lee Ann thought she could see the corners of his mouth twitch, but she wasn't sure.

He raised a glass and tinged it with a fork to get everyone's attention. "I hope last night's hoe down was enjoyable to everyone. I wanted to thank you all for your help. Before you go, don't forget to pick up a package of beef for yourselves out of the freezer. It's good aged beef. It doesn't begin to pay for all you've done here over the past few days, but I wanted to thank you all now, if I don't catch you on your way out. You brought in every last cow, bull, and calf, and I'm grateful. The Silver Rock will make it another year, and I couldn't have done it without you. Every one of you knows if you need a hand just call me, and I'll be more than happy to help you with your spreads."

Nods and smiles showed everywhere. "Two weeks from now, I will be going to Bob and Josie Lockhart's Diamond Dee, and I hope to see some of you again."

Bob raised his hand and added, "Each and every one of you's welcome to come."

"So the good Lord watch over you, and happy trails." The boss ended his speech and sat to have breakfast.

Lee Ann watched him for a moment and wondered how many of his kind were left in the world. Just then, Clay wandered into her field of vision, and she nearly sprayed coffee laughing at the vision he made.

THE WORK WAS ALL but over by the end of the day, and most folks had moved out hours before. Clay sat on a tree stump and continued to repair a rein someone had busted. It was going to be a little shorter than the other one, but it would still do. He had just risen to put it back in the tack barn when a small hand on his shoulder stopped him. Orange blossoms drifted by his nose, so he knew who it was before he turned.

"Hey. I wanted to thank you for this morning." Her eyes were on her hands, which were nervously twisting a hoof pick around. "I was a shrew and ..."

"You were also perfectly right." He lifted her chin and looked into her gorgeous turquoise-green eyes. "It was my turn."

"Still." Lee Ann looked out somewhere over his shoulder.

"Look." He turned to gaze out over the mountains where the clouds rambled along, white and puffy and in no particular hurry. Big deep blue patches in between caused the contrast to be sharp, and he had to squint. "You never hesitated to do your share and more. Why should I?"

Apparently, she thought he deserved a reward because the next thing he knew, she had nearly climbed on top of his toes and jerked his head down for a swift kiss. In the next instant she took off, racing over the still-damp ranch yard.

It stirred something wild in him, and he responded by running flat out to catch her. He caught her just inside the horse barn. Breathing a little hard, he drew her to fit against him and pinned her there by placing hands on either side of her and shoving her against the wall. Her panting aroused him, and he felt the familiar fullness in his britches that happened now whenever she was near.

God, he was bad as some pimple-faced lust stud. He decided that he would just have to live with it in his head, even while his lower body pushed against her denim-covered hips. He rocked against her as he looked into her eyes. Her pupils dilated, and her nostrils flared. He lifted her hat off her head and closed in for the kiss that he wanted so badly. He lifted her to get a better angle at her mouth, and she settled against him straddling his hips. It did unbearable things to him, and the ancient rhythm escalated. He deepened the kiss and felt her respond by allowing him access to all of her mouth and neck.

Her tongue tentatively touched his, and he chased it back into her. He couldn't seem to get enough of her taste, the feel of her. He wanted to stop pushing against her, wasn't sure how much more he could take, had never been this out of control. He pushed harder and felt the pressure of her lower back against the hand that was between her and the barn wall for support. He realized she had tilted her hips to feel him better, and he almost lost it completely.

He bit his own lip to control himself. He had

to have her. Had to find a place. Instinctively, he glanced around for a private spot. The trophy room was behind them, usually locked, but for some reason it was open. He took her with him and crabbed sideways until they were inside. He pulled the door closed and locked it. She took a shuddering breath as he laid her on some clean blankets piled in one corner.

As she lay back, he noticed the upward thrust of her breasts softly outlined by her sweatshirt. He eased his hands under the shirt and pulled it off. All she had underneath was a flimsy sort of silky thing. The light shafting through the partly open shutters was enough that he could see the outline of her nipples, dark through the shirt. He lipped first one nipple, then the other. She cried out, causing him to suckle them in earnest desire.

"Clay, we have to stop."

His hand found her jean snap and flipped it open with dangerous dexterity as he rubbed against her.

The delicious friction he kept up the whole while had brought Lee Ann to the edge, over and over, and the dampness she felt signaled that she was ready. "Someone is going to find us."

His hand found the spot where she had soaked

through her underclothes. He pushed against the fragile barrier, shoved it aside, and slid an exploring finger inside. She bucked upward and wet him with her honeyed warmth, helpless to stop it.

"Mmm-hmm. Everyone's gone."

She listened for a second, momentarily sated, and realized he was probably right. "This isn't right. We're on the job." She pushed him back, and her hand grazed his bulging jeans.

His hips jerked, and he hissed through clenched teeth. "Watch it."

Her eyes rounded as she saw the size of him. "God, I am." Slowly she pulled back. As hot as she was, he looked too, too. . . . "No."

"Clay, Lee Ann. You back here?"

Lee Ann panicked and sat straight up. Suddenly, she felt as if she were fifteen again and Charlie was her dad. She lurched to her feet and zipped her jeans in record time. Clay sat at her feet with a dazed look on his face.

"Get up," she hissed. "As soon as he gets to the corrals, he'll turn around and come back."

"Damn, Lee Ann. If you think I care what Charlie Bruce thinks . . ." He handed her sweatshirt to her.

She jammed her hat on her head and flicked her

hair to rid it of anything it might have picked up. "You might not. I do. I've known him all my life. I swear, if you don't get up . . ."

He reluctantly got to his feet and whistled. "Does this look as bad to you as it does to me?"

She let her eyes focus clearly on their surroundings. The shelves were empty. All that was left was little rings of dust where silver trophies of all kinds had been. She raced for the door, yanked it open and hollered, "Charlie! We're back here in the trophy room. We've been robbed!"

Footsteps could be heard heading their way, fast. "What?"

She pointed him into the room and flicked on the light. "Look!"

He stood for a moment, stunned. "I'll be damned. When did you find this?"

"Just now," they chorused.

He looked from one to the other of them. "Uh-huh." He took just a little too long to continue. "How did you get in?"

"It was open," Clay offered.

"Well," he rubbed his jaw, "it's not quite as bad as it looks." He sat down on one of the old chairs in the room and continued to look around. "Though some's gone. Maybe four or five."

"What do you mean?" Lee Ann counted more than twenty empty dust rings.

"I've had them melted down for one thing or another through the years."

"Why in the world?"

Charlie laughed. "Oh, for silver jewelry. Had an Indian friend who would do them up real pretty, with turquoise and such. Quite a hit ·with the ladies." He winked conspiratorially at Clay. "Especially if they knew the history behind the piece. But you can't with the later ones. They're just pot metal or plastic." He twirled the padlock around his finger, then stopped and looked at it. "Yeah, it's been jimmied. If that don't beat all." He swung around and opened the door to herd them through it.

Once out into the open air, Charlie motioned them to the tables set up by the cook shack. Some folks still milled around, loading up their livestock and gear, but except for a friendly wave now and again, they left the three pretty much alone. Lee Ann and Clay settled themselves on one side and Charlie on the other of the picnic-style table. He seemed fascinated with his hands, which he held steepled before him. Lee Ann remembered from childhood that this meant business. Suddenly, she knew. He had decided. She glanced over at Clay, who had stuck a piece of straw in his mouth and sucked on it with the fervor of a dedicated smoker, gazing into the clearing sky. He didn't have a clue.

"Well, I've decided." She had to strain to hear him.

"Huh?" Clay leaned forward, suddenly all ears.

"Wasn't easy." Charlie looked up and made eye contact with each, slowly, in a two-beat measure. "You both could run this place all by yourself."

Had he stayed focused on Clay just a second longer? Did he have the job? Oh, Lord, what would she do now? Somehow, she managed to nod and mouth, "Yes, sir." Her insides shook and her mouth glued itself together.

"Clay . . ."

Her heart dropped to her gut and shot back up to dam up her throat. "No," she whispered behind her hand, which had somehow found her way to her mouth.

"You figger you got yourself back under control?"

A glimmer of hope shimmied through her.

"Yes, sir." He frowned and took his turn looking at his hands.

"Well, then. Seein' how either of you could do the job, and you have a fine career waiting for you . . ."

"Yes, sir. I do. And I know now I can handle it. Just needed to get my own two feet back on the ground. I've done that." Strong man gazed at strong man.

"Wait a minute." Lee Ann stood when they did and watched dumbfounded as they shook hands. "I, I . . ."

With a laugh that seemed to come from somewhere deep, Clay reached out to shake. "You won, pure and simple, buckarette."

Words wouldn't come. She just stood there letting him shake her hand like a limp noodle. Shouldn't she be enjoying this more? Finally, she burst out of her nerve-induced paralysis. "No. No, that's simply not true." She turned to Charlie, whose eyebrows crept up to his hairline.

"You tellin' me I made a mistake, youngster?"

"No, sir. That is, I can do the job; it's just that . . ." She looked back and forth from one to the other. They just waited. She started to get a crick in her neck. Finally, she looked down, scuffed her boot in the dirt. "I still have a lot to do, and I had counted on his help." That last wasn't strictly true, but suddenly the prospect of the Silver Rock without Clay Carter seemed a lot less wonderful.

"He sure can stay on another week, if he's a mind

to, but as a hand. You're the foreman now, Lee Ann."
That said, he took his hat off, wiped out the brim,
and ambled out into the ranch yard to say good-bye
to the last of the round-up help.

19

Absence Makes the Heart

CLAY'S HEART POUNDED, HIS lungs heaved, and sweat poured off him in sheets. The cardiologist smiled an evil smile. "Just one more mile."

"No problem. Could do it in my sleep." He knew a sneer lifted his lip, but he couldn't seem to stop it. He picked up the pace on the treadmill.

"Make it two, then. This is supposed to stress you." The man in the white lab coat with "Dr. Lint" emblazoned in red on the pocket turned his back and scribbled more in the chart. "You say you haven't needed anything for pain in the past month?"

"More than a month." He wiped the sweat out of his right eye and pounded on. Truthfully, he could have used something right now, but he wasn't going to admit it. He knew if he had tried this a month ago, he would have been in a lot more pain. But the ranch work had given some muscular support to his back. Well, his granddaddy had always said that work did a body good. The thought about the ranch bred a thought about Lee Ann. The cardiologist stepped closer to the monitor and glanced his way after assessing it.

"You all right?"

Clay came back to his surroundings. "Sure. Why?"

"Your heart sped way up for a couple of seconds there . . . but now it seems okay." Still, he stood and kept his eyes fixed on the monitor as Clay finished up.

"You want me to go another mile?"

Dr. Lint smiled. "No. You have already way out-performed the other guys in the precinct."

"Does that mean I'm back on duty? Not desk jockey, but the real thing?"

"Don't see why not. Your psych eval is as good as the rest." He twirled his stethoscope above his head for a second before he placed it on Clay's chest. "*I* always wanted to be a cowboy."

Clay assessed the man's slight stature and white, soft hands as he took deep breaths. When the stethoscope was lifted, he answered, "I'm sure you could do it. Just takes grit."

"Grit? Oh, yes, *True Grit*. John Wayne. Great movie."

THE WIRE WHIPPED BACK and hit her full force across the bridge of her nose. Even as she wrestled it back onto the fence post and gave the splice one more twist, she could feel blood trickling down her face. Mentally, she calculated the last time she'd gotten her tetanus shot as she eyed the rusty barbwire. Must have been six, eight months ago. It would do. She whipped off her bandanna and wet it from her canteen. Pressure ought to stop the bleeding, she thought.

"Whoa." She reached for the saddlebags the rangy roan gelding carried. He snorted and backed when a breeze tickled his nose with the scent of her blood. "Here, you." She wiped a drop of it into his nostril, and he quieted. It was a hunting trick she'd learned from her father. The constant smell of blood desensitized horses to it and they calmed. Didn't always work, but mostly it did.

Her hand lingered for a moment over the wound powder she kept for the horses. The stuff could stop bleeding on all but the biggest cuts. But a quick check told her that her sliced nose had quit bleeding and that further, it was just an odd little nick and not the slash she'd thought, so she just dabbed the wound with first aid ointment and left it open.

Returning the ointment to the saddlebag, she patted the big rangy roan. Clay had preferred this horse for fence work. No wonder. Thinking of his young horses leaving him standing alone out in the wilderness brought a smile to her face and pictures of his lean hard body to her mind.

He had stayed that week as she had wanted, but it deteriorated into their picking at each other like kids and, when he'd left, they were almost fighting. She wouldn't blame him if he never came back. Or called. 'Cause she sure thought he'd have called by now. But Charlie's big mobile set-up remained quiet, and she was sure Charlie would have told her if a call had been left on the machine.

She replaced the fence tool in the special leather holder she'd made and swung up onto the tall horse, with the help of a good-sized hunk of granite. A deep breath drew in the smell of warm horse, cattle droppings, and creosote. Heaven. She remembered the first time she had ever spoken about how she loved the smell of horse and cattle at the grade school she attended in the town nearest her father's ranch. "Ewwwww," the little red-haired girl had squealed. "That's disgusting." *Oh, well,* she thought, *no accounting for taste.*

By the end of the day Lee Ann was disgusted with folks who thought it just fine to cut fence if it happened to be in the way of their all-terrain vehicles, dirt bikes, or trucks. It amazed her that they seemed to think that when they purchased the vehicle, they purchased the right to Arizona's state lands. Not many seemed to know that when a rancher leased that land and fenced it, they shouldn't be on it without permission unless they were hunting, and even then they had to have a license to hunt and the game animals had to be in season. She had repaired six new cuts just today.

With a sigh, she took down her hat, wiped out the brim, and replaced it. It was hot and airless in the deepest canyons and way too early to be this warm. She wet her bandanna with water from her canteen and was just dabbing it on her face and neck when she heard a rifle blast on what seemed to be the next rise.

As she heeled her horse into a lope, she wandered if Charlie had shot a varmint. There was talk of a big old male tom mountain lion taking the late calves. It was nasty business. He would eat a few bites, it was said, and then move on to the next kill, taking as many as three in one day. A cougar like that could decimate a calf crop in no time. As she topped the rise, a Jeep spewed gravel and dust as it sped away from a downed cow. All she could see was a man's profile in the cloud of dust raised as the vehicle sped away. She raised her binoculars to get a better look. It was useless; he'd raised too much dust, but the man had looked very tall to her. She heeled her blowing mount closer to the cow.

"Aw, damn." The cow was losing blood by the gallon from the hole in her ribcage. A distressed bawling was taken up by beef near enough to catch the scent of blood. A cry much higher than the rest was where she aimed her gaze.

"Maaaaw, mawww." The little black calf with huge knobby knees and a white patch on its forehead kept advancing toward her a few wobbly steps at a time. That he wasn't even dry yet gave Lee Ann hope. He might be so young, she could catch him up. She crooned reassuringly to him as she moved forward in a crouch.

"C'mon, Little Blackie." Just a few more feet would do it. He gazed at her myopically with newborn vision and blinked. A hand laid on him just caused another bawl, but he stayed put. She gathered him and stood, groaning with the weight. Even brand new, these little ones were not light.

Stopping for a moment by the cow, she checked the ear tag number, then strode over to the big roan. Carefully, she arranged the calf over the horse's lower neck and swung up in one smooth movement. Little Blackie kicked for a moment or two, causing her mount's ears to flatten, but the roan quieted as they stepped out into a long, ground-eating walk.

When she got to the top of a rise, she looked back to check how the vehicle had left the ranch. She squinted, but could make out the gate hanging wide open. With a sigh, she headed that way and made a mental note to get padlocks for all the gates. It would be a pain to have to get down each time you drove a vehicle through, but maybe it would stop this latest idiocy. Little Blackie stayed where he was laid, and she pulled the heavy pipe gate closed. Gathering him back up, she remounted. Her back and the backs of her legs ached with the extra burden.

Shadows slanted long over the ranch yard by the time Lee Ann got back to headquarters. She put Little Blackie in with a couple of cows that had lost their little ones during roundup. She hoped he would mother up with one of them. Resting her weight on one leg, she leaned forward onto the pipe corral and stretched out her back.

Little Blackie cried as if his heart were breaking, and one big old orange cow ambled slowly over to him. When he wouldn't quiet, she took to licking him from head to toe. His little tail started wriggling and slapping back and forth, and he happily nuzzled her full udder. When he began to tug enthusiastically, she bumped him with her bony head but allowed him to stay. By the time she relaxed and began to chew her cud, it was nearly dark. Satisfied that all was well, Lee Ann made her way to the house. If her nose didn't deceive her, it was pork chops tonight. Charlie was just putting down the chow as she came in.

"Looks good."

He nodded and sat, content to wait while she washed up at the sink. "Beginning to think you might not show. Then I saw the big roan and realized you were here somewhere."

Her stomach prefaced her answer with a growl. "Glad you went ahead and cooked, though it's my turn and I owe you one."

"You don't worry about that. If we start keepin' track and owin' meals and all, we'll get so mixed up, no telling what could happen." He helped himself to the mashed potatoes, then offered her the bowl. "What kept ya?"

"Trouble, maybe." She chewed and swallowed. "Number 461 is gone. Shot."

"Too early for hunters." He drew on the beer he had. "See anything to identify the shooter?"

"Not really. Except this: He was a big man, tall, not fat, just big. And he drove a Jeep, an open Jeep. Couldn't get the license."

"Durb Gleeson drives a Jeep. Was it him?"

Lee Ann tried to picture Durb. "Maybe, but why would Durb pull such a stunt?"

Charlie shrugged. "Why does Durb do any of the weird things he's done? Did the cow have a calf? She should have by now." He shook his head, and a grimace twisted his rough features. "She was a good cow, though she always calved a little late."

"Little Blackie."

"You named it?"

"Him, and yeah, what of it?"

A smile tugged at the corners of his mouth, just like Lee Ann had hoped. "I mothered him up with that old cow of yours whose calf got trampled, um, number 241."

This time a full grin lit his rugged features. "The other cow you named. Peaches?"

"Yep. Peaches."

"Well, that's real fine. She has been known to nurse other cow's calves before. She ought to do the job right."

"Yep. The little fella's belly was being filled when I left."

"Let's stop all this gabbin' then, and get yours full."

Lee Ann took his suggestion and concentrated on the creamed peas for a few minutes.

The boss got up and made notes in his records, then came back with the coffee pot and a pan of cobbler. "Save room for Josie's cobbler."

Lee Ann thought the day might not end so badly after all.

"And before I forget again, Clay called again and mentioned that he wanted to speak to you."

"Again?" It was all she could do to stay seated. "As in he's called before and asked for me before and you forgot? Or, he's called again and this time he wanted to talk to me?"

"Whoa there, young'un. As in he called earlier this week and asked for you, but it slipped my mind."

In her haste to get up she nearly tumbled the coffeepot. Taking a deep breath, she calmed herself and stood poised by the phone. "Did he leave a number?"

"Seems like he might have done." He pointed to a scrap of paper next to the phone.

What was the matter with her? Her heart was pounding like a teenager's. Any minute now, she was going to pop a zit. Her fingers punched the number. The lazy hello that sounded in her ears made her heart flip.

"Clay?" She grinned like a fool at Charlie and gave him the thumbs-up sign. "What's that? You'll have to speak up. Reception's not so good." Her boots weren't touching the ground, she was sure.

"I say, I have Friday and Saturday off, and there's a rodeo up in Agua Fresca. Can you go?"

"I think so. One of those days, sure." She tried to picture him in his police uniform, but all that would come to mind was the lean, hard-muscled, denim-clad Clay that she knew.

"No, Lee Ann, both of those days. I could get us a room at the hotel." Her heart shot to her throat, nearly choking off her reply.

"Both?" she squeaked. "Overnight?" Heat filled her throat and then her face. "Let me check with the boss."

For just a moment, she felt as if she were asking

her dad if she could go out, and her embarrassment at what the invitation probably entailed made a bead of moisture trickle down between her breasts. "Charlie? I have an invitation."

He waved her off. "I know, I know, for Friday and Saturday. The rodeo. Sure, you're pretty well caught up around here."

"You know?"

Clay's heart missed a beat as he recognized her tone. "Oh, no," he whispered to himself. "She's fixin' to get a mad on."

"I heard that, Clay Carter. What do you think? That he's my dad? That I'm some little kid who has to have permission?"

Here he hadn't talked to her in almost two weeks, and it sure wasn't going the way he'd hoped. "No, Lee Ann. Not that. Just ..."

She cut him off ruthlessly. "Just what? You two men were just going to arrange my life and let me know later?"

"He's your boss and ..."

"And what? Did you consider that I might just hate rodeo? Did you consider my feelings at all?"

He winced as this last was nearly shrieked. He heard a door slam.

"Was that Charlie?"

A slightly subdued tone answered him. "So? You think I care?"

"Yes." His voice sounded very calm, even to him. "I do."

"Just a minute." The phone clattered in his ear, as he wondered what she was doing. He could hear Charlie Bruce's deep tones now and Lee Ann answering him, soothing him. "It isn't you I'm mad at, it's him. He should know better. Sorry I shouted." A few seconds later she was back on.

"I'll think about it and call you tomorrow night." The phone went dead in his hand.

"Well, shoot. I won't be here tomorrow night, you little wild cat. I'll be on duty." He shrugged as he pulled off his T-shirt. "Guess you'll just have to find that out." Even angry, she turned him on in a bad way, and now he needed to cold shower if he was going to have any hope of a good night's sleep. And he was going to need one.

Seemed that springtime brought the crazies out in force, and today's duty had been tough. Trying to be reasonable to people without reason was always hard. Just today, he'd been driving down Washington Avenue and been stopped by a naked man doing somersaults across the crosswalk.

He chuckled and shook his head at the memory.

The man had seemed supremely happy. They had hauled him in, done a Breathalyzer, and watched for signs of drugs, but it became evident that he was clearly delusional, not chemically challenged. It was tough to ID him without benefit of rational conversation and clothing, so they just sent his picture out online to the other agencies. They would have a better idea what to do with him when they heard. Since he had been somersaulting in front of oncoming traffic, it wouldn't have been kind to leave him to his own devices.

The cold shower was working its magic so he reached down and warmed it up a bit. Turning it off after a good soap and soak, he stepped out just in time to catch a call.

"I just realized you might be on duty tomorrow night." *Smart girl.*

"You figured right." A smile softened his words. "Do you like rodeos?"

"If the livestock is treated right." Her tone was still stiff.

"It's supposed to be a good one." He couldn't believe he was holding his breath. He forced it out.

"Okay. What do I need to bring?"

"Oh, just whatever you might need to wear . . ."

"What does that mean?" A note of warning alerted him.

"Maybe it would be better if I just told you what I have planned, you can say yay or nay, and then you'll know what you need." He swallowed a huge lump in his throat. "Okay?"

"Hmmm." She purred. "Go on. I'm listening."

"Breakfast Friday morning at Eggfries."

"How did you know that I love Eggfries?" He thought maybe he could hear a smile in her voice.

"Didn't really. Just hoped. Then, I'll get a basket from Picnics to Go and we'll stop in the pine forest on our way for a cool lunch. I know a place where we can dangle our feet in the creek."

"Sounds wonderful right now. My feet are burning up." Her laugh tinkled over the line, raising his hopes.

"The rodeo starts late afternoon for the opening ceremonies, a Native American Pow Wow and Prayer Meeting."

"Hmmm." Doubt sounded in her voice.

"We can just walk around the grounds. They are selling jewelry and fry bread."

"Uh, oh. Sounds like I might just gain weight this weekend . . ."

"Don't worry. You could stand a few pounds."

"What?"

Her sharp reply reminded him painfully, again,

that he needed to be careful what he said. He wasn't talking to one of his partners here. "You look great. I just think you lost a little too much over roundup." In truth, he thought that the more delicate look it made in her face was attractive. It was just that he had seen too many women without curves and didn't like it. Truth. He knew the truth always worked with her. "I love your curves."

"Oh." Softly, she breathed the word. "You're right. I could stand a high-calorie weekend or two."

"I'll take you any way I can get you." Oops, that may have been too far.

"You won't take me, cowboy, until I say so." Her words held a hard edge.

"I've never, uh, taken any woman that didn't want it, Lee Ann, and I won't start now." His own words sounded hard.

"So, you've had a lot of women?"

That shrewish note was definitely back. He had about had enough. "Do you want to hear about the rest of the weekend?" His last ounce of patience was trickling away.

"Oh." She puffed. "Sure."

"We'll be staying at the Tall Pine Inn, and they serve breakfast in their dining room as part of the deal." There. He'd gotten past the tough part. The night.

"Okay. Will I have my own room?"

Or maybe not. "If you want it."

"I want it. Call me old-fashioned."

"Okay, Old-Fashioned, you've got it." This was not going the way he'd planned. But he'd been telling the truth when he said he would take her any way he could get her. He had gotten way too used to having her within reach way too fast. Missing her was a physical ache that tortured him every minute of every day. "Then the rest of the day is pretty much rodeo, shopping at the tents, and, uh, dancing. I should have you home before dark Saturday."

"Now that's better. I'll scare up the appropriate duds. I think it all sounds like fun."

20

Things That Go Bump in the Night

THE ALARM WENT OFF, and Lee Ann stretched her arms above her head. Anticipating two whole days off sent a delicious sense of decadence cascading through her. For a moment, she lay still, just enjoying the feel of it. Then, she swung her legs over into the pre-dawn chill and padded barefoot toward the bathroom door. Her foot hit something wet and unyielding on the floor.

"Ugh, what the heck?" All she could make out was a dark form. A breeze wafted across her feet. For seconds she didn't get it. "The door is open!" As she stepped over to close it, the hair on the back of her neck rose, and instead she pulled it wide. The light revealed a sight that made her gag. The smell of iron assailed her senses. She knew blood when she smelled it. At that moment, she wished with all her heart that she was a screamer, but not a sound would come from her closed throat. She grabbed her gun and her boots and stumbled out the door. Finally, her voice worked. "Charlie? Charlie! Come quick!" Trying to keep her eyes on whatever could be behind her, she bumped into him in the middle of the ranch yard. She found a scream. At least part of one. "AAAAAhhhhh . . ."

"What's wrong? You near scared ten years off me." Charlie grabbed her by the upper arms and made her face him. "What?"

All she could do was dumbly point back at the open door. Finally, she was able to spit it out. "In there. Something dead."

A look of understanding filled his face. "Mouse?"

She rapidly shook her head. "A—a—bigger."

"Oh, a rat." Her voice wouldn't work, but her hands did. She pulled him toward the door.

He peered inside, then stepped in to squat beside the mound. "Well, it could be worse. It's just another calf."

"But *in my room*, Charlie."

He stood to face her. "I know. That's the troublesome part. Got a rope?"

Numbly, she reached to the wall where her rope hung by the door and handed it over to him. He calmly reached down and looped it around the hind legs of the calf. She tugged on her boots and then grabbed hold to help, and together they pulled it out into the ranch yard. Bum slunk over, sniffing at the carcass.

"You're a failure as a ranch watch dog, you big mutt." Cowed, he slunk away. She pulled on her Levi's jacket over her long johns.

"Well, now. That's another troublesome spot. He didn't raise a ruckus. Means he knew whoever did this." Goosebumps rippled up Lee Ann's arm. "Help me find out if we've worked it." She knew he was asking her to check to see if the calf was branded and ear-notched.

As they turned the carcass, straight strips of flesh hung in precise, two-inch tatters. It became apparent the calf was unbranded, unworked, and very young. "There weren't many that were still carrying by the end of round-up. We should be able to figure out who its mother is."

Lee Ann hugged her arms to herself. Charlie didn't seem nearly shook up enough about this. Her dad would have been. But then, she reflected, he wasn't her dad. And she was the foreman. "Have you ever seen anything like this before?" She took a deep breath and looked away.

"Yep. Out back of the barn, during roundup." He stood, rubbing his chin.

Her hands went to her hips, telegraphing her aggravation at not being told. "What?"

"Oh, sorry I didn't tell you. Clay was right there, and he just hooked his horse up to it and took it up the hill for a coyote dinner."

"Well, that should have called the varmints in." Charlie had to have known better.

"Just seemed the easiest thing to do. Didn't want folks getting spooked."

"Did the two of you come up with any ideas?"

"Just that the carcass was carried there by one good sized man, size thirteen or fourteen boot."

She shivered at the thought of someone that large having been in her room, looking at her while she slept, defenseless. With an effort she shook off the fear.

"Think I'll take to locking my door at night." Charlie looked at her pointedly. "You might do well to."

"I will. Want me to take this up the hill?"

"No, no. I think this time we want to report this to the authorities."

"Want me to make the call?"

"No. I'll do that. I'm going to look around a bit, not that I really expect to find anything. You need any help cleaning up?" Lee Ann shook her head and headed for the barn, calling back over her shoulder, "I'll cover it up with a tarp."

Inside, the barn was still shadowy in the early morning light, and Lee Ann was extraordinarily aware of every little sound. When Booger trumpeted from the end of the barn in an ear-splitting blast, she nearly came out of her skin. The tarp, she remembered, was in back of the grain bins. As she reached back and strained to pull it forward, something bumped her from behind. The shriek she sent forth nearly equaled Booger's in volume.

Pounding boots told her Charlie was headed her way. At the door, a fuzzy, gray mass collided with him, nearly sending him sprawling. "Bum, you worthless cur!"

A nervous giggle erupted from Lee Ann's throat as she realized who made her scream. "Come here, Bum, it's okay." The big dog stole in with tense glances at his owner.

"Are you okay, Lee Ann?"

She nodded. "I guess I'm a little more upset by this than I let on. Guess knowing it happened before is a little, uh, unnerving." She yanked on the tarp and it flipped free, bringing a shower of dust and hay that made her sneeze.

His large hand settled for just a second on her shoulder. "Don't get spooked. We'll catch this guy."

CLAY PULLED IN just as Lee Ann finished cleaning the stain off the floor. He stood framed in the doorway, the denim-clad cowboy she remembered. Her first impulse was to run to him and wrap her arms around him to feel the solid comfort of his presence. Instead, she tossed the wadded paper towels into the trash, basketball-style. "Hi, Buckaroo."

He tipped his hat toward her and smiled his easy smile. "Buckarette. You ready to go?" He looked down at the wet floor. "Accident?"

Abruptly out of energy, she sat, shaking her head, dangerously close to tears. She hoped he couldn't tell.

"Hey, what's all this?" He tipped her head back. "Are you about to cry?"

She stiffened her spine. "Of course not. A little trouble, that's all." Briefly, she recounted the early morning event.

"I guess we won't be going much of anywhere after all." He had squatted at the stain ring the water had left. "Sounds exactly like what Charlie and I found."

"I know." She softly punched him in the arm. "Why didn't you tell me?"

He glanced up at her and stood. "If I recall correctly, I had a lot of distractions." He turned and walked slowly, head down to the floor, and went on out. After a second, she followed. He was bent over and walking slowly forward, eyes glued to the ground. He stopped and pointed. "There."

A very large boot print could be seen in the deeper dust beyond the corner of the building. Again, the goosebumps rose on her arms and she shivered.

"Big son-of-a-bitch." He shook his head and continued walking to the back of the building. His trail took him to just behind the barn, where he stopped and pointed. The bootprints stopped abruptly in a mass of hoofprints. "He got off here and carried that thing the rest of the way. Was that it under the tarp?"

Lee Ann nodded. "Took a big man to do that, huh?"

He put an arm around her and pulled her close. "Yes, sweetheart, it did."

She relayed what she had found the day before out on the range.

"Points to Durb Gleeson, more and more. Jeep, you say?"

She dug in the dirt with the toe of her boot and nodded. "Could be Durb."

"Charlie doesn't think so, you know."

She shook her head. "No. I didn't."

"But I say he had the motive." Clay suddenly looked a lot more policeman than cowhand.

"What's that?" She tried to imagine. It came to her about the same time he said it.

"You shamed him in front of folks, and Charlie, well, he supported you. Men can be mighty touchy about such a thing."

She chewed her thumbnail and thought. "Could be. I guess. But why cut them the way he does? That sort of thing would take time and precision."

"Seems crazy. Person would have to like doing it, or at least take pride in it or something." He walked out and lifted the tarp. "Yep. Same MO. Charlie want you to haul this away?"

"No. He's reporting it, I guess to the livestock board and the sheriff. That's who I'd call, anyway."

"Lee Ann?" He turned her to face him. "I'm spending the weekend here."

"I can handle this." It rankled her that he didn't think so.

"I know you can, but I don't think we should go and leave all this for Charlie to handle, so I might

303

as well stay." Clay hated to think what might happen to her if the man known as the "Pink Ribbon Killer" had a copycat imitating him. Several years ago, that man had been committed as criminally insane, never to be released. So it had to be a copycat of some sort, or the weirdest of coincidences. In any case, if Lee Ann wouldn't let him stay, worrying about her might just drive him insane. He hugged her, and when he did, he knew he'd made the right choice, because she clung to him.

Bacon frying was their first clue that Charlie had started breakfast, and they joined him. Clay was glad to be seating himself at the table.

"Heard you pull up. Hope you're hungry."

Clay pulled out a chair for Lee Ann, who sat without complaint. He saw Charlie raise an eyebrow about the lack of sass. Breakfast was completed in companionable silence with no one speaking his or her thoughts. About the time the last bite had been eaten and the coffee cups had been refilled, the dog took up barking like the world was coming to an end.

Charlie pulled open the door and the three stepped out to wait for the sheriff's 4X4. Clay knew it would be a trick to get Lee Ann away so he could ask the officer to follow up and see if he knew the whereabouts of the Pink Ribbon Killer. He would rest a lot easier if he knew for sure the killer was still incarcerated.

After Charlie had recounted what they knew and the sheriff had viewed the carcass, they all had to answer some questions. Clay didn't think the questioning was terribly inspired and, while he didn't expect the seasoned sheriff to be surprised, he was unprepared for the total lack of interest.

"Have you had any other kills like this?" The man didn't even look up from his clipboard.

"No. Just these two." He turned away and measured the boot mark.

Clay couldn't help it. "Just how many kills do there have to be before you get interested?" He knew his voice held an edge, but he couldn't help it. Indifference ticked him off. He felt Lee Ann tuck her hand in the crook of his arm.

His words seemed to make some kind of impression on the lawman. "Look. They're calves. Just calves."

Clay tensed, the steel springing into his voice. "And one of them was not two feet from my girlfriend while she slept, alone and defenseless."

The other man stopped, turned, and faced him, legs apart, arms loose at his sides, clipboard forgotten. The voice was soft, but undershot with warning. "Maybe you ought to take better care of your girlfriend."

"That won't be necessary." She stepped purposely forward, between him and the sheriff. "I can take care of myself. I'm the foreman of this place, and the only reason we called is because the law requires us to. I *will* find out who did this, and it *will* stop."

Clay got goosebumps watching her, knowing the courage it took to say it, to back it up. He could see that the sheriff couldn't quite deal with the twentieth century staring him in the face. "She's your foreman?" He didn't even compliment her with a glance.

Charlie nodded and tipped his hat. "Yep. Darn good one, too. If she says she will take care of a problem, it'll get done. You need anything else, Sheriff?" He waited.

The sheriff looked her up and down, and Clay stepped to her side. He wanted to say that he was going to stay and keep an eye on her, but he knew better.

That familiar notch up of her chin came and she repeated Charlie's question. "Anything else you need, Sheriff?"

He glanced at Clay then back to her. Taking his hat off, he shook his head and held out his hand first to her, then to Clay. "No, ma'am. I expect that will about do it. Do you have any more questions for me?" Clay knew he couldn't ask about the Pink Ribbon Killer now. He would just have to call later.

"No, sir. I don't." She shook his hand just once and turned to Clay and Charlie. "Well, I won't leave the place while something like this is going on, so I may as well get to work. I want to ride fences today and get padlocks on the gates. Charlie, I saw some with keys in the trophy room. Want me to use those?"

"That would be fine, Lee Ann. But you should take your weekend with Clay. You deserve it."

She smiled brightly at her employer and made sure she sent one Clay's way, too. "He's welcome to stay, if that's okay with you, boss, but I'm going nowhere. One man could decimate a whole herd in a couple of days, if he'd a mind to. Though," she added with a wry chuckle, "he'd have to give up the pretty carving."

Darned if she couldn't make them both smile. Clay followed her lead to the barn.

THE WARM SMELLS of the barn did as much to soothe her jangled nerves as Clay's presence did, and, by the time Lee Ann had Star haltered, she felt she had things back in proper perspective. This didn't even compare to some of the problems she had dealt with on her dad's place. Maybe it was a little weirder, but it wasn't anything she couldn't handle. Now the cowboy who followed her into the stall—that was another matter. She faced him, hands on hips, Star at her back.

"You fixin' to follow me around all weekend?" She smiled up into his concerned gaze. Lord, he smelled good.

"I'm *fixin'* to." He seemed to be laughing at the way she spoke.

"Are you funnin' with the way I talk, buckaroo?" She knew he had the same battle with speech that she did. It felt good to know that he was ranch-raised like her. He toed the dirt in a good farmboy imitation.

"Shucks, ma'am. You jess make my tongue go purely wild, you do." The glint in his eyes reminded her of a small boy's. She wanted to hug him badly. Instead she shoved him aside as she passed to go out with Star. She almost made it. He scooped her up and sat her in one smooth motion on Star's back and led them both out into the sun. For a moment while the sun blinded her she just sat, like a little owl, turning her head, trying to see.

The next thing she knew, he had pulled her down into his arms and she felt his whole long, hard, dangerous length slide against her. Her breath lodged and hung up in her throat. How long had it been since he'd kissed her? As his lips settled over hers to claim them, she decided it had been entirely too long. He hadn't let her feet completely touch the ground yet, so she dangled, only anchored by his hips and arms and the tips of her toes.

His warm tongue touched her lips, probing, seeking. She let him in. His coffee-sweet breath tasted way too good, mingling with hers. She met his tongue with hers, and he answered with a satisfied hum that filled her mouth with a moment's vibration. Her hands rested on his shoulders, then crept back around his sun-warmed jacket, one finger finding warmth under his hairline. His hair was silky but resilient and strong, like him. She twirled it while she tilted her head as he deepened the kiss.

The strange vertigo descended on her that she had only ever felt when he kissed her. It was good he held her so tightly. The kiss went on and on. A nudge finally brought her back to some sense of reality. Star whickered her impatience.

His deep chuckle ended it. "I guess the audience wants us to move on."

She nodded and dropped to the ground, suddenly bereft of his arms, his support. "That—that's okay." She couldn't seem to get enough of looking at him. He stood so straight, so strong, so tall. Yep, it was a sure thing: She had a real weakness for cowboys. "Who do you want to ride?"

His smile caused an ache somewhere in her chest. She hadn't noticed before that he had a very slight overbite and decided that she liked the way it curled his lower lip a bit, making it appear fuller, more sensual. She really wanted to kiss him again and concentrate on how it felt.

"You're the boss. Who do you want me to ride?" he asked.

"Oh? Uh, Ranger, I guess." He tipped her head up to gaze into her eyes.

"You guess? Are you okay?"

Not with you around, she thought. Not anymore. "Sure. I mean, Ranger. He gets along great with Star, and he is good in rough country." Mentally she chided herself to get her mind back on her job. Tying Star, she rabbited to the trophy room to get the locks. She turned to run back and slammed into six foot of solid cowboy.

He growled. "I think we have some unfinished business here first." Deliberately, he closed the door and locked it with a door lock she had never even noticed. Her eyes adjusted to the gloom of the room. The only light came in through the shuttered window in the wall behind her. One look into his eyes, and she felt like prey. His eyes devoured her. She felt small and defenseless. She backed away, looking for a way out; even though she knew she wanted him, a primitive part of her yelled "run."

She reached for the door, and the knob turned in her hand. His large brown hand clamped over hers and pulled it off, finger by finger. He drew her hand to his mouth and kissed each fingertip while he removed first her hat, then his, and threw them aside to land on the trophy saddles in the corner with a puff of dust. Wrapping one arm around her shoulders he pulled her forward and staked his claim on her mouth with his. In two-step timing he eased her back to the pile of blankets in the corner. She couldn't have said how she ended up flat on her back if her life depended on it.

"I want you, and I intend to take you." Vaguely, she wondered what happened to her snappy comebacks, all her defensive lines. She reached for what had worked before. He wanted her job. *No, he didn't, not anymore,* a little devil in her mind answered.

He had started moving against her, insinuating

himself between her legs, rubbing his arousal where he must have known it would do the most to her. Her pelvis tilted to receive him, and her face flamed at her body's instinctual response. Her arms flailed out in attempt to dislodge him, to find something to grip to roll him off.

Neatly, he pinned her arms above her head with one hand while he unbuttoned her shirt with the other. She made the mistake of making eye contact. His look said he adored her, he cherished her, he loved her, and he meant to have her. But he hadn't said it, and she recalled with the last shred of her sanity that she had seen this look before, in cowboys who had come and gone. She had gotten away from all of them but one and had lived to regret that one. With supreme effort, she dislodged him and scrambled to the door. By the time she had wrenched it open, he was up and beside her.

"Hey, hey. What is this?" He tipped her chin up and searched out her gaze. For just a second her eyes met his.

The warmth of her tears startled Lee Ann into belligerence. "I'm not just another roll in the hay, cowboy." Her lip lifted. "I'm very sorry you think so."

With a vicious yank, she ripped the door wide open, hitting him hard on the shin. Out of the door with a bound, she strode down the breezeway to where she had Star tied and, even though she could hear his yowl of pain, she didn't stop until she began to groom the mare. So intent was she that she didn't hear his approach over the rasping of the brush as she cleaned away the hay and dust.

"I'm sorry."

She angled herself so she didn't have to look at him. She wouldn't make that mistake twice.

He grabbed her by her upper arms. She stared down at his boots. "Did you hear me?"

She just stood there . . . waiting. He just wanted someone, anyone. She was available.

"I haven't told you what you mean to me." Here it comes, she thought. Here is where he uses his best lines. Stubbornly, she gave no indication she heard.

"I want it all, Lee Ann."

Yeah, she thought, *sure. Of course you do. What cowboy with an urge doesn't?* She pulled away, kicking at the dirt and throwing the brush savagely. She might as well face it, and him. Hands on hips, she sneered, "Oh, yeah, I just bet you do." His startled look might have caused her to reconsider, if she hadn't heard it so many times before. She readied her hand to slap him if he came closer.

Abruptly, he dropped to his knees. "God, I

don't know where to begin. One of the most important moments in my life, and I can't think what to say."

Her hand dropped. "What?"

He looked up from below her, a funny bemused grin on his face. "Rugrats. A big house. You, with a big belly, me kissing it and loving you . . ." He looked down at his hands, spread them and turned them over as if he'd never seen them before. "Giving you every damn thing you ever wanted that's in my power to give and not taking a thing back until we have said our vows, proper-like, with a minister and the church . . . the whole nine yards."

He was good; she had to hand it to him. "Why don't you stand up and say that?"

He tried. "I can't."

For a long moment she waited. In her mind's eye, she remembered when Andy had told her he loved her, and she also remembered how she was powerless to move. "Why not?" Not that she would believe him.

He looked up at her and she saw, to her astonishment, a tear in his eye. "I don't know."

The simple honesty in his reply undid her. She dropped to her knees and held out her arms. He came to her and she cradled his head against her chest. Something deep within her tore, and tears sprang forth, healing tears.

Suddenly, he towered above her, strong again. Holding her again, though this time as if he could shield her, protect her for all time. "You're kinda destroying my ego here. You're not supposed to cry."

"You don't understand. Sometimes a heart has to break to heal." Sobs poured out of her like she was dying.

"Shush, shhhhhh." He murmured. "I think I do."

Did she dare to hope? Could she trust him? She sniffed loudly and worked hard to stop the tears and the sobs. "If this is a proposal, I want to hear the words."

He pushed her back and lifted one knee. His lopsided grin sent ripples of warmth through her. "The ring is back in the truck. I don't think I can get up to get it yet."

She managed a shaky laugh. "Say the words, cowboy."

"I want the job, Lee Ann Waters." His eyes were the true blue of honesty. "And I promise you, I am the best man for the job."

She waited, rooted, unable to speak or move. In this one way, she was entirely old-fashioned.

"Will you do me the honor of becoming my

wife?" He looked at her with incredible intensity. His eyes burned, probed.

She nodded happily and threw her arms around him.

He pulled slightly away. "I want the words, Lee Ann."

"I'll marry you, Clay Carter, if you promise never to drink or gamble again."

He grinned and looked deep into her eyes. "That sounded seriously like sass, but I'll do it. You know I will."

All she could do was nod and bury herself in cowboy. Finally, he stood and pulled her up.

As soon as Lee Ann could stand, she pulled away from him. "Hope you don't think this changes the plans. We still have some serious riding to do today."

He laughed and leaned down to get his hat. Settling it on his head, he spun around to stroll down the aisle toward Ranger's stall, whistling a tune.

As she turned to saddle up Star, it dawned on her that he was whistling "You Light Up My Life." Patting the good mare on the head, she looped an arm around the warm neck and watched while the man she now knew she loved gathered the horse he would ride along with her and Star today.

21

The Rules of Engagement

BY A LITTLE AFTER six, all the gates had padlocks on them and Lee Ann felt a little better about things. Not that a padlock out in the middle of nowhere was a real big deterrent, but it was something. The sun was beginning to set, and the whole world took on a bright glow that intensified the colors on the mountains, just before they turned purple in the waning light. She never failed to hum "purple mountain's majesty" when she saw the change.

"Nothing prettier, is there?" Clay sat the big range horse easily, with his hip hitched to one side to ease his seat. His total attention was on the frontage range.

"No." She turned to catch the sherbet-colored sky turn into a fiery conflagration that would never be believable in an artist's rendition. "Look at that. It just doesn't look real."

He turned to catch the light show. "No. But there *is* one thing prettier." He lifted his leg over the neck of his grazing horse and jumped down. "You."

Her breath caught in her throat as it had a hundred times that day. It happened each time she looked at him and realized that he meant to be hers. He reached up for her and she let her reins go, her legs loose so when he pulled her forward she went easily. "You hold me like I weigh nothing."

"I wouldn't say nothing. There's some real muscle here." He gave a lopsided grin that sent her heart into overtime.

She managed to land her lips on his as she slid down. The heady scents of sunshine and cowboy filled her senses, and the feel of hard muscle and denim did the rest. If he asked for her now, she knew she couldn't deny him. Each time she had looked at him that day, she knew with increasing conviction that, at last, she had found one she could trust. That he came packaged so attractively hurt not at all.

To her startled surprise, he pushed her back. He pointed to a downed log, worn smooth with time. "Stay there." He walked over to his saddlebags. "I have to get something."

Bewildered, she sat. He kept himself between her and whatever he was doing. She heard the clank of glass. When he turned he held a couple of blue tin splatter-wear cups and a chilled bottle of wine. A scowl began to form on her face.

"It's sparkling cider, Lee Ann. I wasn't sure it would stay cold, but look." Holding up the glistening bottle, he turned it this way and that, showing off its pale green clarity and the sheen of drops that looked like cool temptation. He laid a red-and-white checked cloth on the ground in front of the low log. It glowed in the deepening dusk. He arranged the cups and the bottle and popped the cork. Carefully he poured them half full. He handed her one as he seated himself next to her.

She held the cup to her nose and smelled the snapping fresh scent of the brew. The bubbles tickled her nose and made her laugh. "What's the occasion?" She sucked air as he pulled a little black velvet box from his jeans.

"Ah, here it is." He glanced up at her, and his deep blue-gray eyes crinkled with laughter. "It about rubbed a hole in me, but that was okay, 'cause I at least knew I hadn't lost it." He knelt in front of her, suddenly serious, and laid the box to one side of her on the rock. He picked up his drink and held it to her in a toast. "To us and the grace of the good Lord that helped us find each other."

"Hear, hear," she whispered. "By the way, don't you think I should know at least what religion you are?" Sipping the sweet drink, she felt her heart trip as he took his time to answer. How could she not have considered something so important before she said yes to him?

"I expect about the same as yours." He settled next to her and sipped his drink quietly. "Granddad usually just took us to whatever church was closest and open."

She nodded. "I used to tell Dad I thought we were Bap-meth-o-lic."

His chuckle sounded deep and sexy. "That's a good way to describe it. So, did you go to a lot of different ones, too?"

"Um-huh." She felt the need to be closer and so slid up against him. He took her drink and set it beside her.

"Is that a decision we have to make now?"

Dumbly, she shook her head. He reached down and picked up the black velvet box, angling his body so he cold hold it about chest level between them. He opened the lid and tilted the contents toward her. Before her lay the most perfect marquise diamond she had ever seen. It sparkled brilliantly and, even in the dim light, blue and rainbow glints shot though the air. It was held to the band in two strong arcs of gold that swirled around the stone, anchoring it surely.

She wanted to say a hundred things, poetic and beautiful. "It really looks strong."

He grinned at her and lifted it out of its slot in the white velvet. "It is. A strong ring, for a strong lady. I don't ever want you to leave it off because you're afraid you'll hurt it." He lifted her left hand and slid it on the ring finger.

She angled it one way, then the other. "It's a perfect fit."

He pulled her to him in a crushing embrace, leaving no space between them anywhere. "So are you," he whispered, then kissed her deeply, claiming her.

All doubts were erased as he deepened the kiss. She looped her arms up around his neck, stretching sinuously, standing on her toes. Over his right shoulder, she glimpsed the ring. Its fire seemed to send a shard right into her, deepening her mounting excitement. His warm breath in her ear sent goosebumps cascading down her arms.

"Do you like it?"

"Oh, Clay. *Like* doesn't begin to describe it." She planted little kisses all over his cheeks, eyes, lips, then his neck. It only seemed natural that she unsnap his shirt as she rained more down his chest, his belly. She found herself kneeling as she worked to undo his belt buckle. Now that her doubts were laid to rest, she couldn't get to him fast enough. His large brown hands grabbed her wrists.

"Whoa, there, wildcat." He stepped back from her and turned to his horse. He threw down his bed roll and tied his horse to the tree closest to them.

On her knees, she felt like a beggar. "Star won't go anywhere. Come back here, cowboy." She didn't care that she seemed shameless. He shook out the roll and she smoothed it with trembling hands. He turned to her and eased her back with infinite tenderness.

"We can wait." His husky voice made her breasts tighten. Wordlessly she shook her head.

His groan came from deep within him as he levered himself over her. He managed to cover her without crushing her, angling onto one hip to keep his weight off center. The next thing she knew her shirt slipped off, followed shortly by her bra. The desert breeze signaling nightfall washed over her skin. His moist tongue and lips worshipped the hardening buds now nearly painful with need. She brushed aside his maddeningly slow hands to undo her own belt and jeans. Her boots dumbfounded her for a moment, until he helped.

Finally, she lay nude beneath him. His jeans rubbed roughly against her as he rocked in a rhythm telegraphing his need. She shoved his shirt back off his shoulders and tossed it away. Her hands curled into his crisp chest hair, black and sparse. She wanted to feel it against her and ran her hands around to his back. Slick, warm ridges of muscle undulated under her exploring fingers as he pushed against her over and over. She nipped his shoulder in frustration and let one hand slide around front to undo his jeans. "Please, I want . . ."

A gunshot fragmented the night, exploding in the dirt at their feet. Star screamed and tore off and Clay shoved her under the log all in the same few seconds. He crouched over her, his gun appearing in his hand. His lips lifted in a snarl, he commanded, "Stay down. I mean it. Stay put."

He lifted his arm and shot in the direction the rifle fire had come from. An answering retort rang off the rocks around them. His horse danced at the end of its reins, desperate to be away. Clay lunged for the horse and mounted it in one smooth leap. The thunder of horse hooves echoed sharply as he raced off in the moonlight toward the danger.

Rifle shots retorted one-two-three. A horse screamed agony in the night. Lee Ann's hand stopped as she struggled to pull her jeans and boots on. Tears clouded her vision. She dashed them away and continued her mad rush to be clothed. Seconds seemed like hours. She strapped on her holster and prayed Star had not gone far. "Clay?" she screamed. "Answer me. Clay?" Abruptly, Star loomed before her, softly snorting in alarm.

Whispering, she sought to calm the animal as she grabbed for the reins. Her shirt remained unbuttoned, but she had ceased to care. All that mattered was to get to Clay. He could be hurt or worse. . . .

Frantically she pumped her heels at Star's sides, and the good mare responded with a fearless lunge in the direction Clay's horse had gone. It was only a couple of hundred yards to the downed horse. She pulled up sharply on Star's reins and circled the heaving horse, whose legs aimlessly thrashed. "Clay!" Again she screamed his name.

A shot echoed loud and sprayed dirt at her dancing mount's feet. She flattened herself over the horse and headed in the direction of an overhang she spied ahead. If only she could make it. She jerked the reins back and forth, causing the mare to zigzag in a path she hoped would make a hard target to hit.

She made it, jumped to the ground, and crouched down, straining in the early moonlight to see something beyond Ranger. The big horse's movements quieted, and she suspected death was not far away. Her stomach twisted in deep sympathy and pain for him.

The sudden quiet was eerie. Nothing moved. At first, no more than a sense, she could hear something moving almost silently through the underbrush. A large form loomed to her right, and she lowered her pistol to aim directly at it. A whisper brought her up short. "Lee Ann. It's me."

"Oh, thank God." Her knees buckled, and tears made him swim in her vision. She wrapped her arms around him and dragged him back into the shadow of the overhang, with her. She tried to chuckle. "I thought for a second there that I had had the shortest engagement on earth." He pulled her into his bare arms, and held her close while he watched out for anything he might be able to see.

"Damn this bare hide. I'm afraid I make too good a target in the moonlight."

His skin did glow, even though he had a tan. Experimentally, he rubbed dust all over. It did little good as it slid right back off as soon as he moved.

"I can go."

He turned sharply toward her. "Don't even think about it, little girl."

Her chin jutted and she hissed, "I am not a little girl . . ."

He clamped a hand over her mouth. "You listen here. This is my line, darlin'. I do this for a living, and I'm good at it." He dropped her and grabbed her canteen from Star's saddle. He sucked air as he poured the contents all over himself. Then he flung dust on top. Seeing what he was up to, she knelt to gather dust and helped sprinkle it all over him. If he was determined to be the one, she could at least help him. He kissed her once, hard. "I mean it. Stay put. If I have to worry about you, I'll get distracted and could get hit." With that, he disappeared into the underbrush.

Seconds turned into minutes and minutes turned into nearly an hour. Lee Ann had a big thirst on. She knew Clay's canteen was hooked to Ranger's saddle horn. She also knew that whoever was out there had a clear shot at her if she came out from under the overhang. She decided she could wait. Everything in her wanted to sneak into the bush and follow Clay, but his words had effectively chained her to the spot. It was unthinkable that she should cause him to be distracted. She prayed that he was as good as he thought.

A low form slunk in the shadows beyond Ranger. Another joined it. Shortly there were several more. In a rapid assault, all the forms attacked. Coyotes swarmed Ranger. Her arm flew up to wave them off, and she considered shooting at them. A thought stayed her finger on the trigger. What if she needed her bullets to save Clay? The coyotes would have Ranger sooner or later, she reasoned.

Her heart hurt as the animals swarmed the good horse lying on the ground. It dawned on her that he hadn't moved at all, and she prayed it meant he was gone on to better pastures before they got to him. In the distance she thought she could hear a truck, maybe two. The sound came from behind the attacker's position. Could it be that help was here? Unlikely, since they were so far out. Still the sounds came closer, then closer yet.

Finally, she heard Clay's voice, so close she nearly jumped out of her skin. "Give it up, Gleeson. That's Charlie and the sheriff coming. There's no way out." She nearly gave in to the urge to poke her head up, but wisely she waited until she heard the vehicle's doors slam. A minute later, she heard Clay.

"C'mon out, sweetheart, we've got him." She scrambled around the overhang in time to see the sheriff handcuff Durb Gleeson.

Charlie Bruce shined his flashlight on Clay, then her. "Looks like you're a little underdressed for the occasion, son."

Lee Ann found she was happy to have buttoned her shirt back up. Underdressed or not, she was happier to see the men before her, alive and unhurt, than she had ever been in her life. She ran up and plastered herself onto the man she now thought of as her fiancé. He held her close.

The sheriff read the man his rights. "Durb Gleeson, you have the right . . ."

Charlie held up a hand. "Just a minute, Sheriff. Better start over. That's not Durb."

With the light shining full on the man's face it became apparent it wasn't. A quick search for ID revealed the man was Ed Gleeson.

"My Lord." Charlie wiped out the brim of his hat. "That's right. Ol' Durb has a twin brother. I had plum forgotten." The grimy man acknowledged Charlie with a nod.

The sheriff started over, did it right, and took the man to his 4X4. Locking him in, he came back and took the rifle Clay had confiscated. "I'll be back later to question you all. Is everything else okay?"

"Not really, Sheriff. He shot Ranger." She shot a look Charlie's way. "Sorry, boss, he's dead."

"Don't you worry, Lee Ann. I'm just happy this varmint's caught and neither of you are worse for wear. He could've done a lot more, if you and Clay hadn't gotten him."

The sheriff ambled over to look at the horse. He squatted for a moment to run his hands over the sleek hide and shook his head. "It's a crying shame." He glanced up at Lee Ann, who stood watching. "Was he a good one?"

"Yes, sir. He always did what was asked." Her insides trembled as she contemplated the loss.

"That's better than some people I know." The sheriff stood. "I assume you all will press charges."

"I'll ask Charlie." She came to where the two men were looking into the back of the Jeep that Ed had obviously driven. She glanced down into the back of the open vehicle and shuddered at what she saw. Dried gore and blood covered everything.

"Boss, the sheriff wants to know. You want to press charges?"

"I'm of two minds, Lee Ann. Ed there is known as crazy Ed. He's never been right in his head, and Durb has mostly been able to keep him out of trouble. I think I want to talk to Durb some, before I decide. Ed disappeared about four years ago. I guess it's time to find out where to."

"Anyone who can do this is pretty near the edge, boss." Clay indicated the Jeep. "And I'd say he stepped over it when he put one of his pieces of handiwork in Lee Ann's room."

"You've got a point there." Charlie stood gazing at the cruiser and its occupant.

Clay stepped over to the sheriff who was talking on his radio. "Are you running a background check on him?" Lee Ann followed him.

The sheriff nodded, and she strained to hear the conversation over the crackle on the air. He turned to them after he replaced the headset. "He's just barely out of prison. He had been serving time for aggravated assault."

"Could you humor me, sir, and check if he had any way of being involved with the Pink Ribbon Killer?" A foreboding caused Lee Ann's pulse to jump.

"Why do you ask?" She searched Clay's face for a sign.

"It may be nothing." He looped a hand around her waist and pulled her close.

The sheriff reached for the headset again and minutes later they had their answer. "Ed should never have been put with The Pink Ribbon Killer." He bent in and peered at the man in custody with visible disgust. "Seems he asked to be bunked with him, and someone decided there was no harm in it." He shook his head as Charlie joined them. "Seems Ed was proud of rooming with him and often said he liked the killer's style."

Lee Ann's hand flew to her face as she sought control over her thoughts. "Oh, my Lord. Do you know that they say most serial killers start on animals?"

"Yeah, I do. I was hoping you didn't." Clay pulled her close and turned to face Charlie. "Boss, if you don't press charges, I will."

Charlie Bruce reached for the clipboard the sheriff had offered earlier. With a shrug he started filling out the form on it. "Who knows? Maybe we'll be doing Durb a favor."

Lee Ann shivered and was suddenly acutely aware that she enjoyed Clay's strong arms around her. She looked up into his face as he stared one last time at the calf killer. "How long will he get?"

"Probably not long enough. I'll ride Star back, boss, if you'll take Lee Ann with you."

"You two. Still trying to take care of me. Knock it off. I'm the foreman. And I can do my job." She strode over to Ranger and managed to get his bridle off. Clay helped with the saddle. These they loaded into the back of Charlie's truck, when he stopped them.

"I know there's no separating you two." He grinned and pointed to the ring adorning Lee Ann's left hand. "I'll take poor old Star home, so you don't kill her riding double." He called out over his shoulder as he headed for the mare, "You can call it an engagement present if you like." Lee Ann barely had time to catch the keys as a glint in the moonlight warned her they were coming.

22

Best Man

IT ONLY SEEMED RIGHT when Clay followed her into her room in the bunkhouse that night. "I would have thought you'd moved into the main house."

She eyed him as he stood outlined in the door by the bright moonlight. Briefly, she shook her head. "No. I've always treasured my privacy, and I think Charlie Bruce is the same way."

He stood rooted, stupidly unable to think of a thing to say. He knew heaven and earth couldn't move him from her side tonight, but she had just said she wanted her privacy. He watched as she shook off her boots and pulled her shirt out of her jeans and ambled over to the little burner.

He couldn't do anything but watch as she pulled the works out of an old-fashioned coffeepot and added a filter and ground coffee. It seemed like the most important thing anyone had ever done, as she poured water into the pot and delicately inserted the stem and basket and replaced the lid. Hands on hips, she turned and faced him.

"Now, it will be ready when we get up in the morning." She slid forward on quiet cat feet, muffled by loose boot socks. "*If* we get up in the morning." Her hands worked their way around his neck and tugged on his hair in the back. The feel of her warm hands on the back of his neck and her supple form on his chest and belly electrified him and lit his senses.

He noticed the unusual slant to her eyes as she looked into his own. Their emerald clarity drew him into her. Her tongue-moistened pouty lips invited him. He loved the way her lashes fluttered slightly as she gazed at his face, first his eyes, then lingering on his mouth. He pulled back, then closed on her to pull her fully to him. His breath stirred the glistening hair by her ear. He lifted her hair away from the back of her neck and nuzzled the fine hairs at her delicate nape. He inhaled her scent, sort of like lemon flowers, peculiar to her alone.

If he lived to be a hundred he would never forget it. She stood on tiptoe to kiss him, finding the one clean spot under his chin. Abruptly, he remembered the dirt he had covered himself with. He pushed her back and noted the fine dust that had transferred itself to her. "May I use your shower, ma'am?"

She grinned and whirled to lead him to the shower, which was just off the sink in the kitchen of the bunkhouse. With a rapid twist, the old shower sputtered to life and poured forth a surprisingly hot stream of water. She pulled a towel from some stacked orange crates that served as a linen closet. "Here, and hurry up. I want to take one, too. I'd join you if there was room."

Even as his mind tossed around what she implied he realized that it was no exaggeration: The shower was tiny, and he knew it would take someone his size some wild gymnastics to get to all his parts and get them clean. Even so, he got done in record time, even for him. He wiped the water out of his eyes and opened them. He started rubbing down his arms, then knew a moment of surprise when he figured out he was being watched, closely.

She had apparently been getting out clean sheets when she had peeked, because there she stood, staring, flushed, and adorable. He lowered the towel to his waist and wrapped it securely. He stepped out, banging his knee on the shower wall, and pulled the curtain back in invitation. "Your shower awaits, madame."

Suddenly, she was all nervous giggles. "Th—thanks. I'll just lay these on the bed." She was at a total loss with what to do with two hundred pounds of wet cowboy. The utter perfection of his body fired an image to her mind, sort of shell-shocking it. She knew policemen were fit, but he was, well . . . unreal. "You can just go get in my bed . . . I mean, er uh, sit in the chair by the television, er . . ."

"Lee Ann, it's okay. Now you just get your shower." He pulled her forward in quick, hot kiss that promised more, then sent her with a gentle push toward the shower.

It wasn't until she was under the hot stream of water, washing away the tension and dust of the day, that cohesive thought returned. Excitement rippled up and down her belly when she thought of what waited for her outside the shower. Her gaze lit on the glistening diamond that spoke of permanency, and her breath caught in her throat. Finally, she could stand it no longer. She shut the shower off with a snap and wrapped her hair in a towel, turban-style. The other towel she managed to wind about herself. Turning, with her heart firmly lodged in her throat, she pulled back the shower curtain and looked toward the bed. He was there, hitched up on one arm, lying on his side, his blue-gray gaze firmly fixed on hers. "Come here."

She shook her head. Shyness enveloped her, reminding her of every awkward moment she could ever remember. "No," she whispered. Yet her traitorous feet moved forward.

"Lie right here." He pointed firmly, right in front of himself, to the old crazy quilt.

"No." This time she shook her head vigorously, then lay right there.

"Kiss me, right here." He pointed to his lips.

"Never . . ." The word ended on his lips. His warmth suffused her as he took her mouth in a deep, delicious, nearly criminal kiss. Then he flung away the towels that only seconds before separated them. She melted into him as they got so close she couldn't tell where she ended and he began. Somewhere, it registered on her mind, a radio played. Moisture made each movement sinuous and slick, slightly sucking, in rhythm with the song that played. And still the kiss went on.

Caught in a vortex spinning down, down, down, another song began to play and time shifted and spun, no longer making any sense. Finally, she threw her head back and sucked air. All that mattered was what she felt. The springy hair of his chest lightly abraded her nipples. She felt his hot, seeking mouth at her neck, nipping, tasting. His hands where everywhere at once, touching everything, no holds barred. She loved his firm, stroking touch.

His salt teased her tongue as she let the tip explore his chest. He kissed his way over one shoulder and down her chest, to light on one nipple and tantalize it with his tongue. His warm brown hand splayed on her belly, and he kneaded it as he suckled. Though he was slightly drawn back, the evidence of his desire lay large and hot along her leg. As she wondered what he would feel like, he suddenly invaded her in the very spot that longed for him. He rubbed her with a firm tenacity that robbed her of her ability to think. She arched and bucked as the strongest sensations she had ever experienced took control.

Impossibly, his touch heated even more. She glanced down to see his head there. "No," she whispered, but, not to be denied, he deepened the intimate caress. Her world shattered then, and she careened out of control and screamed his name. "Clay!" As he claimed her mouth with a kiss, he claimed her body with his in one sure, savage thrust. She nearly bucked him off in response, but he held her tight and sure and rocked her with his instinctual rhythm.

He filled her so, she seemed on the edge of pain, and she knew a *frisson* of fear. A moan escaped her lips, only to be stifled by his. He demanded entrance there, too, and plunged in and out in a synchronized dance of need. She felt her body swell and yet at the same time open to accommodate him. She shifted to take him to the fullest and knew the need to mate with him, to make him spill his seed into her. She wanted his babies. Yet they hadn't discussed it. With a herculean effort, she dislodged him and pushed him back. Panting, she strove for sanity—at least the ability to speak two coherent words.

"Want babies?" She held him back.

"What?" His eyes focused, and he shuddered. "Yours? Yes." He pulled her back to him. "Not a good time to make this decision." His shoulder muffled his voice as he reached for something on the floor. For a second, the sound of tearing foil registered on her still-whirling senses. The subtle difference when he rejoined her made her glad, for she knew that he had healed and was back in complete control once again. If he could control himself in this situation, she knew he could in most any. With that thought cascading joy through her, she gave herself to him without reservation, free at last to love and live.

Six Weeks Later

THE WHITE WOODEN TRELLISED arch was placed just in front of the bunkhouse porch. On either side of it, large oak barrels held the green cat-claw vine with yellow flowers that twined throughout, dripping off in places in verdant abundance. Guests sat on white wooden benches positioned in two columns, six rows deep, facing the porch. Bougainvillea and palo verde blossoms covered the ground, making a crazy quilt of purple and yellow underfoot. Orange blossoms from branches of trees torn off to grace the ends of each bench scented the air with spicy sweet aroma. Everyone wore his or her finest Western wear. An organ played the light strains of a classic waltz as a signal to the woman and man who waited behind the main house. The bunkhouse door opened, and suddenly silence reigned, with every eye on the man that emerged.

"I know you were all expecting Lee Ann. But

you'll just have to make do with me." A ripple of amusement swept the group. "I'm the Reverend Bill Matthews and have the honor of joining these two fine youngsters today." The classic waltz ambled into something softer. "It has been my distinct honor to get to know these two, who will eventually become members at our church up in Carterton, Colorado. That is, because to Clay's granddad's great delight," he gestured to the white-haired man in a dark blue western suit at the head of the groom's side, "the soon-to-be man and wife will join him in Colorado to run the family ranch, the Double C."

Clapping and shouts of cheer filled the air. "So if you would now please join me in welcoming this fine young couple to the ceremony of their joining together as man and wife." He extended his arms to indicate behind them.

Gasps signaled Clay's arrival as he came from the barn on a jet black prancing stallion adorned in black tack with heavy silver adornments. He was dressed in a solid black three-piece Western suit, hat, and boots. Women fanned themselves and men hooted their appreciation. One uniformed policeman called out, "Clay Carter, you're out of uniform."

Clay tipped his hat at the men in the police force

who stood on the groom's side and grinned. He pulled the horse to a stop just at the back of the aisle and waited, his smile gone, his gaze fixed to the corner of the main house. He dismounted and handed the horse off to Bob Lockhart, who stood with Josie at his side, dressed in spring green and holding a bouquet of tiny perfect pink tea roses.

Clay walked up the aisle and joined his granddad. The two swung in unison to face the back as the wedding march's melody filled the air. Behind the house a man on a brown horse spoke to the incredible beauty at his side. His voice slightly choked. "I sure am happy you picked me to give you away, Lee Ann. It's an honor." Charlie Bruce took her gloved hand and raised the back of it to his lips. "I'm asking this for Duke Waters now. Are you sure of him?"

Lee Ann nodded, tears forming in her eyes as she gazed at him. "Yes, Charlie." She raised her eyes to the heavens. "And yes, Dad. Clay Carter is the best man for the job."

He chuckled and kissed her hand, pulled her veil over her face, and took just a second longer to behold her in her white lace dress as she sat the saddle of her palomino mare in solid perfection. "Duke and your mama are watchin', I know for sure, and they are *so* proud." He took his hat down and wiped out the brim. "I guess I knew the first time I saw you two together, I wouldn't be able to stop this. I'm losing a darn good foreman."

Wiping suspicious moisture from his eyes, he firmed his hold on his reins, cleared his throat, and heeled the brown horse forward. "Let's do it." She lined up beside him on the prancing golden mare, whose white mane and tail flowed in ripples in complement with her dress and veil, as they floated out behind in a white perfection.

Lee Ann's heart leapt to her throat as she rounded the corner of the house and caught a glimpse of the gorgeous cowboy that was to be hers. Her excitement must have communicated to the mare, because she reared up, pawing the air. The crowd sucked in air and murmured alarm until the bride settled the mare expertly back on the ground.

No such sound came from Clay Carter. He knew he was looking at one of the finest horsewomen he had ever known, knew it would take a heck of a lot more to unseat her. Besides, his voice was locked up by the white vision before him, who had managed to get to Bob and Josie and dismount.

She took the bouquet and advanced up the aisle, with Charlie on her arm and Josie attending her as matron of honor. The closer she got, the more Clay shook. He despaired of being able to say his vows and prayed for a miracle.

The miracle came in her smile as she stood before him. She whispered, "I just told Charlie that you're the best man for the job." She took the bouquet from Josie and a hug from Charlie, who handed her to him. Suddenly, he was fine. Strength poured through him as he vowed then and there to be her everything. Together they turned and faced the preacher as one.

Six Years Later

THE LONG, LOW RANCHHOUSE stood in the shade of the hardwood trees. Abruptly, the door opened with a bang and discharged three hollering children, a hound puppy and one rather harried-looking older woman, flapping her apron, shouting instructions. "Don't go far now, Clinton, Chet, and Annie, you hear me? Your ma and pa will be in soon for dinner, and I don't want to go hunting you."

As usual Annie was in the rear, her tiny three-year-old legs pumping furiously to keep up with her older brothers. "Hey, don't forget me! Hey, you two . . ." Her scream warbled with frustration.

Suddenly, a rider swept past the older woman and swooped up the little girl. Overcoming the boys, they raced past to the fort in the big oak tree that seemed to be the little ones' objective. From the height of the palomino mare, the mother easily placed the little girl on the platform. Giving a smile as bright as the Colorado sunshine, the little girl squealed and clapped her hands. "Thank you, Mama. I win! I win!"

Lee Ann Carter turned to see how the boys were doing and spotted her husband coming on his black gelding. His face looked like thunder.

"Darn you, Lee Ann, you're in no shape to be doing that. You shouldn't be lifting *or* galloping on horses." As he got nearer though, his face softened. "And neither should Sugar, you know. You're both getting too far along." The mare's bulging sides proclaimed her pregnancy, as did her rider's softly rounding belly.

"Don't you worry about me and little Maggie here." Lee Ann softly patted her belly, then dismounted.

Clay slid off his horse to join her and the boys. He ruffled the boys' hair. "Hear that, boys? You're going to have a little sister again." Annie hopped up and down and reached for her father, who lifted her and put her on his hip.

"Aw, Dad," they chimed in unison. "Girls ain't no fun."

"Sure they are!" He chuckled and put his other arm around his wife. "And one day, you'll find out that they can do things just as well as boys." He winked at his wife and daughter. "Even if they do things a little different."

About the Author

One fine spring day when the air was aflutter with every kind of songbird, Susan's mother, Bessie, decided she would bundle her up and take her for a ride in the stroller she'd just gotten from her sister Martha. With some trouble she bundled the busy toddler into a sweater and trousers and a warm knit cap and trundled outside. "Look around you, sweetheart. This is what spring smells like. What do you think?" At the absence of a reaction, Bessie looked down to see her nearly two-year-old daughter with arms reaching out, standing in her stroller. Two words came from her little rosebud mouth as Susan strained toward her objective. "Give me." In dismay, Bessie gazed towards the object of her daughter's desire. Horses. Ponies, to be exact. Susan was born next door to a pony farm, and this was the first time she'd seen them. And now she wanted them. What was a poor, divorced mother to do? She simply couldn't afford a horse. Couldn't think of any way. Being a practical woman, Bessie decided, with a shrug, that her daughter would surely outgrow the desire.

Bessie was still telling herself that Susan would outgrow her desire a year later when Susan announced she wanted to write stories (another wish Bessie was pretty sure Susan would outgrow), and again when Susan was thirteen and working at a horse farm specializing in Quarter Horses, and again when Susan got her first horse from a divorcing friend, and again when Susan bought her Arabian horse at an auction, and again when Susan reached thirty and was riding all over the Sonoran desert with a doctor friend.

Well, Susan never did outgrow the desire to ride, or to write, and now she cheerfully does both. Susan lives with her husband Joe and a constantly varying number of horses, dogs, cats, birds, and a variety of wildlife in the Superstition Mountains of Arizona where they love, laugh, and live.

Susan Yarina's website is www.SusanYarina.com. Send email to SYarina315@aol.com or susan@SusanYarina.com; send snail mail to Premium Press America, Attn: Susan C. Yarina, P.O. Box 159015, Nashville, TN 37215-9015.

SPECTER OF DEATH

Ben Raines and the company of Rebels walked into the town just as dusk settled over the land. The surrendering Blackshirts sat on the curbs and sidewalks, their hands on top of their heads. None of them would meet Ben's eyes. They were terrified of him. More than a few crossed themselves when he drew near.

Ben turned to Lieutenant Ballard. "Jackie, what's going on here?"

"We haven't been able to figure that out, sir," she replied. "At first, we thought it might be some sort of trick."

Another Rebel walked up. "They believe you have supernatural powers, General. They think you're a shape-changer."

A low murmuring began as the Blackshirts spotted Ben ambling along, carrying the old Thompson.

"El Lobo! El lobo espectro!"

Ben caught the phrase being used and it amused him. They were calling him Ghost Wolf.

BATTLE
IN THE
ASHES

WILLIAM W.
JOHNSTONE

PINNACLE BOOKS
Kensington Publishing Corp.
http://www.kensingtonbooks.com

PINNACLE BOOKS are published by

Kensington Publishing Corp.
119 West 40th Street
New York, NY 10018

All Kensington Titles, Imprints, and Distributed Lines are available at special quantity discounts for bulk purchases for sales promotions, premiums, fund-raising, and educational or institutional use. Special book excerpts or customized printings can also be created to fit specific needs. For details, write or phone the office of the Kensington special sales manager: Kensington Publishing Corp., 119 West 40th Street, New York, NY 10018, attn: Special Sales Department, Phone: 1-800-221-2647.

Pinnacle and the P logo Reg. U.S. Pat. & TM Off.

ISBN-13: 978-0-7860-2024-9
ISBN-10: 0-7860-2024-5

First Pinnacle Books Printing: May 1993

10 9 8 7 6 5 4 3

Printed in the United States of America

BOOK ONE

The Rebels had sailed tens of thousands of miles, fighting pitched battles on island nations from Ireland and England, south around the Horn, then northwest up to Hawaii and back to America. They had freed hundreds of thousands from the yoke of slavery and tyranny and thought that when this voyage was over, they could rest for a time.

That was not to be.

The war-weary Rebels were returning to America to begin preparations for what would soon be the largest guerrilla action ever undertaken in modern history.

They had discovered while fighting halfway around the world that a massive army had been training for years in South America. The army's mission: to conquer what was left of North America and reeducate its citizens . . . those that would be left after a savage purge of men, women, and children they considered to be inferior.

Nazism had once more reared up its ugly face and was on the march, goose-stepping its way north. But the new leader making use of Hitler's ravings was more subtle in his indoctrination methods. Within the ranks of the New Army of Liberation could be found men and women of all races, all nationalities, all colors. The man behind the movement knew that he must use people of all colors in order to win. After the battle was won, then he would purge his ranks of those he considered inferior. But in order to do that, once the battle was won, he would need the help of a certain type of North American . . . a rather ignorant type of person. Unfortunately, that type still existed in large numbers in North America, for as much as some Rebels might want to, they couldn't just shoot anyone who did not subscribe to their way of thinking.

Even though the world would be much better off had they done just that.

Years before the Great War ravaged the world, offshoots of nearly every terrorist group operating around the globe had learned of the new movement and rushed to South America to join the ranks. A terrorist lives for terror, to kill and maim and destroy. Terrorists don't particularly care what cause they're fighting for (many soon forget their original passion and live only for the blood-letting), as long as they are causing pain, spilling blood and blowing this and that to bits . . . including old people, babies, animals, and other innocents. But terrorists almost always share one philosophy: they hate America and Americans with a red-hot passion. So when the world's many terrorist groups learned that an army was being secretly formed and trained to take over America, they jumped at the chance.

Then the Great War blew the world apart. The New Army of Liberation stayed down and low and continued training in small bases all over the jungles and mountains of South America. Soon after the germ and nuclear strikes, one man emerged out of the rubble and panic and confusion and chaos of war.

He was an American, and his name was Ben Raines.

Now the terrorists and the bigots and the hate-mongers and the lawless and the ignorant and the lazy and worthless of the world could really have someone to hate.

Ben Raines.

Ben soon formed a small gathering of like-minded people. They spread out all over the country, seeking others who shared their philosophy of living and their dreams of rebuilding the shattered nation. While the central government (politicians) of the United States were still staggering around and pointing fingers of blame at each other and appointing and forming seemingly endless (and useless) committees to study this and that, Ben Raines and his growing band of followers, soon to be called Rebels, were cleaning out and setting up their own brand of government in the Northwest. It was called Tri-States, and before the nitwit politicians who made up the new central government of the United States, its capital now in Richmond (Washington, D.C. had been destroyed, and many Americans, whether a part of the Rebels or not, felt that was long overdue) knew what was happening, they discovered that there was a country within a country, and everything was just fine in the Tri-States.

The Tri-States had zero crime, zero unemployment, clean, pure running water, electricity, social services, schools that really taught the young, medical care for all, and all the other amenities that made life good for the law-abiding. And things just hummed right along in the Tri-States. And they did it all without help from the central government, and even had the audacity to tell the central government to keep their noses out of the business of Tri-States.

"My God!" cried the politicians, blithering and blathering about in Richmond. "We can't have this. Why, this is positively *un-American!*"

Then the central government in Richmond learned that criminals were actually being *hanged* in Tri-States, for such innocuous things as murder and rape and armed robbery and other such minor offenses that everyone knows is not the fault of the perpetrator, but rather the fault of everyone else. After all, if the homecoming queen won't date a person, or the coach won't let a person play in the big game, or if somebody has a nicer car or newer tennis shoes or flashier jacket, a larger TV set, or a better boom box or Walkman, why it makes perfect sense for that less fortunate person to go out and steal a gun and blow somebody away, for the mental scars left there by these horribly traumatic situations would certainly justify violent acts against an uncaring society.

So after the liberals in Congress ceased months of blubbering and snorting and weeping and stomping on hankies, and after forty-seven committees had concluded 5,593 meetings and fact-finding tours (all at taxpayer expense), the central government reached its decision: The Tri-States would have to cease and desist and disband and stop all this foolishness.

The citizens of Tri-States, through their elected leader, Ben Raines, told the President of the United States and the members of both houses of Congress to go fuck themselves.

Well! Nobody tells Congress to do *that!*

The government of the United States declared war on the Tri-States. They thought they had wiped out all those malcontents who had the nerve to think they knew more about running a government than professional politicians.

They were wrong.

Ben Raines gathered a handful of survivors around him and proceeded to rebuild his army. Once that was done, the Rebels proceeded to kick the crap out of the thugs and bully-boys the central government sent after them.

The Rebel philosophy spread and the Rebel army grew in numbers. Just when Ben Raines and the Rebels had seized control of the central government, tragedy struck the world in the form of a rat-borne plague, and when it was over, there was not a stable government left intact anywhere in the world.

Anarchy reigned. Gangs of thugs and warlords ruled the cities and countryside, wreaking havoc and misery on the battle-torn and weary population. Everywhere except inside the borders of the new Tri-States, that is.

Ben Raines had gathered his Rebels around him and started all over, in the Deep South. When they had their sector cleaned out and running smoothly, the Rebels began the job of sweeping out the nation, coast to coast, and border to border. It would take them years.

And down in isolated areas of South America, Field Marshal Jesus Dieguez Mendoza Hoffman continued building and training his army of Nazis, staying low and out of sight. Their time would come. They waited.

Now it was time for Ben Raines and his Rebels, and Field Marshal Hoffman and his NAL to meet.

The battleground: North America.

The stakes: Freedom.

ONE

"Arms in the hands of citizens may be used at individual discretion . . . in private self-defense."

John Adams

Ben Raines stood alone—as alone as the Rebels would ever let him be—looking south from his temporary CP in Texas. Everything was packed up in Hummers and cars and trucks, and his personal company of Rebels were ready for him to give the word. Ben was dressed in denim work shirt, jeans, and lace-up boots. Gone were the famous tiger stripe BDUs of the Rebels. Every Rebel now dressed in civilian clothing. Their uniforms had been laundered and packed away in plastic bags and stored in the Rebels' many underground bunkers, located all over the lower forty-eight.

For the moment, Texas was clean of any members of Hoffman's goose-stepping, black-shirted NAL. But Ben knew that was about to change, and that change was more than likely only moments away.

This upcoming fight came as no surprise to Ben, for he had always predicted—even years before the Great

War, back when the world was more or less stable—that the final action was going to take place on American soil. Only who they were fighting came as any surprise to him.

Ben stood and clenched his big hands into fists. "Goddamn you mealy-mouthed politicians," he swore, smoldering anger behind his words. "Goddamn you all. You brought us to this. Everything that happened is your fault. Everything that we now face is your fault. I should have gone along with the plan years back and toppled you bastards in Washington. I regret now that I didn't."

That those hated political leaders were long dead in their graves held little consolation for Ben. He wished they would all rise up from the ground so he could personally shoot them.

"Only a handful of you had the good of the tax-paying, law-abiding majority in mind," he muttered darkly. "I hope you bastards are burning in hell with hot pitchforks jammed up your asses!"

"The general is pissed," Cooper, Ben's driver, said, standing with Ben's personal team a few yards away.

"No kidding, Coop?" Jersey, the diminutive dark-eyed, dark-haired little beauty who was Ben's self-appointed bodyguard replied. "Here we are, about to be attacked by several hundred thousand goose-stepping Nazis—who only have us outnumbered about two hundred to one. The entire Rebel army is spread out over four or five states, and with all of us dressed like people getting ready to go to a rodeo, or a country music honky-tonk. We have the supplies for a long operation but getting to them is going to be a bit of a problem. He knows the Rebels are going to take a lot of losses over the months ahead. Intelligence says about fifty to sixty percent of us are going to die, Coop. And that's weighing heavy on his mind. In addition to all of that, General Raines knows that none of this would be happening today if the damn politicians of America had paid attention to the demands of the majority of citizens back umpteen years ago and let the Constitution be the road to travel instead of their own stupid mumblings. And you think the General is pissed, Cooper? Naw. Why would you think that?"

Cooper winked at her and tilted her ball cap down over her eyes. Jersey laughed and took a mock swing at him.

Corrie stood wearing a light backpack radio, earphones covering one ear to catch any messages. Beth, the historian and records-keeper of the team, had Ben's Husky, Smoot, on a leash. The animal had filled out and matured, now nearly a full-grown Siberian husky of about seventy pounds. She would get bigger still. The husky got her name because, as a pup, she made sounds that sounded like she was saying, "Smoot! Smoot! Smoot!"

Suddenly Ben's team, to a person, stiffened when they realized just what they were seeing. Ben was once more carrying his old Thompson SMG, the old Chicago Piano slung over one shoulder. And belted around his waist were two Colt .45 auto-loaders.

"Son of a gun!" Corrie said. "We haven't seen those in a long, long time."

Ben heard and turned around and looked at them. "I carried this old dinosaur when it all began, years back." He sighed. More years than he liked to think about. So many good friends dead. Hundreds and hundreds of men and women who gave their lives for the Rebel cause. "So I'll be carrying this old Thompson when it ends . . . one way or the other."

Actually, the Thompson had been reworked so many times by Rebel armorers there was not an original part left in it. It was still a slow-fire weapon when compared to an Uzi or HK, but that monstrous slug it spit out would inflict horrible damage upon a person.

All of Ben's team knew that just the sight of those .45-caliber monsters would be a great morale boost to all Rebels, and that was probably one of the reasons General Raines had done it.

Ben had put aside the old Thompson a long time back, because many people—including a lot of his own Rebels—were beginning to think the legendary old submachine gun had magical powers, and many of them wouldn't touch it. They were just as much in awe of the SMG as they were of Ben. Ben had convinced most of his people that he was not some sort of God. But there were many living in the battered nation who felt he was just that, and no amount of talking would ever make them believe otherwise.

"What's the word on Thermopolis and his bunch, Corrie?" Ben asked.

"All set up and dug in deep and tight in Arkansas, sir."

"Did he take Emil with him?" Ben asked with a smile.

"Very reluctantly, sir."

"At least that will keep the little con artist out of trouble for a while."

Thermopolis and his band of hippies made up part of Ben's HQ's Company. It would be their job to keep track of all units of Rebels. A demanding and nerve-wracking job. Ben had handed that to Therm because

16

he was a fine detail man and had never liked the killing involved in fieldwork. Thermopolis had a staff of just over 250 men and women. And the finest communications equipment known to exist in the world.

"Latest position of Herr Field Marshal Hoffman and his New Army of Liberation?" Ben asked, contempt thick in his voice. Then he spat on the ground.

"About five miles south of the border, sir."

General Jesus Dieguez Mendoza Hoffman was the commanding general of the NAL. Spelled Nazi. He was the grandson of a very infamous Nazi SS general who escaped to South America after the Second World War. Hoffman had been schooled from birth to despise America and everything Americans stood for. His sole purpose in life was to destroy the very last vestiges of America and establish a new Nazi order that would ultimately rule the world.

But first he had to kill Ben Raines and the Rebels, and that was something that thousands had been attempting to do for years, with no success. Yet.

Field Marshal Hoffman was looking forward to mixing it up with Ben Raines and his Rebels. He paid little attention to his advisors when they warned him not to become overconfident. True, he had suffered some minor losses shortly after the Rebels returned from Hawaii, but those were only very unimportant skirmishes. There was not a doubt in Hoffman's mind that this upcoming campaign would be a short one. There was simply no way the Rebels could stand up to his mighty army. No way. That was so ridiculous a thought it was laughable.

"All of General Payon's people over the border, Corrie?" Ben asked.

"All that's coming across."

Ben again turned to face the south. The Rebel commanders had looked over, discussed, and rejected dozens of plans on how best to confront the Nazi hordes fast approaching what had once been called the United States.

"Loosely united," Ben muttered, disgust in his voice. "And ruled by federal judges."

Even before the Great War cast its long darkness over the land, Ben had written that the United States was no more than a slightly benevolent dictatorship, and anyone who believed that the American people had any real power over their own lives was living in a dream world.

"General," Corrie called. "Buddy wants to know why in the hell you are still here with Hoffman's scouts less than five miles away?"

Buddy Raines, the powerfully built and brutally handsome son of Ben.

"I'm surprised that Tina hasn't put in her two cent's worth, as well," Ben said.

"She has," Corrie told him. "And so has Dr. Chase. I just didn't tell you. What do I tell Buddy?"

"Tell him to worry about his own ass. I'll take care of mine."

"Rat," Corrie whispered Buddy's code name, "the Eagle says to thank you for your concern and that he will be along presently." Corrie was forever rewriting and rewording Ben's remarks from the field.

"I'm sure that is exactly what he said," Buddy responded.

"Would I lie?" Corrie replied sweetly.

"Tell that middle-aged Rambo-type to get his butt out of there!" Dr. Chase thundered over the air.

Dr. Lamar Chase, Chief of Medicine, a man well into his seventies, had been with Ben since the Rebel dream of true liberty and justice for all law-abiding citizens began, years back.

"Yes, sir," Corrie acknowledged the transmission.

"That must be Dr. Chase bitching about me being here," Ben said, without turning around.

"Ah . . . right, sir."

"Tell him to clear the air and leave it open for emergency transmissions only."

"The Eagle says we are bugging out of this area very soon, sir," Corrie radioed.

"I just bet he did," Chase snorted. "You're a sweet girl, Corrie. But you're a terrible liar! Chase out."

"Feels funny not being in uniform," Jersey said.

Ben heard her. "We are in uniform, Jersey. From this moment on. But I know what you mean. Does feel odd. The Hummer all packed and ready to roll, Coop?"

"Yes, sir."

Ben walked back to his group and knelt down, petting Smoot for a moment, rubbing the husky's head. "You're going to Arkansas, Smoot. You'll be safe there." He stood up. "Take Smoot to the airstrip, Beth. Coop, drive her there. Smoot will be safe with Therm and his bunch."

Ben had cut his personal detachment down to his small team and one platoon of Regulars, all of them hand-picked by Ike McGowen, the Russian, General Striganov, Dr. Chase, the mercenary, Colonel West, the former SAS Officer, Colonel Dan Gray, and Ben's children, Buddy and Tina. That one platoon had the fighting capability of approximately a full company of any other soldiers in the world.

Ben squatted down in the shade of a truck and rolled a cigarette. "We're all standing on the darkened and scorched edge of history," Ben muttered. "Waiting for the flames to destroy it all."

"Beg pardon, sir?" Corrie said.

"Nothing, Corrie. Just talking to myself. When is that damn Nazi son of a bitch going to make his move?" he said irritably.

"General Ike says if you don't get your butt in gear and get out of here, he's going to come down here personally and kick it for you," Corrie said, after ten-fouring a transmission.

"Tell Tubby to watch his own ass," Ben replied. "He's got a lot more to look after than I do."

Ike was a bit on the stocky side. The ex-Navy SEAL was another who had been with Ben since the beginning.

"Shark," Corrie radioed, "the Eagle is just about to fly."

Ben smoked his cigarette, thankful that Dr. Chase was miles to the north and not standing here bitching and raising hell about Ben's few cigarettes a day.

"General," Corrie's voice held a different note. "Scouts report Hoffman's Blackshirts are moving north. All columns on the roll."

"Tell the Scouts to bug out and rejoin us here," Ben said quietly, standing up. "Tell them to push it." When Corrie had radioed the orders, Ben said, "Advise all units Hoffman is moving. Tell Ike to blow everything from San Diego to El Paso. We'll make those goose-stepping bastards work for every damned inch of American soil they choose to be buried in."

"Is anybody going to say, 'well, this is it?'" Cooper asked.

"You do, and I'll hit you, Coop," Jersey warned. "I swear I will."

Herr General Field Marshall Jesus Dieguez Mendoza Hoffman stood several miles south of the Mexico/U.S. border, felt the ground tremble beneath his polished boots, and watched the huge clouds of dust rise into the air. The dust clouds stretched for as far as the telescope-assisted eye could see. The Blackshirts of the NAL could all accurately guess what had just happened.

Hoffman was not impressed. His cold black eyes were startling to see beneath his very blond hair and pale skin. Many of the NAL were a mixture of Spanish and German blood. Hoffman lowered his binoculars and let them dangle from a leather strap. "Bridges and roads," he said. "So we will be delayed for a few days in crossing. Does the famous General Ben Raines think this action will strike fear into our hearts? Nonsense. What are the very latest intelligence reports from our friends north of the border?" he asked an aide.

"Still very confused, Field Marshal. No one seems to know just what Ben Raines is planning. He has spread his forces all over several states, from small units to large ones."

"I personally think it is some sort of trick," a senior aide spoke up.

"What kind of trick? Be more specific, Karl."

"I don't know, sir. But his actions make no military sense. They run contrary to every rule of engagement."

Hoffman smiled. What Raines was doing made perfect sense to him. He was going to wage a campaign of terror and harassment against the NAL. A purely guerrilla action just as soon as they crossed the border. No matter. They would amount to no more than a stinging bee.

But what Hoffman didn't know was that the Rebels were pure killer bees, not for the most part docile honey bees. The NAL was about to learn a hard lesson concerning Ben Raines's Rebels.

"Order patrols across," Hoffman said. "Let's see if the famous Ben Raines has the courage to face us."

But Ben was heading straight up Interstate 35 toward a preset destination some sixty miles from Laredo. Ned Hawkins and a contingent of his New Texas Rangers had laid down a trail a drunken city slicker could follow, heading up Highway 83 toward Carrizo Springs. Buddy and his people had taken off toward Freer, and Tina and a contingent had left quite a trail as they headed toward Hebbronville.

Twenty miles away from each of their positions, other contingents of Rebels lay waiting. Twenty miles further on, yet another ambush was lying wait . . . and so on for a hundred miles in all directions.

Hoffman's patrols reported back by radio. "We are across into North America. No resistance. Both cities are deserted."

"Surely everything is booby-trapped?" Hoffman questioned.

"Nothing is booby-trapped," his people radioed. "We have found nothing. But large forces of Rebels have scattered in all directions, using all the highways leading out."

Hoffman smiled. "Oh, Ben Raines. You are a devious devil, you are. You want me to head straight up your Interstate system and then you and your Rebels will fall in behind us and attack from all sides. I see your plan. It is a good one, but I am too smart for you."

All his aides and flunkies and gofers smiled and nodded their heads. Field Marshal Hoffman would never fall for something so obvious.

"Four battalions across the river," Hoffman ordered, picking up a map. "Each battalion to be backed up by armor."

"Gunships, Field Marshal?"

"No," Hoffman said drily. He had sent a dozen gunships across the Rio Grande a few days before to harass the Rebels. He discovered then that the Rebels had the most sophisticated surface-to-air missiles known to the world. Even better than his own. Everything from Stingers to the SA-14 Gremlin. None of his gunships had returned. "We shall keep them on the ground for the time being."

The Rebels had reached their destinations and were working furiously to get into position, hoping that the Blackshirts would fall for this ruse.

Hoffman had his trailer pulled up, and he sat with his boots off, feet up, sipping tea and relaxing. His people were resting, all certain that in a few hours, the battalions would report back—victorious, of course.

Miles down each road, Rebel Scouts lay concealed, waiting to signal their friends of the approaching Blackshirts.

"Hoffman may be a jerk-off," Ben said to his team, as

they waited for word of pursuit. "But his troops are sea-soned veterans. We don't ever want to make the mistake of selling them short. What happens on this day is going to make the rest of his people very cautious."

Ben had ordered his people to ground several miles outside of the deserted town. This was brush country, at one time the site of many ranches and farms. Now it was all grown up. The Blackshirts would be expecting an ambush in the towns; they would not be expecting Rebels to pop up out of the ground in open fields and meadows and start hurling rockets at them—Ben hoped.

The Rebels had the finest rocket launchers, every-thing from the German Armbrust to the American TOW. They had AT-4s, Carl Gustafs, and Milans. And they were skilled in their use.

They waited.

"Everyone is in position," Corrie reported. The ambush sites were all approximately the same distance from Laredo, the furthest one being sixty-eight miles, the nearest one fifty-six miles. But the nearest one was located on the worst road, so the Blackshirts should arrive at all sites within a couple of minutes of each other.

At least that's the way Ben planned it.

The Rebels were still outside their hastily dug holes, and Ben looked over at Jersey and smiled. She had turned her ball cap around, bill to the back, and looked about fifteen years old.

These kids, he thought—and they were kids, at least to Ben—have seen precious few moments of joy and peace in their lives. Take those guns and knives and grenades and battle harnesses from them, and they'd look like young people on their way to a square dance. But Ben knew these young men and women were among the most

24

brutal, savage and skilled fighters in all the world. And their loyalty toward him borderlined on the fanatic.

Cooper was chewing on a weed. "Coyote probably came along right before we got here and peed on that thing, Coop," Jersey told him.

Cooper spat out the weed and gave her a dirty look.

Beth was writing in her journal, and Ben knew it would be in the neatest handwriting he had ever seen, and very concise. Corrie was dressed in jeans and pull-over shirt, an earth-tone bandanna tied around her head. She felt Ben looking at her and smiled at him. He winked at her.

"Jersey," Ben said. "What time is it getting to be?"

She grinned. "Kick-ass time, General!"

"Damn right," Ben said.

The Rebels were dug in 250 meters from the interstate. Their vehicles hidden about a mile away. Ben did not want to risk hiding them in the town, for fear the Blackshirts would first shell the town.

Ben looked across the way and chuckled softly. Those Rebels who were in sight certainly did not appear worried about facing a force of Blackshirts that would outnumber them ten or twenty to one. Several of them were sleeping, their ball caps or cowboy hats over their faces. Others were reading old paperbacks or hardcover books. Several were working crossword puzzles.

"Large force, approximately battalion size, just passing by the Scouts' position," Corrie said.

"Head's up!" Ben called to his people. "Give it all to me, Corrie."

"Open and canvas-covered trucks, deuce and a halves, escorted and trailed by main battle tanks."

Ben looked over at Jersey. "Kick-ass time," she said.

TWO

The battalion commander of the Blackshirts rode in an open scout car, behind several main battle tanks, which were not buttoned up. The BC was an experienced soldier, a veteran of many, many battles and a devoted follower of Hoffman and his wacko philosophy. The BC was also a very arrogant man who believed that the Blackshirts were invincible in battle. After all, they had never really lost a battle. True, they had experienced some setbacks against General Payon's forces, but in the end, had been victorious. And they would be victorious against these stupid Rebels as well. He firmly believed that.

His final thought was that no force on earth could defeat the Blackshirts. He took that thought with him into eternity as a slug from a .50-caliber sniper rifle blew away most of his head. The BC's brains splattered all over the driver and in a horrified panic he spun the wheel just as a rocket struck the vehicle and turned it into a burning, smoking, twisted mass of junk.

Some of the tanks were rendered inoperable as rockets blew the treads off; others took hits that exploded the fuel tanks and set off the ammunition storage bins, turning the inside of the tanks into a man-made hell.

The troops riding in the trucks had no chance at all as rockets blew them to bloody chunks and heavy machine guns chopped up what was left. Eight hundred men and women of the Blackshirts' infantry and eight tanks and crews were killed, badly wounded, or frightened out of their wits in less than thirty seconds.

"Mop it up," Ben ordered. "And bring me any prisoners."

Ned Hawkins and his New Texas Rangers turned the highway outside of Carrizo Springs into a smoking mass of twisted metal and broken bodies. They began gathering up what weapons and equipment were still useable and stripping the bodies of boots. At Ben's orders, they took what uniforms were not burned or shot or blown to bloody rags. Ned did not have the foggiest notion why the General wanted the uniforms, but he was not about to question Ben's orders.

"Help me!" pleaded one Blackshirt with both legs blown off.

"There ain't nothin' I can do for you, partner," a Ranger told the man. "I'm not gonna waste pain-killers on you."

"You're devils!" the man gasped.

"No," the Ranger corrected. "We're Americans. And you fucked up bad comin' here."

Outside of Freer, Texas, Buddy and his teams gave the Blackshirts a very deadly surprise and left their broken, burned, and bloody bodies on the road and shoulders and ditches. On the east side of Hebbronville, Tina and her Rebels ripped into the Blackshirts' column with the ferocity of a pack of angry wolverines. So complete was the ambush, not one Blackshirt in any of the four columns had the chance to get off a single radio transmission to warn Hoffman what was happening.

The four Rebels teams piled up the bodies, poured gasoline on them, and set them afire, to disguise the fact they had stripped the bodies of uniforms, then slipped back to their vehicles and drove away.

In the once lush lower Rio Grande valley, Rebels had set fire to everything that would burn. They left a smoking, charred, and burning hell behind them, leaving nothing of value for Hoffman and his Blackshirts. So intense were the flames that the advancing forces of the Field Marshal had to back up and cut west in the hope of finding another way across the river.

In his lushly appointed trailer, Hoffman sipped tea and waited for news.

Worried aides haunted the radio operators for reports that never came. All the frantically working operators could pick up were the undecipherable slurping sounds of burst transmissions from Rebel units.

"An entire regiment simply does not vanish from the face of the earth!" a colonel yelled at a frustrated and browbeaten radio operator.

"I know, Colonel. I know. I'm doing all I know to do."

It fell on the shoulders of Hoffman's top aide to carry the silence to Field Marshal Hoffman. The aide was not looking forward to this—at all.

To the north, west, and east of Hoffman's position,

great black carrion-eating birds were ceasing their endless circling and gliding to earth for a feast.

"You have good news at last, my friend?" Hoffman
asked with a smile.

"I . . . have no news, sir."

Hoffman stared at the man.

"We cannot make contact with any of the battalions."

"What you are saying is impossible."

"We have lost contact, sir."

Hoffman slowly pulled on his boots and stood up,
straightening and buttoning his uniform. "Ridiculous!"
he snorted, and opened the door, stalking out of the
trailer.

Ben ordered all units to fall back to a line that
stretched west to east, following Highways 57 and 87,
from Eagle Pass to Victoria, Texas. There was now a
long, loose Rebel line stretching from California to the
Gulf of Mexico, and Hoffman's Blackshirts were beginning to realize they had one hell of a fight facing them.
Reports poured in to Hoffman's CP.

"That's sixteen hundred or so miles!" Hoffman
stormed. "It's impossible. Raines doesn't have that many
troops. It's a damn trick. And where in the hell are those
four battalions I sent out? Have any patrols reported
back?"

"Not yet, sir. We're expecting word any minute."

It came. And Hoffman appeared to be in mild shock.
He stood for a moment, speechless, his mouth open.
"All of them?" he finally spoke.

"All of them, sir," the radio operator said softly. "All
four battalions destroyed."

"Survivors?"

"A handful. They are being transported back here as quickly as possible."

Field Marshal Jesus Hoffman stared at the man, his black eyes burning with fury. "Give me the actual number of personnel lost."

"Over twenty-three hundred, sir."

Hoffman sat down hard in a chair, clearly stunned. A handful of Rebels had wiped out four full battalions of top combat-seasoned troops along with their escorting armor. Impossible. But it had happened. *How* was the problem Hoffman knew he had to solve. And how to prevent it from ever happening again.

"Hoffman has ordered an immediate halt to all advancing troops," Ben was told. "They moved up to a line about thirty miles inside our borders and stood down."

Ben nodded. "He's busy working out mind-problems. He's trying to figure out what his best move would be and he's not going to commit any more troops until he does. We clearly won the first round, but let's not get cocky about it. Hoffman's people are going to kick the shit out of us before this is over." Ben paused for a moment, and those around him knew he wasn't through. He tapped a folder lying on the battered old table in the dining room of the once fine home about thirty miles outside of San Antonio, just off Interstate 35. "Bad news, people. This is the final analysis of months of intelligence work by our people. They conclude that thousands and thousands of Americans, all of them living outside of Rebel zones, have gone over to Hoffman's side. Copies of this report have been sent to all of our batt coms. From this moment on, we don't know who to trust."

"But we damn sure know the types of people who rolled over," Ned Hawkins said. "At least, I do. I used to be one of them. I can spot them at five hundred yards without binoculars."

Ben smiled. "Yes," he said drily. "So can I, Ned."

The Rebels all knew the type. Their numbers were made up of people of all colors, who, before the Great War, blamed everyone except themselves for the problems facing themselves and the nation. Whites who hated blacks. Blacks who hated whites. People of all colors who wanted something for nothing. Give me money for doing nothing. I demand this and I got a right to that. All niggers is lazy, they stink, and they're cowards. All honkies is racist and out to get us brothers and sisters. The only good Indian is a dead Indian. We were here first, the land belongs to us and by God we want it and to hell with everybody else. I demand more social services from the government but I want big government to stay out of my life. I got more bills than I can pay, I done it knowin' I was doin' it, I had a fine time doin' it, so now I'll just declare bankruptcy and to hell with my creditors. I got a right to party down and screw anybody I wants to screw, and if I get pregnant, the taxpayers can just damn well pay my medical bills and support my child'en from cradle to grave and give me welfare. I got a right to eat, I got a right to have proper housing, I got a right to have money in my pocket, and you can't make me work if I don't want to. Give me money, money, money. For if you don't, I'll boycott, I'll picket, I'll disrupt services, I'll blow up your house or

31

your store, I'll burn a cross on your lawn. I demand government subsidies for this, that, and the other thing. I ain't gonna send my kids to school with no goddamn nigger or spic or Jew. I don't want my kids to associate with a lot of racist honkies. All niggers is bad. All whites is good. All Blacks are good. All whites are bad. You're picking on me. I'll sue you. Just 'cause you caught me breakin' into your home, that don't give you the right to use force against me, and if you do, I'll sue you and there are sure as hell a lot of lawyers around who'll take my case and win it. On and on and on.

Oh, yes. The Rebels knew the type well.

Ben leaned back in the chair and closed his tired eyes for a moment. He wished there was a place he could take his Rebels and to hell with everybody else. A place where they could live and prosper in peace.

But he knew there was no such place.

He knew that wherever they went, they would have to fight for their right to exist. He smiled at that. Our *right?* he thought. Let's don't be hypocritical, Ben. Don't start sounding like all those protesters of years back, demanding this and that. What you and the Rebels are doing is attempting to rebuild a nation. Moral issues can be hashed out later.

Ben opened his eyes: "If those groups out there, which we all know comprise hundreds of thousands of people, would put aside their hate for one another and band together, they'd have a damn good chance of defeating us."

"They won't do that," Tina told him. "They hate each other more than they hate us. Our best hope is that they wind up killing each other."

Ben stared at the Rebels crowded into the room.

"We're not going to wait for Hoffman and his goose-steppers to get a firm toehold in America. Corrie, order all units to immediately launch a full-scale guerrilla action against the Blackshirts. Coast to coast. Get geared up, people. We're taking the attack to them!"

General Payon, the commander of all Mexican forces, ordered teams of skilled guerrilla fighters to head back into Mexico, swing around, and attack the Blackshirts from the rear, stinging them and then quickly withdrawing.

From Texas to California, all along the border, Ben's Rebels began quietly getting into place to raise some hell with Hoffman's Blackshirts.

"Lovely night," a Blackshirt commander said, stepping out of the abandoned house along the New Mexico border. "I love this climate here." He smiled and breathed deeply. "I shall ask to be permanently assigned here once we have defeated Raines' Rebels."

Those were the last words he would ever say as three fire-frag grenades bounced on the patio and blew, spreading him and two others all over the rear of the house.

His personnel ran onto the blood-slick patio and began firing wildly in all directions. They hit nothing. The dark shadows melted into the night.

In a once lovely home just south of Tucson, along Interstate 19, two squads of top-notch battle-hardened Blackshirts had just finished their supper. Their last supper. They were looking forward to a group of ladies coming over for a little entertainment. The "ladies" were from a Ben Raines-hating group who called themselves CRAPO. The Committee for the Removal of All Political Opposition. The ladies would come over, but the two squads of Blackshirts would be in no condition to entertain them. Not after three rockets from Armbrusts tore into the house and blew it to bloody bits.

Fifteen miles away, a ten-man Blackshirt patrol in two trucks pulled up behind a man working on his old pickup truck along the side of the highway.

"What's the problem, friend?" the team leader asked.

"Worn out," the man replied. "Everything is just worn out." He smiled at the men, his teeth flashing in the night. "Forgive. I forget my manners. I have fresh fruit in the back. Apples and oranges and melons. I would be honored if you would take my small offering."

"We couldn't take your food, senor."

"Please. I would be offended. Nothing is too good for the people who would finally relieve us of the yoke of oppression placed on our necks by that damnable Ben Raines and his filthy followers."

Hiding in the ditches alongside the highway, the battalion commander of Thirteen Battalion, Raul Gomez, stifled a groan. Amelio was a natural born ham and on this night he was really putting on quite a show.

"Ah," the Blackshirt team leader said. "We were told this area had a lot of people who were sympathetic to our cause."

"Oh, my, yes, patron. Many, many of us welcome your coming. Words cannot express my true feelings," Amelio added with just a touch of irony.

The Blackshirts slung their weapons and flipped back the tarp over the bed of the truck. They stood dumbfounded, for the bed was empty. They looked for Amelio. He was gone. The last thing they would experience on this earth was the pain as bullets from M-16s ripped into their bodies.

The Rebels took their weapons and what uniforms could be patched up, tossed the weapons in the Black-shirt trucks, and headed out into the desert, leaving the bodies for the buzzards.

It was only the beginning of what was to be a very, very bloody night.

THREE

When the news of the night's work reached Jesus Hoffman early the next morning, the man very nearly lost his composure. He forced himself to be civil to the messenger and sat back down at his table, looking at his breakfast. He pushed it from him; his appetite was gone.

They had not yet penetrated forty miles into North America and already the losses were unacceptable. And casualty reports from the bloody night just past were still coming in.

It was impossible, but yet it was happening. Then Herr Hoffman said what people had been saying for years about the commander of the Rebel Army. "I hate that goddamn Ben Raines!"

Hoffman bathed and shaved and splashed on cologne. He dressed in a field uniform, tan pants, and black shirt, and stepped out of his trailer to face his most senior commanders, gathered at his orders. He had prepared a speech in his mind, but looking at his commanders, found the speech not what he really wanted to say. He waved his people to follow him to where a large canvas had been stretched to offer protection from the

36

elements; it was open on all sides. Under the canvas, he turned to face his people. Following a decidedly discouraged sigh, he began to speak.

"You all know that Raines' Rebels struck last night. Reports are still coming in. Many of our most forward units have been virtually wiped out or bloodied badly. I have ordered those still functioning to bunker in until further orders. Now then, certainly none of us expected the taking of North America to be easy. But none of us ever dreamt the offensive would start on such a dour note." Jesus Hoffman paused for a moment, then blurted, "Gentlemen, I am open for suggestions."

The hundreds of small teams of Rebels scattered all over the country didn't need any suggestions. They knew what to do: Kill Blackshirts and anyone who supported them, overtly or covertly. And those many hundreds of citizens who were on the side of Hoffman learned this very quickly and vacated Texas posthaste. They knew better than to waste time trying to explain to the roaming Rebel patrols why they chose to support Hoffman and his Blackshirts. The Rebels were not interested. The Rebels had a nasty habit of hanging or shooting collaborators. On the spot. They also knew all the ways of extracting information from recalcitrant suspects. The Rebels did not use physical torture—under physical torture, the suspect will tell his or her questioners anything to stop the pain. Instead, the Rebels used polygraphs, Psychological Stress Evaluators, drugs, and hypnosis. It was unpleasant.

John Masters was the leader of one such group of people who dreamed of the day Ben Raines would die and the Blackshirts would rule. He fantasized of a world free of blacks. And free of Ben Raines and his goddamn Rebels. John believed that everything bad that had happened to him and America could be traced right back to blacks. His followers numbered just about ten thousand and they lived in a town in North Texas.

Luis Carrero was of Spanish descent (although he was fourth generation American), and Luis dreamed of a world free of everyone except Spanish speaking peoples. He hated people like Ben Raines. And he hated the Rebels. Everyone around him hated Ben Raines and the Rebels. Luis's followers numbered about ten thousand. And Luis dreamed of the day Jesus Hoffman and his Blackshirts would take power.

Moi Sambura hated everyone who was not black. Moi (real name Charles Washington) held sway over a following of about ten thousand spread over several counties in what used to be Eastern Mississippi and Western Alabama. Moi and his followers had caused no trouble and managed to stay clear of the Rebels over the years, even though they were well aware the Rebels knew of their presence. General Cecil Jefferys, himself a black man and second-in-command of all Rebel forces, detested Moi and everything he and his followers stood for. Cecil had bluntly stated for years that someday the Rebels would have to go in and wipe that bunch from the face of the earth. Ben had held him back.

"They're not causing any trouble, Cec," Ben had cautioned.

"The hell they're not," Cecil would reply. "They've either run off or killed every white person in eight counties. They're in a constant squabble with Wink Payne and that bunch of white trash that follow him."

"We'll get to them all in time, Cec," Ben would say. Now was that time.

"General Jefferys on the horn," Corrie told Ben. "He sounds unhappy about something."

"Moi Sambura and Wink Payne," Ben said, walking across the living room of the house in Texas, about seventy-five miles north of Hoffman's command post. "He's found out they both have linked up with Hoffman's Blackshirts. God, what an unholy alliance that must be."

"Go, Cec."

"Ben, we've got to move against Moi and Wink. They've both linked up with Hoffman—for totally different reasons—and having them at your back is unacceptable."

"And what do you propose, Cec?"

"Leading my forces against them. All-out ground and air assault and wipe them clean once and for all."

"Cec," Ben said patiently. "You are still recovering from heart surgery. How many pacemakers do you want installed in your chest? And even if you were a hundred percent, your pulling out would leave Base Camp One unprotected. No. We'll deal with these splinter groups when the time comes."

"You're making a mistake," Cecil warned.

"Cec, we're spread too thin as it is. I've got eyes and ears on Moi and John Masters and Wink and Luis. And that silly-assed CRAPO bunch in Arizona. They're a threat, but not much of one. They all have high numbers of followers, but they're all too lightly armed to pose much of a threat. We've got our hands full dealing with Hoffman."

"All right, Ben. It's your show. That was good work last night."

"We made him bleed, for sure. How are you feeling?" Cecil had undergone emergency heart surgery just a few months back.

"I'll be one hundred percent in a few weeks, Ben."

Ben knew that was bull and so did everyone else. But they also knew that Cecil would push it to the limit unless Ben kept a tight rein on him.

"You do what the doctors tell you to do, Cec," Ben warned. "I need you right where you are."

"That's ten-four, Eagle. Out."

And Ben knew Cecil would follow orders. He might not like it, but he was a soldier's soldier. And Ben knew too, that Cecil was irritated at not being able to get into the field. But Ben needed Cecil right where he was.

To the south of Ben, Hoffman sat behind his desk looking at General Hans Brodermann. Brodermann stood before him, in full dress uniform, but not the uniform of the regular army. Brodermann was dressed all in black, with the silver death's head insignia of the old Nazi SS on his collar and cap. If there was a crueler man anywhere in the world, Jesus Hoffman was not aware of it. Hans detested everything about America, for it was the American army, fifty years back, who had hanged his grandfather, who was one of Mengele's assistants at the death camps. And Hans's mother and father had never let him forget that fact. Hans, unlike Field Marshal Hoffman, had no Spanish blood in him. He was aryan. Pure aryan, he chose to think. And while he had many nationalities serving under his command, his personal detachment of soldiers were all Germanic . . . or at least gave that appearance.

40

Hans was one of the select few who knew that once North America was taken, many now serving faithfully in Hoffman's Blackshirts would be disposed of. Especially the Arabic, Oriental, and Negro . . . the fate of any others was negotiable.

Hans smiled at Hoffman. It was not a condescending smile, for Hans truly admired and liked the young field marshal, some fifteen or so years Hans's junior. Hans had studied Ben Raines extensively over the years, as had every officer in Hoffman's army, and knew that he and Ben were about the same age, and very nearly the same height and weight. He also admired General Raines. He detested him, but he admired him as well. "So you have decided to pit me against General Raines, mein Field Marshal?"

"Ja, Hans," Jesus momentarily slipped into German. "Your SS division will spearhead the America invasion, Hans. Crush everything in your path. Bring any resistance to their knees, and strike fear in the hearts of anyone who even remotely believes in the Rebels."

Hans clicked the heels of his polished riding boots in reply.

Hoffman stood up and walked to a huge map of the United States, secured to the wall of his trailer office. With his back to Brodermann, he thumped his fist against Texas. "I want this place secured, Hans. I don't care if the ground is so soggy with American blood it slops under my boots. Secure it!"

Again, the click of heels.

Jesus turned, a cold look in his black eyes. "How you do that is of no consequence to me, Hans."

"Carte blanche, Field Marshal?"

"Exactly."

"When do I leave?"

"Forty-eight hours." He gave the Nazi stiff armed salute. "Heil Hitler!"

"Heil Hitler!" Hans shouted, then spun around and walked out of the trailer.

Ben sat silently in his chair for a long time, staring out the window, or where the window used to be. He was alone in the room and had given orders he was not to be disturbed for anything short of a nuclear strike. He doodled on scraps of paper, drummed his fingertips on the table, paced the room and cursed and prayed. When he made up his mind, and it was only after the most agonizing hour of his life, he stood up and called for Corrie and the rest of his team to come in.

"Corrie, do we know the frequencies of the known groups aligned with Hoffman and is it possible to jam them for any length of time?"

"Yes, sir. Those people aren't really that smart to begin with. They don't know that we've broken every code they've ever devised within a hour of their transmitting it. They could easily be jammed. For however long you wanted it."

Buddy and Tina were in the general vicinity, and General Georgi Striganov had radioed that he was on the way in.

"I want the rest of the batt coms here ASAP," Ben said. "Transmit that by burst and tell them to get here by fastest means possible. I will not make this decision alone."

Four hours later, the fifteen battalion commanders, including Ben, were seated in the large room. They had all looked at and studied the clear plastic covered U.S. map on the wall. Ben had drawn a line east to west, from the Virginia coast clear over to the California coast.

Ben sat on the edge of the heavy old table, staring at his commanders. "I will not make this decision alone, people." He pointed to the map. "The thirty-sixth parallel. If possible we're going to contain Hoffman's people below it. Above it will be all those who, while they might not agree with our philosophy, at least are not aligned against us."

"A mass evacuation, Ben?" Georgi asked.

"Yes."

"That leaves Cecil with his ass hangin' out in the wind, boy," Ike drawled.

"No, it doesn't," Ben spoke very softly. "For only we have the antidote to the gas our scientists perfected."

Pat O'Shea, the Wild Irishman, as he had promptly been dubbed, whistled. "And if the winds were right . . ." he trailed off.

"Yes," Ben said. "Hoffman's people would die by the thousands. So the entire state of what used to be known as Louisiana will be a neutral zone. We have antidotes for every type of gas Hoffman has, and he knows it. We have nuclear weapons, and he knows it. Bet that Hoffman and his top people have studied me extensively. They know I'll use both if pushed to it."

"And any who refuse to go north?" Jackie Malone, commander of Twelve Battalion, asked. She and Tina were the only female batt coms. Not that there weren't more females qualified, the Rebels just didn't have the personnel to field any more battalions . . . yet.

"We cannot guarantee their safety, and neither can

we guarantee that we won't shoot them on sight, mistaking them for the enemy or enemy sympathizers."

"I like it," West, the mercenary, said. "It would certainly give us a wide-open field of fire, so to speak."

The others nodded their heads in agreement. Danjou, the French Canadian and commander of Seven Battalion, said, "The evacuation would have to be started immediately. I mean, like this evening."

"Yes. Provided we are all in agreement on this plan. Let me see a show of hands."

Every hand went up.

"All right, that's it. I don't know that we can contain them at the thirty-sixth parallel. I only know that we'd better give it our best shot."

"I hate to be the one to throw cold water on this plan, father," Buddy spoke up. All heads turned to him. "But there is no way we're going to evacuate all innocent people out of hundreds of thousands of square miles. It is, simply put, impossible."

"I agree," Ben said. "But what choice do we have, son, except to try? Hoffman has not yet turned his mad dog loose. But it's only a matter of time before he does. General Payon says that General Hans Brodermann is a monster. Totally ruthless. He will kill anything or anybody who gets in his way. Brodermann commands a full-size division. He has more men in that one division than we do in our entire army. Payon, who by the way could not attend this meeting because he is . . . ah, busy this afternoon . . ."

Everybody laughed at that. They knew that Payon and his teams were harassing the hell out of pockets of Blackshirts.

". . . told me that Brodermann is the cruelest man he

has ever seen. He loves torture; enjoys seeing men and women and children humiliated and degraded. This man would make Sam Hartline look like an angel."

Ben had killed the torturer, Hartline, in hand-to-hand combat several years back.

Ben said, "We'll be lucky if we can get forty percent of the population above the thirty-sixth parallel. Fifty percent will be nothing short of a miracle. But we have to try. Let's go, people. We have a lot of work to do."

After the others had exited the room, Ike walked to Ben's side and said, "It's a grand and noble plan, but it ain't gonna work, Ben."

"I know it," Ben spoke quietly. "But we have to give it our best effort." He smiled at Ike's attire. The man was dressed in bell-bottomed jeans and wore a sailor's cap on his head. He resembled a fat Popeye. "You know what you look like, Ike?"

"Don't say it, you stringbean," Ike told him. "Ben," Ike's tone turned serious. "You take care, now, you hear?"

Ben held out his hand and Ike shook it. "Luck to you, old friend."

"Same to you, Ben."

Ike turned and walked out into the fading light.

"We're sure going to need all the luck we can grab," Ben muttered. He picked up his Thompson just as the gas lantern sputtered and died. "I hope that's not an indication of things to come," he said.

FOUR

The Rebels broke up into small teams and began scouring the countryside, going house to house and alerting the people there. It was a futile gesture, and they all knew it, but all felt it was something that must be done. They asked each person they contacted to alert at least two more families. Most survivors agreed to move north; some refused to leave.

"Your funeral," the Rebels told them, and moved on. They had neither the time nor the inclination to argue.

Hoffman's intelligence people knew something big was going on north of their position, but didn't, as yet, know what. On the morning that Brodermann and his SS troops were preparing to pull out for the first big push, Ben broke the news to Field Marshal Hoffman.

Hoffman read the communique several times, then handed it to Brodermann, who read it and passed the paper around to the other commanders.

"He's bluffing!" a tank commander said. "Raines would never use poison gas or nuclear weapons."

"Ben Raines doesn't bluff," Hoffman said, meeting the eyes of Brodermann and seeing the slight nod of agreement from the man. "If he says he'll do something, he'll do it. Don't *ever* sell this man short. He's ruthless. But in a strange sort of way, a fair man." He turned to the map. "Raines says we can use this area of Louisiana to set up hospitals and long-term patient care and no one there will be bothered as long as it is used as that as nothing more. Everything else is a free-fire zone. Advise our medical personnel that this designated area is to be a non-combat zone. We will also respect all of the Rebels' medical facilities. After all," he said, "we are not barbarians."

Ben read the communique and nodded. "Brodermann is on the march. He's moving on three fronts. Heading up Eighty-three, Eighty-one, and Fifty-nine. Armor and heavy artillery. Approximately seven thousand men per column. And the columns are staggered." Ben sighed. "All right, people. Start blowing every bridge south of Highway Ninety. Burn every town, every village, every house. We'll not leave one scrap of useable material. We can't stop the bastards, but we can damn sure make life miserable for them."

"Hoffman is attacking along the borders of California, Arizona, and New Mexico," Corrie said. "Pouring across in large numbers. Intell says we vastly underestimated the size of his army."

"We, hell!" Ben said. "Intelligence did, not us. What's the latest estimate?"

"Probably two hundred thousand."

"God*damn!*" Ben said. "We're outnumbered two hundred and fifty to one. And that's being optimistic."

Ben looked over at General Payon, who had just

pulled in that morning. The Mexican commander was dead tired and his clothing grimy from the road, but he managed to smile sadly. "It is a grim time we live in, my friend."

Ben was silent for a moment. "We have three Rebel battalions to the west of us, and six battalions here in Texas. I'm going to hold the rest in reserve to the north of us. But close enough so they can come busting in if we need them. Order your people to fall back and join those battalions north of us, General. They need the rest."

"They are weary, General," Payon admitted.

"General, I hate formality. What do your friends call you?"

Payon smiled. "You'll hear it sooner or later. My nickname comes from my early days in broadcasting. Mic the Mouth. Like in microphone. I used to get quite excited at soccer games."

Ben laughed. "Mike it is."

General Hans Brodermann halted his column just south of the now fiercely burning town of Cotulla and ordered his break-off columns to stop and hold their positions. They were just south of the ambush sites at Freer and Carrizo Springs. Both of those towns were also blazing. Gas fumes in long unused buried tanks were exploding, sending debris flying into the smoky sky.

Brodermann stood up in his armored scout car and looked at the scene through binoculars. "Ruthless man," he murmured. "Ben Raines is going to be a formidable enemy. I like that. He'll give me a good fight." He sat down and spoke to an aide. "Be certain we don't outdistance our supply trucks. Have the scouts found a way around this inferno?"

"Yes, sir. But the roads are very bad and we won't make good time."

"We shall take all the time we need, Peter. This is going to be a very long campaign."

The column moved on, its speed reduced to a crawl. Which is what Ned Hawkins and his small team of New Texas Rangers had counted on. There were half a dozen armored scout cars in the column, so they had no way of knowing which one Brodermann and the senior officers were riding in. Besides, General Raines had told them to concentrate on the supply and support vehicles. A column can't move if it doesn't have fuel.

Ned's team put four rockets into huge, lumbering tankers and the old rutted highway was enveloped in a massive ball of fire. Vehicles near the tankers exploded, both incinerating and blowing body parts in all direction.

Ned and his team jumped into stripped down fast attack vehicles and took off across the country, weaving and zigzagging and presenting no targets at all for the guns of Brodermann's SS troops. The fast attack vehicles were well out of range in under a minute, almost silently speeding across the brush country, the wide fat tires digging into the earth. The exhaust systems of the vehicles were muffled down to near silence.

"No pursuit!" Brodermann was quick to tell his radio-operator. "That's what they want. They'd chop any pursuers to bits. Secure the immediate area and let's check damage." When his men assured him the area was clean—and it was—Brodermann got out of his armored scout car and stretched his joints and muscles, looking all about him.

"Get my camp chair and place it over there," he told his driver, pointing to a shady spot. "And establish radio contact with Field Marshal Hoffman."

"On scramble, sir?"

"It doesn't make any difference," Brodermann said. "I suspect that Raines's Rebels have the capability to decode anything we might transmit." He told his senior people to come with him. Out of the fierce Texas sun, Brodermann spoke. "We have to start thinking like Ben Raines," he told the assembled group. "We will not be fighting a conventional war. We shall be fighting a very unconventional war. It will be like no war we ever waged. Oh, we all have experience in guerrilla tactics, but on a much smaller scale. I suspect Raines has probably twelve to fifteen thousand Rebels. He's broken them up into tiny units and sent them all over the nation. Day after day, week after week, he's going to peck at us. And if we let him, he will inflict horrible damage. He's not going to fight us on our terms, so we have no choice but to fight him on *his* terms."

Brodermann chuckled without humor. "Years ago, we thought we would walk into this nation and seize the cities, thus controlling the countryside. Raines burned the damn cities to rubble. Then we changed our method of operation and decided to concentrate on the Rebel outposts. We managed to destroy a few, but now Raines has disbanded all of them south of the thirty-sixth parallel and sent them scattering in all directions. We know that the Rebels have huge underground supply caches, but only the most senior officials of the Rebels know the locations. It would be amusing to torture a

50

Rebel, to see how he or she withstands pain, but nothing constructive could come of it. Those supply caches can keep the Rebels supplied for years. Raines's Base Camp One is off-limits to us. His factories there are working day and night in the manufacture of munitions and supplies. If we attempt to interfere with any of that, he will unleash his poisons upon us, and we have no antidote for them." Aides brought them all coffee, and they sugared and creamed and stirred and sipped for a moment.

Brodermann said, "Most of those Americans who refused for years to come under the rules of the Rebels now have no choice in the matter. They have to follow Raines. This is one smart bastard, people. He's not only a ruthless warrior, but he is a damned intelligent one."

"Then we must destroy Ben Raines," a colonel said.

"Oh, very good, Wiesenhofer," Brodermann said, sarcasm thick in his words. "That's excellent thinking. You have a plan, I suppose?"

"Ah . . . no, sir."

"I thought not. Colonel Wellmann?"

"No, sir."

"Colonel Marke?"

"No, sir."

"You have all read the dossiers compiled on General Raines. He has no family that we are aware of. At least not outside the restricted area. There is no leverage to use against him and the bastard wouldn't yield to any if we had it. Captain Blickle, what was that message you spoke of about an hour ago? Something about motorcycle thugs attacking a patrol of ours?"

"Yes, sir. Yesterday a gang of biker hoodlums, male and female, attacked and wiped out a patrol of ours working over in Florida. Two of our people pretended death and heard them talking. The group is heavily armed and commanded by two people: Leadfoot and Wanda."

"Leadfoot?" Brodermann asked, arching one eyebrow.

"Yes, sir. Obviously a code name of some sort. They are all operating under code names. But I don't know why that is. The survivors said others were called Beerbelly, Hoss, Sweetmeat, Sugar, Hognose, and Pisser."

"My word!" Colonel Wellmann said.

"Have our people in intelligence analyze those names," Brodermann ordered. "They have some significance, surely. Pisser?" he muttered, shaking his head. "Well, I have to confer with Field Marshal Hoffman. It would be futile to continue pushing forward with great armies. We'd be all bunched up fighting shadows."

"Then what do we do?" Colonel Wellmann asked.

"Come up with a better plan," Brodermann said simply.

"You bastard!" a man told Ben. Everything the man and woman and the three children owned was piled into the beds of two old pickup trucks, parked in front of a freshly painted and well-kept house.

"Oh?" Ben said, smiling at the man and not taking offense, for he knew what the man was referring to, and it wasn't Ben's ancestry.

"I hate you and your damn harsh right-wing rule, Raines. But even you're better than those Blackshirts. I think."

Ben laughed. "Right-wing, huh? It's been awhile since I've heard that phrase. You're way too young to be a part of the old peace and love generation. You weren't even born then, I don't imagine. So what's your problem?"

"You've forced me to pick up a gun and fight, that's what's wrong!"

"Are you telling me that you have lived here since the Great War and never had to take a human life?"

"No. I can't say that. I've defended home and family when it was necessary. But I didn't take some perverted delight in killing."

"And you think I do?"

"Yes."

"Well, to a degree, you're right," Ben admitted. "I enjoyed killing Sam Hartline. I think I did the world a favor by destroying Sister Voleta and Khamsin and Lan Villar and Kenny Parr and Ashley and Matt Callahan and all the rest of those terrorists. I enjoyed wiping out most of the Night People. But what you may not know is this: we have about three thousand or so former criminals in our ranks. I offered them amnesty and they took it. They've turned into top-notch fighting men and women. And at least they are fighting for this country. What are you doing, except running your mouth."

"There are about two hundred or so of us here, General. We've done pretty well so far and we haven't asked you people for a damn thing."

"Yet," Ben said. "And don't think you've done your kids any favors, for they haven't been vaccinated for any of the childhood diseases. I know. For you people don't have the capability to make the vaccine—any of it. We do. Disease is rampant in this nation, mister. But with

53

your mentality, if your kids get sick and die—God forbid—you'll probably blame me for it."

The man stared at Ben. There was no hate in his eyes, only disgust. "And you think you would be blameless?"

Ben smiled and leaned up against a fender. Brodermann and his forces were a hundred miles south, and Ben was in the mood for a good argument. Since Thermopolis had moved part of Intell and HQ to a secure position in Arkansas, Ben had not had a good headbutting difference of opinion.

"You mean," Ben said, "you want it like before: free rides for everyone?"

The man, who had told Ben his name was Charles, shook his head and grimaced. "You right-wingers always have an easy explanation, don't you?"

Ben carefully rolled a cigarette before replying. "If you mean that I don't believe in something for nothing, yes."

"I . . ." Charles shook his head. "No. No, I'm not going to argue with you, General. You've got us right where you want us, so what is the point?"

"You disappoint me, Charles. I was so looking forward to a spirited debate." Ben sighed. "Well, go on, take your family, and get them across the thirty-sixth parallel. Draw weapons and learn how to point them in the right direction. There'll be medics there to vaccinate your kids and see to any of your needs. Big Brother's back now, Charles. But you don't seem very happy about it."

Charles stared at Ben. "You . . . goddamnit, Raines. None of us wanted Big Brother in our lives!"

"Really? Why, Charles, your kind wanted cradle to

grave protection from all things. You wanted the best law enforcement but you paid many of our cops shit wages and saddled them with so many rules and regulations they couldn't function. Your kind talked out of both sides of your mouths. On one hand, you bawled and squalled and stomped on hankies everytime a punk got killed. You bellered and roared because you couldn't be safe in your homes or on the streets, but then you filed lawsuits about overcrowded prisons and jails until they were being run not by the corrections people but by federal judges. You wanted adequate health care but you slapped doctors with so many lawsuits many of them either had to quit or raise their rates so high it was unaffordable to a great many people. Then you started hollering about a universal health plan and the goddamn ambulance-chasing lawyers and lobbyists and attorneys for the doctor's organizations stalled it in committee for years. You want me to go on, Charles?"

"You're twisting things all out of context, General."

"Am I really, Charles? Am I?"

The man refused to reply. He spun on his heel and stalked away, getting into the lead pickup and driving off, heading for the north. And safety. In the dreaded hands of the Rebels, whom he professed to despise.

"Didn't bite, did he, General?" Jersey asked, standing close to Ben.

Ben cut his eyes and smiled at her. "Wasn't because I didn't try, Jersey."

"Why do they hate our way so much, General?"

"You can't make a fair comparison. None of you. Because you've never known any other way, Jersey. You, Beth, Corrie, and Cooper never knew—or have blocked out—the way it was before the Great War."

"I remember just a little bit of it, General," Corrie said. "I have this picture of my parents sitting around the table—I think it was the kitchen table—once a month and wondering how they were going to pay all their bills. Isn't that funny? I can't even remember what they looked like. But I remember that."

"Yes," Beth said. "One of the few things I remember clearly was my mother and father saying often that taxes were killing them. And that something was dreadfully wrong with our government. I don't even know what they did for a living. I don't really know how old I am."

"My granddad used to say this country was going to hell in a hand basket," Cooper said. "Of course, I didn't know what he meant. But I've listened to the older Rebels talk for years. I sure as hell don't want to go back to the way it was before the Great War."

Thoreau's line about leading "lives of quiet desperation" came to Ben's mind. But how to explain that to these young people who had never had the chance to experience that quiet desperation?

And when I am gone, and war is over, what kind of world will these young people build? Or will they still be young when peace reigns? Will they live to see peace?

Ben shook his head and opened his map case. They were a few miles north and west of the ruins of San Antonio, in the hill country not far from the deserted town of Bandera. The group had stopped and set up camp at one of the many old dude ranches in the area. Bandera, Ben had read in an old brochure, had once been called the dude ranch capital of Texas.

Bands of wild horses now roamed the area, descendants of the tame horses that city folks once came to ride and play cowboy with for a week or so. Half-wild cattle could be found everywhere, and the Rebels never lacked for fresh meat.

And neither will Brodermann's people, Ben mentally added.

But Ben couldn't see any way to prevent that.

"Scouts report that more and more people are leaving the area and heading north," Corrie broke into his thoughts. "But a lot of them are joining up with John Masters and his people up in the Panhandle. He's got quite a following, General."

"Estimates?"

"Ten thousand."

"That's men, women, and children. How many fighting personnel can he field?"

"About thirty-five hundred."

"That's still too many to have at our backs. Tell Buddy to regroup his Eight Battalion and get ready to strike from the north. I'll pull together my One Battalion and hit them from the south. We've got time. Brodermann is still trying to devise a battle plan. Saddle up. Let's go deal with Mr. Masters and his hate group."

FIVE

John Masters looked the part. And he played it well. He was one of those quasi ignorant, heavy-jowled, pus-gutted, piggy-eyed loudmouths who had an unshakable opinion on everything and was given to thundering Godlike pronouncements through a bullhorn, which his followers hung on breathlessly. To say his followers were just slightly less knowledgeable than John would be like saying fire is hot.

Since the Great War, dozens of groups, large and small, made up of people who blamed everything bad that had befallen them on those who were not the same color, religion, race, or whatever, had sprung up all over the nation. If they did not get in the way of the Rebels, or draw too much attention to themselves, Ben had pretty much left them alone.

Then groups such as Masters's began embracing the puke from the brain and mouth of Jesus Hoffman, who preached the somewhat diluted teachings of Hitler.

That was more than Ben Raines could take.

"Raines ain't a gonna do nothin' to us," Masters boasted, when he learned that two groups of Rebels were approaching his location, one from the north, the other from the south. "They's too many of us. 'Sides, Raines has got his hands full tryin' to deal with the Blackshirts, and they gonna walk all over Ben Raines and then we'll be shut of that nigger-lovin' bastard forever."

It never seemed to occur to people like Masters that armies numbering hundreds of thousands had been trying to 'walk all over Ben Raines' for a decade. Ben was still very much alive and very much in command.

And as far as Ben being a "nigger-lover," Ben didn't place a whole lot of emphasis on the color of a person's skin. It was what was in the individual's heart and brain that mattered to Ben. Ben and his Rebels had fought Blacks, Whites, Hispanics, Asians, and just about any other ethic group one could think of . . . if they were stupid enough to declare war on the Rebels.

The Rebel Army was made up of men and women of all nationalities, all religions, all races. Ben's critics, and they were many, had accused Ben of taking the cream of the crop and ignoring the rest. That was true in part.

For the most part, the men and women who made up the Rebel Army were a tolerant bunch who used a great deal of common sense in day-to-day dealings with their peers. Anyone could do it; most simply would not. And that included people on both sides of whatever color line was involved. Whatever the color or faith.

So in that respect, Ben did have the cream of the crop.

But even among Rebel ranks, many had to continually work at being tolerant of others. Sometimes tempers flared and violence followed. It was not often, but it did happen. As Ben had pointed out many times, the men and women who made up the Rebels were not perfect . . . they just tried very hard to be.

John Masters looked at the communique handed him by a runner from his communications center. He wadded it up and tossed the crumpled note to the ground. "Brodermann says for us not to engage the Rebels. He wants us to cut and run. Hell with him!"

"Why, goddamn, General," a follower of Masters said. Masters insisted on being called General, even though he had no prior military training and could not even make it through the first few weeks of Boy Scout training, back when such organizations existed. He was kicked out when he said he wasn't sharin' his tent with no goddamn Jew-boy. "We'll just whup Raines proper and have done with it."

"Damn right!" Masters replied. "Git ever'one to arms and in position around the town."

"How many's comin' at us, General?" Sonny asked.

"Brodermann says two Rebel battalions. That's about fifteen-sixteen hundred Rebels. I figure each battalion's got at least three-four hundred women and niggers and Jews and spics and the like. They can't fight and ever'one knows it. So that means we're prob'ly lookin' at no more'un a thousand people. It won't take us long to deal with this. I just can't figure how come ever'body is so scared of the Rebels."

For years, Masters and his hate group had been isolated in one corner of the panhandle of Texas. They had grown their crops, maintained the oil rigs and refineries in the area, and kept their heads down. They had communications equipment, but had never been able to break even one of the Rebel codes. Masters and his people had no knowledge of burst transmissions and no concept of military tactics. Their slogan was Stay White And Pure. SWAP. It was a mystery to Ben how Masters and his SWAP people were going to get along with Hoffman and his mixed bag of fighters. But since few radical racists had the ability to see past the ends of their noses, that small obstacle had probably never occurred to Masters.

Masters and his fearless fighters grabbed their guns and got behind barricades, ready to defend their wimmin an' child'en against the dark hordes of racial equality, common sense, and justice.

Ben and his son Buddy pulled their battalions up to within a mile of the town and circled it, out of range of anything Masters had in the way of armament.

Behind the barricades, General Masters stood, a green beret on his head—he had taken it away from a little boy years back—and his trusty .30-.30 at hand. "Our moment of glory is here, men!" he shouted. "We'll go down in history as the first to defend our right to live white and free and pure."

Actually about a half a million had gone down under the guns of the Rebels. Six feet down in most cases. Mass graves.

"Stand ready to repel the charge!" Sonny shouted. He remembered that line from his high school lit class.

"Aw, shit, Sonny," Bubba said. "I was gonna say that."

But no charge came.

Ben leaned against the fender of his Hummer and viewed the town through long lenses. Paul Blair, a Cherokee Indian and a graduate of the University of Tennessee stood beside Ben. Paul was a company commander in Ben's One Battalion. He had found a chicken feather and stuck it in his cowboy hat.

"Take plenty scalps this day," Paul grunted, a twinkle in his eyes. "Paint face and dance. Then count coup."

Ben looked at him. "What are you going to use for a coup stick, O Great and Noble Red Man, your economics degree or your minor in education?"

Paul grinned and showed Ben a child's rubber tomahawk he had found amid the rubble of an old five and dime. "Will this do?" It was surprisingly realistic.

Ben laughed at the man. "That thing is going to get you in trouble someday, Paul."

"The dossier on John Masters says he hates Indians."

"Masters hates everybody. What else is new?"

"I want to get close to the man, wave this tomahawk, and yell some Cherokee words at him."

"I wasn't aware you knew any Cherokee."

"I know how to say 'good morning' and 'it looks like it might rain.' " He pulled out several tubes of lipstick and knelt down, looking at his reflection in the outside mirror of the Hummer. He began carefully streaking his face with purple and red and orange.

Jersey looked at him and slowly shook her head. "How come One Battalion always gets the people who are full of shit?" she questioned.

Paul cut his eyes. "Look, Little Bit, you're about a quarter-breed Apache, yourself."

"You're right," Jersey said. "Let me use that lipstick when you're through."

"Jesus," Ben muttered. "You people better start taking this seriously. John Masters is a certifiable nut, but his guns are very real."

"Buddy on the horn, sir," Corrie said.

"Go, Rat," Ben said.

"What's the poop, Pop?"

Ben chuckled. His kids took every opportunity to take as many liberties as possible, knowing that Ben didn't mind and the other Rebels got a kick out of it. "We wait. Intell says there are lots of children in there and I want to keep collateral damage to a minimum."

"That's a big ten-four, Big Daddy. Rat out."

"A whole battalion of jokers," Ben muttered. "Corrie, order snipers up with their .50s. Start picking off SWAP people on sight."

"Yes, sir."

When Ben turned around, he was momentarily startled. Paul Blair had taken off his shirt and had painted his chest with the lipstick.

"Are you going to take off your shirt, too, Jersey?" Cooper asked, standing well away from her.

Jersey told him to go commit an impossible act upon his person.

"Request permission to take some of my people in after dark, sir," Paul said.

"Your people being those of Indian heritage, I'm sure," Ben replied.

"Well . . . that's a possibility."

"Permission granted. Now get out of here." He looked at Jersey. "And, no. You're not going."

"The thought never entered my mind, General."

"What the hell are they waitin' on?" a SWAP member asked, wiping his sweaty hands on his britches.

"They're just standin' out there lookin' at us. All they've done is call for our surrender."

"And General Masters told them what they could do with that, didn't he?" his buddy replied.

"Damn shore did."

That was the last thing he would ever say. A sniper's bullet took him in the center of the face and blew out the entire back of his head. The force of the .50-caliber slug slammed him backward and knocked his body into a staring, horrified, and blood and brain-splattered SWAP member. He dropped his rifle to the street and it went off, the bullet striking a man in the knee and sending him howling to the ground in pain. His rifle clattered to the street but did not discharge.

"Goddamn!" a team leader yelled. "Fire at them Rebs. Far, goddamnit, far!"

"Far, hell!" a SWAP member hollered. "Far at what? I can't see nobody to far at?"

With good reason. The sniper teams, laying a mile to a mile-and-a-quarter out of the city limits, were using ten-power scopes and firing the .50-caliber Haskins M500. A monstrous powder charge blows the 1.5-ounce slug out of the muzzle with five to six times the energy of a 7.62 mm NATO round. Using various types of rounds, the Haskins can deliver slugs that will either pierce four-inch armor or explode on contact, turning the steel body into flesh-shredding shrapnel. The bullet arrives at its target long before the sound of the rifle can be heard, and at that distance, sometimes it is not heard at all.

"Order the sniper teams to use armor-piercing rounds," Ben ordered. "Let's liven up the day for the SWAP members."

The streets of the town had been barricaded with old junked cars and trucks, rusted out and useless. The .50-caliber armor-piercing rounds blew right through them and tore great gaping holes in the flesh of the defenders crouched behind the rusted hulks, sending the SWAP members hollering and racing for better cover.

"Sir," Beth said to Ben. "Sergeant Hanks requests permission to speak to the General."

"Beth," Ben said. "What is with all this sudden formality? We've never stood much on . . . Jesus Christ!" Ben yelled, as he turned and eyeballed something that looked straight out of an African jungle movie.

"Easy, General," Sergeant Hanks said, jerking off his grotesque wooden mask. "It's me, Hanks."

Ben stepped back and looked at the man. He was speechless. The black sergeant from upstate New York was naked except for a loincloth and a whole bunch of chicken feathers he had glued to his body. He held the sun-bleached skull of a cow in one hand and a horribly ugly ceremonial mask in the other. He was smiling at Ben.

Ben found his voice. "Robert . . . what in the name of God is going on around here?"

The words had just left his mouth when the sounds of tom-toms reached him. He listened for a moment, looking all around him as the sounds drifted through the early summer air.

Corrie spoke into her headset and said, "Buddy wants to know if you're having a dance over here and why he wasn't invited?"

"Oh, that's Captain Blair, sir," Hanks said. "He's got about a dozen of his Indian buddies with him and they're doing a war dance. I thought I'd dress up like a witch doctor—I found this mask in a house down the road—and do some psychological warfare on the folks in the town. They've got nothing in that town that will reach this far."

Ben knew that for a fact. His Scouts had already gone in, scratching themselves and hawking snot on the ground, cussing blacks and Mexicans and Jews and everybody else they could think of. They had looked around, had a meal, and sized up the situation. Small arms only, and that was not unusual.

Years back, Ben and his people had swept the nation clean, seizing and storing weapons of all descriptions. They had left very little for others.

Wild yelling and chanting came over the sounds of the tom-toms.

"Where in the hell did Captain Blair get tom-toms?" Ben asked.

"Oh, those are fifty-five gallon drums, General," Hanks said. "We fooled around with various levels of water in them to get just the right sound. Pretty good, huh?"

"Right," Ben said. "And I suppose you have several more of your buddies of . . . color to assist you in this, ah, witch-doctor dancing?"

Hanks grinned.

"Oh, go on," Ben said, doing his best to hide a smile. "While you're at it, see if you can conjure up a plate of fettuccine for me."

"General Masters!" an aide yelled, busting into Masters's house. "They's a whole bunch of damn nigger witch doctors a-whoopin' and a-hollerin' on the road. Shakin' skulls at us!"

Masters spilled his coffee all down the front of his shirt. He heaved his fat ass and his pus gut out of the chair and lumbered after the man. Using binoculars, he viewed the scene.

"By God!" he breathed. "Them's real Africans out yonder. They's callin' down some curses on us."

"Do they work?"

"How the hell do I know. Folks say they do. That voodoo's some powerful stuff, boy."

Sergeant Bob Hanks and a few of his buddies had a really nice dance step all worked out. Sergeant Hanks had to threaten to shoot two of his friends before they'd agree to do it. And it was a good thing they all wore old Halloween masks, for they hid their embarrassed grins.

The four men, all nearly naked except for loincloths and chicken feathers, would take three steps forward, hold up cattle skulls in the direction of the town, shout "Ugh!" and back up.

"This is terribly repetitive," one of the men said. "Not to mention embarrassing."

"Just shut up and go 'Ugh!'" Bob told him.

"Boy, that's playin' dirty," John Masters said. "I mean, that's dirty even for Ben Raines."

"I don't feel good," a SWAP member said. "My stomach hurts. I think they done caused me to come down with some terrible disease."

A doctor among the group looked at the men in disgust. "Don't be stupid!" he admonished them. "Just ignore all that ranting and raving. It can't hurt you."

Then the sound of tom-toms reached the defenders of SWAP. Wild Indian yells followed that.

"What the hell is that?" Masters demanded.

"Injuns!" he was told. "Look through these here field glasses and you can see 'em. All painted up and doin' a war dance."

Cooler and more intelligent heads among the SWAP forces tried to prevail. But it was no use. Ignorant and misinformed to begin with, bitter and hate-filled long before the Great War, now isolated for years, with little emphasis placed on learning, many of the SWAP people began to unravel. Children began crying and that only added to the confusion.

"Shut them goddamn kids up!" Masters hollered. "I cain't hear myself think with all that catterwallin' goin' on. I got to think, y'all. Damn!"

A sniper's bullet slammed through a concrete block and sent stone splinters into Masters' face and neck. He bellowed in fright and pain, hit the ground and flattened out. As much as his pusgut would allow.

Hanks and his dancers were really getting into the rhythm of it, and getting very innovative. The tom-toms were banging and Blair's Indians were yelling.

Ben was sitting in a camp chair by his Hummer, drinking coffee and thinking this was a hell of a way to fight a war.

Both Buddy and Ben had sent some of their Scouts in close and they were now flitting among the buildings on the edges of the town. In a hour's time, the Scouts had grabbed about sixty young kids and passed them back to their lines, turning them over to the medics.

"The kids are in pretty good shape, physically," a Rebel doctor reported to Ben. "But they're filled with hatred toward anybody not of their color. It'll take a long time to bring them around."

"I'm not going to try," Ben said, surprising those gathered around him. "Base Camp One is very nearly overwhelmed now. And we've only had limited success in working with the kids of outlaw and hate groups. When this is over, we'll reunite them with their mothers and let them go. It's the best we can do under the circumstances."

He stood up and again looked at the town through binoculars. He scanned the town for a few seconds, then lowered the field glasses and turned to face his team, a hard look in his eyes. "Beth, tell Blair and Hanks to knock it off. They've had their fun, now it's time to get serious. Corrie, tell Masters to send out the women and kids. We don't want to hurt them. Get the mortars set up."

The tom-toms ceased their drumming and Hanks and his now nearly exhausted "witch doctors" vanished from the long lenses of the SWAP members.

"What the hell's Ben Raines up to now?" Masters questioned. The cuts on his face from the stone splinters had been dabbed with iodine and he looked like he was suffering from some horrible pox. "Where'd all them niggers and Injuns go to? What the hell's goin' on out yonder? What's all them wimmin back yonder squallin' about?"

" 'Bout sixty-seventy kids is gone," he was informed. "The Rebels done been in the town and snatched 'em. They cut a bunch of throats and they used silenced guns to kill more of ourn, too. Nobody saw nothin'. Bastards move like ghosts, they do."

"Raines is tellin' us to send out the women and kids," a radio operator said. "Says he don't want to see them hurt."

Masters felt something cold and slimy roll around in his guts. He'd spent years boasting about how he and his people would kick the crap out of the Rebels should they ever show up. Now they were here and Masters had lost about fifty people to sniper bullets, the Rebels had arrogantly slipped into his town and kidnapped dozens of kids, cut throats, and killed his people without being seen, and his SWAP forces had not been able to fire an effective round against the Rebels.

"Send out the women and kids, John," a doctor urged him. "We can then make our stand, if that's what you want to do."

"What do you mean, *if?*"

"You want to die for nothing?" the doctor questioned.

"What do you mean, nothin'? Our cause ain't nothin'. We got a free white society. We got what we always wanted. This is what we worked for, even before the Great War."

"And when we die, we will have a cold lonely grave," the doctor said. "I don't take much comfort in that. General Raines let some of his troops have a little fun at our expense. That's how confident he is. I'm taking my wife and family and leaving under a white flag. The rest of you can stay here and die. For your cause." He walked away.

Masters leaned against the wall of a building. He hated Ben Raines almost as much as he did niggers. But the idea of dead kids and women didn't appeal to him. "Send out the women and kids," he ordered. "And everybody else that's turned chickenshit. Me . . . I'm stayin'."

"They're showing a white flag," Ben said, looking

through long lenses. "Corrie, ask Buddy if he's receiving the same signal."

"That's ten-four, General. Women and children and a few men in the bunch."

There were six highways leading into the town. The Rebels had blocked them all. 60 mm mortars had been set up and the crews were standing by, ready to drop the rockets down the tubes.

"Tell those surrendering to get their vehicles and drive out of here," Ben said. "Jesus, we can't handle all those people. Tell them to head down to Interstate 40 and then cut west. I don't ever want to see any of them again. There must be four or five thousand of them. My God, they could overwhelm us by sheer numbers."

"Hell of a way to fight a war," Jersey muttered.

SIX

The old cars and trucks smoked and rattled and rolled on, the occupants staring silently through hate-filled eyes at the Rebels as they drove past.

"We'll probably have to fight those kids someday," Buddy radioed to his father.

"I'm certain of that," Ben replied, watching as a boy of about ten gave him the middle finger from the back seat of a car. Ben resisted an impulse to return the bird.

"The children sure have lovely manners, don't they?" Jersey remarked.

"Yes. Remarkably well-behaved," Ben replied drily. "They have certainly been steeped in the social graces."

"What will happen to them, I wonder?" Beth asked.

"Oh, they'll drive until they find some deserted and isolated little town," Ben replied. "Then they'll set up there and once more start teaching and preaching hate against people not of their color or faith or personal opinion or whatever. Years back, those of us with any sense knew that laws and legislation alone could never erase hatred and prejudice and bigotry . . . anymore than governments could effectively legislate morality. It was going to take education and a hundred percent effort on all sides of the color line."

"But none of us had to go to school to be able to get along with others," Corrie said.

"True," Ben said. "So maybe there is hope for the human race after all. But not for that bunch holed up in the town. Corrie, tell them to surrender. They'll have one chance and one chance only."

Corrie did and listened for the reply. She smiled sadly. "They said for you to go to hell, sir."

"Start dropping in mortars," Ben ordered.

"Here we go," Jersey said.

Mortar teams had ringed the town from about 2,500 yards out, and their crews started dropping in M734 preset rounds of HE. Some exploded on contact with earth. Others detonated near the surface, and still others were used as proximity rounds, killing anything within a predetermined range.

Still other mortar crews dropped in willie peter, and the white phosphorus rounds soon had flames leaping into the dry air and thick smoke billowing up from the burning town.

Those inside the town had the Rebels outnumbered, but anytime a fighting force bunkers themselves in tight with no escape routes, the outcome of the battle is nearly always predictable.

John Masters was only minutes away from learning a hard lesson about the fighting savagery of Ben Raines and the Rebels.

There were those who tried to run from the flames. Snipers cut them down. Confusion was the order of the day as the mortar rounds never stopped coming in. Each mortar crew was throwing six to twelve rounds a minute at the town, and it was a constant roar of deadly booming thunder. Old burning buildings were collapsing all around the SWAP defenders and flying rubble was causing as many casualties as anything else. Men were being buried alive under tons of brick and mortar. The Rebels had come with plenty of supply trucks following them, and planes were ready to fly in more rounds if needed.

"We gotta surrender, John!" a weeping man screamed at Masters. "We're all gonna die in here if we don't."

"Hell, no!" Masters shouted. His face and head were dripping blood from minor wounds caused by flying debris, he had lost his beret and his rifle, and was armed only with a .357 revolver, which was about as effective as a club since the Rebels were still a good mile and a quarter away, most of them lounging on the ground, smoking or reading or gossiping or catnapping.

"John, goddamnit, look around you!" his friend shouted. "The damn town is bein' destroyed around us whilst we talk. Can't you see what them Rebs is doin'? They're walkin' mortar rounds in, John, startin' at the outskirts and workin' in. They're pushin' us back to the center of the town. Once they have us all within a two or three block area, they'll just pour it on and kill us down to the last man."

Masters looked at the pistol in his hand and threw it to the rubble-strewn street. "Git on the horn and tell Ben Raines we give up. Go on, do it." When his friend had raced away, Masters turned and looked toward the south. "Goddamn you, Ben Raines. I hate you!"

"You ain't never gonna make me take orders from no nigger, Ben Raines!" Masters declared, standing in front of Ben, who was sitting in a camp chair, drinking a cup of coffee. "I ain't never took no orders from a coon and I ain't about to start now. Not you, not God, not nobody can make me do that."

A Rebel psychiatrist was seated a few feet away, observing and listening to Masters. As for Ben, he hadn't as yet made up his mind exactly what to do with the prisoners, about fifteen hundred of them, but he was working that out in his mind.

"You might as well go on and shoot me now, Raines," Masters stood his ground. " 'Cause there ain't nothin' gonna convince me that niggers is good for anything cther than bein' a white man's slave. And what are you doin' with all them goddamn witch doctors, anyways?"

All the Rebels standing around laughed at that.

"Y'all quit laughin' at me!" Masters hollered. "Stop it, now, you hear?"

That just got the Rebels laughing all that much harder and louder.

"What are we going to do with all these people, father?" Buddy asked.

"Put them on trucks, send them to California, put them on a couple of those ships we have out there, and dock them at San Carlos, Baja, Mexico."

"Are you serious?"

"You have a better idea?"

"Unfortunately, no."

"You ain't sendin' me down to live with no damn bunch of lazy-assed, greasy beaners!" Masters hollered.

"On second thought," Buddy said, "I approve of your plan. Wholeheartedly."

"Thank you. I think those warm, friendly, and very

pleasant people down in the Baja will know exactly what to do with Mister Masters and his ilk."

"I think General Payon is going to get a big laugh out of this," Jersey said.

"I hate Mexican food," a SWAP member said. "Makes me fart."

"We have lost a stronghold in North Texas," Jesus Hoffman was informed. "Raines and his Rebels wiped out John Masters and his group. It is unconfirmed, but reports are he killed them to the last man."

The Rebels had sent out that report.

Field Marshal Hoffman sighed and shook his head. This campaign was not going well at all. "What is General Brodermann's location?"

"Just south of San Antonio. But the Rebels have put the city to the torch. They have destroyed it. General Brodermann reports that there is little left."

"Order him to halt there." Hoffman was thoughtful for a few moments, staring out the window of his trailer. He wanted North America, but he wanted it whole, not the charred useless remains of it. The U.S. had factories he could reopen; but not if Ben Raines kept putting them to the torch.

Hoffman thought he knew Ben Raines' long-range plans, and they distressed him. Ben Raines was looking far to the future; planning for decades after his own death. The man was not looking for immediate personal creature comforts and glory, he was thinking of his grandchildren and his grandchildren's grandchildren. Ben Raines' plan was to tear it all down and rebuild from scratch, politically, judicially, and economically.

He must be stopped.

"What Masters said back there, General," Beth asked. "Before we shipped them out. Was any of that true?"

Ben and Buddy's columns were heading south, to take up positions just north of San Antonio. Ben had received word that Hoffman's columns had stopped and were bivouacked just south of San Antonio, about forty miles apart.

"To a degree, yes," Ben replied. "But people like Masters always take things out of context. The government did put in place a number of programs aimed at helping minorities, and some of them were blatantly unfair. Anytime the government forces private industry to hire someone or promote someone based on color instead of ability, that's wrong . . . on the one hand. On the other hand, many companies would not have hired or promoted minorities had the government not put those laws in place. It was a Catch 22 situation.

"But Masters was right when he said that too many times minorities cried racism when none existed, or was intended. And he was right when he said that the welfare system was abused. It was. By too many people, of all colors. And he was right, again, to a degree, in saying that the government—when we had a government—pandered to minorities and crapped on the white middle class. Just before the Great War knocked everything down, race relations were at their lowest point in three decades. The much-put-upon middle class had grown weary to the point of armed rebellion by seeing certain types of minorities burn and loot and riot every time some decision or event went against their beliefs. And he was right in saying that you didn't see white Americans taking to the streets and looting and burning and acting like crazy people when a black person shot a white person. People like Masters are uncomfortably correct on a lot of points, as far as they choose to take the issue.

"But, Beth, up until the 1960s, many blacks, and other minorities, in certain parts of the country, weren't even allowed to vote. They had to pay taxes, serve in the armed forces, and obey the laws, but they couldn't vote, go to a school of their choice, sit in the front of public transportation, eat in a public restaurant, stay in a white hotel or motel, or walk in certain parts of town. They were beaten, lynched, tarred and feathered, castrated, raped, falsely imprisoned, kept from holding public office, and forced to suffer all sorts of other indignities. Most received substandard education, using hand-me-down textbooks and were taught in dilapidated, poorly maintained buildings."

Ben looked out the window at the seemingly deserted countryside. "Takes a long time for people to forget. It doesn't excuse lawless behavior or preferential treatment, but I don't blame them for not forgetting."

"But on the other hand . . ." Corrie said with a smile, wanting Ben to warm further to the subject.

Ben laughed. "What do you want me to say, Corrie? That we all have a streak of bigotry or racism in us? Well, we all do. Anyone who says they don't is a damn liar. What we have to do—black, white, yellow, red, tan—is work to overcome that. The white people can't be expected to work at one hundred percent in overcoming it, and allow the blacks to work at fifty percent. It must be a joint effort, pulling in double harness all the time. But it wasn't, it isn't now, and it never will be. Cultures will always clash. But what we can do—the Rebels—is attempt to teach people to clash gently, not violently. To talk it out instead of duking it out. Or shooting it out. To convince people to stop pointing fingers and saying 'you owe me something for what your ancestors did to mine.' That's bullshit. What's past is past. Let's bury it, stand side by side, and look toward the future." Ben smiled. "Just please turn down that goddamn boombox!"

The Rebels headed south, with a lot of laughter coming from Ben's command vehicle.

The battalion commanders met at Ben's CP north of San Antonio. Payon, the Russian, Striganov, Rebet, Danjou, Ned Hawkins of the New Texas Rangers, and O'Shea, of the Free Irish.

They commanded some 6,000 men and women. Against some 21,000 elite SS troops under the command of General Brodermann.

After greeting everyone, coffee was poured and the commanders sat down, while Ben moved to a large wall map of Texas. "Here is the latest from Intell, and it's easy to see what Brodermann has in mind. Green denotes where his main forces are located, ready to thrust north. Highways 83, 35, and 37. Orange denotes his smaller units—trained and experienced guerrilla forces. They are poised on Highways 181, 123, 80, and 183. Well, Brodermann just made his first fatal mistake. He split his forces to meet us at our own game. He fails to realize that we've been playing this game for years. He's a comparative newcomer at it. But it won't take him long to learn. He's an experienced commander. Now then, his men are still in bivouac. So we're going to get in place and hit him hard at first light day after tomorrow. Buddy is in place over here, on Highway 90, in hiding and ready to strike from the east the instant we hit from the north. Georgi, I want you and Payon to launch full battalions in what will appear to be a major assault at the westernmost column along Highway 83 at 0535. At the same time, the rest of us will hit the smaller units over here, from the north, while Buddy's people come at them from the east.

"The instant the attack begins, preset charges will be blown, knocking out the bridges across the Nueces, the Leona, and the Frio, west of Brodermann's CP, which is here, on 35. Bridges will be blown on the San Antonio and the Atasosa. Brodermann's two centrally located columns will be cut off, unable to head straight east or west. They'll have to detour far south and then cut across. By that time, our work will be done and we'll be gone." Ben sighed and then smiled faintly. "Hopefully. If we do this right, we will have eliminated a very elite part of Hoffman's army and demoralized the hell out of the rest of it. There is no point in taking prisoners." That was said very flatly and it left no doubt in any commander's mind. "There will be no circling around or prolonging this affair. We hit them hard, gather up as much equipment as we can in a very short time, and get the hell out of there. If the enemy wants to pursue us, that's going to be their funeral. I don't think they will. But if we're successful, Brodermann just might be so angry he'll throw caution to the wind and come chasing us." He smiled. "I hope he does."

Beth and Cooper passed out briefing kits to the commanders and they sat for a time, studying them. Jersey sat in a chair in a far corner of the room, her M-16 across her knees. She was expressionless. Jersey made even hardened commanders nervous.

Striganov finally turned his head and stared at Jersey. "You don't trust us, girl?" he rumbled.

"When it comes to the General's life, I don't trust anybody," Jersey said.

Payon laughed at the expression on the Russian's face. "With a battalion like her, we could win the war in a week, hey, Georgi?"

"Less than that," Georgi replied.

Payon had noticed that Ben's team always positioned themselves at separate locations around any room he was in, offering him the maximum of protection. Outside any building Ben was in, there was always at least one full squad of heavily armed Rebels, and a hundred yards away, ringing them, another squad or two.

"You ready, my friend?" Georgi asked the Mexican.

"Yes. It is going to be payback time for my people."

"You want to lead the assault?"

"I would be honored."

"So it shall be."

The Russian and the Mexican left the room.

Soon the others filed out, until Ben was sitting alone at the scarred old once-lovely dinner table in the huge dining room of the big ranch house. Cooper walked over and refilled Ben's coffee cup. Ben thanked him and rubbed a palm over the wood. "A lot of good times were had around this table," he said aloud, speaking to no one in particular. "Families gathered for anniversaries, birthdays, family reunions, Christmas, Thanksgiving. From the old pictures we found scattered about, several generations have sat around this table. Years of meals were enjoyed here. Families were planned, futures all mapped out, engagement parties held here, wedding gifts were shown here and baby shower presents piled high. Today, I sat here and planned the deaths of hundreds, perhaps thousands of men. And tomorrow, the home will be burned to the ground. Is it the end of one era and the beginning of another, or just the end, period?"

"You always get this way before a campaign, General," Beth said. "Go have a drink or two."

Ben's eyes widened, for Beth was the quiet one. Then he started laughing, for what she had said was true. He quickly sobered when Corrie said, "Dr. Chase is here, General."

"Chase! Hell, he's supposed to be in the neutral zone in Louisiana, setting up hospitals for the wounded."

"He's pulling up right now. He flew into that strip on the Llano and had a driver bring him here."

"Goddamned old goat. Doesn't he realize this whole area is only hours away from being a free fire zone?"

"Oh, shut up, Raines," Dr. Chase said, stomping into the room. "You don't have enough medical people here to handle the job and you know it. You're going to have badly wounded and you know that too. So stop bitching about it and pour me a cup of coffee."

Cooper was terrified of the old doctor. Jersey just sat and stared at him. If she was afraid of anything, no one knew what it was.

"You, girl," Chase said, looking at her. "Stop giving

me the evil eye. I've known this middle-aged Don Quix-
ote a lot longer than you."

"So what does that make you?" Jersey popped back.
"Sancho Panza?"

Lamar Chase blinked and Ben laughed at the expression on his face. "So let's hear your comeback to that,
Lamar."

"Impudent child," Chase grumbled, and sat down.
He glanced over at Jersey, smiling at him. "You really
read Cervantes?"

"Sure."

"I would have thought your tastes would be more in
line with *Cosmopolitan.*"

Jersey blinked. "What the hell is that?"

SEVEN

After chatting for a few minutes, with Lamar bringing Ben up to date on conditions in the neutral zone, he asked, "Where do you want my MASH units, Ben?"

"I've got dust-offs and fully set-up medivac planes spotted around the area north of both battle sites. Put your field hospitals here at Junction and at Caldwell. Landing strips at both places. I've made agreements with Hoffman to honor his field hospitals and he has agreed to honor ours."

"Do you think he will?"

"For awhile. Until the battles start turning sour on him. And they will."

"You are a supremely confident man, Ben. Considering all that we're up against."

"It's been written that the right cause always wins, Lamar."

"Oh, yes. God on our side and all that," the doctor said. "I just hope somebody remembered to tell *Him* about it."

"Didn't Joan Baez sing a song about God On Our Side, or something like that?"

"Raines, how the hell would I know? You listened to Joan Baez?"

"Sure. And Bob Dylan and Procol Harum . . ."

"Do you have something stuck in your throat?"

"No! That's the name of a group. They did "A Whiter Shade Of Pale." Good tune."

"*You* listened to Bob Dylan?"

"Sure. I can borrow Cooper's guitar and sing you some of his songs?"

"Oh, God, no! The last time you tried to sing your dog ran away from home, women miscarried, and it rained for a week straight. Spare me your dubious vocalizing."

"Now you've hurt my feelings, Lamar."

"Nobody can hurt your feelings. You're an insensitive oaf." He looked at Ben and shook his head. "Don't pout, Raines. It doesn't become you."

"Can I giggle and simper instead?"

"You're making me nauseous. Do you have anything to drink around here?"

"Water."

"Now you can add lying to your other faults," Chase said. "There hasn't been a time in all the years I've known you that you didn't have a bottle stashed somewhere."

"Sorry, Lamar. You're out of luck."

"Isn't it about time for your annual visit to the proctologist?" Chase asked sweetly.

"The booze is over there in my knapsack," Ben said quickly, pointing.

"I knew you would never even consider refusing an old man a drink of whiskey," Chase said, chuckling as he walked to the knapsack.

"You're an evil old man, Lamar," Ben told him.

"I'll never deny it. But it sure has been fun on the journey to that point."

Stretching out east to west for almost two hundred and fifty miles, the Rebels quietly got into position. They moved out in tiny units of two and three vehicles, too small for detection. Hoffman had learned not to put helicopters in the air, for the Rebels had the most sophisticated SAMs in the world, and not one chopper Hoffman sent out had ever returned to the pad.

There were still a lot of people in Texas, and in every other state, whose loyalties did not lie with the Rebels, but they had learned that the Rebels, in this fight for survival, dealt very harshly with collaborators. If a turncoat was not shot or hanged on the spot, they were shipped to California, put on board ship, and off they went to some godforsaken island thousands of miles away, and dumped. And Ben Raines had lots of ships and lots of crew for them.

Those who supported neither Raines nor Hoffman were advised in the strongest of terms to keep their mouths shut. Just behave like those three monkeys: hear nothing, see nothing, and do not speak. And after seeing the cold killing grimness in the eyes of the Rebels; those who wished to remain neutral, and not make the retreat north to the thirty-sixth parallel, quickly agreed that it would be best if they saw nothing, heard nothing, and spoke not a word.

On the night preceding the attack, aides came to the trailer of General Hans Brodermann. Brodermann had a headache and was in no mood to listen to the gloom and doom reports.

"Don't be ridiculous!" he snapped at his people. "The Rebels are not going to attack us. We're too strong and they are too weak. Raines made a mistake in breaking up his battalions into small guerrilla units. He rendered himself nearly impotent. He'll realize that mistake in time, but by then it will be too late. We will hold our positions until long range artillery can join us. Then we shall begin the forward march, clearing out great swatches of territory as we advance. Now return to your commands and get a good night's sleep. We have forward observation posts on alert, and they are manned by the best people we have. Raines and his little mosquito bands will not trouble us here."

Brodermann was correct to a degree. He did have forward observation posts, and they were manned by some very good people. But not as good as the Apache, Pina, Navaho, and Zuni Indians who made up Ben's Special Operations Teams. While Ben and his Rebels had been overseas, those units had been training Stateside in preparation for this. Brodermann's SS units were about to discover what the U.S. Army had learned more than a century past: never underestimate the fighting skills and the stealth of the warriors who made up the Southwest Indian tribes. The SP teams had learned that the SS forward observations teams, with predictable Germanic precision, reported in at 00 hours and again at 0030 hours. On the dot. To the timed second. Which was why Ben had timed the assault to begin at 0535. For at 0531, the forward observation people would be dead in their bunkers. Brodermann would learn to never underestimate the savage and unorthodox fighting techniques of Ben Raines.

The fast attack vehicles of the Rebels had driven to within a couple of miles of the forward observation posts and then cut their muffled down engines and waited. Strict noise discipline was being observed. No one moved, no one talked, no one lit up smokes. At 0525 radio operators turned up the volume and began listening more intently to their earphones for the clicks that would tell them the outposts were cleared of all hostile living things. Except for perhaps a stray scorpion or a rattlesnake.

The sky was just beginning to tint a faint silver in the east when Corrie said, "There it is, General. Two clicks. Repeated. We're clear."

Ben looked at luminous dial of his watch. 0533. "Two minutes to go. Start engines."

Brodermann was beginning to stir under his blankets. He opened his eyes and stretched, reluctant to leave the warmth, for the night had turned unusually cool.

In about sixty seconds it would, quite unexpectedly, warm considerably.

"One minute," Ben said.

Cooper slipped the Hummer into gear. The bolts of mounted .50-caliber machine guns were pulled back. Big Thumpers were armed. Mounted 7.62 M-60s were readied. Grenades were taken from battle harnesses. People swallowed to relieve the mouth-dryness of tension.

"Go!" Ben said.

Corrie relayed the orders as the FAVs lunged forward, big fat tires digging at the ground. Cooper floorboarded the HumVee as Beth stood up and worked her way into the harness behind the roof-mounted M-60. She was bulletproofed from her head down to her hips. The material wouldn't stop a .50-caliber slug, but it would stop anything up to that.

The FAVs sped past the silent forward observation posts and silently screamed toward the still-sleeping camp of the elite SS troops south of Interstate 10 and east of Interstate 30. Ben and his battalion were taking the heaviest unit of SS troops, on Highway 181, next to the San Antonio River and the closest unit to Brodermann's location. Rebet was tackling the SS troops located on 123, east of Cibolo Creek. Danjou and Ned were attacking the SS forces bivouacked on Highway 80, and Buddy was roaring in from the east, hitting those along the Guadalupe River and Highway 111–183.

All units struck within seconds of each other. Striganov and Payon had slipped in and set up old 81-mm mortars and gave Brodermann's camp a full 90 seconds barrage of HE and willie peter as they were storming in.

Hans Brodermann heard the fluttering of mortar rounds and was out of bed and jumping into his trousers and boots just as the first round hit.

"Mein Gott!" he muttered. "It can't be. Raines wouldn't dare!"

But then he had no more time to think as a round exploded very near his quarters and tipped the trailer over. Brodermann went rolling and sliding ass over elbows on the tiled floor and banged his head on the base of the commode, knocking himself goofy for a few minutes.

Outside, the scene was chaos, highlighted by tanker

trucks being ignited, vehicles burning, and the area filled with racing Fast Attack Vehicles and pickup trucks and Hummers, the vehicles scooting around, the machine gunners pouring out heavy fire at anything that moved. Big Thumpers were knocking out grenades and spreading death and confusion all over the place.

The central command of Hans Brodermann was in total chaos. Commanders were trying to rally their troops amid the clattering of machine guns and the roaring of 40 mm grenades. No one could believe it was happening. Something like this was simply not done to the elite troops of the SS.

But it was being done. And being done devastatingly well. Along and south of a two hundred and fifty mile stretch of highway, the Rebels were kicking the shit out of the troops of Field Marshal Jesus Hoffman and enjoying the hell out of it.

The Rebel vehicles made one long pass through the camps and when they pulled out, they left behind them a scene of burning, ruined confusion, the camps littered with dead, dying, and badly wounded.

Ben and his teams hit the SS camp and caught the elite troops of Brodermann with their pants down . . . many literally so, with their bare butts hanging over the edge of the latrines.

It was a dangerous but highly successful move on the part of the Rebels, but also one that in all probability they could never pull again. After this attack, Brodermann would reassess his security and tighten it down.

But that wouldn't help him a bit on this bloody gray Texas morning.

Buddy and his battalion slammed into the SS camp

from the east and caught Hoffman's finest completely by surprise. It was a rout. Many of the SS troops weaponless, caught walking to or from the latrines, to or from the mess tents, or just getting out of bed. Some were naked except for a towel around their waist, ready to walk to the portable showers.

At every location, the Rebels roared up and down between the lines of neatly pitched tents and chopped those SS troops still in their sleeping bags or blankets to bloody rags with automatic weapons' fire. Many of the drivers of the heavier Hummers just took dead aim at the arrow-straight rows of tents and drove right over them, crushing and maiming those unlucky ones still inside.

Hans Brodermann struggled to his feet and fought to claw his way out of the overturned trailer, which he knew could turn into a death trap at any second. He crawled out of the front door, now facing toward the sky, and tumbled to the cool earth, landing heavily on his belly and momentarily knocking the wind out of himself. Cursing, he fought his way to his feet and stood for a moment, shocked and stunned by the sight in front of him.

The early morning grayness was torn by sounds of the deadly surprise attack. Fires were burning out of control and the dead and wounded were sprawled anywhere and everywhere he looked. It was chaos on a scale that he had never before witnessed. His people simply could not get a handle on it; they could not get organized enough to mount even a small counterattack.

Brodermann hit the ground as a FAV came roaring past. The machine gun on the open roof, mounted on the roll-bar, opened up in his direction and the lead howled over his head, tearing great holes in the floor of his trailer. He could do little else but curse Ben Raines. And that he did, with great feeling.

Danjou and Ned ripped through the SS camp at high speed, Rangers in the back of the fortified pickup trucks throwing grenades, manning heavy machine guns, and using Big Thumpers to hurl out their deadly charges.

As Striganov and Payon were completing their final swing of Brodermann's main camp, they gave the orders for the 81 mm mortars to resume their shelling of the camp, using HE and willie peter. Brodermann and his SS troops could do nothing except keep their heads down and try to survive this bloody, terrible, and totally demoralizing Texas morning.

In every Rebel battalion, Ben had issued orders to certain teams to do nothing except concentrate on crippling or destroying Brodermann's vehicles. When the assaults finally ended—the attacks lasting no more than three or four minutes maximum—the Rebels left behind them a scene that was enough to make even the most seasoned combat veteran weep.

Flames were leaping upward, the smell of burning rubber offensively harsh in the cool air. The smoke from the many fires was thick, hanging close to the cool earth, and nearly blinding. The screaming of the wounded was awful. Many of those caught in their tents had crushed limbs from the Rebel vehicles running over them. Stores of ammunition were cracking and popping and for any of the SS troops to move was a danger from the exploding rounds of their own stockpiles.

The Rebels had killed or wounded nearly fifty percent of Brodermann's SS troops. They took no prisoners. They showed no mercy. The Rebels were ruthless and savage and to the survivors of the early morning attack, it told them what they had to look forward to in fighting Ben Raines and his people. Most did not relish the thought.

An aide came running up to Brodermann as he was slowly getting to his feet. Brodermann was badly shaken. Nothing like this had ever happened to him. It was . . . unthinkable. Gnats like the Rebels were supposed to be merely irritating, certainly not deadly and dangerous.

"Do we mount a counterattack, General?" he yelled to be heard over the roaring of the fires and the cracking and popping of small arms ammunition.

Hans Brodermann stared at the wild-eyed man with blood from a slight head-wound trickling down one side of his face. "No," Brodermann finally found his voice. He coughed to clear his throat of the nearly choking smoke that swirled all around the camp. "Raines would love that. You may be sure he has planted ambush teams all along the roadways, hoping for us to pursue. Are we in contact with the other battalions?"

"All units seem to have been attacked. The Rebels struck at every location. We have reports that bridges were blown all around us."

"Send out small patrols to assess the damage. Check the forward posts. I have a hunch you will find only dead men."

"Yes, sir. I will send men over to right your trailer and start repairs."

Brodermann turned and looked at his bullet-pocked quarters, lying on its side like some dead prehistoric beast. "Leave the son of a bitch where it is," he said bitterly. "You can bet Ben Raines does not have such luxury with him. We can no longer count on fighting a conventional war, Willie. When all damages have been tallied, report to me. Then I must report to Field Marshal Hoffman. It is a bitter day, Willie. A bitter day."

Hundreds of yards away from Hans Brodermann, two senior SS sergeants looked at one another. One said, "I think we made a mistake in coming to North America. A very fatal mistake."

EIGHT

The Rebels lost five people, with a dozen wounded, two of them seriously. Miles north of the burning camps of Brodermann's troops, they quietly buried their dead in secluded places and conducted simple ceremonies.

Then they mounted up and pulled out, heading for a central rendezvous point.

"Spread out," Ben told his people. "From the Devils River in the west to the San Jacinto in the east. Hit whatever you think you can successfully tackle. I want these goose-stepping bastards held below the twenty-eighth parallel for as long as possible. The longer we can contain them down here, the stronger our people get above the thirty-sixth." The Rebel commanders shook hands all the way around and took off.

Ben and his teams moved to just outside Kerrville, secured their vehicles in several of the many buildings in the old religious encampment, and settled in, monitoring the still-frantic radio transmissions from the Black-shirts.

Even Ben was stunned to learn that the attacks had killed or wounded nearly half of Brodermann's forces.

His eyes touched the eyes of his team and several other Rebels attached to him. The eyes were smiling, hard warrior smiles.

It was then that Ben realized the Rebel movement would never die, never be defeated. As long as there was one Rebel left alive, the movement would live. The Rebels did not consider their way to be perfect. They were not striving for perfection. The past system of justice and law and order and all that went with the forming of a society had deteriorated to a confusing and nonworkable mess when the Great War came and wiped the slate clean. Then the Rebels spent years cleaning out the scum and the dregs of society, the human predators. They knew their system of government worked; they had seen it work for nearly a decade. Not for everybody, for a system of laws and rules cannot be devised that will please everyone. But enough people agreed with the Rebel way to try to live under it, with more coming in every day.

It would not die. The Rebels would not, could not, let it die.

And Ben knew they wouldn't let that happen.

"Company coming," a guard called out. "Forward people are bringing them in."

Ben stepped out to meet the people, and pegged them at once. Religious fanatics. He'd never met a religious fanatic yet who didn't share, to some degree, the same look of arrogant smugness, of a closed mind to all opinions save what they personally embraced, and they all irritated the hell out of Ben.

"General Raines," the Rebel said, "these people are from something called the Church of the Only Holy Way."

"Wonderful," Ben muttered. "I guess that means if you don't belong to their faith you will be denied entrance to Heaven."

"Exactly, sir," one of the younger men in the group said.

"Horseshit," Ben told him.

The young man blinked. "I beg to remind you there are ladies present, sir."

"If you say so." Ben looked at the dozen or so men and women, most of them in their late twenties or early thirties. They all looked healthy and well-fed. And Ben didn't like or trust any of them. "What do you people want?"

"Protection from the advancing hordes of mongrels."

"Where are your weapons?"

"We don't believe in violence, sir."

"Then turn right around and carry your butts on out of here," Ben replied. "I'm not your nanny."

"General," a rather pretty woman said.

"I'm not going to argue the point with you, lady. If you don't place enough value on your life to fight for it, then I have no use for you. Now is there anything else you want?"

"I was told you were a cruel man, General Raines," a beady-eyed young man said, waving a Bible at Ben. "But until now, I did not realize just how cruel."

Ben stared at the young man. It has been noted by everyone who ever got personally close to Ben that when he stared at you, his eyes could take on the predatory stare of an eagle just before it sank its talons into prey. The young man suddenly got a case of the twitchy-itches.

"I may be cruel, sonny-boy. That's not for me to decide. But what I really am is a realist. And you are beginning to get on my nerves. Now it would be a very wise thing for you and your little group of religious bigots to get in your jalopies or on your bicycles and drive or pedal the hell north. Up to the thirty-sixth parallel. That is roughly a line stretching east to west, right across the center of the nation. It goes through some fascinating places. Roanoke, Louisville, St. Louis, Colorado Springs. Of course, few of those cities are standing now, but I'm sure you could find some converts among the rubble. I'm equally certain they would rape your women, butt-fuck you men, and then turn you into slaves, swap you off for a good horse, or have you for dinner. And if you're so stupid you won't pick up a weapon to save your own lives, then I want nothing to do with you. Now get the hell out of here."

"May God strike you dead, Ben Raines!" a woman shouted.

Ben laughed at her. "Now that is interesting, lady. First you tell me you don't believe in violence, now you're imploring God to strike me dead. You're not very consistent, are you?"

She stood and glared at him.

Ben said, "Get them out of here and on their way north. Somebody up there will look after them."

"Suppose they won't go?" the Rebel asked.

Ben shrugged his shoulders. "Then that makes it their problem, doesn't it?"

"You'll burn in the hellfires for this, Ben Raines," the beady-eyed young man shouted, waving his Bible "God is on our side."

"I do believe I've heard that one before," Jersey muttered.

Ben smiled and waved at the group and stepped back inside the building. Some of the religious fanatics tried to follow him. Jersey stopped that movement by applying the butt of her M-16 to the belly of the beady-eyed follower of the Church of the Only Holy Way. He folded up like a piece of paper and hit the ground, coughing and gagging.

"You'll suffer mightily for that, sister!" a woman shouted. "For you have struck a messenger from God."

Jersey narrowed her eyes and opened her mouth to give the woman a personal message. A very personal message. Cooper could attest to the fact that when Jersey decided to verbally unload on a person, it was like firecrackers exploding around one's head.

"Let it alone, Jersey," Ben said from the open doorway. "It just isn't worth it. Believe me, I know from experience."

When Jersey gave the beady-eyed messenger the butt of her rifle, the area around the front of the house suddenly filled with armed Rebels. The group who had confronted Ben very quickly got the message: their lives were on the line, and they were toeing that line awfully close.

"Peace, brothers and sisters," one of the group said. "Allow us to leave and we shall depart quietly."

"Haul your butts, then," Cooper said.

The group got their messenger up on his feet and led him away. He was a little pale and a tad shaky.

Ben was studying a map when his team joined him in the large office of the old complex. A seasoned Rebel medic, but a newcomer to Ben's personal detachment, said, "You don't like those kinds of people very much, do you, General."

Ben looked up and smiled at the Rebel. A medic that Doctor Chase had transferred to Ben's command. "Book-burners," he said. "Self-appointed censors hiding behind their own narrow interpretation of the Bible. In their own way, they are no better than the worst racist group we have ever encountered. We demand a lot from our own people, but there is no one religion among our ranks. I don't care if you worship a kumquat. Just don't try to force me to do it. I've disliked those kinds of people ever since I was old enough to reason. They're bullies and cowards waving a Bible. I don't give a damn what happens to them." He put his reading glasses back on and resumed his studying of the map. The subject was closed.

Field Marshal Jesus Hoffman sat in his quarters and looked at the wall. The report transmitted from General Hans Brodermann and typed up by his staff lay on his desk. The most elite and combat-experienced of all his troops had been overrun and their numbers cut in half by a Rebel sneak attack during the predawn hours. Tons of equipment lost. Vehicles destroyed. Hundreds of weapons and thousands of rounds of ammunition gone, much of it taken by the marauding Rebels. His people were badly demoralized. The advance had been brought to an abrupt halt.

What manner of men and women were these Rebels?

He called out at the knock on his door, and the office filled with his most experienced commanders, from Captain to General. They sat at his gesture and waited in silence.

Hoffman stood up and looked at the group. Finally he

said, "We have marched thousands of miles. We have faced and overcome savage Indian tribes and armies whose numbers were ten times greater than those of the Rebels. Now we have scarcely advanced one hundred and fifty miles into North America and our losses number into the thousands. And they have been inflicted upon us by a band of men and women whose numbers don't even equal one of our divisions.

"To the west of us, a mere three battalions of Rebels have effectively halted our advance into California, Arizona, and New Mexico. A very magnificent advance of ten to fifteen miles, I might add. The entire way drenched with blood. Our blood—not theirs. Disgraceful. To date, a rag tag band of North American malcontents, led by a middle-aged man, have managed to bring down the government of the United States, wipe out most of the bands of outlaws and mercenaries, kill off the world's best known and respected terrorists, defeat and destroy the armies of Khamsin, Lan Villar, and others, then sail halfway around the world and defeat Jack Hunt and his armies in Ireland, move to England and destroy the gangs there, free Hawaii, and now they have stopped us dead in our tracks. How?"

His commanders remained silent. They no more had the answer to that than did Field Marshal Hoffman.

Hoffman did not let up. "And to further worsen the situation, Ben Raines has not defeated us with mighty salvos of artillery and huge tank battles. His people are attacking in small numbers in pickup trucks and light vehicles. And on at least two occasions my armies have been stopped and humiliated by a bunch of goddamn Texas cowboys on *horseback!* We are the finest equipped army on the face of the earth"—Wrong! He just thought that. Ben's Rebels had equipment that Hoffman and his people did not even know existed—"and our people are being defeated by mounted Texas Rangers. On *horseback*, for God's sake! Charging us with six-shooters blazing!"

"Ah, actually, Field Marshal," a general dared contradict, "most of those Rangers were using 9-mm semiautomatic pistols and H&Ks or Uzis."

"They were still riding goddamn horses, weren't they?" Hoffman flared, sitting down behind his desk.

"Ah . . . yes, sir. Twice, that we know of."

"What do you mean: 'that we know of?' "

"They don't take prisoners, sir. And they seldom leave survivors."

"Well, don't just sit there with your long faces hanging out. You are among the finest minds I have. Give me some suggestions and solutions."

A young major stood up. "Sir. What Ben Raines wants us to do is break up our forces and fight him guerrilla style. I feel that would be a grave mistake."

"State your objections to that," Hoffman ordered.

"General Raines and all his commanders know the country. They know it from coast to coast, border to border. They have supplies hidden in hundreds, perhaps *thousands* of secret caches. They have millions and millions of gallons of fuel hidden. Probably *billions* of rounds of ammunition and explosives. Several years ago our intelligence people reported that Raines' doctors and scientists have antibiotics—in powder form, sealed in air-tight containers—which will last for years. All they have to do is set up a portable lab, add water, or a few chemicals, and go from there. General Raines planned for this invasion, all the while hoping it would never come, but he was certainly going to be ready for it if it did occur. Our supplies are right now days behind us, struggling to reach us. And that's if we don't move from this location. I realize I am the youngest and least experienced man here, Field Marshal. But you asked for suggestions. I am afraid I do not have any solutions."

"Thank you for speaking your mind, Major." Hoffman knew the young major was brilliant, and felt that he had not spoken everything on his mind. He smiled at the major. "What would you do if you were sitting in this chair instead of me?"

"I honestly do not know, sir. And I admit that I have thought of what I might do. I could reach no conclusion."

Hoffman stared at the young major for a moment, then nodded his head. "Thank you, Major Weber. I appreciate your candor."

Weber sat down. He knew he had not won any points with the older commanders present, but he had won some points with the Field Marshal, and that was all that mattered.

Hoffman drummed his fingers on the desk for a moment. "General Brodermann learned a hard lesson about the Rebels. But what happened was not entirely his fault. We had to learn how the enemy would fight, and now we know. With savage ruthlessness. Giving no quarter, asking none. And that's the way we must fight them. We will hold here until our supplies reach us. A week; no more than that. Brodermann has asked that he be allowed to maintain his point position. I have said yes. General Schiller, start our terrorist groups marching at once. Spread them all over the nation. They know what they must do, and being terrorists, they do it extremely well."

"Yes, Field Marshal. At once."

"General Jahn, are your *fallschirmtruppen* ready?"

"Ya, Field Marshal. My paratroops are ready to go at your signal."

"Colonel Barlach, are you ready to receive prisoners for interrogation?"

"Yes, sir."

Hoffman smiled. "General Daimler?"

"Sir?"

"Do be so kind as to bring Colonel Barlach some prisoners. You know how testy he can be when he is not inflicting pain on someone."

NINE

"General Payon's eyes and ears in Mexico say that Hoffman's supply trucks will reach him in less than a week. Planes are already landing at the strip near his CP," Corrie said.

"I wish I knew what he was up to," Ben mused. "Beth, did our people get anything of value from those prisoners we picked up and shipped over to Cecil?"

"Nothing, sir. They just don't know anything of value. Obviously, Hoffman and his top people play it pretty close to the vest."

"And reports of random acts of terrorism are still coming in?"

"Yes, sir," Corrie said. "Savage, brutal, and totally senseless acts."

"He's cut his radical fringe loose," Ben said.

"All those messages we received for years were true," Beth said. "The hate for America never died."

"So it seems," Ben said softly. "Those fruitcake groups still hate America and Americans as much, or more, as before. I didn't understand it then, and I still don't." He smiled at his team. "Don't look so startled, people. There are a lot of things that I didn't and don't understand. Probably never will. Where was the latest attack, Corrie?"

"About a hundred miles northeast of here. A Rebel patrol found what was left of the elderly couples. Four couples. Patrols had tried to evac them but they said they'd lived in that area all their lives and weren't about to move now. They were all tortured to death."

"Let's take a ride," Ben said.

The four couples, all in their late seventies or early eighties, had lived in a large rambling one story home. They had worked a large garden, had chickens and hogs, and kept the place neat and had obviously been living a quiet and contented life. Ben stood in the large living room and looked at the words written in blood on the walls.

"Mideast fanaticism shit," he said, disgust in his voice. "Praise Allah and all that crap. Die in battle and go straight to paradise. Real brave bunch, this group is. Killing a small band of nearly helpless elderly men and women really strikes a blow for their cause. Providing they even know what that cause is, which I doubt."

His team remained silent, for they knew that the harming of helpless children and elderly or innocent animals could push Ben's danger meter over into the red. Cooper, watching Ben's face, had him a hunch that when they caught up with this bunch—and they would, he had no doubts about that—the outcome for this terrorist group would be about as pleasant as a crucifixion.

"Buddy's here," Jersey said, looking out a blood-splattered window. "He's got a prisoner."

Ben stepped outside to face the dark eyed, olive-skinned man with his hands tied behind his back. Father looked at son. "Where'd you find this piece of shit?"

The prisoner hissed and spat at Ben, the spittle staining Ben's shirt.

"About fifteen miles from here. We think he got separated from the main group. The only thing he will say is how much he hates America and Americans."

"Jew-lover!" the man spat out the words, his hard bright eyes staring at Ben.

"And that," Buddy added. "He has a terrible complex when it comes to Judaism."

"Torture me!" the man shouted. "I will tell you nothing. I will soar on the wings of pain to Paradise."

"Oh, you're going to soar, all right," Ben told the man. "But not on the wings of pain." Ben looked at the man and woman from the Rebels' intelligence section. "He's all yours."

The two-person team picked up their briefcases of chemicals and walked toward a small shed. "Come on, Ali," the woman said without looking back. "You're going to sail as high as an eagle can fly."

"I will tell you nothing!" the man shouted.

"Wanna bet?" Ben asked, his smile as hard as flint.

"I think we might have overdone it," the woman said. "We turned him into a babbling idiot."

"I'm very nearly overcome with grief," Ben said, pouring a cup of coffee from the pot on the grate over the small fire in the yard. "I might start flailing myself with ropes and chains at any moment. What'd you learn?"

"His team is working close," the man said, as the

woman poured herself a cup of coffee. "Hoffman sent out several hundred teams to terrorize and demoralize the citizens, all over the United States. Every damn lunatic group that ever existed has linked up with Hoffman. And since you used to work for the CIA, you're a main target, General."

"What else is new?" Ben muttered. "Back when the world was more or less functioning I used to get a half dozen death threats a year . . . at least."

"Didn't the Agency protect you?" the woman asked, looking up from the fire.

"You have to be joking!" Ben said with a smile. "Someone filed some lousy reports on me. They shoved me out in the cold and left me dangling. Said I'd been a bad boy. I told them if I hadn't of been a bad boy, I wouldn't have spent years in Operations. They failed to see the humor in that." He laughed. "It could have been worse. They could have kept me on and assigned me to the Mideast desk."

"What do you want us to do with the sheik of Araby in there?"

"Drag him outside, pump him with enough joy-juice to float him to paradise and leave him for the buzzards."

"And then?" Buddy asked.

"We go terrorize some terrorists. They won't be hard to find. We'll just follow the trail of blood and bodies they leave behind. That's all the hell they've ever known how to do. And they do it well."

Ben split his teams and told them to work every road. Visit every house in every hamlet. Get any people left started north across the parallel—if they chose to go— and kill terrorists. Continue burning anything that

108

would torch. Leave nothing behind for Hoffman's Blackshirts.

Ben's team drew first blood. A forward FAV, ranging miles ahead, radioed back that they had spotted what appeared to be very furtive movement in a tiny hamlet that had been reported totally void of life only a few days back.

"Hold it there," Ben said. "Don't give away your position. We're on the way."

It was dry rolling hills country. Ben and team parked, hiding their vehicles carefully and walked to the Scouts' position on a rise that overlooked the dusty little hamlet.

"We've counted eighteen so far," the Scout leader said. "We think there's maybe double that. It appears to be a meeting of some sort. Two groups have joined the ones already here. They work in six person teams."

"All right," Ben said. "We'll wait and see if more join them. We'll send as many as possible of these cowardly bastards to hell. Spread out. Work low and slow."

"General," Corrie said. "Buddy is in a firefight with some sort of hostile group about thirty miles west of here. He says they'll be able to contain the situation, but won't be able to lend us a hand for several hours, at least."

"I don't recall asking for his help. My God, but he's getting to be as worrisome as Ike. Tell him to mind his own business."

Corrie turned her head and bumped Buddy. But she softened Ben's reply, as Ben knew she would.

The Rebels crept into position and waited. The terrorists below them were fruitcakes and screwballs, but they were also professionals who, judging by their movements, had received extensive amounts of training in their deadly art. The Rebels soon pinpointed the location of the guards and as the day wore on, knew to the minute when they would be changed. Four more six-person teams drifted in, all coming in from the north and the east. That made at least forty two terrorists in the small village and possibly as many as sixty, or more.

Ben smiled at the number. He had twenty four people with him, having eluded the others that Ike had saddled him with. It should be a real interesting fight.

"We have to assume there are no civilians down there," Ben said. "And if there are, they're there willingly. We have heard no screams of pain or shouts of protest." He looked at his watch. Two hours had passed since the last team had checked in. "Those people made one big mistake, gang. There is but one road leading in and out of that village. And we have it covered. Tell the mortar crews to start shelling, Corrie."

The town must have been where the terrorists were storing supplies. Perhaps they had returned there to re-supply. The Rebels would never know. The third mortar round landed in the center of an old service station/garage and when it blew it took nearly all of that side of the block with it. Bodies and body parts were flung in all directions and the blast was so heavy the concussion from it flattened two frame structures located directly across from the garage, on the other side of the street.

Wounded and dazed and confused terrorists staggered out of the remaining buildings and the Rebels shot them down where they stood. The memory of those tortured and butchered elderly people was vividly fresh in their minds.

Ben and his people left their positions and walked down to the tiny town, now devastated, the streets slick with blood spots. Ben stood over a woman with more than a tad of Oriental blood in her . . . and all around her. Ben guessed her age at about thirty five. It was hard to tell. Her eyes shone hate up at him. She spat at him, the bloody spittle landing near Ben's lace-up work boots.

"What nitwit group did you belong to?" Ben asked her.

She cursed him in very fluent English.

Ben picked up her Uzi, handed it to a Rebel, and walked away, leaving her to die with a curse on her lips and hate for America in her heart. "Be sure and strip the ammo belt from her," Ben called over his shoulder.

"Sure is a mixed bag," Jersey remarked, walking beside Ben. "Oriental, Black, Hispanic, and Arabic." She looked around at the dead and dying and the ripped and shattered bodies. "They must have had a ton of explosives in that garage."

Ben squatted down and rolled a cigarette. He watched as his two medics went from terrorist to terrorist, checking them. He offered them no pain killers, no medicines, no patch jobs. They had dedicated their lives to inflicting pain on innocents; they could die the same way.

There was an occasional shot as some of the less seriously wounded terrorists tried to make a fight of it. It was not much of a fight.

"Buddy just a mile out of town," Corrie said.

Ben ground the butt of his cigarette out under his heel. He didn't feel like putting up with another antismoking lecture from his son.

"Father, where is the rest of your detachment?" Buddy asked, walking up. He sniffed the air suspiciously and looked accusingly at his dad. But he sensed Ben was in no mood for a lecture and left it at that.

"I sent them to another suspected terrorist site. It's rather difficult to move about unobtrusively with a god-damn platoon following me."

Buddy looked around him at the devastation. "What did you drop on this town, a mini atomic bomb?"

"Three mortar rounds, kid. The third round landed in a storage area filled with some sort of explosives and drums of gasoline. It was a rather large boom."

"So I see. That group we came in contact with mistakenly thought we were part of Hoffman's army. They did not like our surrender terms."

"And?"

"Well, after negotiations failed, we eventually stacked the bodies in several buildings and set them on fire. It was a dreadful smell."

"Before or during the burning?"

"Both."

The Rebels talked casually of the deaths of their enemies. Most would work feverishly to save the life of a hurt dog or cat. They would weep over the body of a fallen buddy. They would risk their lives a hundred and one times a day to save any innocent person. But their unofficial motto was an eye for an eye plus the head of an enemy. A Rebel would crawl through his own blood, holding his guts inside his shattered stomach with one hand, just to kill an enemy. Ben had told them once that was the unofficial motto of the old Israeli Mossad, and it fit the Rebels rather well. Which was why they had never been defeated and never would be defeated. They would lose battles, but not the war.

One final shot was heard at the far end of the mangled street. A Rebel walked over to investigate. "Another terrorist, General," he called. "She shot herself in the head rather than surrender to us."

"Gather up everything we can use and load it in the trucks Buddy has tagging along with him."

"Thank you very much, father," Buddy said sourly.

"You're quite welcome, son. What are you doing with those deuce and a halves, looting the countryside?"

Buddy walked off, muttering to himself.

Ben was not nearly as charitable as his son. He ordered the bodies left where they were. "Let the buzzards have them," he told his people. "Mount up. We've got to hunt a hole and stay down for a time."

"Twenty eight teams have failed to check in," Field Marshal Hoffman was informed the next morning. "Including most of the Syrian teams."

"How overdue are they?" Hoffman asked, as his stomach abruptly turned sour. He belched and patted his lips with a napkin. He looked down at his breakfast and suddenly lost his appetite.

"A full twenty-four hours."

Hoffman sighed and pushed back from the table. "They're lost, then. Goddamn that Ben Raines. Goddamn him, you hear?"

The Blackshirt heard, as did anyone else within a hundred yards of the lavishly appointed trailer, for Jesus Hoffman was shouting.

The word quickly spread and the commanders of the thousands of troops gathered in the huge miles-long encampment rushed to the trailer, to stand outside and listen to the Field Marshal rant and rave.

"No more!" Hoffman shouted. "No goddamn more! I will not tolerate it."

The news of the Field Marshal's tantrum quickly spread and the entire encampment soon grew eerily silent. Mechanics put down their wrenches, cooks turned the fires low, infantry personnel stopped the cleaning of weapons.

"We did not march thousands of miles to be held at bay by a ragged bunch of malcontents led by an idealistic dreamer!" Hoffman thundered.

"No, sir," the messenger said. He wished he was facing a band of Rebels at this moment. He wished he could be anywhere except where he was.

Hoffman lost what was left of his composure. He picked up his freshly poured cup of coffee and hurled it against the wall of the trailer.

Hoffman whirled to face the young messenger. "Without Ben Raines, the Rebel movement would crumble. Chop the head from a snake and the snake dies." Hoffman looked at the messenger as if seeing him for the first time. "What do you want? Send someone in here immediately to clean up this mess. Get out of here!"

The messenger hit the air.

Jesus Dieguez Mendoza Hoffman clenched his fists, forced himself to take several deep breaths, and calmed his raging emotions. He stood for a moment, staring out of the window of the trailer. For the first time since his outburst he was aware of the hundreds of troops all gathered outside, quietly waiting. He looked at his commanders, standing close to his quarters. Hoffman walked to the door and slowly opened it. He waved to his senior commanders, motioning them to his quarters.

His composure fully restored, Hoffman sat down at his desk and waited until his people had taken seats. "Gentlemen, we have been held at bay by a pack of barking dogs long enough. We have allowed ourselves to be frightened and cowed by this tiny band headed by Ben Raines. Effective this moment, that will cease. The greatest army on the face of the earth has been forced into a defensive position. Think of the absurdity of that. The ridiculousness of it. Impress that upon your troops. Show them how they have been humiliated by a tiny band of men and women in blue jeans and cowboy boots, racing about in little puny vehicles . . . and on horseback," he spat the last. "Brandishing six-shooters and waving the flag of Texas."

Hoffman stared at his commanders, crowded into the room. He smiled at the group. "Three days from now, at dawn, we move out. In force. We launch a full-scale attack against the Rebels. In one week, I plan to have the entire state of Texas under our control."

TEN

"Not damn likely," Ben said, after reading the communique just decoded by his people. He laughed softly. "So Herr Hoffman plans to strike fear into our hearts by flexing his muscles, eh? All right. We'll let him flex his muscles. Corrie, has this communique been sent out to all our people?"

"Waiting for your orders to do so," she replied.

"Do it. Then tell them to stand by for further instructions."

Ben walked to a map thumbtacked to a wall of the old church rectory and studied it. He smiled and looked at Beth, standing by with pad and pen at the ready. "As soon as Hoffman makes his move, have all our people fall back. Have our people immediately begin gathering up all the broken weapons we've picked up, all the wornout clothing and boots. All the patched and useless tarps and ground-sheets and shelter-halves. Gather up all the ripped and torn underwear and socks. Pile up busted canteens and rusty eating utensils and the like and get ready to scatter them along the way. I want this to look like a complete rout on our part. We are fleeing for our lives, people. We are turning tail and running away from the awesome forces of Hoffman. We are frightened to death of the Blackshirts. Their advance has demoralized us all. Their might has turned us into rabbits. Order everyone to fall back to the thirtieth parallel. Start all the battalions I've held in reserve working their way south. Right now. Tell them to stay at least a hundred miles east or west of Hoffman's northern push." Ben chuckled, but it held an ominous note. "So come on, Hoffman. Show me what a brilliant strategist you are. Strike fear into my heart, you evil bastard!"

"Ike reporting, sir," Corrie said. "He says that the Blackshirts are pulling away from their lines and heading east, on the south side of the border. Hold on, sir. Colonels Gray and West calling in. They say the same thing."

"Get hold of our eyes below the border, Corrie. Ask them what Hoffman has left down there for reserve. He's got to have stretched himself pretty damn thin."

"I did, sir. He's left behind small garrisons of troops in selected towns. But mostly he's depending on the local bully-boys to keep the people in line."

"We know he has several more divisions down in South America," Ben mused. "But we also know he's short on wheeled transportation. Like us, he has plenty of prop-planes, but damn few jets and fewer pilots to fly them." Ben paced as he spoke. "We'd be wasting explosives blowing airports. You can land most of those old transports of ours, and his, on practically any runway a crop-duster could use."

Ben walked to the everpresent coffee pot and poured a mug. He sugared and stirred and sipped. Then he smiled. "Hoffman anticipated my move. He felt I would swing troops around to nip at his sides, so he's pulled his western troops in to protect his flanks. And he's hoping I wouldn't pull my battalions out of the west and give him a hole that I'm wagering he had no intention of using. Well, the Nazi son of a bitch guessed wrong!"

"Order our three battalions in, sir?" Corrie asked.

"You bet." He smiled once more. "Float like a butterfly and sting like a bee."

"Sir?" Beth asked.

"A champion prizefighter used to say that . . . or something to that effect. It fits us rather well, I think. Because that's exactly what we're going to do."

Jersey and Cooper exchanged glances, Cooper whispering, "Now it's gettin' down to the way the General likes to fight."

"Yeah," Jersey returned the whisper. "Kick-ass time!"

There were those in Hoffman's command who questioned his decision to launch a full-scale attack deep into the heart of Texas, but only the most brave questioned it aloud, and then only among the closest of friends:

Brodermann was not one of those who questioned his Field Marshal's order. He looked forward to this massive thrust of men and machines of war. Hans had a very personal score to settle with Ben Raines, and the sooner the better was his philosophy on the subject.

He had asked to spearhead, and was given the green light. His people were ready, and he now waited for the word.

"What is the status of those Rebels in California, Arizona, and New Mexico?" Hoffman asked, on the night before the pullout.

"They are still there. Your plan worked, sir. They remained in position, afraid to leave the route unguarded."

Hoffman smiled. It was going to work.

Actually, the three battalion commanders did leave some people behind. Seventy-five from each battalion. They kept cook fires burning, kicked up dust running around in cars and trucks, played catch with baseballs and footballs and so forth, and in general maintained a very high profile.

Since the black-shirted troops left behind to watch the Rebels were fewer in number than those they spied upon, neither side was in very much danger from the other. It was just a variation on the game of hide and seek, so to speak.

Albeit a deadly one if those south of the border ever caught on to what was actually happening north of them.

Brodermann radioed back to Hoffman, excitement in his voice. "It's a rout, Field Marshal. A complete rout. They're leaving equipment behind in their haste to retreat. Our people are stocking up on field rations—cases of them. We've tested them and they have not been tampered with. They're really quite delicious."

The Rebels had been only too happy to throw away the goop that Dr. Chase's lab boys and girls had dreamed up for them to eat. It was highly nutritious and packed with vitamins and minerals and tasted like shit.

"They abandoned clothing and weapons and canteens. Many were so frightened they left their boots.

They left behind cases and cases of field rations. More than enough to sustain my people for a week or more."

The only hitch the Rebels' lab people hadn't worked out was that the rations tended to make one constipated. As Brodermann's people were about to discover.

"Maintain your position," Hoffman ordered his spearheader. "I want to see this personally."

"They took the bait," Corrie reported, after all the info was in from communications. "They sound elated."

"I hope they eat all that goopy shit," Ben said, aware of Dr. Chase standing close, scowling at him. Ben turned to meet the frowning chief of medicine. "And I'm telling you for the last time, Lamar: have your people come up with something less nutritious and more on the tasty side."

"I've already ordered that, Raines," the crusty old doctor popped right back at him. "The first shipments should be arriving by planes within hours."

"Good. Green eggs and ham was wonderful in book form. It isn't worth a damn at four o'clock in the morning."

"You are belaboring the point, Raines. Shut up about it. And where did you get that sombrero you've plopped on your head? You look like Hoot Gibson."

"Who the hell is Hoot Gibson?" Jersey whispered to Cooper.

"He's taking a hell of a chance," Thermopolis spoke to a few of his staff members at one of their communications and HQ bunkers deep in the Arkansas mountains. "This could backfire on him. But I can see why he's doing it."

120

Emil Hite, the little ex-conman turned loyal Rebel, was not his usual joking self. He was serious as he studied the big board, denoting the positions of all the Rebels, all around the shattered land that was once called the United States. Someone was constantly changing the board.

"But if Hoffman continues to fall for it," Emil said, "he'll be in one hell of a bind, once the General starts attacking from all sides."

"Big 'ifs,' Emil," Therm said softly. "Real big 'ifs.' "

Ike, Dan Gray, and West were moving east, staying on secondary roads and keeping Scouts ranging far out front at all times.

Leadfoot and Wanda had cleared their sector of Hoffman's Blackshirts and all the collaborators they could find and were now barreling west. They had taken the southernmost route across Louisiana, staying in the bayou country, and had crossed into Texas on what remained of old I-90. The ex-outlaw bikers had picked up dozens of other bikers who wanted to be a part of Raines' Rebels, and it was an awesome sight as the several hundred strong bikers, all heavily armed, came roaring westward on their choppers and custom motorcycles. In the old Sam Houston National Forest, they pulled in and made contact with Ben's HQ.

"Leadfoot on the horn, sir," Corrie said.

Ben took the mic. "Go, Leadfoot."

"Got nearly four hundred bikers now, Eagle," Leadfoot radioed. "We're in the southernmost trees named after one of the commanders at the Alamo. You ten-four that?"

"Sam Houston National Park," Beth said, lowering a map.

"I copy that, Leadfoot. Straight west of you is a MASH unit. You know their frequency. Head there and await orders."

"That's a big ten-four, Eagle. Give 'em hell. Wolf Pack out."

"Hoffman and Brodermann just think they've seen unconventional warfare," Ben said with a smile. "Wait until they tangle with that bunch of outlaws."

"You have done well, Hans," Hoffman said, beaming with satisfaction at the seemingly endless trail of discarded equipment left behind by the "fleeing Rebels." "I am now certain we shall be in full control of Texas in a week's time. After that, it's just a matter of tracking down the retreating Rebels and disposing of them. Do try to take General Raines alive. Colonel Barlach is so looking forward to interrogating the good General Raines."

"I shall do my best, sir."

"I know you will."

Dr. Chase had moved his MASH units about a hundred miles north, to Ballinger on old Highway 83, and to Hillsboro on 35. Ben and his Rebels carried on with their systematic destroying of towns and cities and the blowing of major bridges.

If at all possible, Ben intended to hold Hoffman south of I-20. But with the massive firepower of the man, he didn't know if that was possible.

Like the mule, all he could do was try.

"It's time to pull the plug on Hoffman's advance," he told his team. "We've got to knock out some of his tanks. Once that's done, we can uncork our own tanks and meet his on a equal basis. Our tanks are far superior. They're better armored, have heavier firepower, and are faster. What are the latest reports?"

"Hoffman has committed eight divisions north of the border," Beth said. "He has four divisions in reserve."

Ben shook his head. He had been stunned when he had heard the rumor of the revised figures of Hoffman's strength. He had been shocked when he found out they were true. "Twelve full divisions," Ben said softly. "Approximately two hundred thousand men. Minus about fifteen thousand that our little ragtag bunch of boys and girls have managed to send to that great Nazi heaven in the skies."

Ben walked to a map. "The arrogant bastard has spread himself over three hundred miles of territory, committing a full division up eight routes. Look at what's he's done. We've stopped him dead bang cold on 163 just north of Barnhart by blowing those bridges. We've stopped him at the ruins of San Angelo. We've trapped him and stopped him between the Llano and the San Saba. We've blown every bridge on 87 and stopped him dead. Same on Highways 16, 281, 81, and 77. He's most vulnerable on Highway 77. His people are exposed and in danger and the silly bastard can't see that. Order Buddy, O'Shea, and the Wolfpack to start hammering at that part of the division that someone foolishly placed over here on 36. They're cut off. We've blown all the bridges between 77 and 36. Get them moving, Corrie."

There was nothing Hoffman could do except pace up and down as his engineers, now stretched pitifully thin along three hundred miles, worked feverishly to lay temporary bridges across rivers and creeks. None of his commanders dared approach him to point out that several battalions of his troops were cut off and dangerously exposed. Hoffman was in no mood for a critique of his strategy.

Hoffman ordered spotter planes up; the Rebels brought them down with SAMs. Rebel long-distance shooters, armed with .50-caliber sniper rifles lay hidden along the north shores of the rivers and creeks and terrorized the Nazi engineers.

Hoffman dared not send teams across to hunt down the snipers, not after the first few attempts. Ben had anticipated that and had Scouts and Recon teams in place to ambush the Blackshirts as they tried to circle around the snipers, who were firing from as far away as a mile and a half.

Hoffman ordered his artillery to lay down covering fire in an attempt to kill the snipers. As long as the bombardments lasted, the snipers were quiet and his engineers could work. Once the bombardments ceased, the snipers popped up and started shooting. Hoffman's engineers finally had to build thick shields and work behind them, which slowed them down to less than a snail's pace.

Hoffman's massive army had been stopped cold.

On the easternmost flank of the Blackshirts, Buddy, O'Shea, and the Wolfpack quietly got into place along a seventeen mile stretch and waited for the fall of darkness. The Blackshirt commander knew he was exposed, knew that he was light when it came to tanks, and suspected the Rebels would try to hit him sometimes during the night. But where? was his main concern. And how would they do it? He spread his men thin, all along the seventeen mile stretch of old highway.

Knowing how the Rebels loved risk-taking and doing what was least suspected of them, the commander made a fatal decision and faced the bulk of his troops to the west, thinking that the Rebels would probably slip up *between* the two cut-off armies.

"We're dealin' with a bloody fool," O'Shea said to Buddy. "Did the man think we'd walk into a box like that?"

"He just had to make a choice," Buddy said. "And he made the wrong one."

"He'll ne'er get another chance to choose," the Irishman said grimly.

"Count on that," Buddy finished it.

The sun slipped over the horizon and deceptive shadows began creeping and lengthening. Field Marshal Hoffman ordered all work stopped and all men to take up arms. There was a sick, tight feeling in his belly. His early supper lay like a slimy blob in his stomach.

"What's wrong?" General Schiller radioed, irritation evident in his voice. "My engineers are nearly finished. Another hour and we can cross."

"No," Hoffman radioed his reply. "Every man behind a gun. I feel the Rebels will make a charge this night."

"From the *front?*" Schiller questioned. "That would be suicide, Field Marshall. Ben Raines would never do anything like that."

"Don't question my orders!" Hoffman snapped. "Every man on the line."

"Yes, sir," his generals acknowledged. And to themselves: But if Raines does come, it won't be from the front. We are not dealing with a fool.

"Make them use up ammunition," Ben told Corrie. "We've got them ahead of their supply trucks. Let's wear them down. Get them shooting at shadows."

At full dark, the Rebels began lobbing mortar rounds in the general direction of Hoffman's lines and the Blackshirts panicked, immediately opening fire, pouring rounds into the darkness, hitting nothing but rocks and trees and empty air. All along the three hundred miles of front lines, the Blackshirts wasted thousands of rounds of precious ammunition. The early night sparked and sang deadly songs, the ragged tune coming from the Blackshirts side of the rivers and creeks. The Rebels kept their heads down and let the lead whistle and howl.

Buddy, O'Shea, and the Wolfpack had worked their way so close to the lines of the Blackshirts they could hear them talking. They could practically smell the fear emanating from the cut-off Blackshirts.

"Now!" Buddy shouted.

The Rebels slammed into the eastern side of Highway 36 with the savagery of hungry piranhas.

The commander of the Blackshirts on the eastern edge of Hoffman's northern push got off one short radio message. Hoffman's face drained of blood and his stomach churned as he read the message. GOD HELP US ALL.

ELEVEN

The Rebels were all over the Blackshirts before they could reposition from west to east. This was bloody and brutal hand to hand fighting, something the Rebels had perfected over the long years of war. This was pistol and knife and hatchet and club warfare. Back to the raw basics.

The Blackshirts had never, ever, encountered such savagery. The Rebels did not come screaming over the top—they came like deadly silent wraiths and it was that very silence that panicked and broke the enemy line.

The disciplined soldiers of Hoffman's army looked at outlaw bikers, bearded and leathered and tattooed, swinging deadly barbed lengths of chain; their female counterparts armed with silenced machine-pistols, spitting out quiet death.

The soldiers of Hoffman broke and fled for their lives, running toward the west. Those that chose to stay and fight died. The Rebels took no prisoners.

The Rebels smashed through the thin lines and split up, working north and south along the rutted old highway. They captured hundreds of assault rifles, fine weapons, and thousands of rounds of ammunition. They captured machine guns and light vehicles and mortars and cases and cases of mortar rounds. They captured hundreds of boxes of field rations, which to the Rebels, after years of eating their own highly nutritious but crappy-tasting goop, were like gourmet meals.

The Blackshirts even abandoned half a dozen of their big battle tanks—the crews running off into the night. The Rebels promptly cranked them up and drove off, along with the trucks and other light vehicles, after loading them with guns, ammo, food, mortars, boots, and anything else the Rebels felt they could use.

The Rebels did not come out of the battle unscathed. They had their dead to carry off and bury and their wounded to transport to Chase's MASH units. But the Blackshirts suffered terrible losses. All who did not run off were killed and many of those who tried to flee were gunned down.

It was wasn't a matter of being callous. It was merely a question of chopping down the enemy to a more manageable size. Every Blackshirt killed now was one less the Rebels would have to someday fight.

By the time troops from Hoffman's Eighth Division got over to the battle site, there was nothing left but the silence of the dead.

General Ramos Schleyer, CG of the Eighth Division, stood in the center of the carnage and was stunned speechless. The dead were sprawled everywhere. The Rebels left behind no wounded.

"Barbarians!" Ramos hissed, finally finding his voice. "Filthy savages." Strange words from a man who took great delight in raping young girls, violating young boys, and killing anyone who did not agree with his political views. He pointed his riding crop at an aide. "The Rebels will pay dearly for this, Hugo. Dearly, I say. Mark my words."

"Field Marshal Hoffman, sir," a radioman handed the general the field phone.

"No, sir," Ramos said, in reply to Hoffman's very direct question. "They were wiped out to the last man. The filthy barbarous bastards left no wounded behind." He listened for a moment. "No, sir. The Rebels took all the equipment. Guns, vehicles, boots, food, mortars, tanks, gasoline . . . everything." Again, he listened. "Yes, sir. I will see that our people are properly buried. I have chaplains coming in now to insure proper burials."

After Hoffman had broken the connection, Ramos said, "Get me General Krosen at the Second Division. We have to make plans to rid ourselves of Ben Raines. *That* and nothing else, must be top priority. We have to convince Field Marshal Hoffman of that. We must."

"We are now dirty filthy barbarians," Corrie told Ben, who was sitting behind his desk, his stocking feet propped up.

He smiled and lifted his mug of coffee at her. "I'm glad to hear it. Obviously, Buddy's report was factual. What officer called us that?"

"The CG of the Eighth Division. General Ramos Schleyer. He is furious and saying that he will have your head on a pole for this atrocity."

"That would be unpleasant," Ben said. "What else?"

"We've decoded some rather odd transmissions and cryptography is trying to make sense out of them now."

"And they all concern me, right?" Ben asked, a strange smile on his lips.

"Yes," Corrie said. "How did you know?"

"Like so many others we've faced, Corrie, the leaders of the Blackshirts believe that if I'm killed, the Rebel movement would collapse. They just can't see that I'm merely a part of it. I'm not the whole. But we're going to have to be careful from now on. For if the generals convince Hoffman of their theory, assassins will be coming out of the woodwork after me." His eyes swept the room, lingering for a moment, touching all the members of his team. "And that includes all of you. And don't ever forget that."

"Well, if that's the case, Ike oughta be storming in here at any moment," Jersey predicted. "That ol' mother hen will be wanting to relocate you up way up in North Canada."

Ben smiled. Jersey had pegged the ex-SEAL correctly. Ike was very protective of Ben. As soon as the decoding experts did their work and reported the news to all Rebel commanders, Ike would be rolling in and raising hell about Ben's safety.

"The Blackshirt generals are requesting a meeting with Hoffman," Corrie called out. "They want to meet first thing in the morning at Hoffman's First Division HQ."

"It's started," Ben said. "Fine. That will give us another day to shift troops around and make plans. I . . ."

"General Ike on the horn, sir," Corrie said. "He says it's very important."

Ben laughed and walked to the radio. "I bet it is," he said, taking the mic as Corrie flipped over to speaker.

Ike was already yelling. "Goddamnit, Ben. Pack it up and get gone from there."

If they were not transmitting from a "fixed" base, to improve the range of communications, and to prevent the enemy from getting any accurate fix on locations, in the field the Rebels used a very upgraded version of the suitcase repeater.

"Where would you have me go, Ike?"

"Away from where you are," Ike said simply, calming down.

"That's not a bad idea," Ben said, but not to Ike. "But we'll do it on the Q.T." To Ike: "No, Ike, I think we'll just stay put for a time. But I will take your very fine suggestion under advisement."

Ben never said things like "taking your very fine suggestion under advisement," and Ben knew Ike would grab the hidden message immediately.

"No way I can convince you, huh?" Ike said, a very subtle change in his voice.

"Not a chance, Ike." Ben knew other Rebel communications people would be monitoring the transmissions and they would put it all together.

To insure that everybody knew what was going on, Ben and Ike began conversing in double-talk, using terms that would lead the Blackshirts—if they could unscramble the transmissions—to believe that Ben was staying in his present location.

When they had spoken enough gobbledygook to tip off even the sleepiest of Rebel communications operators, Ben hooked the mic and said, "Pack it up, people. We're pulling out."

Within minutes, the team had packed their gear and

were heading out. They rolled into Dr. Chase's HQ a few hours later.

"Get your MASH units down and moving," Ben told the chief of medicine. "To just north of I-20. And don't argue. I think Hoffman will be mounting a major offensive very soon."

"Me, argue?" Chase said innocently.

Ben rolled his eyes. "Move!"

"Most of them can move," Chase said, becoming very serious. "I've got two who can't be moved for seventy-two hours. And that's final."

"All right, Lamar. It's your show."

"You staying here, Ben?"

"Until dawn." Over coffee, he explained what he felt the Blackshirts were going to try next.

Chase nodded his head. "That's the way it always is, Ben. Back to playing cat and mouse." He refilled their cups and looked hard at Ben. "The game is just about to turn deadly serious, isn't it?"

"Yeah. We're going to start taking casualties now. Hoffman will make fewer and fewer mistakes counting on the day when he feels we have to stand and slug it out."

"And will that day come, Ben?"

"Oh, yes. It'll come, Lamar. We can't hit and run forever. But that time must not arrive until we've killed off a lot of his troops. This has got to stay a guerrilla-type action. We just don't have the people to stand nose to nose."

Lamar toyed with his coffee mug for a moment. It was very late, past midnight, and the MASH tents set up around the small house Chase was using as his quarters and office were silent. The doctor lifted his eyes, looking at Ben. "Old friend, are we going to win this one?"

"I don't know," Ben said softly. "The movement itself will never die. I know that. But whether you and I and those close to us will live through this fight . . . that's up for grabs."

Lamar sighed. "Well, I'm an old man." He smiled. "With a reasonably young gal and a baby to look after. It won't matter much if I don't make it. You, now, you've got a few more good years ahead of you." And . . ." He paused and frowned. "If you'd quit smoking cigarettes, that is."

"I haven't lit one in your presence so far, have I?" Ben said with a smile.

"No. But you'd like to. Oh, go on and roll one, Raines. You're beginning to fidget like a virgin in a locker room."

"And *what,* Lamar?"

"What do you mean, Raines?"

"You started to say something then paused and started your usual harangue about my smoking."

"I do not harangue anyone, Raines." He took a sip of coffee. "Ike's right, you know."

"Oh, Lamar, not you, too!"

"Listen to me, Ben. You've *got* to listen to me. You talk of the movement. Ben, you are the movement. I know all the times we've discussed this. I know all your arguments: Buddy and Tina will take over, blah, blah, blah. And I know that someday they will have to assume the lion's share of what you now do. But not yet. The time is not now. You said it yourself, Ben: we are facing the most crucial time since the Great War. Now, more than ever before, we need you."

133

It was said with such sincerity, such quiet emotion, Ben sat and stared at the older man for a moment. "What do you want me to do, Lamar?"

"I can't ask you stay out of the field, Ben. That's in your blood. But do so with caution. Don't spearhead. Don't lead wild charges. And don't get careless and let yourself get boxed in somewhere."

Ben slowly nodded his head. "All right, Lamar. I'll rein in my horns. I won't go looking for a fight, but damned if I'll run from one."

"That's good enough for me, Ben. Go get some sleep. We'll talk more at breakfast." He smiled. "Fresh eggs and ham."

"That's an invite I'll accept."

Far to the south, Hoffman sat in the darkness of his trailer. He felt he knew perfectly well what his generals wanted to discuss in a few hours. The taking of Ben Raines. But Hoffman, even though he was younger than Raines, and did not have near the experience, was nonetheless a very intelligent man. He knew that should he, Hoffman, die, his army would fight on. And so would the Rebels. Perhaps not with the cunning that Raines possessed, but fight on they would. And he felt that Ben Raines knew that, too.

Any of Raines' colonels or generals could step in. He knew. He had studied the dossiers on them all. Dan Gray was a brilliant leader of men, as was Ike McGowen. General Payon was tough and smart. General Georgi Striganov, the Russian Bear, was a tough old soldier with years of experience behind him. The mercenary, West, was as mean as a cornered panther.

Ben's son, Buddy, was fearless in a fight and showed great potential as a leader.

No, Hoffman concluded, his generals were wrong. Very wrong. But they were right about one thing: they could not continue to allow the Rebels to chip away at them. How to stop the bastards and bitches from doing that had caused Hoffman endless hours of sleeplessness. But there had to be a way. There just had to be a way.

Hoffman ordered every division to hold their positions and not to attempt any advance. Every commander in Hoffman's army doubled and sometimes tripled security on the edges of their perimeters.

Ben ordered his own people to back off and take a wait and see attitude until after the generals met with Hoffman. It would be interesting to see what came out of the high-level meeting.

"Gentlemen," Hoffman kicked off the meeting. "Let's face facts. And the overriding fact is that our eight divisions and Brodermann's short spearheader division are surrounded by a thin line of Rebels. Now I do not perceive that as much of a threat; we could punch through at any time. However, when we do punch through, and we will, Raines will simply order his northern-based troops to fall back, and realign his forces to the east, west, and south. We will conquer nothing, because Raines is destroying everything in his path. We will kill no Rebels, because Raines will not allow any face-to-face fighting, except on his own terms. And we all know that is savage surprise ambushing."

He paused and looked at his commanders for a moment. "And we have learned some hard lessons about ourselves and the Rebels during this short campaign. I myself have learned that up until we crossed the border, I was an arrogant fool. I believed that we would just roll over the Rebels and march on to glory. I said that Texas would be ours in a week. Well, comrades, Texas will be ours, but it certainly will not be ours in a week, and probably not in several months. Unless we are very, very careful, Texas could very easily be our Russian front, our Waterloo, our Dunkirk. If we don't succeed here, we're finished. Think about that for a moment."

Hoffman waited until the sudden babble of voices had fallen back into silence. "Gentleman, Raines is not going to fight us on our own terms. He simply will not do it. And if we continue fighting him, using the tactics we have thus far practiced, he'll eventually defeat us. Look at the facts. For every Rebel we've killed, they've killed five hundred of our people. At least. We thought, I thought, we could occupy the towns and cities and turn the people against the Rebels. I did not count on Raines evacuating everybody and relocating them north. And north of the thirty-sixth parallel he has Rebels training many of those evacuees, whipping them into an army five or six times our size. That son of a bitch Raines is the most unpredictable goddamn bastard I have ever encountered in my life!"

Hoffman stomped to a window and stared out, struggling to regain his composure. He turned slowly, looking at his men. "Who among us ever dreamt General Raines could very nearly successfully evacuate an entire *state?* That's impossible! But he did it."

Hoffman paced the room like a caged animal, around and around the neatly aligned chairs.

"Field Marshal," General Timmermann spoke. "Does

not that prove what we here maintain? Kill Ben Raines and the movement dies?"

Hoffman shook his head. "No. It does not. Raines is the driving force. But the Rebel movement—no, their philosophy—is ingrained. The death of Ben Raines will not cause the Rebel movement to dissolve. They would falter for a step or two, and then, I believe, grow even stronger. For then, Ben Raines would not be a leader, he would be a *martyr*. I sure as hell don't want that. Many of the people of the United States who presently dislike the man would pick up a gun to fight us."

The more Hoffman spoke, the more frustrated he became. He felt like going away where no one could see him and jumping up and down and screaming in a temper tantrum. He could not remember ever feeling so helpless.

Taking a deep breath, he said, "Ben Raines has approximately fourteen battalions. About eight hundred to a battalion. Eleven thousand men and women, and those badly outnumbered forces are *kicking the shit out of us!*" he screamed the last. "They are doing what tacticians would claim is impossible."

"We could kidnap his son and daughter," General Schmidt suggested.

"Raines does not negotiate with criminals," General Maihofer said. "And he would call that a criminal act. Besides, we don't even know their location."

"Hell," General Kroesen said. "We don't know the location of *any* of Raines' people. We send out patrols, they never return. We send up planes and helicopters, they're shot down. Hunting the Rebels is like searching for a single ship on the ocean. You know it's there, you just can't find it."

"We had dozens of collaborators in this state," General Schleyer said. "Feeding us very good information. Raines hanged some of them, shot a few more, and the others got the message. They now claim to have no knowledge of anything. The three monkeys personified."

"Take some of them to Colonel Barlach," General Mohnhaupt suggested. "He'll get whatever is in their heads."

"It would be of no use by the time they were transported to him and he did his work," Hoffman nixed that. "Raines and his Rebels do not stay long in any one spot. What we have to worry about is whether our former spies are now spying on us!"

General Jahn had remained silent thus far. Hoffman met his eyes and said, "Something on your mind, General Jahn?"

"Break my paratroops up into small, highly mobile guerrilla teams and drop them far behind enemy lines."

"The planes will be shot down!" General von Hanstein flared.

"Shut up," the tough paratrooper told him, steel in his voice. "I have that problem all worked out."

General Jose Schmidt then uttered what every person who had ever fought Ben Raines and the Rebels had said at one time or the other. "I hate that goddamn Ben Raines."

TWELVE

"Our Scouts on the western and eastern fringes of Hoffman's position report hearing planes go over last night," Corrie told Ben. "They did not return."

"What do our people at the thirty-sixth parallel report?"

"Nothing. Their radar picked up no air traffic at all."

Ben thought about that for a moment. "How many planes, Corrie?"

"A large number."

"Well, Hoffman is either dropping supplies to the few of his people we know still remain north of us, but I think that's unlikely. I think he probably dropped paratroopers north of us, then the planes took a wide half circle back home and none of our people heard them."

"Somebody down there finally got some brains working," Jersey remarked. "I was beginning to think this was going to be a piece of cake."

"I knew it was too good to last," Ben said. "All right, Corrie, have communications alert all our people for impending guerrilla action. These boys and girls are going to be tough. From what our intell people have managed to find out, General Jahn is smart, tough, mean, and a damn good soldier. And you can bet this, too: Jahn jumped in with them. The German authorities arrested him and kicked him out of the German army just before the Great War because of his Nazi views. He was an up and coming career man, too. Only the Great War prevented the Germans from putting him in prison. But he's a top-notch soldier."

After Corrie had done her work, she turned in her chair and said, "Speaking of Germany, Thermopolis up at communications is getting some strange signals in German. He just bumped me about an hour ago. He says that Germany is now stabilized—kind of like we thought we were in the States—and the messages are saying something about you to hang on, two units of GSG 9 are on the way to help us. Therm says he has no idea what GSG 9 means."

Ben's boots hit the floor and he jumped to his feet. "GSG 9? Hell, that's Colonel Wegener's old outfit. I think Uwe Dee was commanding officer when the Great War came. GSG 9 is, or was, a top antiterrorist unit. You get Therm on the horn and have him find out who's commanding these units and then have our people in England verify it. Man, oh, man. I hope these boys are on our side."

"Are they that good, General?" Beth asked.

"They're tops, Beth. Or were. I imagine they still are. Come on, boys," Ben urged. "We need all the help we can get."

It did not take Corrie long to determine that the GSG 9 people were for real and they were on their way to assist Ben and the Rebels. They were still a few hundred miles off the South Carolina coast, and Ben ordered trucks from Base Camp One to be there to meet them.

"Who's in command?" he asked.

"A Colonel Lenz is in overall command," Corrie told him. "The battalion commanders are Major Streicher and Major Dietl."

"So this gives us about two thousand more people, right, General?" Cooper asked.

Ben smiled. "Well, not . . . quite, Coop. I figure about four hundred."

"Four hundred!" Jersey blurted. "But you said two battalions."

"No, I didn't. I said two units. Their combat units consist of two hundred men per unit . . . or at least they used to. But don't worry, gang. Those four hundred will more than carry their weight."

Ben was silent for a time, standing by a boarded up window, staring out through the cracks in the warped old boards hastily nailed up years ago. The old home showed signs of having been involved in several battles over the long, bloody years. He turned from the window.

"Corrie, bump Thermopolis on burst and ask him to start contacting other countries that we know are free of the plague and have stabilized their governments. We know of several."

"Yes, sir. What are we asking those governments for?"

"Help," Ben said simply.

Hoffman's forces began inching forward, sometimes no more than a mile or two a day. Ben's people harassed them every inch of the way. But harassment was not enough to stop them. The Rebels fought hard, but constantly lost ground, as they were now fighting Hoffman's massive divisional thrusts, and also guerrilla actions on all sides. General Jahn's tough paratroopers were popping up and striking all over the place.

The GSG 9 people had landed and were on the way. Poland had responded to Ben's plea for help and was sending a battalion. The governments of Denmark, Finland, and Norway were hurriedly putting together a force of men and equipment. Australia had answered the call and they were sending a small force of volunteers. Iceland was sending 250 men. Korea was sending men and equipment. England was sending over a short battalion. Holland was putting together a small volunteer force of their Royal Netherlands Marines Corps.

For the moment, at least, no one else could send anything except prayers. France had been virtually wiped out by the plague, as had Spain and several other European countries. But Ben knew that many other countries around the world were functioning and could send help. For whatever reasons, they remained silent, not responding at all to the pleas for help.

"They better get their act together," Ben said grimly. "For if we don't stop Hoffman here, right *here,* that Nazi son of a bitch will conquer the world."

"General," Corrie said, turning from her radio. "Israel has come on board. They're up to their eyeballs fighting the Arabs, but they're going to send a small force of paratroopers."

Ben nodded his head. "God knows of all countries they can least afford to send help. But I felt they would. Anyone else?"

"Not yet."

"Tell Thermopolis to keep sending out the call for help."

"Yes, sir."

The next day, Spain came through. They were sending a special force of their GEO, the Spanish antiterrorist unit.

Ecuador, Peru and Venezuela asked if they could not be of more help by combining their forces, to try to block Hoffman's supply line from the south.

"Tell them it would be much appreciated," Ben said.

Beth added it all up. "Just under five thousand personnel, General."

"There may be more coming," Ben said, rubbing his face. "But don't count on it."

None of the older Rebels said anything, but Ben knew they were, to a person, thinking about all the countries America had helped over the years, countries who now were remaining silent. Some of those countries were, Ben knew, just simply unable to send any help. But more than a few just chose to ignore America's plight.

"You will be remembered," Ben said, a very ugly note to his voice. "Tattoo that on your arms, assholes."

"Ike on the horn, General."

Ben took the mic.

"You'd better split, Eagle," Ike warned him. "Hoffman's first division is exactly twenty miles from your location."

Ben sighed in frustration and anger. The Rebels were not accustomed to retreating. "All right, Shark. We're bugging out now. We'll set up north of I-20."

Ben turned to Corrie. His team could easily read the

anger and despair on his face. "Corrie, order all units to retreat north of I-20 and regroup there. The rest of you, start packing up."

"Yes, sir," she said softly.

Hoffman was euphoric when the news of the Rebel retreat reached him. He actually felt like singing and dancing around his office. He had not conquered all of Texas in a week, as he had boasted he would, but his people now controlled a large chunk of it. His bubble of euphoria burst when he was given the rest of the news.

He was stunned silent for a moment. "German troops are coming over to aid Ben Raines?" Hoffman gulped for air and screamed at the aide. "*German* troops will fight against me? I do not believe that. That is impossible. We are fighting for the Fatherland. They must know that."

"Yes, sir. I'm sure they do," the aide said diplomatically. "But units of GSG 9 are rapidly approaching what we think is General Raines' current position."

"There must be some mistake. Surely they are coming to aid us?"

"No, sir. We intercepted messages from the German chancellor. He said we must be stopped at all costs. Nazism must not be allowed to flourish again."

Hoffman fell back into his chair, his mouth hanging open. He stared at the young aide for a moment. "That cannot be! It's a lie someone made up!"

"No, Field Marshal. It's true."

"How many German troops?"

"Approximately five hundred, sir."

Hoffman started laughing. "Five hundred? That's ridiculous. Five hundred troops. That's funny, my friend.

Five hundred troops. Oh, thank you. I needed a good rousing laugh."

The aide waited until he had stopped his laughing and was wiping his eyes with a clean handkerchief. "Also troops are on the way from Poland, Denmark, Finland, Norway, Australia, Iceland, Korea, England, Holland, Israel, and Spain."

Hoffman's butt left the chair in a hurry and the aide backed up quickly, thinking the field marshal was going to jump clear over the desk. "What the hell did you say?" Hoffman yelled.

"I said troops are on the way from Poland, Den . . ."

Hoffman waved him silent. "I heard all that! I'm not deaf. How goddamn many troops?"

"Our intelligence says that to send less than five divisions would be useless."

"Five divisions!" Hoffman yelled, his face paling. "Five fucking divisions?"

"Yes, sir."

Hoffman cleared his throat, composed himself and sat down, smoothing his hair with his hands. "We are talking of full combat divisions."

"Yes, sir. That is what intelligence thinks."

"That would be approximately one hundred thousand men. Why then, is Germany sending such a token force?"

"Intelligence thinks they are only an advance team, sir."

"Yes. Yes. That makes sense. Now I want you to leave me. I must think."

The aide left. Happy to do so.

Hoffman leaned back in his chair and put his hands behind his head. So, he thought. We are once more fighting the world, as Hitler—God rest his glorious soul—did so many years ago. They are fools to fight us. Fools! This plan that I am now carrying out was fully planned years before I was born. Victory was assured me by the very blood that runs through my veins. I cannot fail. That is not only unthinkable, it is impossible.

He thought for a long time, wrote out a message, then rose and walked to his communications building. "Order all commanders to halt their advance immediately. We must prepare for a major assault against us." He handed the message to the radioman. "This will explain everything. Send this in code to all commanders. Immediately."

"Yes, sir."

Corrie sat for a moment, trying to make some sense out of the communique just radioed to her from communications central. It just didn't make any sense. Finally, she handed her headset to another Rebel and walked into Ben's office, a room just off what had once been a den in the old home.

"Makes no sense, General," she said.

Ben rubbed eyes weary from hours of staring at maps. "What doesn't, Corrie?"

"We just decoded this. Hoffman has ordered an immediate halt to all advances. He has instructed his troops to prepare for a major counteroffensive by the Rebels."

Ben looked at her for a few seconds, then shook his head in confusion and disbelief. "Would you repeat that, Corrie."

" 'Rebels being reenforced by five divisions of troops

unfriendly to our goals. Preparing to launch major counteroffensive against us on all fronts. Stand or die. Heil Hitler.' It's from the headquarters of Field Marshal Jesus Hoffman."

"Do they know something we don't, Corrie?"

She shrugged her shoulders as the rest of Ben's team gathered around. "Do you suppose Ike or some of the other commanders sent out false information?"

"Not without first clearing it with me. I do not understand this at all."

"All our batt coms are requesting orders," Corrie said. "What do I tell them?"

Ben leaned back in his chair and smiled. "Tell them to mount up. We attack!"

THIRTEEN

The Rebels punched at Hoffman's lines from all directions, using mortars, rockets, and light arms. Every Rebel who could carry a rifle took part. It was hit hard and run like hell. They didn't really inflict a lot of physical damage, since the majority of Rebels had moved north of I-20, but the psychological effects on the Blackshirts was significant.

"We have repulsed the first wave!" Generals Schleyer, Maihofer, and Schmidt proudly radioed to Hoffman. "Our casualties are very light."

But General von Hanstein wasn't buying any of it. He didn't believe Ben had five divisions coming to his aid. He didn't believe there were five solid divisions of troops anywhere in the world except for the troops they were already fighting.

He sent a patrol north of his position to check it out. They reported seeing only very small bands of Rebels. They guessed they were Rebels—they couldn't be sure since those they spotted were in no regular uniform. None of those they saw showed any inclination to stand and fight. They requested permission to pursue and engage.

"Negative," General von Hanstein quickly nixed that. "Return to base." He got Field Marshall Hoffman's HQ. "This is a ruse, sir," he informed Hoffman. "I don't know what Raines is doing, but he does not have five divisions of additional troops. It's some sort of trick."

"Nonsense!" Hoffman snapped. "I shouldn't have to remind you that our intelligence is the finest in the world. They have been on top of this situation since the first transmission. You are wrong, General von Hanstein."

Von Hanstein held his temper and his tongue. He had always been of the opinion that Field Marshal Hoffman's intelligence people would have difficulty finding their own asses with both hands and a seeing eye dog. But he knew better than to argue with Hoffman.

"Yes, sir," von Hanstein said. "As you say, sir." Von Hanstein walked outside and stood for a moment. "Ben Raines is up to something," he muttered. "I know you're up to something, Ben Raines. But what?"

Ben didn't know himself until he stood facing a map. Then he started smiling.

"We're in trouble," Cooper whispered to Jersey. "The general's grinning."

Ben turned around. He smiled at his team. "I have a plan," he said, then started laughing.

"GSG 9 people are in camp," Corrie said. "And Ike's on the horn and he's hot."

"Go, Shark," Ben keyed the mic.

"Goddamnit, Eagle!" Ike roared. "You're supposed to be north of I-20 by now."

"GSG 9 people rolling up, sir," Jersey called, looking out the window. "They look pretty damn tough to me."

"They are," Ben said. "Shark, we're been delayed some. We'll be packed and on the road within the hour. That's a promise." Ben was careful not to tell him in what direction they'd be heading, however.

"That's good, Eagle," Ike said. "General von Hanstein is not fifteen miles from your location."

Ben grinned. "That is a fact, Ike. Yes, indeed. That is a fact. Eagle out." He stepped outside and shook hands with a smiling Colonel Lenz of the German GSG 9.

The two men spoke for a moment and Colonel Lenz laughed. "Everyone said you had more than your share of courage, General Raines," he said. "This proves them correct. It's a fine plan. Let's do it."

"You've got some memorizing to do, Colonel," Ben said. "We'd best get to it."

A half hour later, Ben gathered his team around him and laid it all out. There was just about one minute of silence after Ben had told them what they were going to do. Jersey finally found her voice and summed up the feelings of everyone present. "Holy shit!"

Von Hanstein finally but reluctantly followed orders and prepared for an offensive from the Rebels, spreading his people out along a line east to west. The easternmost units were side by side with men of the Fifth Division, the westernmost units talking with personnel from Hoffman's First Division. Ben and his Rebels, and Colonel Lenz and his GSG 9 men, all of them now dressed in seized Blackshirt uniforms, with Lenz spearheading, headed south and just drove right up to the first checkpoint on Highway 67 and stopped.

"You there!" Colonel Lenz barked at a guard. "We're

from General Schleyer's Eighth. We're trying to get to Field Marshal Hoffman's HQ with a personal message from General Schleyer and this idiot driver of mine took the wrong road. Can you help us?"

"Certainly, sir," the guard said. "Just stay on this road for about twenty more miles. You'll come to Highway 87. Turn west and you'll run right into the field marshal's HQ. Have you seen any Rebels, sir?"

"We've seen nothing. I think it's a ruse and so does General Schleyer. But . . ." He smiled and shrugged his shoulders. "We are only soldiers, hey. What can we do?"

"Yes, sir," the sentry said with a grin. "I imagine General von Hanstein would be glad to talk to you. He shares your views about this so-called assault. His CP is only a mile past the intersection. He's pretty thin down there. All our troops have been deployed along this line."

"Certainly, we shall speak with him," Lenz said. "Do call the General and advise him we are on the way."

The sentry waved them on through. "Heil Hitler!" he stiff-armed.

Lenz forced a smile, returned the stiff-armed salute, and mouthed the hated words. Then he spat out the window. "Up yours, asshole," he muttered, when they were past the checkpoint. He grinned at his driver. "He'd probably shit on himself if he knew he'd been standing this close to a Jew, Zuckerman."

Zuckerman then proceeded to heap some highly uncomplimentary remarks on the heads of the Blackshirts and Lenz laughed aloud. Down the road, the convoy pulled over and he ran back to Ben's vehicle, an armored car seized from one of many Rebel ambushes of Blackshirts. "That's the hard part," he told Ben. "Von Hanstein will have fresh coffee and cake waiting for us."

"I can't believe that sentry didn't smell a rat," Ben said. "We're not exactly a small force."

"I must admit, I was a bit apprehensive. You ready?"

"Let's do it."

Lenz chuckled. "If we pull this off, it'll send this Hoffman bastard spinning right through the ceiling."

Von Hanstein stood for a moment after receiving the message from the checkpoint. Something bothered him about this. Why did this officer take the northern route instead of the much safer southern route? "Oh, well," he finally muttered. "Make fresh coffee, Carlos," he told a Blackshirt. "Company is on the way from Schleyer's Eighth."

The sergeant paused and narrowed his eyes. "From a hundred and twenty five miles east of us, sir?" he questioned. "At this time of high alert?"

"Odd, isn't it, Carlos?" von Hanstein said softly. "Ah! I have it. The party must have set out long before the alert. That's it."

"Yes, sir. I'm sure that's it." But the sergeant was far from convinced as he set about making fresh coffee and laying out cookies and small pastries. Something about this just didn't feel right to him. His duties done, he checked his sidearm and made certain his rifle was close at hand.

Carlos looked outside. Not enough men, he thought. The camp is nearly deserted. General Raines is crazy enough to do something this daring . . . Bah! He shook his head and pushed those thoughts from him. The guards at the checkpoint would not have allowed the convoy through if anything had seemed out of the ordinary. You're letting your imagination run away with you, he silently admonished himself.

"Sergeant Rogillo!" the voice broke into his thoughts. Carlos looked up. "Sir?" he said to a lieutenant.

"Daydreaming, Sergeant?" the lieutenant asked, a smile on his lips.

"I . . . ah, guess so, Lieutenant," Carlos admitted, red-faced.

"That's not like you. What's the matter?"

"Nothing, sir. Nothing at all."

"Be alert then. We don't want a bad report going back to General Schleyer, now, do we?"

"No, sir." On this last day of his life, Carlos busied himself setting out cups and saucers.

General von Hanstein sat in his office, behind his field desk and drummed his fingertips on the wood. He again read the message. Odd that the officer did not give his name. Perhaps he should give General Schleyer a call? He opened his mouth to call for an aide, then sighed and shut his mouth. What was he thinking of? Schleyer would think him a fool!

He rose and walked into his communications room. "Have there been any further attacks from the Rebels? Anywhere along the front?"

"Just a few skirmishes, sir. Nothing of any significance."

Something is wrong, von Hanstein thought, returning to his office. Something is very, very wrong.

Sergeant Carlos Rogillo had gone to communications and spoken with the guard at the checkpoint. The guard had been very indignant. Of course, he was certain the men were from the Eighth. He'd recognized Sergeants Zimmerman and Rozas. And the colonel was SS.

SS, Carlos mulled that around. SS? No way. Why would an SS colonel be acting as a messenger boy? Those turds thought themselves to be above such mundane tasks. Especially a colonel. Carlos felt eyes on him and turned, looking at Major Schlosser, looking at him.

"What's the matter with you, Sergeant?" the major asked. "Your behavior is quite odd."

"I . . ." The sounds of approaching vehicles cut off his reply.

Major Schlosser waved him silent.

General von Hanstein stepped out of his office, straightening his tunic.

"SS troops, sir," Lieutenant Bachman said. "A lot of SS troops."

"SS?" von Hanstein said. "That explains a few things. Those arrogant bastards think they're invincible. That's why they took the northern route. Showboating. Do you recognize any of them, Hans?"

Hans Bachman peered out the freshly cleaned window of the old farmhouse. He shook his head. "I . . . I'm not sure. I think I know this colonel, sir. I mean, I've seen him around."

"Show them in," von Hanstein said, then walked back into his office. "Bring *them* to *me.*" He'd be damned if he'd grovel to a colonel, even if he was one of those goddamned SS people.

Boots sounded on the porch.

Sergeant Carlos Rogillo opened the front door for Major Schlosser to greet the visiting troops. The major stepped out, smiling. Carlos stepped to one side and looked around the Major. There were women in this group. That's odd, he thought. The SS did have women in its ranks, but they were usually office personnel. The colonel and his senior officers were probably making a lark of this trip, carrying their personal cunts along with them. That's usually what those perverted SS females were used for. All of them were twisted in some deviant manner. Carlos looked for a familiar face. He knew Sergeant Zimmerman. He couldn't find him in the milling crowd. Odd, the SS troops seemed to be taking up a loose defensive position. Paranoid bunch of bastards.

Carlos turned around and walked to his desk, automatically straightening his uniform. Like most regular troops, he was slightly afraid of the SS. They just were not normal people.

"Good afternoon, Colonel," Major Schlosser said. "Please come in. You must be tired. After you've freshened up, we have coffee and cake."

"Danke, Colonel," Lenz said with a smile.

Schlosser stepped to one side. The man behind the colonel seemed somehow familiar to him. Tall, with a lot of gray in his hair. Hard mean eyes, too. Old for a major. Probably fifty. The man stared directly at him and Schlosser was suddenly very uncomfortable under the hard gaze.

He was only seconds away from becoming a whole lot more uncomfortable. For a very brief period of time.

Colonel Lenz and Ben Raines stepped past Schlosser and entered the command post.

General von Hanstein looked up from his desk, stared at the tall major, and felt the blood drain from his face. "That's Ben Raines!" he screamed.

Jersey gave Major Schlosser a burst in the belly from her H&K and the slugs knocked the major backward. Sergeant Carlos Rogillo grabbed for his pistol and Major Dietl shot him through the heart. Carlos fell across the pastry table and died with his face on a cookie platter.

General von Hanstein felt the muzzle of a .45 not too gently touch the side of his face. He cut his eyes and stared into the face of Ben Raines.

"Welcome to Texas," Ben said. "You asshole!"

FOURTEEN

The battle for the headquarters of General von Hanstein was very short and very brutal. The Rebels and the GSG 9 men took only a few prisoners, General von Hanstein among them. The Rebels and the GSG 9 personnel gathered up all the weapons, ammo, and food, loaded up the beds of trucks, and took off, heading south. The radio operator had been killed in the first burst of gunfire, so it was doubtful he managed to get off any messages . . . but Ben wasn't going to take any chances.

"We'd never make it by heading north," he told Colonel Lenz. "So we head south and cut east once past Austin, then cut north once we're clear of Schleyer's Eighth Division lines. I've marked maps in case we get separated."

"And if we meet enemy long the way?" Colonel Lenz inquired, a hard glint in his eyes. The commander of the German troops liked the way Ben Raines fought a war.

Ben smiled. "Why . . . I guess we'll just have to engage them, won't we?"

The two men laughed, shook hands, and ran to their vehicles.

General von Hanstein, trussed up like a pig, lay in the bed of a deuce and a half. He glowered at everyone who came near him, and refused to speak a word.

"They've discovered the camp," Corrie told Ben, monitoring on a Blackshirt radio. "Hoffman's ordered a full-scale search underway immediately. He's ordered planes up."

"Head straight for the ruins of San Antonio," Ben said. "They'll never expect us to do that. We can't make it tonight, but we can make this state park a few miles down the road and camouflage the vehicles. The roads are in too bad a shape to try running at night without lights. Step on it, Coop."

The convoy made the old overgrown state park, hurriedly camouflaged their trucks and armored cars, and settled in for a very tense night.

"Do we bump Therm and tell him where we are?" Corrie asked.

"Negative. No transmissions of any kind. No fires, no smoking. Cold camp. We just sit tight and silent."

"Ike is going to be screaming and climbing the walls," Corrie reminded Ben.

"Good," Ben said, opening a field ration packet and smelling it before tasting it. "Maybe he'll lose some weight."

Ike McGowan wasn't the only one screaming and climbing the walls. Field Marshal Hoffman was having a temper tantrum. Hitler would have been proud. Between violent fits of temper, which included breaking glasses, cups, and one very old bottle of brandy, Hoffman ordered a replacement commanding general in to take over von Hanstein's division, a massive air and land search underway, the sentry who let the Rebels and the GSG 9 men through put up against a wall and shot, and then a bottle of aspirin and two tranquilizers. When he finally managed to calm down, he called a meeting of his staff officers. None of whom were looking forward to the meeting.

"The few wounded the Rebels missed during their coup de grace said many of the attackers spoke German," Hoffman told his people in a surprisingly calm voice. "That means the GSG 9 people have linked up with Raines. The goddamn filthy traitors. The wounded also heard General von Hanstein scream out Ben Raines's name from his office. They also confirm that General von Hanstein was taken prisoner. Thrown into the back of a truck. The nerve of that bastard Raines. Taking a small force deep into our territory and carrying out a successful raid."

Before he could continue, an aide rushed into the room and handed him a slip of paper, then quickly departed before Hoffman could read the radio message and once more fly into a fit of rage.

Hoffman read the message and barely managed to contain his anger. He took several deep breaths and composed himself. He said, "At least a full division of Ecuadorian, Peruvian, and Venezuelan troops have closed our highway supply routes. Those supplies that we were expecting will not arrive. The convoy was ambushed and all supplies seized. There were no survivors. All supplies will have to be flown in from this point on." He was silent for a time. "The world seems to be mass-

159

ing against us," he said finally, his words softly spoken. "But we expected that. All right. I anticipated something of this nature. I will shift Eighth Division down to guard the airport and roads around what is left of San Antonio. Supplies will be flown into there and trucked out into the field. Eighth Division will also have the responsibility of providing guards for the supply convoys. From this moment on, we are in no rush. We advance daily, but we do so slowly and carefully."

"Then we are standing down from our defensive positions?" a staff officer asked cautiously, knowing the question had to be posed.

"Yes," Hoffman said, no anger in his reply. "I overreacted and will admit it."

"What about the message we received from the commander of Base Camp One?" Hoffman was asked.

Cecil had sent word that Hoffman could, under the terms agreed to earlier, freely and safely staff hospitals within the boundaries of what used to be Louisiana— and was now a neutral zone—but under no circumstances would he allow any SS troops to be treated in that area. He had issued orders that any and all SS troops were to be shot on sight, no matter what their physical condition might be.

Hoffman merely shrugged at that. "We will provide care for our elite troops. We do not need the protection of a neutral zone for them. The Rebels in the field will not attack a hospital. General Cecil Jefferys's orders came as no surprise. Considering what he is. All combat troops will stay out of the neutral zone."

Hoffman met the eyes of his staff officers. "Let's return to the matter of Ben Raines. That son of a bitch!"

* * *

Ben and his command, deep in enemy territory, hit the small patrol of Blackshirts very swiftly and very hard. The five vehicle patrol had made the mistake of entering the old state park. It was their last mistake. Five rockets from Armbrust launchers turned the trucks into blazing death traps. Within seconds the Rebels and the GSG 9 personnel had put out the flames so the smoke would not be seen and had dragged away the searingly hot rubble, the bodies entombed forever in the twisted and melted metal.

"For years I have heard of Ben Raines and the Rebels," Major Streicher said to Ben, as they sat in the darkness of the cold camp. "At first we thought it was just a rumor. Then rumor became fact as more and more countries—splintered and torn as they may be— began adopting the Rebel philosophy. Those countries who are sending troops here are now virtually free of crime and are rapidly rebuilding their societies. Those who have not adopted the Rebel way are nothing but raging battle zones. They will have to be dealt with at some future point. By us."

"I'm afraid you're right," Ben agreed, grimacing as the night breeze picked up and brought with it the odor of freshly charred human flesh. "That is, providing we manage to knock the blocks from under Hoffman and his Nazis."

The major smiled in the night. "Oh, we will, General. All of us sensed that the moment we met you and your people. Your movement is unstoppable. We might die, but the movement will live on."

"Ike's raising hell, General," Corrie said, walking up. "He's getting everybody else all worked up, too."

"Let him holler," Ben said, wishing he had a hot cup of coffee and a smoke to go with it. "We'll bump him as soon as we're clear of this box we're in. I don't even want to risk a burst. The damn Blackshirts are all around us. They could get lucky."

"This General Ike McGowan," Colonel Lenz said. "Will he send out rescue patrols?"

"No," Ben said quickly. "He'll bluster and beller but that's just for my benefit. He's letting me know how he feels about my taking chances."

"He's right, you know?" Colonel Lenz said softly.

Ben chuckled goodnaturedly. "My God! You and Ike are going to hit it off famously."

At first light, Hoffman's troops began their slow northern advance along seven fronts. There was little the Rebels could do to stop them. Ben had ordered his heavy artillery moved north and hidden. For every big gun and battle tank the Rebels had, Hoffman had thirty. The Rebels just could not stand toe to toe with the Blackshirts and slug it out. Not yet. They had to wear them down, little by little.

Ben and his command pulled out, heading east and staying on little used county roads, getting lost more than once, for many of the roads were not on any map. Dusk found them camped along the banks of a large creek or a small river—none of them were sure about that.

"I think it's the Blanco," Cooper said, looking at a

map. "This road is not marked. If it is, we've got to cross Interstate 35 tomorrow."

"And we know from radio intercepts that Hoffman is shifting his Eighth Division over to San Antonio," Jersey added. "We might run into them."

"I think we'd better stay right where we are," Ben ended that discussion. "We've got good cover and water. In a couple of days we'll be in the clear. Stand down, gang."

Forward people both saw and heard Hoffman's Eighth Division on their way southwest to San Antonio. And it was a massive movement. At noon of the third day's hiding, the recon teams reported no more movement of troops and equipment. The highways were silent and empty.

"Let's go, people," Ben ordered. "We'll be in the clear in two hours."

Luck was with them and two hours later, they were rolling up 77, big and bold as brass, heading for Waco . . . or what was left of it.

"According to these reports," Major Dietl said. "Hoffman's Seventh Division is only a few miles to our west."

"Sure," Colonel Lenz said with a smile. "That's why General Raines is taking this route. Who would think to look for us here?"

Dietl grinned and shook his head. "Working with the general is going to be interesting."

"To say the least."

The words had just left his mouth when the words of forward Scouts screamed into Corrie's ears. "Gunships heading south. Following the highway."

"Over there," Ben said, pointing to the ruins of a

small town. "Duck in between those buildings. Order Stingers readied."

As she always did, Beth had slipped on another headset and was monitoring the frequencies used by Hoffman. "They're calling in our position now, General," she said.

Cooper pulled into an old service station. The gloom was comforting.

"The choppers are beginning a slow circle, General," Corrie said, after speaking with forward recon. "Staying out of range of SAMs."

"I wondered when Hoffman's boys and girls would smarten up," Ben said, getting out of the armored car and stretching. "Well, we can expect some sort of company pretty damn quick. What kind of gunships are they, Corrie?"

"Scouts don't know. Say they've never seen anything like them. But they resemble our Apaches. They say the firepower looks awesome. But the choppers are not making any hostile moves. They are staying well away from the Scouts position, maintaining a slow circle."

"Dig in for a fight," Ben ordered. "We can't move from here. Those gunships would cut us to pieces."

Corrie was calmly setting up her radio, Jersey was standing in the open door of the service part of the old filling station, Cooper was checking out his M-60 machine gun, and Beth had taken up a position at the rear of the building. Other Rebels had spread out up and down the ruins of the small street. Stingers were readied in case the circling gunships of Hoffman did come into range.

Men of the GSG 9 had quickly appraised the layout of the town and taken positions without having to be told. In less than three minutes, the town appeared to be deserted.

"Blackshirt units are on the way," Corrie said. "From the north, west, and south."

Ben nodded his head and checked his Thompson, then checked his sidearms. "How many of them?"

"Too damn many," Corrie replied. "And coming as fast as road conditions allow."

Ben smiled at her initial reply.

Cooper unwrapped a candy bar from a ration packet and took a bite. Jersey popped a fresh stick of gun into her mouth. She glanced at Ben. He winked at her and Jersey laughed and signaled thumbs-up. Beth was laying out thirty round clips of .223 ammo for easy reach.

"Colonel Lenz reports his men are in position," Corrie said. "Recon staying in place and asking if there is a way to get a Stinger to them?"

"Negative," Ben told her. Ben walked around the shop area a couple of times. He stopped and said, "Corrie? Now you can bump our people and tell them where we are and that we just might be in a little bit of trouble."

Jersey rolled her eyes at that, then grinned and said, "And tell them if they want to get in on the action they'd better hurry. We're about to kick Nazi ass all over the place."

FIFTEEN

Hoffman was ectatic as he studied the huge wall map of Texas. He could not hide his wide smile. He actually felt like dancing. He controlled that unseemly urge and rubbed his hands together and chuckled. "We have that arrogant rogue bastard now," he gloated, for he had correctly anticipated what route Ben might take back north. "He cannot slip out of this box. Shift units of the Seventh Division north and south of Raines's location to prevent Rebels from coming to his aid. I want gunships up immediately to cover the area east of his position. Nail the lid down tight. Now, General Ben Raines. Now, I have you." He turned to face an aide. "Just as soon as all troops and gunships are in position, kill that son of a bitch. Blow that damn town to bloody splinters and dust."

The staff officers surrounding Hoffman all applauded at the brilliance of their field Marshal. He accepted the loud accolade with modesty.

"Corrie, belay the message to our people. Maintain radio silence. Cooper, pass the word: Take two day's rations, as much ammo as each person can comfortably carry, and leave everything else. We were using Blackshirt vehicles so let's leave some presents behind with them."

Cooper grinned and nodded his head in understanding. The vehicles would be booby-trapped.

"Split up into four or five person teams and head for the river bed and work east toward the Brazos. But don't try to follow the river north. They'll be expecting that. Keep working east until we reach our units along I-45. Do it right now. Move, Coop. And get back here quickly. Let's get our shit together, gang. We've got to bug out. I have a feeling Hoffman is going to use heavy artillery on this old town."

Teams began exiting the town within a minute. Ben's team waited, knowing they would be the last to leave.

"I must insist that you leave now, General," Colonel Lenz told Ben.

"Take off, Colonel," Ben said with a smile. "Godspeed."

Lenz gripped Ben's shoulder for a moment, then saluted. "We'll take General von Hanstein with us."

Ben nodded. "If he gets to be too much trouble, shoot the son of a bitch."

Lenz laughed. "It will be my pleasure to do so, General." The German GSG 9 commander was gone at a silent run.

"And so once more, it is with regret that we leave a lovely scenic spot," Beth said straight-faced. "What a delightful time we've had here."

Even though Beth was not prone to wisecracking, ever since she had seen an old travelogue tape she had mimicked the announcer whenever they got into a tight spot.

"Make a note in your diary to return here someday," Ben said with a smile.

"Hell, there won't be anything *left* in an hour," Beth replied.

"Or less," Ben added.

"That's it," Corrie announced, taking off her headphones and slipping into the straps of the back-pack radio. "We're alone. All teams have gone."

"Bug-out time," Ben said, looking at Cooper. He was just finishing his booby-trapping of the armored car. "Did you leave a nice surprise for them, Coop?"

"They'll get a bang out of it."

Jersey groaned at the old joke.

"Let's go, gang," Ben said.

They slipped out and headed for the river. Ben's piece of a map did not give a name for the stream. It was the San something; that part of the map was creased over and not legible. Ben's team had not gone half a mile before the artillery barrage started. They paused and looked back as the old town exploded.

"Another fifteen minutes and we'd have been chopped meat," Jersey said.

"Speaking of meat," Cooper said.

"You're always hungry, Coop," Ben said. "Come on. It's hours before we can stop for that."

"I'll die of starvation!"

"You'll get shot in the ass by me if you don't move," Jersey warned him.

Cooper took one look at Jersey and moved right out. Smartly, as the British say.

The four Scouts had left their forward positions and

moved out first, under orders from Colonel Lenz. He told them to head for the river fast, like bunny rabbits, and stay there until they linked up with their General and stay with him. He didn't have to tell them he was doing that without Ben's notice. They guessed that.

A mile from town, Beth spotted the Scouts waiting for them. "Don't fuss at them, General," she said. "I bet you Colonel Lenz ordered them to link up with us."

"You're probably right." Ben waved at the Scouts to take the lead and they set a route step that was not uncomfortably fast, but covered a lot of ground. The small group held to cover as much as possible, avoiding open fields.

Ben was the first to hear the unmistakable whapping of rotor blades. "Down!" he called. "Choppers."

Corrie was listening intently to her earphones. "Teams have been spotted," she said, lying beside Ben. "Hoffman knows we bugged out."

"We're in for it now," Ben replied. "He'll be throwing everything he's got at us."

"We're spotted!" Beth shouted, listening to the Blackshirt's frequency.

"He'll be coming in for a strafing run," Ben called, watching the chopper begin a slow turn. "Good God, look at the armament on that damn thing."

Then the helicopter disintegrated in the air as a Rebel Stinger, fired from a hidden Rebel team about a half a mile away impacted against it. Metal parts and body parts were flung in all directions and the ball of fire fell out of the sky and crashed to earth.

"Let's go!" Ben shouted, jumping to his feet. "Head for that stand of timber."

Reaching the timber and pausing to catch their

breath, the small band of Rebels listened for the sounds of more choppers. None came.

"Probably a lone wolf," Ben said, after taking a small sip of tepid water from his canteen. "You picking up any enemy chatter, Beth?"

"Negative."

Corrie didn't mention that Ike and other Rebel commanders were raising hell about Ben's disappearance and continuing silence. Ben already knew that.

"Let's cover some ground while we can."

By nightfall, they had put the destroyed town far behind them. They ate cold rations and Ben told them to get some rest. He had some thinking to do.

Should they move on? That just might be a dandy way to get seriously dead by the guns of their own people. Before they had bugged out of the little town, passwords had been chosen: *Alamo* and *Bowie*. But with very nervous trigger fingers, there might not be time for words.

Ben slept for a few hours and then roused the others. "We'll chance it. Let's move out. Everybody remember the challenge? OK. Heads up."

They had not gone a thousand yards before the point man dropped down, the others following.

The point Scout silently wriggled back to the main body. "Blackshirts," he whispered. "Looks like a big bunch of them."

"Go around them," Ben said. "To the east. Coop, pass the word. Anybody makes a noise, we're all dead."

It took them nearly half an hour of slow and silent moving, being very careful where they put a boot down. By the time the Rebels had worked their way clear of the Blackshirt encampment, the smell of nervous sweat was becoming sharp in the surprisingly cool night.

A mile away, behind them, hard gunfire splintered and fractured the night. A few hundred yards in front of them, sudden movement and the sounds of boots hitting the ground flattened the Rebels out, still and silent, hearts thudding heavily. Sharp commands came to them and then a Blackshirt patrol came running past, heading for the gunfire. They were running so close all the Rebels could feel the impact of boots upon the earth.

"Move out," Ben whispered. "Straight east. These sons of bitches are all around us." He didn't have to add "be careful."

A hour later, the Rebels came to a tiny creek, the water no more than a few inches deep, and took time out to splash cold water on their faces.

"Where in the shit are we?" Cooper whispered.

"Alive," Jersey told him.

They walked on. They were bone tired and nerve-taut, but each careful step put them that much further away from enemy territory.

Just before dawn, during a much needed rest period, Beth suddenly perked up, sniffed, and asked, "What's that smell, General?"

"The river. I smelled it a few minutes ago. That's why I called this break. I want to wait until light to look it over. I think we're clear. I think I know where we are. If it hasn't been blown, there should be a bridge about two miles to the east of here."

"I sure could use some hot food, clean socks, and a bath," Cooper said.

"The bath, I certainly agree with," Jersey stuck it to

him. "But stay close, you smell so bad you're keeping the mosquitos away."

"You're just too kind to me, Jersey," Cooper popped back, putting a hand on her knee. "I always knew that deep down you really cared."

Jersey looked down at the hand on her leg. "I'll break it, Cooper."

He removed his hand. Quickly.

"Sleep," Ben put an end to the harmless bantering that had been going on between the two for years. "All of you. I'll stand first watch."

The team slept until the warm rays of light filtering through the trees woke them. They looked around. Ben was gone.

The first team to have bugged out of the town had reached a Rebel patrol and reported. Ike had flown in to where Ben was supposed to have been, a few miles north of I-20, and was studying a wall map.

"If they made it through all those patrols and gunships," he said, "I figure they should be at the river by now. We know there are Blackshirts east of the river, but only in very small patrols. We have more patrols working there than they do."

"Settle down, Ike," Dr. Chase told him. "If anything had happened to Ben, one of his team would have radioed in. You know that."

"Unless the whole team was whacked," Ike said grimly. "And we've got to consider that." He started pacing the floor and cussing.

"I swear to God, Ike," Chase said. "If you don't settle

down, I'm going to tranquilize you. And with a butt like yours, I couldn't miss with the needle."

Ike tried to look hurt. He couldn't pull it off. "I'll have you know I've lost a few pounds, Doc."

"Well, you found them again. Sit down, Ike!"

Ike stopped his pacing and sat down. Chase poured him half a glass of bourbon. "This was found buried a couple of days ago. Several cases of it. I can't think of a better time to get loose. Drink up, Ike. Ben will make it. He always has."

"Luck has a bad habit of running out on a man, Lamar. And Ben's been doing this for a long time. Too long, I'm thinking."

"I stopped trying to get him out of the field entirely a long time ago. He'll die in the field, Ike. You know it, and I know it."

"Yeah," Ike said softly and cut his eyes to the silent field telephone on the desk.

Hoffman had been in a blue funk since his troops had found no bodies in the rubble of the old town. That elusive son of a bitch Raines had slipped out like a silent snake. Hoffman had poured twenty thousand troops into that area and still Raines had slipped away. It was quite impossible, of course. But Raines had certainly done it.

Incredible. The man and his Rebels moved like ghosts and fought like possessed demons. And obviously they took General von Hanstein with them. They would probably torture him. Poor von Hanstein. He would have the divisional chaplin hold a service for him. Yes. That would be the Christian thing to do. And Jesus

Hoffman certainly considered himself to be a Christian man. He went to mass every Sunday. And didn't he have the good of everyone in mind? Certainly he did. It was just that some people were born to lead and others were born to serve. Or be exterminated. Hoffman didn't consider that unchristian at all.

An aide knocked and entered. Hoffman looked up. "What is it, Lieutenant?"

"That fellow up in Mississippi and Alabama, Moi Sambura? He wishes to speak with you on the radio, sir."

A grimace passed over the fine Christian features of Field Marshal Hoffman. "I thought the Rebels were jamming all their frequencies?"

"They have stopped. Momentarily, I'm sure."

Hoffman rose to his boots. "Oh, very well. I wonder what that damn nigger wants now?"

BOOK TWO

ONE

The Constitution preserves the advantage of being armed which Americans possess over the people of almost every other nation ... where the governments are afraid to trust the people with arms.

—James Madison

"What are you listening to, Corrie?" Ben asked.

"Some interesting exchanges between Hoffman and that nut that General Jefferys hates so, Moi Samburu. You want to listen?"

"No," Ben said. "You can tell me the gist of it after those two clowns stop their babbling." Ben paused in the rolling of a cigarette. "I thought Moi was being jammed?"

"I got a burst from Base Camp One about five minutes ago. General Jefferys ordered the jamming stopped for a time so he could find out what Moi is up to."

"Good idea." Ben lit up and watched Corrie take notes of the conversation between the Nazi and the nut.

Ben and team were about fifteen hundred yards from a bridge that spanned the Brazos, the Rebels hidden amid the thick vegetation. So far, Scouts had reported no signs of life on the other side, but Ben was not convinced. If they were caught under fire while crossing that bridge, it would be over for them. Rainfall had been heavy and the river was up.

Corrie rolled her eyes and grimaced. Ben smiled. Moi must really be on a verbal rampage. Back before the war he was an extreme militant who advocated and preached loudly that blacks should declare war and kill all whites. Just as Wink Payne hated all blacks and wanted them all dead. Now they were both aligned with Hoffman against the Rebels. Neither man had enough sense to understand that if the Rebels were defeated, Hoffman would turn on them and kill them both. It was, as Ben had said before, a very unholy alliance. Not to mention very unstable. Both Moi and Wink possessed unpredictable and volatile personalities. Ben had hoped for several years now that they would meet and kill each other. No such luck.

Corrie sighed and removed her headset. "Moi and Wink have had a major falling-out. Moi wants to attack Wink's position and Wink wants to declare war on all blacks. Hoffman told both of them to maintain peace or he'd send troops in to be sure it was done."

Ben was reflective for a moment, then he smiled. "Now that is interesting. When we get out of this hole we're in, we'll just have to see if we can agitate them both a little bit."

"Rebels coming in!" a lookout passed the word. "About forty of them."

A half a dozen teams of Rebels and GSG 9 troops, all looking weary and bedraggled entered the camp. Ben stood up and shook hands with Major Dietl.

"It certainly is good to see you alive and well, General," the major said with a smile. "It's been a rather dicey couple of days."

"It has for a fact," Ben agreed. "Sit down and rest. Eat. We'll cross over just as soon as I'm sure we're not walking into an ambush."

Major Dietl sank to the ground with a sigh of relief.

A Scout walked into the encampment. "Barry's back, General. He said it was an easy swim. He says it's clean on the other side."

"Easy swim for him," Ben said with a smile. "He's Ike-trained. He's got web-feet and gills. All right, Paul. Take your Scouts across and cover the other side for us. We'll be along presently."

"Right, sir."

The Scouts secured the east end of the bridge while Ben and the others packed up their meager supplies and began the crossing. They marched for another ten miles and saw no signs of human life. They passed only a few deserted farms; most had been destroyed by the retreated Rebels. Ben had left precious little for Hoffman's army.

Ben called a halt and told Corrie to start sending out very short coded messages. "Let's see what we get in reply."

They got nearly every team that had bugged out of the old town. The teams were all within a five mile range of each other.

"Tell them to start heading north," Ben said, pointing to a spot on the map. "We'll link up there."

Cecil had Rebel personnel on the Texas-Louisiana border and intercepted the coded messages. He sent word to Ike and planes were waiting on the small strip when Ben and his group arrived. Two hours later they were back in Ben's CP just north of I-20.

"Where you worried about me, Ike?" Ben asked with a smile, removing his filthy shirt and tossing it aside.

"Not a damn bit," Ike said stiffly. "I'm tired of worryin' about you."

Ben laughed at him and Ike exploded. He outlined, for the umpteenth time, all the reasons why Ben should stay out of the field and start acting more like a commanding general. Lamar Chase came in and sat down, after pouring himself a cup of coffee. He listened and chuckled occasionally at Ike's antics. He knew that Ike's words were bouncing off Ben like water off a duck.

Finally, Ben, showered and shaved and dressed in clean clothing, looked at Ike. With a bland expression on his face, Ben said, "I'm sorry. Were you speaking to me, Ike?"

Ike stood sputtering and stammering and flapping his arms like a fat bear. He finally stalked out of the room, muttering about associating with crazy people. He slammed the door behind him.

"You going to lecture me, too, Lamar?"

"Nope," the doctor said. "It wouldn't do any good, would it?"

"Not a bit."

"So our little talk of a few weeks ago is right out the window, huh, Ben?"

"Not entirely, Lamar. But if I see that my taking a chance will accomplish something, I think it's worth the risk. You want to argue that?"

"No." The doctor was strangely quiet.

"Are you sick?"

Lamar smiled and shook his head. "No. Just glad

you're back, Ben." He lifted his coffee mug in a salute in Ben's direction, then left the room.

"What the hell's wrong with him?" Jersey blurted.

"He's getting mellow in his old age, I suppose. Have our spooks gotten any information out of von Hanstein?"

"Nothing that we didn't already know," Beth said, her hair still damp from the shower. "I talked to one of those weirdos from intelligence, and it's like we thought all along: Hoffman doesn't really have much of a plan. The spook thought von Hanstein was telling the truth."

"Beth, you make damn sure the general is not physically harmed. Some of our people are certain to be taken prisoner, and I want to be able to have something to swap . . . unharmed."

"Field Marshal Jesus Hoffman on the horn, General," Corrie said.

"No kidding?"

"No kidding, sir."

"I'll be damned," Ben said, taking the seat Corrie just vacated for him. He keyed the mic. "This is Ben Raines."

"General Raines," Hoffman's voice sprang into Ben's ears. "This is Field Marshal Hoffman. I believe you have one of my generals."

"That I do."

"He is an old and dear friend of mine, General."

"General von Hanstein has not been harmed nor will he be, Field Marshal. I expect the same treatment to be accorded should any of my personnel be taken prisoner."

"I assure you that will be the case."

"Thank you."

"Now, then, General Raines. Shall we discuss the release of General von Hanstein?"

"Oh, I think not, Field Marshal. Von Hanstein is really quite comfortable here and we have many, many things to discuss."

"He will tell you absolutely nothing, General." Hoffman's tone turned a bit cooler, losing some of its geniality. Ben felt all that buddy-buddy crap was forced anyway. "Not even under torture."

"Field Marshal, I have no intention whatsoever of torturing von Hanstein. He is in comfortable, if not lavish quarters. He is eating the same food we are, and except for some sore feet from all that walking we did bugging out of that little town before you starting shelling it, your general is in fine shape." Ben chuckled and that seemed to infuriate Hoffman. Ben heard his sharp intake of breath.

Hoffman's tone turned to ice. "You cannot win, General. Your position is quite unenviable. I assure you of that."

"Oh? That's news to me, Field Marshal." Ben smiled and winked at his team. In order for them all to hear, he had turned on the speaker and cut the volume low to prevent feedback. "Seems to me like my people have been kicking your goose-stepping ass all over the place."

Hoffman almost lost it at that. Ben could practically feel the hate coming over the airwaves. Hoffman took several deep breaths and said, "You will live to regret that remark, General Raines."

"I doubt it, Hoffman." Ben dropped all pretense of formality, since neither of them meant any of it. "But I will tell you something I really believe: this just might be the end for both of us."

Hoffman was silent for a time. Then he sighed. "All right. I will admit that has crossed my mind. But it does not have to be, General."

"I don't much care for any of the options you're about to present me, Field Marshal."

"Surely you recognize I represent the master race?"

Ben laughed. "The master race. You've got to be kidding. You're just like the rest of us, Hoffman. All mixed up. You've got German, Spanish, Indian, and no telling what else coursing through your veins. Where do you come off with this master race crap?"

"I think, General, that you are trying to bait me," Hoffman replied, avoiding the question. "You know exactly what I mean."

"This conversation is beginning to bore me, Field Marshal. It's just about time for dinner, and I'm hungry. Is there anything else on your mind?"

"Your arrogance will defeat you, General Raines." Hoffman could scarcely keep his anger in check. He was so angry his voice trembled, for he had radioed on an open frequency and knew that thousands of people—including many of his own—were listening to the exchange. And he was not making a very good showing. "I will bury you all!"

"A Russian leader said pretty much the same thing, decades ago," Ben reminded the Nazi leader. "He was wrong, and so are you. You might kill me, Hoffman, but the Rebel movement will go on, and eventually, be victorious. You don't have much sense, but I think you have enough to know that."

Hoffman lost it. He exploded in anger and started cursing Ben, in German, Spanish, and English, the profanity all jumbled up in languages.

Ben laughed at the man and signed off. He turned to his team and said, "That will blow the lid off, gang. He's got to recoup his verbal losses. He'll hit us hard and hit us soon. Put everybody on full alert."

"I can't understand why he radioed on an open frequency." Beth said.

"He's so arrogant he felt his troops would get a morale lift by listening to the conversation," Ben said, moving to a wall map. "It never occurred to him that he would come off second best." He studied the map for a moment. "I'm guessing now, but I'll bet that he'll probably move up artillery and start pounding us. All along this line. He'll try to punch through. Corrie, send a runner and tell Chase to pack up and move out. Have him shift all his MASH units back twenty miles. Right now!"

Ned Hawkins of the New Texas Rangers had entered the room and was standing quietly, listening. "Have we lost Texas, General?" he asked.

Ben shook his head. "No." He studied the map for a moment longer. Then he smiled grimly. "But we're going to let Hoffman have some territory. We'll let him punch through," he jabbed a finger at the map, "along this line, and commit his troops. While he's doing that, we'll be doing an end-around and harass the hell out of him on three fronts. From the south, east, and west. But we won't be able to do much in bumble-bee size teams. We'll reform in company strength and make him fight us along a line that conceivably could stretch for a thousand miles. He'll have to match us unit for unit or we'll be all over and around him by infiltration."

Ike had walked in with Doctor Chase. "Just as soon as we do the end-around and counterattack, Hoffman will order General Jahn's paratroopers to surface and hit our northern people hard," Ike said.

"Yes. So, Ike, you and Rebet take your battalions and all the latest reinforcements and move north, up to the thirty-sixth parallel. That'll put nearly seven thousand people under your command. You've got to keep Jahn's paratroopers contained and off our backs. As soon as Hoffman makes his push, Jahn might regroup into a major force and strike . . ." His eyes searched the big wall map north of the thirty-sixth parallel, ". . . somewhere. And he might decide to stay in small units and wage a guerrilla war. I don't know."

"Whichever way he goes, we'll hold them, Ben," Ike said. "But where does this put you, Ben? As if I can't guess."

Ben smiled. "In the field, Ike. I'm reforming my company and heading south. We can't afford to let even one able-bodied person stay back in this fight." He winked at Ike. "And I do a pretty fair job out there in the field."

Ike nodded his head. "I won't try to talk you out of it, Ben. I'm through with that." He stepped closer and stuck out his hand. "Good luck, Ben."

Ben shook the hand. "Same to you, Ike." He dropped the hand and smiled. "Maybe someday we can all sit around and reminisce about this."

Ike returned the smile, but like Ben's smile, it was forced. Both men knew this was root-hog-or-die time. That they would never see each other again after this moment was a real possibility.

Chase knew it, and walked to the table and poured three drinks, about two fingers each. "Drink up, boys. This is no time to be maudlin."

The men clinked glasses. Ben said, "To victory." He looked over at Jersey. "Right, Jersey?"

She smiled. "Kick-ass time, General!"

TWO

At dawn, Hoffman's big guns had been moved into position and opened up. From the ruins of Forth Worth-Dallas west over to Midland, Hoffman's gunners lobbed in rounds. But they fell on no Rebel positions. Ben had guessed accurately and shifted his troops. The incoming rounds created a lot of sound and fury but the Rebels sustained no casualties. And as Ben had predicted, when the big guns fell silent, Hoffman's troops massed for a northern push across I-20. They surged across, and found nothing.

Hoffman stood just north of the smoking ruins of Abilene, a look of confusion on his face. That was quickly replaced by fury when a runner handed him a message.

"Rebels are attacking our flanks and hitting hard to the south of us," Hoffman said. "Have we had any word from General Jahn?"

"General Jahn has been forced to regroup in order to combat the multinational force operating to the north of us," Hoffman was informed.

"Five Division is ranging far ahead of the other columns, sir," a young captain said, excitement in his voice. "The swastika is flying proudly over the cities of Dallas and Fort Worth. We are victorious!"

Hoffman stared at the young man. "How many Rebels has Five Division killed?"

"Why . . . ah . . . none, sir. But they have taken prisoner a group of people believed to be agents of the Rebel government. They deny it, of course. They claim to be from something called the Church of the Only Holy Way and they are demanding protection."

Hoffman continued to stare at the young captain. "Protection from what?"

"Us, sir."

"Send them to Colonel Barlach," Hoffman ordered. "He'll get the truth from them."

That would be the last time anyone would ever hear from the members of the Church of the Only Holy Way, whose members believed in nonviolence and who would not pick up a gun and fight for their dubious beliefs.

Hoffman clenched his fists in anger. "Have there been any Rebels reported killed?"

Hoffman's aides stood in silence. Their muteness gave the Field Marshal the answer to his question. His thousands of men had not killed a single Rebel.

"We have conquered nothing and we are victorious over destroyed cities and miles of desolation," Hoffman said. "We have not spilled one drop of Rebel blood." And I have led my troops into a box, he admitted silently.

Hoffman walked away from the group, to stand silently in the shade provided by what remained of one wall of a burned out building. "Ghosts," he muttered under his breath. "I'm in a battle with shadows and invisible whirlwinds. I can't win this way. It's impossible. How can we be victorious over an enemy who will not stand and fight?"

An aide approached him. "Sir? Your quarters are ready and the battle maps are up and accurate to the hour."

"By all means," Hoffman said, sarcasm thick in his voice. "Let me view this ravaged land and all its conquered and beaten people."

Hoffman stood in his quarters and looked at the huge map. He shook his head. "We're in a box," he finally spoke. "I led us right into a box."

"But one that we could break out of anytime we wished," a staff officer said.

"And go *where?*" Hoffman asked, touches of desperation in his voice. He sat down at his desk and rubbed his face with his hands. "Call in my generals," he said. "We have to have a meeting. We cannot continue like this. We are accomplishing nothing."

"We could advance, sir," a colonel spoke. "We could move right up to the thirty-sixth parallel."

Hoffman looked at the older man. They just don't understand, he thought. But I do. In all our years of war, we have relied on massive troop strength to conquer the people.

We should have stayed in South America.

He pushed that thought from him. But it wouldn't go far. It stayed in the back of his mind, nagging at him like an invisible but very vocal old hag.

We should have stayed in South America.

Shit! Hoffman silently raged.

Our supply lines have been cut, Hoffman thought, swiveling in his chair to face the map that he hated to look at. We have outdistanced what few trucks are getting through from the south. My elite shock troops are fighting for their lives against General McGowan and the multinational forces a hundred miles to the north and if I try to send troops in to beef up my paratroopers, the Rebels will ambush them. Most of my terrorist teams have been found and wiped out. Those two idiots to the east, Moi Sambura and Wink Payne are no help at all. Luis Carrero and his followers have proved to be less than worthless. All talk and no action. That's what I get for putting much faith in a former Los Angeles street gang leader, a black radical, and a white redneck.

We should have stayed in South America.

"Get my generals in here," Hoffman said wearily. "Order all troops to halt advances." He slammed a hand on his desk. "Goddamnit!"

Ben and his company had worked their way up close to the southernmost contingent of General Schmidt's third division. The rolling prairie country along the North Concho was very deceptive, and the Rebels had used that to their advantage, leaving their vehicles several miles away and advancing on foot and crawling on their bellies. Dusk was settling over the land, and the Rebels smelled fresh blood.

"Scouts report no more than two companies occupying the town," Corrie said. "Nearest reinforcements are forty-five miles to the northwest, thirty-five miles to the east, and forty-five miles to the north. The south is empty."

"Field Marshal Hoffman has called for a meeting of

his generals," Beth reported. She was monitoring the Blackshirts' frequencies. "Hoffman is slightly pissed."

Jersey, lying beside Ben, said, "Hoffman stepped on his dick this time."

Ben softly chuckled. "How close in are the Scouts?"

"Inside the town at five locations," Corrie said. "They'll create a diversion at your orders. Blackshirts are digging out their field rations now and getting ready to settle in for the night."

"Five minutes," Ben said. "We'll let them enjoy a few bites of their last supper. Any word from Ike?"

"Kicking the hell out of Jahn's forces. Ike says the multinational force is some of the best he's ever seen. The countries really sent the top people. Fifty of the Israeli IDF captured two hundred and fifty Blackshirt paratroopers."

"What'd they do with them?" Ben asked.

Corrie just looked at him.

"That's what I figured," Ben muttered. He took a sip of water and checked his Thompson, pausing as Corrie held up a hand and listened intently to her earphones. "What is it?"

"The troops in town just surrendered to the Scouts."

"They did what!"

"Packed it in. Gave up. Scouts say come on in. The town is secure."

The company of astonished Rebels stood up and walked into the tiny town just as dusk was settling over the land. The Blackshirts sat on the curbs and sidewalks, their hands on top of their heads.

A low murmuring began as the Blackshirts spotted Ben, ambling along, carrying the old Thompson. Ben caught the phrase being used and it amused him.

"El Lobo! El lobo espectro!"

They were calling him the Ghost Wolf.

Ben stopped in front of one young officer, a lieutenant, and stared down at him. The young man refused to meet Ben's eyes.

Ben turned to Lieutenant Ballard. "Jackie, what's going on here?"

"We haven't been able to figure that out yet, sir," she replied. "At first, we thought it might be some sort of trick. But now I believe these men are really scared to death of you."

A Spanish-speaking Rebel walked up. "They believe you possess supernatural powers, General. They think you're a shape-changer. And apparently so do a lot of other Blackshirts. But we can't get a fix on where it started."

An idea sprang into Ben's mind. "Make sure someone is monitoring the Blackshirts' radio at all times. Start interrogating these people. Find out if these men joined Hoffman willingly, or were conscripted. I've got a hunch it's the latter. I also have a hunch they don't have much in the way of education. We just might have found the fatal flaw in Hoffman's armor. He's spent years building a mighty army, but he forgot to educate his people. Get cracking."

Ben walked the line of Blackshirts. None of them would meet his eyes. They were terrified of him. More than a few of them crossed themselves when Ben drew near.

Ben heard mutters of "Silent Death," and "Ghost Walker," when he came close to the surrendered soldiers. He paced up and down the line, saying nothing, just staring at the men, who still refused to meet his gaze.

Jackie Ballard walked up and motioned Ben to one side. "You called it, General," she said. "These are conscripts. About half of Hoffman's army are draftees. They have no stomach for this fight. Most of them despise Hoffman and his methods. But the army was the only way to receive food and shelter and medical care for themselves and their families. It seems that Hoffman has taken over several South American countries and one either serves Hoffman, in one way or the other, or gets himself or herself enslaved or dead. The troops serving in the southern sector are nearly all conscripts. Only the hard-core are at the front."

"I'm getting the impression Hoffman's army is built on shifting sand," Ben replied. "How about education?"

She shook her head. "Very poorly educated. Many can neither read nor write much beyond a third grade level. They're very superstitious."

Ben nodded his head in understanding. The average age of Hoffman's troops was about twenty-one or so. That meant that when the Great War struck the earth, these men were children, and mentally, had not grown much beyond that.

All right, Hoffman, Ben thought. You still have us outnumbered, but I've found the chink in your armor.

"What are we going to do with these people, sir?"

"I don't know. Yet. But I'm working on it. Let's get something to eat and bed down. First thing in the morning, I want to speak with the officers and senior sergeants."

* * *

Ben and his team pulled out of the town at dawn, and headed for another location, taking the two companies of Blackshirts with them. The captured troops had proved themselves to be friendly and cooperative and seemed very much relieved to be prisoners of the Rebels.

The Rebels headed south, stopping about twenty-five miles later at the ruins of a tiny town. They were deep in enemy territory, but the bulk of the enemy was far to the north of them, and Ben felt they were in little danger. He was not surprised to find nearly a platoon of Blackshirts in the ruins of the town. Upon sighting the Rebels, they threw up their hands and grinned. Captain Garcia, commander of the surrendered Blackshirts, had told Ben to expect it.

"They do not wish to fight North Americans, General," Garcia said. "What they wish to do is to join your Rebel army."

"They would fight their friends?" Ben asked.

"No," Garcia said quickly. "But they would fight against the regular troops of Hoffman. Their friends will all surrender if you give them a chance to do so. Field Marshal Hoffman made a very bad mistake in forcing these men to join his army. Perhaps if he had not threatened their families if they did not join, things would have been different. Many of these men are from the many Indian tribes of South American countries. They can be very fierce fighters, for that is their heritage, but only if they choose to fight. You see, General, Hoffman deliberately kept these people uneducated. But just because one has little formal education does not mean that person is *estupido*. These people have seen that in your army, there are people of all colors, all faiths, all working together. Hoffman is a smart man, but he is also a very arrogant one. And he is surrounded by arrogant men."

The lieutenant in charge of the platoon of Blackshirts who had just surrendered approached Garcia and Ben, a package in his hand. Jersey leveled her M-16 at him.

"Wait!" Garcia said. "He means your general no harm. He has very little English, so he is going to show you his intentions." Garcia spoke in rapid-fire Spanish, too fast for Ben to follow, and the lieutenant nodded his head and opened the package and smiled.

The package contained civilian clothes.

The lieutenant pulled at a pocket of his black shirt. *"Muy malo,"* he said. He pointed to the civilian clothes and then to Ben's denim shirt. "Ver' good!"

Ben understood the simple message. He looked at Garcia. "All your people have civilian clothing?"

Garcia smiled. "Si. We have been waiting for you. Many more would like to join you, but they are afraid that El Lobo will shoot them before they can make their intentions known."

Ben looked at Garcia for a very long moment. If he made the wrong choice, the situation could well turn into a massacre for the Rebels. For once the surrendered black-shirts were armed, they would outnumber the Rebels in Ben's immediate command.

He looked at Lt. Ballard. "Jackie?"

She shrugged her shoulders. "I believe them, General. I think we've just found ourselves some much-needed allies."

Ben nodded his head slowly. He looked at Jersey. "How about you, Apache?"

"I say we go for it, General," Jersey told him. "If we

could come up with two or three additional battalions, and stay to the south of Hoffman's lines, we could really start kicking the shit out of him."

Ben opened his map case and spread the map out on a fender. "Captain, show me where you know there are troops waiting to join us."

Garcia pointed to a half dozen locations, running toward the east. "All along here, General. Two, maybe three thousand men and women. One to two companies at each location."

"The ranking officer?"

Garcia shrugged as only a Latin can do. "I guess that would be me, General. I was to be promoted to Major next month. My papers had already been approved. I am jump-qualified and jungle-trained. The equivalent to your old American Army Ranger."

"All right, Jorge," Ben said. "You're now a Colonel in the Rebel army." Jorge Garcia's mouth dropped open in shock. "Get out of those damn Blackshirts and into civilian clothes. We've got a war to win."

THREE

With the surrender of half a dozen of Hoffman's battalions—and the Blackshirt battalions were full strength battalions—Ben now not only had sufficient troops to be a real problem to those loyal to Hoffman, he also had captured large numbers of weapons and vehicles, and one of those battalions coming over to the Rebel side was a towed artillery battalion, with dozens of 155-mm howitzers and the heavy 6 × 6 trucks needed to pull them, and the eleven man crews needed to make them fully operational. The 155s had an enormous range and Ben was smiling as he inspected the guns and crews, who had burned their hated black shirts and were now dressed in a variety of colors.

"El Lobo!" one senior sergeant shouted, and soon the call was thundering all around the encampment. "General *El Lobo!"*

Ben let them shout until they got it out of their systems. He figured he'd sure been called a hell of a lot worse. Ben waited until they quieted down and stood silently, all eyes on him. Ben was not much on speeches, so through an interpreter, he kept it short.

"Welcome to the Rebel Army, and welcome to America and to Texas. When this war is over, and it will be and we will win . . ." He waited until a new round of cheering had faded, with many of his own people caught up in the spirit of the moment and joining in. ". . . You can return to your own homes, or bring your families up here and stay with us. The USA is a big empty country, and we need new people."

He paused for a moment. "We won't all make it through. We will have casualties. We will all lose friends and loved ones. I've helped bury more than I care to think about over the long and bloody years. Friends and loved ones," he said, his voice suddenly husky with emotion. For a moment, he thought of Jerre, buried on a lonely lovely ridge a thousand miles to the northwest. "It's the price we pay for freedom. Freedom is never cheaply won. The right to be free, to live and love and raise your families and attend the church of your choice and defend what is yours and work the earth or whatever your vocation might be, is always paid for with the blood of brave men and women. Men and women just like you.

"All of you have decided to reject the hateful and brutal philosophy of Nazism and join us against that terrible rebirth. Even though your commanders have made it clear to you that if you are captured, you will be shot, on the spot, by Hoffman's forces. Field Marshal Jesus Hoffman issued those orders yesterday morning and they were immediately passed along to you. I'm proud to say that not one of you elected to leave the ranks." He paused for a few seconds. "I'm not much on speeches, so I'll end with this: I welcome you all."

Ben stood alone—Jersey three steps back and to his

right, the butt of her M-16 on one hip—in front of several thousand troops and all the equipment of war, and listened to the wild cheering. They were certainly an enthusiastic bunch, but in the back of his mind, Ben was wondering if they could fight.

Well, he thought, that was going to be determined very quickly, for in his pocket he had the message Corrie had handed him just moments before he addressed the new troops. Hoffman was sending battalions of his elite SS troops against them. They were about twenty five miles away, to the north, and pressing hard.

"Colonel Garcia," Ben called.

"*Si*, General?"

"Position your troops and get your artillery in place. We are going to stand and slug it out."

"*Si*, General!"

Ben walked back to Lieutenant Ballard. "Position your people to the rear, Jackie. This is the fight of our new people. Let's see how they work."

"Yes, sir."

Ben walked the lines, and was impressed at how quickly and proficiently the new battalions worked. He concluded that they had been thoroughly trained by experts. Up to now, the only thing lacking had been motivation. Now they had it.

Colonel Garcia approached him. "General . . ."

"It's your show, Colonel," Ben cut him off. "You call the shots. I'm just an observer."

The young colonel knew that he and his command were being tested by the experienced older warrior. And he knew this was one test that none of them could afford to fail. He had looked into the eyes of all the Rebels, young and not so young. Jorge Garcia had seen years of combat experience in those eyes. These Rebels were experts at war. Even now, with hordes of SS troops advancing toward their position, many of the Rebels were resting on the ground, some reading worn books, some eating, some even asleep. They were, amazingly, utterly, totally calm. Jorge had never seen anything like it.

"Si, General Lobo," Jorge said. "We will not fail you."

Ben smiled, not taking offense at being called a wolf. "I'm counting on that, Colonel. The last thing I want is a Nazi bayonet up my butt."

"That will not happen," Jorge said.

Ben nodded and watched as the colonel trotted off, yelling orders in rapid-fire Spanish. All of the new people had some English, but Ben had okayed the use of Spanish until all of Jorge's people could master a new language.

"Ten miles out, sir," Corrie called. "Coming hard. They have towed artillery."

Colonel Garcia had his own spotters out with Ben's Scouts, and he was receiving the word at the same time as Ben. Ben sat down in a camp chair and rolled a cigarette.

"Preparado," Garcia spoke into his mic, his voice calm. Ben was a thousand or so meters behind the lines, monitoring Garcia's orders by radio.

The crews manning the 155s locked in HE, WP, and M449 antipersonnel rounds. The M-449 rounds each contained dozens of grenades and they were highly effective rounds.

"Good choice of rounds," Ben said, after thanking Cooper for a fresh cup of coffee.

The SS troops were well in range of the 155s, and still

Colonel Garcia held his fire. Ben smiled at that. Jorge knew his business. At eighteen miles this type of 155 could be accurate within approximately one hundred yards of its target. But the closer the target, the more accurate the big guns became.

The Rebels had stopped their reading and sleeping now, and were watching the crews preparing their howitzers for battle. The infantry battalions were dug in deep, the positions staggered in the shape of a huge and very wide U. This country was perfect for concealment and surprise, and Colonel Garcia was using it to its utmost.

"Six miles out," Corrie said. "And closing." She paused, a thoughtful expression on her face. "Whoever is commanding those SS troops is an arrogant fool, General," she added.

"You're right," Ben said. "They should be stopping and getting their artillery in place to soften us up. Instead, they just keep barrelling on. Right about now they're entering the first perimeters of the U. Jorge knows what he's doing. He's impressing the hell out of me. Jorge is going to give those SS troops a real nasty surprise."

Lieutenant Jackie Ballard leisurely strolled by. Cooper noticed with a very appreciative eye that she filled out her jeans remarkably well.

"Down, boy," Jersey told him, noticing the direction his eyes were traveling.

"It ain't no crime to look," Cooper replied. "Is it, General?"

"Damn sure isn't," Ben said. Ben always had an eye for the ladies.

"*Fuego!*" Colonel Garcia shouted, and the ground beneath their boots began to tremble as the 155s roared into action.

Whatever the SS troops expected, it certainly was not this rain of death that began hailing down on them from the skies. Jorge Garcia had aligned his guns with graduated elevation. The first mile of the SS convoy was suddenly turned into an exploding inferno. Bodies were ripped and torn apart and bloody bits and pieces hurled high into the hot smoky air. As those toward the rear began leaping from trucks in an attempt to escape the barrage, Jorge ordered his gunners to fire their antipersonnel rounds. It got real interesting for the SS troops when those started landing. The ground around the panicked SS troops, no matter which way they ran, turned deadly as the grenades began exploding.

Spanish armies have for centuries been big on bugles, and this one was no different. As the last rounds struck, Colonel Garcia shouted, *"Ataque!"* and about twenty-five bugles blew.

Ben nearly left his seat, for he had not noticed the trumpeters gathering a few yards behind him.

"Jesus H. Christ!" Jersey hollered, jumping up and looking wildly all around her.

Cooper had just lifted a coffee mug to his lips and when the bugles blew he spilled the whole cup down the front of his shirt. Beth was writing in her journal, and when the attack bugles blew, her pen went one way and the journal went another. Corrie had just taken off her earphones when the bugles blew, and she fell off the tailgate of a pickup truck, landing on her butt.

Ben looked at his team and started laughing, the laughter just audible over the bugles. Cooper was jumping around hollering, trying to get out of his steaming shirt, Jersey was wild-eyed, Beth looked numb, and Corrie just looked disgusted.

And the bugles continued to blow while Ben was cracking up with laughter.

Ben rode with Colonel Garcia up to the smoky field of death. The colonel's troops were just finishing off the last of the SS troops, and they were not being gentle in dealing with them. Garcia had ordered no prisoners taken, and his soldiers were following his orders to the letter.

A few of the SS troops were begging for mercy, for Heaven's sake. *"Compasion, dios!"* they cried. What they got was a bullet, for the South American allies of the Rebels were well aware of Hoffman's orders should they be taken prisoner, and they knew the SS troops would be happy to execute them on the spot, and take great joy in doing so.

"Gather up all the weapons and other usable equipment, Colonel," Ben instructed. "And equipment that even looks like it might be repairable. That's the Rebel way. We fix it up and store it."

"It is a very good way," Jorge agreed. "And one that we shall adopt, beginning now."

"Your troops were excellent in battle, Colonel," Ben complimented him. "Superb."

Colonel Garcia drew himself up to his full height, which was a good half a foot shorter than Ben. "We are Rebels now, General," he said proudly. "Anything less than perfection would not please me."

Ben smiled and patted the man on the shoulder. "Lighten up, Jorge. In battle, striving for absolute perfection is a good way to get killed. We just do the best we can and then get the hell gone. The Rebels do stand and slug it out from time to time, but we're at our best doing what Jim Bowie advocated. Cut, slash, and run."

"I know who that is!" Cooper said. "He was killed at the Alamo, right, General?"

"That's right, Cooper. He tried to convince Travis to abandon the old mission and launch a guerrilla type of war against Santa Ana. But in the end, Travis, Bowie, Crocket, and a hundred and eighty other men—give or take a few—died defending the mission."

"Was it worth it?" Beth asked.

"That's always been debatable," Ben replied. "I guess that as long as there is someone around with some knowledge of history, it always will be. But if you're asking for my opinion, yes, I think it was necessary; I think the time demanded that sacrifice. It galvanized the feelings of others and that helped win the war for Texas independence." He looked around him. "This is no time for a history debate. Let's get cracking, people, and then put some miles behind us."

Buzzards were circling high above them when the Rebels pulled out, heading east. Even if they were spotted by Hoffman's scouts, no light force would dare attack them, for they were now several thousand strong, and Ben knew that his new Rebels could fight, and fight well.

Far to the north, Hoffman sat behind his desk and silently fumed. The man was absolutely livid with rage, but he had vented his vocal rage and now sat silent. He had sent hundreds of elite troops to crush a few battalions of dissident and ignorant troops, and they had been wiped out to the last man.

"Raines!" he suddenly shouted, leaping to his feet and startling the room full of staff officers. "Raines joined them. Has to be. He's south of us. We've got him and I didn't realize it."

"Got him?" a junior officer questioned before he thought.

Hoffman took no umbrage at the blurted insolence. "Of course. Shift two divisions to the south and engage the bastard and his ignorant new followers."

A senior officer, far too old for the field, was the first to speak. "Jesus, no," he said quietly.

"Uncle Frederich," Hoffman said, looking at the man. "You are questioning me?"

"Yes, Jesus. I am. The rabbit does not pursue the wolf. And Ben Raines is an old gray *lobo*. And those with him are not *lobeznoes*."

Hoffman waved that aside. "I know they are not cubs. They are nothing more than ignorant savages. Many of them can scarcely read and write."

"But they showed today that they could fight," the old man didn't back up. "I, along with others, have warned you about conscripts. I have taken the liberty of purging our ranks of conscripts. It is rare that they make good soldiers . . . for us. Today certainly proved that."

"Uncle Frederich . . ."

"Hear me out, Jesus! I am owed that much."

"*Si, mio tio,*" Hoffman said, and sat down. He could not be disrespectful to a man who had helped raise him.

"I think I know what General Raines is doing. He is making you split your forces, making you fight on many fronts. And that is nearly always the kiss of death. Don't fall for this trick, Jesus."

The other staff officers sat quietly, none of them

wanting any part of this exchange. The old soldier could get away with arguing with the field marshal . . . and he was about the only one who could. The exploding rage of Jesus Hoffman toward anyone who questioned his orders was well known.

"Uncle Frederich," Hoffman said, "even with the addition of these turncoat troops, we still have Raines vastly outnumbered. I feel now is a golden opportunity for us."

The old soldier shook his head slowly, a grim expression on his face. "You heard the desperate radio calls from those dying troops. General Raines now has a new name: 'El Lobo.' And you know how superstitious many of our most loyal troops are. There are murmurings even among them. 'Shape-changer,' is what many are calling General Raines. They roll their eyes and shake their heads just at the mention of his name. My suggestion is this: dispatch enough troops to block the highways and keep General Raines and troops occupied. But no more than that. Shift a division up north to assist General Jahn's paratroopers now fighting those Rebels commanded by General McGowan. Crush those Rebels closest to us. Using massive force, crush them, defeat them battalion by battalion. But don't, *don't*, spread your forces too thin. Don't fall for this plan of General Raines'."

The meeting was interrupted by a messenger. "General Raines on the radio, Field Marshal. He is asking to speak with you."

"Ah!" Hoffman said with a smile, sitting down and turning up the volume on his speaker. In a moment, the patch was completed. Hoffman's mouth dropped open and a collective gasp went up from everybody in the

206

room except Frederich when the voice of Ben Raines boomed throughout the room.

"Hello, Hoffman," Ben said. "You goose-stepping shithead!"

FOUR

Hoffman's face drained of color. Nobody—*nobody*—spoke to him in such a manner. Hoffman sat, momentarily speechless. A small smile curved the lips of the old soldier. He knew only too well what Ben Raines was doing. And he knew without any doubt that his nephew was going to take the bait. Frederich Rasbach started making plans that moment. Even before Hoffman found his voice in retort, the old soldier had made up his mind to take a few troops and leave. North America was about to become very unhealthy. Frederich rose and moved toward the door. There, he paused, to confirm his suspicions.

"I'll crush you!" Hoffman screamed into the mic. "Raines, you bastard! I'll grind you under the heel of my boot."

"Fuck you, Hoffman," came the calm voice of Ben Raines.

Frederich put out his hand toward the door knob and shook his head slowly and sadly.

"How dare you speak to *me* in such a manner!" Hoffman hollered, his face flushed. "You . . . you *trash!*"

Frederich heard fast-approaching boots and stepped aside to let a runner in. The young man rushed to Hoffman's side. "We have his location pinpointed, Field Marshal."

Hoffman nodded his head in understanding and with an impatient wave of his hand, silenced the runner.

"How about you and I settling this, Hoffman?" Ben questioned. "Just the two of us. Man to man. We'll meet and duke it out. Winner take all."

"Duke?" Hoffman questioned the room.

"He means fists, sir," a staff officer said.

"Fist-fighting?" Hoffman said. "How barbaric. But what else should I expect from a low-life with no breeding? Why, the man must be at least fifty years old. He wouldn't offer such a challenge unless he planned some sort of trick."

"General Raines is totally untrustworthy, Field Marshal," another staff officer spoke. "He is not a gentleman."

Frederich smiled. Gentleman, or not, Ben Raines meant every word he had just spoken, and the old soldier hoped his nephew would not take up the offer. Ben Raines would kick the snot out of the younger man.

And enjoy doing it, the old soldier mentally added.

"Two and Three divisions to the south," Hoffman ordered, his face still beet red and his hands trembling with fury. "Immediately. Full armor and artillery."

A staff officer rushed from the room.

You young fool! the old soldier thought. Sending troops right into the wolf's den. And sending them to their deaths.

"How about it, fart-breath?" Ben spoke. "Are you still there or have you gone to the latrine to shit your fear?"

The old soldier by the door had to suppress a chuckle. He despised Ben Raines, but he admired greatly the man's courage and grasp of tactics. And also how well he played on human egos.

Hoffman was so outraged he could not speak. He sat holding the microphone and sputtered.

Say something, you idiot! Frederich thought. Go ahead, step deeper into the trap General Raines is laying out for you. We had such high hopes for you, Jesus. But we failed to see your frailties. You were too coddled, kept too close to the breast. What you are is not your fault, but ours.

"You are a dead man, Raines," Hoffman finally found his voice and composure.

Someday, for sure, as all of us must face that long sleep, the old soldier thought. But not by your hands, Jesus. Resist those orders, Generals, Frederich silently urged.

The officer who had left the room returned, his face flushed with excitement. "Generals Kroesen and Schmidt will be heading south within the hour, Field Marshal," the officer said, waiting until after Hoffman had released the talk key.

"Very good," Hoffman said, then frowned as Ben's voice once more filled his head.

"Hey, Hoffman!" Ben called rudely. "Stop playing with your dick and talk to me."

Hoffman clicked off the radio and turned to face his staff officers. "I will not dignify any remark from that barbarian with a reply."

Several hundred miles south, Ben grinned and handed the mic to Corrie. "Did I talk long enough for them to pinpoint our location?"

"They're probably halfway here by now," Corrie said drily.

Ben laughed and patted her shoulder. "Well, you said you were getting bored, remember? All right," Ben said, rubbing his hands together and pacing as he talked. "Hoffman is going to throw quite a number at us. He's not going to take any chances on us slipping away this time. He'll throw at least one division and probably two at us. What divisions are closest to us, Colonel Garcia?"

"Hoffman's First division is the nearest. But I'd guess Two and Three divisions will be the ones chosen for this. Commanded by Generals Kroesen and Schmidt. They're professionals."

"Not SS?"

"No. That is Brodermann. And we wiped out nearly half his troops." He smiled. "And he was running a very short division, as you may recall."

Ben recalled. "Then for all intents and purposes, the SS troops are but a memory."

"I would guess that he has perhaps four to six battalions left."

"Can he rebuild?"

"Possibly. But not too quickly. He chose his people very well, over a period of years. And Brodermann was not among the dead. At least not that we could identify."

"No. We wouldn't be that lucky, Jorge. All right. We'll say he has five thousand troops left him. That's still a lot of SS crap to have looking over our shoulders."

"I hate those people," a young captain from Garcia's command said. "I loathe them." He shuddered. "They're cruel and twisted men and women."

211

"So were the ones who surfaced seventy-odd years ago," Ben replied. "Nothing changes."

"So what do we do now?" Colonel Garcia asked.

"Why, we wait for the Blackshirts to get here," Ben said calmly. Then he smiled and confused the colonel when he said, "Sort of."

Ben had forced Hoffman to spread his people all over a front that extended hundreds of miles, and Hoffman had no choice but to move his people around in an oftentimes futile attempt to plug holes. He had been forced to send additional troops north of I-20 to assist General Jahn in fighting Ike McGowan and his people. Hoffman's supply lines had been stopped cold in South America and whatever supplies he received had to be flown into the airport at San Antonio and trucked out into the field. Hoffman's grandiose plans to conquer all of North America by fall had been tossed on the scrap heap. Ben Raines and his Rebels had stopped him cold in Texas with little hope of getting out anytime soon.

Hoffman had marched into Texas with just under 200,000 troops, and Ben Raines and his rag-tag bands of malcontents had stopped him dead bang.

Now, to make matters worse, many of his troops were walling their eyes like frightened cattle at the mere mention of Ben Raines's name. There had been talk of some old man who called himself the Prophet popping up all over the place and calling down the wrath of God upon the heads of the invaders.

Nonsense, of course, but many of his troops were getting spooked. And Hoffman did not know how to combat the wild rumors.

And his closer advisor and friend, Hoffman's Uncle Frederich Rosbach, had flown back to South America. Frederich had urged his nephew to abandon his dreams of conquering all of North and South America and return with him. Hoffman, naturally, refused.

One thing Hoffman did know for certain was that when his Second and Third Divisions reached Ben Raines's position in the south of Texas, he would be rid of that bastard forever.

Hoffman might have felt certain about that, but somebody forgot to tell Ben.

Dawn.

"The enemy columns are proceeding very cautiously," Corrie said to Ben.

"Placement of vehicles?" Ben asked.

"Strung out wide and using all accessible roads. ETA of advance troops 1300 hours this day."

"Everybody mounted up and ready to roll?"

"Sitting on ready."

"From this moment on, maintain tight radio silence. If something has to be transmitted, use burst only."

"Yes, sir."

"Let's pack it up and get the hell out of here."

Ben had split his forces, half heading west, the other half east. Colonel Garcia had stepped aside without a word, knowing this was General Raines's show.

When the Second and Third Divisions of Blackshirts had moved out, heading south, Ben ordered four battalions of his Rebels to move east and at his orders, mix it up with the small garrisons left behind. Hoffman had not yet realized it, but he had committed one very large fuck-up. He had left his western flank wide open. Ben could not understand how the man could have made such a terrible error in judgement, but he had, and Ben was going to take full advantage of it.

It was going to be a race for time and distance, one that if Ben lost could spell disaster for his command. But if he could pull it off, he just might be able to knock the boots out from under Hoffman and really give his own people one hell of a morale booster.

"Brilliant," Colonel Garcia said, when Ben outlined his plan. "Absolutely brilliant."

Ben didn't know how brilliant his plan was; he just hoped it would work.

Ben had left behind a small force, armed with howitzers taken from the demolished SS troops. When the two divisions came into range, the small force of Rebels and South American troops would open fire, engaging the Second and Third Divisions in an artillery duel for as long as possible. Ben and his battalions and Colonel Garcia and his battalions would be driving straight north just as fast as road conditions allowed. When they reached the southern edge of Hoffman's First Division, the four battalions of Rebels would attack the small garrisons from the Second and Third left behind from the west. Ben and Colonel Garcia would then strike at Hoffman's First Division, catching them, they hoped, by surprise.

Scouts were already in place, waiting for Ben's orders to neutralize Hoffman's southernmost forward observation posts.

By the time the troops of the Second and Third Divisions overran the positions of the Rebel gunners left behind, who would, hopefully, have bugged out before that happened, the Blackshirt generals would realize they had been suckered. But they would be a good 175 miles south of the surprise attack on Hoffman's First Division, and unable to do anything except cuss Ben Raines. Which Ben felt sure they would do, with a great deal of passion.

Ben was under no illusions concerning the attack. He knew he probably would not get anywhere near Hoffman's HQ. But just being able to strike within a few miles of the man would shake the Nazi bastard down to his toenails.

But General Brodermann worried Ben. His intell people had not been able to pinpoint the man's location. And the thought of that SS son of a bitch launching his own sneak attack against Ben, while Ben was hitting Hoffman with his own surprise attack, was not pleasant.

Then Corrie dropped the news on Ben.

"Brodermann is with the First Division," she said. "Meeting with Field Marshal Hoffman at his HQ. Apache scouts grabbed a Blackshirt recon team and got the information out of them. His battalions have been assigned to Hoffman's division."

"Well, at least we know approximately where he is," Ben said. "Do we have an exact location of Hoffman's HQ?"

"No, sir. Only that he moves it daily. It seems the man is awfully paranoid."

"You have any idea what happened to the Blackshirt recon team?" Ben asked.

"I would imagine they probably tried to escape," Corrie said blandly.

"Uh-huh," Ben said.

"Our gunners are now engaged in an artillery duel

with batteries of the Second and Third Divisions," Corrie said, after listening to her headset for a moment.

The convoy rolled past one of Hoffman's southern-most forward observation posts. Rebel Scouts were sitting by the side of the road, having a late lunch. They gave Ben's command car the thumbs-up sign as it rolled past.

Ben returned the thumbs-up as the convoy rolled on.

"No one's given any alarm yet," Corrie said. "The luck is still with us."

"May the Force be with you," Ben muttered.

"Beg pardon, sir?" Cooper asked.

Ben smiled. "It's from an old movie, Coop."

"Two minutes to artillery drop off, sir," Beth said, working the other radio.

They would drop off the artillery, wait until the guns were ready to fire, and then drive under the overhead arching shells for just under twelve miles. By the time they struck at First Division, the Blackshirts would be softened up . . . considerably.

Ben's forces would then liven things up a bit for the hopefully still-stunned Blackshirts.

"Everybody out and stretch for five," Ben said, as Cooper brought the Hummer to a halt. It would take the eleven man artillery crews just about five minutes to position the 155s and have them ready for firing.

Ben rolled a cigarette and stretched his legs while the artillery crews separated, formed up, and set up. He took a drink of water and checked his Thompson, then checked the bag filled with full drums on the floorboards of the Hummer.

"Colonel Garcia in place," Corrie said. "We will link

up just outside the southernmost edge of First Division's encampment."

"Or what's left of it," Ben said, toeing out the butt of his cigarette. "Everybody knows what they're to do, so there is nothing left to say. Mount up."

The now more than regiment size band of Rebels would roar through the devastation, firing everything they had, including Big Thumpers, until they reached the approximate center of the sprawling encampment. There, they would dismount and take the battle hand to hand.

Those Blackshirts left behind by the Second and Third Divisions had pulled back to the east and joined for greater strength. Four battalions of Rebels were now striking at that small garrison and the plan was for them to punch through and link up with Ben and Colonel Garcia.

Buddy and his battalion, along with the Outlaw bikers, were driving hard for San Antonio. They would stay there and harass the Eighth Division guarding the airport and the ruins of town. Such a small force had no hope of defeating a division, but they could keep them hemmed in and worry the hell out of them.

While Ben was striking from the north, Striganov, West, and Danjou would be hammering hard from the north end of the First Division's lines. If all this worked, Ben's hopes were that Hoffman would be forced to withdraw to the east. Five battalions of Rebels, Dan, Tina, Pat O'Shea, Greenwalt, and Jackie Malone's battalion, were stretching out north to south along Highway 281 and setting up many of the batteries of artillery that Ben had been holding in reserve.

Payon, Paul Gomez, Jim Peters, and Ned Hawkins's bunch were pushing hard to get in position to the south.

If this worked, they would have Hoffman and his men in a box.

If it worked.

FIVE

When the first artillery rounds hit, Hoffman was just sitting down for coffee with General Brodermann. His HQ was several miles from the explosions, but he still heard the booming.

"What the hell?" he said, turning in his chair.

Then rounds started coming in fast and hard.

"We're under attack from the south!" Brodermann said, jumping to his feet.

Hoffman ran for the office and reached it just as an aide opened it from the other side. The door impacted with Hoffman's nose and knocked him sprawling to the floor, his beak bloody. The aide stood frozen, horrified at what he'd done.

"Idiot!" Brodermann yelled at the young man. "Fool! You've injured the Field Marshal. What the hell do you want?"

"We . . . we're being attacked from the west, sir!"

"From the west? What the hell are you blathering about? Are you deaf as well as stupid? We're being attacked from the south. Goddamn it, can't you hear?"

"From the west, too, sir," the aide blurted. Field Marshal Hoffman was just getting unceremoniously to his feet, grabbing at a chair for support, his nose clearly broken and spurting blood. "The garrison just radioed. They cannot hold and are falling back to our position."

"My no' is 'oken," Jesus Hoffman said. "Shit!"

A fat colonel came running into the outer office and tried to stop. The floor of the old home was slick tile, and his leather-soled boots could find no traction. He slammed into the aide, the aide slammed into Brodermann, and Brodermann slammed into Field Marshal Hoffman. All of them went slipping and sliding and tumbling to the floor. For a few seconds, it looked like the Three Stooges meets Danny Kaye.

"We're under massive attack from the north!" the colonel hollered.

"Get off me, you elephant!" Brodermann yelled.

"'et off of 'e!" Hoffman shouted, spraying everybody with blood.

An SS officer came running in. He stood for a moment in the doorway, his mouth hanging open and his face registering his shock.

"What the hell do you want?" Brodermann screamed.

"Ah . . . why, ah, General Schleyer says he is under attack at the San Antonio airport. Why are you all on the floor? What has happened to the Field Marshal?"

Captain Blickle came running in. He blinked at the scene on the office floor. He shook his head and decided it wasn't any of his business. For the moment, at least. "Scouts from General Mohnhaupt's Seventh Division say Rebels are lined up north to south in massive numbers along Highway 281. They have begun shelling his command." He paused. "What are all you people doing on the floor?"

Before anyone could reply—not that anyone was about to—several artillery rounds landed a few hundred yards from Hoffman's HQ. The explosions blew out all the windows on that side of the house and tore off part of the old roof. Captain Blickle joined the others on the floor.

"'Oddamnit!" Hoffman yelled. "'Et off me!"

The rattle of automatic weapons could now be clearly heard.

"Rebels!" someone outside screamed. "Thousands of them. El Lobo is leading the charge."

Brodermann lurched to his feet. "If I hear El Lobo one more time," he shouted. "I'll shoot the son of a bitch who said it."

Together, they all managed to get Jesus Hoffman to his unsteady feet and out the door. "Get the Field Marshal to safety," Brodermann ordered.

"Where?" Captain Blickle demanded, looking around him at the panicked troops, confusion and the exploding artillery rounds.

"How the hell should I know?" Brodermann shouted. "Just get him out of here. Move, goddamnit!"

Blickle and the still nose-bleeding Hoffman rushed to a waiting car and jumped in the back seat. The driver sped off. Brodermann looked around for some of his SS troops, then realized they were miles to the north and probably helping contain the charge of Rebels up there.

"Damnit!" he swore. "Who would have guessed Raines would do something like this?"

Brodermann finally and forever, in the span of only a few seconds, realized that one simply could not second-guess Ben Raines. If you made ready for the norm, he would throw something at you completely off the wall.

Expect something totally unorthodox, and Raines would hand you something right out of a military textbook.

Then Brodermann looked on in amazement as the Rebels began slowing and stopping their vehicles, troops dismounting and engaging the Blackshirts in hand-to-hand combat. "No!" he shouted. "This simply cannot be!"

But it was happening, and Brodermann suddenly got that message and looked around for any officer. He saw one. He jerked his pistol out of the holster and tried to rally the panicked troops. One tried to run past him, all wild-eyed and scared, and Brodermann shot the man. That got the attention of several people. "Throw up a line!" he shouted. "Goddamn you, listen to me. Throw up a line and hold it."

He got the attention of several sergeants, and they quickly began to shout and kick some order back into the troops. A line was thrown up and slowly some semblance of soldiering began to take place. The fighting was now going to be house to house and very close up.

Ben jumped over the sandbags around a machine gun emplacement, jerked the dead body away from an unfamiliar but heavy machine gun, and stitched a deuce and a half from radiator to midway of the bed. Every third or fourth round loaded into the belt must have been incendiary, for the truck exploded and sent body parts flying all over the place.

Jersey and Corrie jumped into the pit with him and Cooper began helping with the belt while Corrie was trying to raise other battalions for a battle assessment.

Ben grinned at her. "When you get Ike, tell him we're having fun down here and wish he could join us!"

Corrie ignored him. She'd been with Ben for years

and nothing he ever did surprised her. She finally yelled, "It was a total surprise, General. All battalions on all fronts reporting we really caught them with their pants down."

"Casualties?" Ben yelled, after cutting down three running Blackshirts. He rested his hands from the heavy jarring of the machine gun.

"Very light."

"Give me a status report on conditions right here, Corrie," Ben requested.

After a moment, she said, "We're stretched out along a line approximately three miles wide. Artillery wants to know should they shell the town?"

"Negative," Ben quickly told her. "Hell, we're on the outskirts of the damn town. Tell the batteries to advance to within a few miles of us and set up and wait for orders."

That done, Ben said, "Corrie, give the orders to go over the top, people. Let's go, let's go, let's go!" And he jumped out of the sandbagged pit and took off running.

"Jesus!" Cooper said, and took off after him, Jersey and Beth and Corrie right on his heels.

Brodermann took one look at the advancing Rebels and cursed as he shook his head. He knew with a soldier's sixth sense that to stand and face that would be pointless. "Fall back!" he shouted. "Fall back to those woods north of town. Move. Quickly, now."

"Secure the town and then advance no further," Ben panted the orders, squatting down behind a brick house.

When he had caught his breath, and Corrie had issued the orders, Ben said, "Set me up a CP and rig for long range transmission, Corrie. Tell supply to get our uniforms ready for us. From tiger stripe to desert cammie. We're back in business!"

When the major five-front offensive was launched by the Rebels in Texas, those Rebel contingents in California, Arizona, and New Mexico rushed the Blackshirts on the other side of the border, while General Payon's guerilleros struck them from the south and the worshipers of Nazism were caught by surprise. No prisoners were taken.

General Cecil Jefferys sat in his command post at Base Camp One with a smile on his face. He had felt all along that when everything fell into place enough to satisfy Ben's mind, he would quit playing cat and mouse all over the state of Texas and really step in close and slap the crap out of Hoffman. And he had done just that.

Cecil made a mental note to go see Ben's dogs that afternoon and play with them for a time. He knew they missed Ben terribly and he needed the exercise anyway.

"Give 'em hell, Ben," Cecil said.

Hoffman and the remnants of his First Division managed to slip through the thin northern lines, running west to east, and hurriedly thrown up by Striganov, West, and Danjou. Hoffman's Second and Third divisions were being held right where they were by Payon, Gomez, Jim Peters, and Ned Hawkins's Texas Rangers. Hoffman's Sixth and Seventh Divisions were taking a real pounding from the battalions of Dan Gray, Tina Raines, Pat O'Shea, Greenwalt, and Malone. Hoffman's Fourth and Fifth Divisions massed and overran

Danjou's position on the eastern edge of the front and pushed into the clear into northern Texas.

Ben ordered those contingents coming from the west to angle south and link up with Raul Gomez who was holding east and west of either side of Highway 277. He also ordered everyone back into uniform and pulled out all the tanks and artillery he'd been holding in reserve.

To the north, Ike ordered teams out to blow all bridges along the Canadian River from the New Mexico line over into Oklahoma, and Cecil sent teams from Base Camp One to blow the bridges along the Canadian from Oklahoma City to the Arkansas line.

Ben leaned back in a rat-chewed old recliner Cooper had found for him and smiled. "Now, Hoffman, you goose-stepping dickhead. Now, let's see you wriggle your way out of this one."

"The Field Marshal does not wish to be disturbed," an aide told the tough paratroop General.

General Jahn looked at the young man and smiled. "Get out of my way, you strutting little REM, before I physically remove you."

The aide blustered, but stepped out of the way. "Sir," he said. "What is a REM?"

Jahn smiled. "It's an American expression. It means Rear Echelon Motherfucker." He stepped into the office and closed the door behind him.

Hoffman's nose had been set and a piece of tape placed across it. He looked at Jahn for a moment. "Well, General Jahn, what is it?"

"Consider surrender terms, Field Marshal," the general said without hesitation.

Hoffman blinked. "Have you lost your damn mind, General?"

"No," Jahn replied shortly. He walked to a sideboard, poured a snifter of brandy, and drank it down.

Far too much brandy, Hoffman noticed. And without taking the time to savor the delicate bouquet. The man was utterly without breeding.

"But it's time to consider our position," Jahn said, his back to the Field Marshal. He poured another brandy, and this time swirled the liquid about and gave it time to breathe a bit.

Then, Hoffman noticed, he knocked it back like a damn drunken roustabout.

"It's better than it was a few days ago," Hoffman said.

"Hell would have been better for us than then," Jahn said. He spoke his mind and damn the consequences. He was a professional soldier, not a diplomat. He turned, facing Hoffman. "Field Marshal, consider this: Eighth Division is pinned down in the ruins of San Antonio. Raines' Rebels there have now been beefed up by about a thousand Mexican guerrillas. Schleyer cannot get out. The Rebels have blown every bridge, every overpass, in a circle around the city. The Eighth is trapped and we cannot get supplies in to them. They are doomed. They will fight until their ammunition is gone, and then they will be forced to surrender."

"We will be victorious up here and then send relief columns to break them out!" Hoffman shouted.

"You're living in a dream world, Field Marshal."

Hoffman jumped to his feet. "You do not speak to me in such a manner!"

"I offer you the truth while your staff officers shield

you and tell you only things they know you want to hear. And you know that is the truth."

Hoffman sat back down and pouted for a moment. He lifted his eyes and looked at General Jahn. "Surrender is repugnant. Absolutely unacceptable."

"Raines is a warrior, a first class fighting man and brilliant tactician, but he is also an honorable man." Jahn sat down in a chair in front of Hoffman's desk. "Field Marshal, you know I only pay lip service to the teachings of Hitler. I am not a Nazi and never have been. No matter what you tell other people or personally think about me, and I know you think you have converted me, I shall never be a Nazi. What am I, what I have been all my life is a fighting man. I am a soldier. You are a student of history, Field Marshal, so think back. Not to the lies and half-truths you were taught as a boy, but to the real truth that you later discovered. The entire world rallied together, seventy years ago, against the man you worship. And now this shattered world is doing the same thing against us. There will be more countries coming in, Field Marshal. Trust me. My intelligence people have monitored other nations' transmissions, and even though they have internal problems of their own, they are putting forces together to assist the Rebels. Even as we speak. I personally don't think they will arrive here in time; I think we will be but a memory before long. But the Gods of war are fickle—they might choose to smile on us for a change. Who knows?"

Hoffman stared at the general for a long moment. His first thought was to immediately relieve the man of command. But he quickly put that out of his mind. Jahn was a fine commander and a brilliant tactician. His men would follow him through the gates of Hell without question. True, the forces of the NAL had suffered a setback, but not one that was insurmountable. He must convince Jahn of that. He needed the paratroop general. Needed him very badly.

"I will not consider surrender, General Jahn," Hoffman reiterated.

Jahn shrugged his shoulders. "In that case, Field Marshal, I am certain that most of my men will fight to the death. But I will not order them to do that."

"You do not believe in our cause, General?"

Jahn smiled. "You mean the torture and oppression and slavery of people, Field Marshal?"

"I am doing no more than Ben Raines is doing," Hoffman replied.

Jahn met Hoffman's eyes. The man is crazy, the paratrooper thought. Why couldn't I see that months ago? He knew the answer to that even before the thought cleared his mind. He saw it. He just ignored it.

"Anything else, General Jahn?"

The paratrooper was silent for a few heartbeats. He shook his head and rose to his boots. "No, Field Marshal. There is nothing else."

"Dismissed."

"Yes, sir."

Hoffman threw out his left arm. "Heil Hitler!"

Jahn looked at him. "Shit!" he said, and left the room.

SIX

Corrie looked up, surprise on her face. "General!" she called to Ben, seated across the room, his eyes poring over maps.

Ben removed his reading glasses and looked over at her. "Yes, Corrie?"

"General Jahn on the horn, sir."

Ben quickly walked the distance and took the mic. "Ben Raines here."

"This is General Jahn. I wish to discuss surrender terms, General Raines."

"On the air?"

"On the air, face to face, or sitting on two burros," Jahn's strong voice came through the speaker. "It makes no difference to me. My only concern is the treatment of my men."

"A trick, Ben?" Lamar Chase asked, standing close.

"I don't think so." He keyed the mic. "If your men lay down their weapons and agree to leave the United States, they will not be harmed, General. I give you my word. But I can't guarantee their safety once out of this country."

"We don't want to leave the country, General. We want to become residents," Jahn replied. "We are not Nazis, General. We are soldiers. But do not ask us to fight against men and women who we, in many cases, have known since childhood. I cannot ask my men to do that."

"I understand, General. I would like to meet with you, General."

"It would be an honor, sir."

"Hold what you have and stay on this frequency," Ben told him. "I'll be back in touch with you in fifteen minutes."

"I shall be waiting. General Jahn clear."

"Get me Ike, Corrie."

"Shark here. Go, Eagle."

"What do you see up there, Shark?"

"White flags, Eagle. Lots of them. My recon teams tell me that Jahn's people all over the place are laying down their weapons and standing in the roads, in the streets, in the fields, hands on their heads."

"I'll be at your location ASAP, Shark. Make a fresh pot of coffee."

"That's a big ten-four, Ben."

Ben put on his beret and picked up his Thompson. "Let's go, people."

Hoffman was clearly suffering from a mild case of shock. That General Jahn, one of the toughest and most capable soldiers he had ever known would surrender to Ben Raines had never entered Hoffman's thoughts.

Hoffman lifted dull eyes to his staff people gathered

around his desk. "What happened?" was all the man could say.

Ben and General Jahn shook hands, and then both men stepped back and studied each other for a moment. Jahn slowly removed his pistol from his holster, all the while keeping one eye on Jersey, who, Jahn quickly and accurately surmised, would be more than happy to shoot him dead on the spot, and handed the weapon, butt first, to Ben.

Ben took it, looked at it, and returned it to Jahn. "Tell your men to keep their sidearms, General. We still have hundreds, perhaps thousands, of outlaws and assorted scum roaming the country. I won't leave you defenseless."

Jahn holstered the pistol. "That is kind of you, General Raines. Some of my men were worried about that very matter. Where would you like us to relocate?"

"Anywhere you like, General. I must advise you that General Brodermann has orders from Field Marshal Hoffman to hunt you down and kill you."

Jahn smiled. "I certainly hope that murderous SS bastard tries it. It will be the last thing he ever does."

Ben laughed. "I believe you, General. Do you know what Hoffman has in mind?"

"No, sir, I do not. And I would tell you if I did. The field marshal and I did not exactly, ah, part on the friendliest of terms the other evening."

Ben chuckled. "You didn't hit him, did you?"

Jahn again smiled. "No. But I would be lying if I said that thought did not occur to me."

Ben sobered and looked at the man. "I have to ask, General. Why did you surrender your men?"

"Frankly, because you are going to win, General Raines. And I felt that any further sacrifice of my men would be criminal on my part."

"Any Nazis in your division, General?"

"Plenty of them. And they did not surrender and will still conduct a guerrilla type action against the Rebels."

"Thank you for your candor, General Jahn. One more thing: If you are serious about joining the Rebels and settling in this country, you will be expected to fight for it."

Jahn smiled. "That is something we do very well, General. Count on us."

The men shook hands and Ben left him with Ike. Just as Ben and Georgi Striganov had once been bitter enemies, and were now friends, Ben felt that given the time, he and Jahn would also become fast friends and allies. Also, though Jahn didn't know all about the meeting, while Ben had been driving up to meet with him, he and his senior officers had been interviewed separately and every word analyzed by some of the most sophisticated lie detector equipment anywhere in the world. Had Ike felt any of them to be lying, he would have shot them on the spot.

Battalions had been reformed and most of the Rebels were back in uniform. For those fighting in the arid parts of the state, they wore desert cammo to better blend in. A few wore tiger-stripe and the rest wore woodland cammo. All were back in black berets when out of combat zone or on stealth patrol, everyone on the line was in helmets and body armor, Kevlared to the max.

Artillery was all in place, gunships were being readied—on both sides, Ben was sure—and the two forces were about to start slugging it out.

And still Hoffman had made no major move to bust his Sixth and Seventh Divisions out of the loose box they were in. Ben had spent several long days pouring over intelligence reports and dozens of maps.

"I just can't believe it," Ben finally muttered. "Hoffman is going to do it." This was said after Ben had studied several bundles of intercepted dispatches between Hoffman and his commanders and then carefully studying a map. "He's really going to stand and slug it out with my eastern battalions. The man is a fool." He straightened up from the table and said, "Corrie, order Dan to launch a full scale artillery attack immediately. Tell General Payon I'm shifting Jim Peters Fourteenth Battalion and Ned Hawkins and his Rangers to the south, with all the artillery they can muster, to prevent the Second and Third from making an attempt to break the Eighth division out of San Antonio. Tell Garcia to shift two of his battalions down to help on the eastern front. The Blackshirts can't run west. There isn't a bridge or overpass intact for hundreds of miles once past this area." He tapped the map. "No point in delaying this any longer." He shook his head. "Damn, but we are spread thin."

Ben turned to Beth. "General Jahn and his bunch cause any trouble up north?"

She shook her head. "Not one incident. While they are being processed by our people north of the thirty-sixth parallel, Jahn ordered his men to turn in their sidearms. Not a one objected. One full colonel was overheard to say if he never heard another shot fired in anger he would be happy."

"But the multinational force have their hands full containing that regiment of Nazis who refused to surrender with General Jahn and company," Jersey said. "Maybe we ought to go up there and lend them a hand."

Ben smiled at her. "Sorry, Jersey. I sort of gave my word I'd run the rest of this show from the safety of a secure position. Relax and enjoy the tranquility."

"But you miss the action, don't you, General?" Cooper asked.

"No comment," Ben replied.

"Dan says he will commence firing at 1000 hours, General," Corrie called.

Ben looked at his watch and smiled. "Fifteen minutes. Dan isn't going to waste any time. How are our stockpiles, Beth?"

"Overflowing, General. But Hoffman can't say the same. He simply won't be able to match us shell for shell and round for round. He's got to conserve his supplies. We have completely stopped any incoming supplies from reaching him."

"Remember, sir," Jersey added. "Our people at Base Camp One worked around the clock for months getting us ready for this. We've got supplies cached everywhere. And the multinationals brought tons of supplies with them."

Ben nodded and began a restless pacing of the office. The office was actually the den of a home located on the Trinity River in East Texas, far from any battlegrounds and out of danger. His team watched him, knowing he was missing the action. Tell the truth, so did they.

Once Ben stopped his pacing and stood for a moment, hands balled into fists resting on his hips. He slowly looked around him at the room, a disgusted expression on his face. Then he walked to the open window and looked at the green landscape. One of the contingent assigned to guard Ben smiled and waved at him. Ben returned the wave and turned around to face his team. "Ike and Chase damn sure couldn't have stuck me in a more isolated place," he bitched.

"Ike didn't do it," Beth said, looking up from her journal. "Your kids picked this place out."

"Wonderful. Never have kids," Ben muttered. "They'll turn on you."

"Hang on!" Corrie said, adjusting her headset. "I've got a transmission coming in. Say again, Recon. Say again. You're breaking up."

She listened for a moment and turned to face Ben. "About a regiment of Blackshirts from the Sixth and Seventh busted through the lines, sir."

Ben's face brightened. "No kidding? Which way are they heading, Corrie?"

"Straight toward us, sir."

"Is that a fact?" Ben picked up his Thompson.

"Dan is urging us to head for the neutral zone and wait it out," Corrie said.

"Way too far," Jersey said, checking her M-16. "We'd never make it."

A Rebel lieutenant had been standing outside, listening. He stuck his head through the window. "What are you talking about, Jersey? It's a good two hundred and fifty miles to the bust out point. We'd be over into the neutral zone long before they even reached here."

"I'm with Jersey," Ben said.

"Sir," the lieutenant protested. "We have a very light battalion here. That's a damn regiment-sized force coming at us."

A sergeant standing beside the lieutenant said, "I can have choppers in here in one hour, General. We've got to get you to safety."

"I don't like helicopters," Jersey said. "They have this tendency to fall out of the sky."

"I agree," Ben said. He gave Corrie a few orders and then, with a smile on his face, said, "Let's see now, what shall we do. Ah! I know. We'll . . ."

"Ike on the horn, General," Corrie interrupted.

Ben walked to the communications set-up and took the mic. "Go, Ike?"

"Ben, you get your long tall skinny ass out of there!" Ike yelled from hundreds of miles away in North Texas. "You hear me, Ben? You head north for the Oklahoma line."

"I thought I'd head for Louisiana, Ike."

The speaker was silent for a moment. "What are you pulling, Eagle?" Ike asked. "I don't trust you."

His team was staring at him, disbelief in their eyes. Ben Raines was going to run from a fight? They didn't believe that for a moment.

"That regiment can't go anywhere, Ike," Ben radioed. "Cecil will have ten thousand home guard people waiting for them at the line. That is, providing they even reach the state line before his artillery blows them off the face of the earth. You're in command here, Ike.

I'm heading back to Base Camp One for a little R&R. You have any objections to that?"

"I don't trust him," Colonel Lenz of the GSG 9 said, standing close to Ike. It hadn't taken the GSG 9 commander long to learn that Ben Raines would go to any lengths to get into a scrap. "He's up to something."

"Tell me!" Ike said. "I been puttin' up with his trickery for years."

"Corrie, have the battalion pack up and mount up," Ben ordered. He winked at Jersey and she smiled, knowing Ben had something wicked up his sleeve.

In Base Camp One, due to repeaters placed all up and down the line, Cecil sat in his office and was able to listen to the conversation, a smile on his face. Ben was sure as hell up to something. But he couldn't imagine what it could be. If Ben told his commanders he was going to Base Camp One, he was going to Base Camp One. How long he was going to stay and what he was going to do when he left was what worried Cecil. For he knew only too well that Ben was an ol' war hoss and he was not going to stay out of action for any length of time. But what in the hell did he have planned?

"He's gonna pull somethin'," Ike fumed. "He's actin' just too damn innocent. I know him, I tell you. He's got somethin' sneaky up his sleeve."

"However," Colonel Lenz pointed out. "He *is* the commanding general."

"Yeah," Ike replied. He keyed the mic. "All right, Eagle. Sounds good to me. With you out of the way, we can stop worryin' about you and concentrate on kickin' Hoffman's butt."

"I thought it was very considerate of me," Ben said drily.

His team was still looking at him thoughtfully, all wondering what Ben really had in mind.

Hundreds of miles away, Ike looked at Colonel Lenz. "He's pullin' somethin'," Ike said. "But for the life of me, I can't figure what it is."

With a smile, Ben handed the mic to Corrie. "Let's pack it up and get gone, gang." Then he picked up his Thompson and left the room, laughing.

Cooper looked at Jersey. "Whatever he's got in mind, you can bet it's gonna be interesting." He paused. "And sneaky," he added.

SEVEN

Ben and his light battalion, actually about three companies strong, pulled out within the hour and headed east. Ben had said nothing about what he had in mind. But everyone in the headquarters battalion knew they were not going to Base Camp One for R&R. Quiet bets were made among the men and women as to their final destination.

When they arrived at Base Camp One late the following morning, Ben told Corrie, "Pass the word that we'll be here for about thirty-six hours. So make the best of it." To Cooper, "Have all our vehicles gone over front to back and top to bottom." To Beth, "Draw supplies for an extended campaign." To Jersey, "Let's go, Little Bit. We've got things to do and not much time in which to do them."

"You think that Ike is gonna figure out what you're up to, huh, and start raising hell about it?"

Ben smiled. "Something like that."

At Cecil's office, Jersey started yakking with old buddies and Ben closed the door to General Jefferys' office. The two old friends shook hands and stared at one another for a moment.

Cecil finally waved Ben to a chair and said, while pouring them coffee, "You must be fairly confident about the outcome of the western campaign, Ben."

"Very. When General Jahn surrendered, that signaled the beginning of the end."

"You took some chances over there." He smiled and held up a hand. "Not that I wouldn't have done the same thing. You had to do something very bold to gain the upper hand."

"I just thank God it didn't backfire on us. And it certainly could have."

Cecil smiled. "But it didn't. You're confident enough to grab at any opportunity to leave and go off head-hunting on your own, so level with me. You're up to something, in your usual sneaky way. So let's have it."

Ben managed to look hurt. Cecil laughed at him. Ben grinned. "You're not going with me, Cec. My first stop was at the hospital to talk to your doctors."

Cecil shrugged. "I have resigned myself to this desk, Ben."

"I'm going to settle the hash of Moi Sambura and Wink Payne once and for all and get them finally and forever off our backs," Ben said.

Cecil drummed fingertips on the desk top. "With how many battalions?"

"Just mine."

"You can't be serious, Ben! Jesus God, man. Moi alone has about ten thousand back-to-Africa followers. Wink has just about the same number of white trash. They're spread all over the top half of Alabama. One faction jumps around and beats on tom-toms and the other burns crosses and has the market cornered on bed-sheets. They're all a bunch of goddamn nuts! But very dangerous ones."

Ben laughed at the expression on his friend's face. Moi Sambura despised Cecil Jefferys and the feeling was certainly mutual. "Oh, I'm going to take along a few tanks and so forth. Maybe some gunships. Don't worry about me. I'm not going in unprepared."

Cecil shook his head and sighed. But he knew that once Ben had made up his mind, nothing was going to change it. "Does Ike know about this?"

"Oh, hell no. He'd be screaming if he did. I'll let you tell him once we're on the way."

"Thanks a lot."

Ben smiled. "That's what friends are for."

Jesus Hoffman sat in his headquarters and brooded. He was not angry. He had vented that and now he was just depressed. Things were not going well. As a matter of fact, things were just plain shitty for the NAL. He swiveled in his chair and looked out the window.

Ben Raines had uncorked all his artillery, and the Blackshirts were getting plastered on every front. Raines had rocket-assisted 155s, both towed and self-propelled, with a range of over 26,000 yards, and Raines had placed them well out of range of Hoffman's largest guns. Every division Hoffman had was tied up, pinned down, or in a box. And they were taking terrible losses. Both in blood and morale.

I should have stayed in South America, he thought for the hundredth time that day. *I should have been content with what I had.* He shook his head. *No, even-*

tually Raines would have come after me, even down there. So if the dream must end, what difference does it make where it ends?

Hoffman stood up and walked around the room several times, to get the blood flowing and the kinks out of his joints and muscles. Then he stepped out of his office and told an aide to gather his staff officers. He told another to make fresh coffee and see if the mess had some cakes or cookies. While waiting for his staff to assemble, he drank a cup of coffee and felt better, refreshed. He sat on the edge of a table he used for a desk and his thoughts were bitter.

"I was going to conquer Texas in a matter of weeks," he muttered. "The whole of the United States in a year." Several of his staff people had gathered silently by the open door and were listening to him mutter. "Now my troops are scattered and demoralized. I would go home, but the way is blocked. I would call for planes, but the Rebels have missiles and would shoot them down. That is, providing they even reached the southern borders of this goddamn country."

One of his staff officers cleared his throat and if Hoffman heard, he ignored it.

"Why?" Hoffman said in a whisper. "More importantly, *how* did it happen?"

"It happened," the voice of a senior staff member broke into his mutterings, "because we were all too confident, too arrogant, and we grossly miscalculated the strength and underestimated the resolve of the Rebels."

Hoffman lifted his eyes and turned his head while the other staff officers braced themselves for a display of temper. But Hoffman merely nodded his head in agreement and softly said, "Yes. Yes, you are absolutely correct. I have to admit it. But do you have any suggestions that would help us turn the battles around to our favor?"

"No, Field Marshal. Sadly, I do not."

"Nor do I," Hoffman admitted. "Come in and sit down, gentlemen. There will be coffee and small treats available in a moment. We have to plan. And do it quickly."

Just before Cecil shut his office down for the day, Ben walked in and checked on what was happening in Texas. His Rebels were steadily gaining ground. Buddy and the bikers and Mexican guerrillas had trucked in some mortars, and had moved in close and were keeping Hoffman's Eighth under a ruthless and steady barrage. Buddy predicted the Eighth was near total collapse and would surrender within the week.

Units from above the Thirty-sixth parallel had moved south and now had a large contingent of Hoffman's troops trapped between Ike's units and their own.

"Down to days now, Ben," Cecil said. "That's Ike's assessment. We sure as hell overestimated the staying power of the Blackshirts."

"General Jahn's surrender knocked the blocks out from under them," Ben replied. "Never in their wildest dreams did they ever envision Jahn surrendering more than half of his division."

"If the Eighth does surrender, what in the world are we going to do with them?"

"I'm readying ships for that now. We'll send them right back to South America."

"The people down there that the Blackshirts enslaved

243

and tortured will surely kill a lot of them once they land," Cecil pointed out.

"I'm counting on that," Ben replied.

Cecil shrugged. "When are you pulling out?"

"First thing in the morning. I'm taking main battle tanks and Dusters and some towed artillery. We'll clear the first decent airport we find close enough in first thing. I want to make peace with Moi and Wink. And I'm going to try. But I'm not going to jack around with either faction for very long, Cecil."

"Good," his friend replied.

An aide came in and said, "This just in, sir." He held up a sheet of paper.

"Read it, Frank," Cecil asked.

"Field Marshal Jesus Hoffman has ordered all troops to fight to the death. Anyone who surrenders will be branded a traitor and shot on sight."

"Thanks, Frank. What do you think about it, Ben?"

Ben shook his head. "It won't work. Hoffman has nothing except Brodermann and a few other battalions of die-hard SS troops to back up that threat. They'll be out of supplies in a week or so. And hungry soldiers don't fight well."

"You're really that confident, Ben?"

"Two weeks ago if someone had said what I just said, I would have thought them crazy. But now, yes, I'm that confident. We've split Hoffman's forces hundreds of miles apart. We've cut his supply lines. We've demoralized his troops. Frankly, I would consider halting all major actions against them and just sit back and starve them out."

"Are you leaving that up to Ike and me?"

"Yes." Ben eyeballed his friend. "But you keep your

244

ass out of the field, Cec. Do I have to make that an order?"

Cecil shook his head. "No. The only way I'll get back into action is if Base Camp One is attacked. And I don't think that's going to happen."

"The regiment of Blackshirts who busted through?"

"My home guards have stopped them cold with artillery and gunships. They broke up into small units and scattered. Some of them have surrendered to Rebel patrols and some have thrown away their weapons. We have evidence that many of them have changed out of uniforms and into civilian clothing and are trying to head south toward home. Latest reports say the Mexican guerrillas are not treating those who cross the border with a lot of kindness."

"Certainly can't blame them." Ben sighed. "Well, it's all over west of us except for the mop-up. The gods of war did not smile upon Hoffman. Luckily for us. It could have turned out very bad." Ben stood up and stuck out his hand. "I'll be pulling out before dawn, Cec. I'll see you all in a few weeks. I'll have mess with the troops this evening. See you."

Cecil sat and watched his friend leave. He could not recall ever meeting or reading about any man who was more of a soldier's soldier than Ben Raines. He slept in the mud and the rain and the cold and the heat with them. He ate the same lousy food and shared every hardship. Which was just a few of the reasons why there wasn't a Rebel in or out of uniform who wouldn't willingly and immediately lay down his or her life for Ben.

Cecil had to chuckle when he recalled first meeting Ben. The man was adamantly resisting becoming any sort of leader. All Ben wanted to do back then was travel the country and write about the Great War and the aftermath of it. He was pushed and cajoled into taking the job. But when he finally made up his mind to do it, he threw himself into it a hundred and ten percent.

The good ol' days, Cecil thought, leaning back in his chair and listening to the silence of the office building. The hum of computers and copying machines was gone. The chatter of men and women at work gone for the day.

"You be careful out there, Ben," he murmured.

As he had done countless times in the past, Ben walked the long lines of trucks and tanks and Jeeps and Hummers, stopping in the darkness of predawn to chat every now and then, Jersey moving like a silent shadow with him. This was One Battalion. Ben's personal battalion. Known throughout the entire Rebel army as the toughest and meanest bunch of men and women in the land. Very few rookies in this battalion. These were bloodied and hardened and seasoned combat veterans. And their name was legend.

"Here we go again, General!" a man called out.

"Damn right," Ben said. "Did you pack extra socks, Sonny?"

"Six pair."

"Did you remember to bring your reading glasses, Jeff?" Ben shouted.

"In an unbreakable case this time!" Jeff said with a laugh. "How about your glasses, General?"

Ben patted a breast pocket. "Right here."

"And I packed an extra pair just in case," Jersey said.

Ben approached the line of big main battle tanks.

246

"You boys and girls ready to go?" he called up to the helmeted head sticking out of the turret.

"Ready to kick ass and take names, General."

"That's my line," Jersey laughed.

A runner panted up to Ben. "Great news, sir. General Ike just radioed in. Hoffman's Eighth division has just packed it in. Buddy Raines is accepting General Schleyer's surrender as we speak."

"Good, good!"

"There's more, sir. General von Hanstein hanged himself last night. Guards found him just about thirty minutes ago. He left a note saying he preferred death over dishonor."

"How very noble of him," Ben said drily. "Are you saving the bad news for last?"

"Yes, sir. Scouts report that numbers of terrorists are still roaming around, sir," the runner stated. "And many of them have joined with Moi Sambura. Wink Payne has vowed to fight to the death."

"How many times have we heard that?" Ben muttered. "All right. Thank you for the news."

Corrie, Beth, and Cooper appeared at his side just as the sky was beginning to lighten. Beth said, "Scouts ranging out, sir."

"Very good. Any breakdowns or other glitches this morning?"

"Negative, sir."

"Bring the Hummer up, Coop."

"Right, sir!"

"We following I-20 this run?"

"Yes, sir," Corrie said. "And recon reports that Moi and Wink are dug in for a fight."

"Then they'll damn sure get one. Right, Jersey?"

"Fuckin'-A."

"Let's do it."

EIGHT

Corrie received messages all that morning about the surrendering of Hoffman's Blackshirts, from squad size to company size, they were laying down their arms and walking out with their hands up. But no one from Hoffman's First Division had surrendered, and not one SS trooper had shown the white flag. So that made Field Marshal Hoffman still a very dangerous enemy. Ben did some head work and concluded that Hoffman could still field about twenty thousand men, perhaps more than that, and all of them hard-core Nazis and dedicated to Hoffman and his dream of a new Nazi empire rising up all over America.

"Bastard," Ben muttered.

No one in the Hummer had to ask who Ben was referring to. They all could pretty well guess.

Once the convoy left the area tightly controlled by the Rebels, the highways were in bad shape and the convoy was slowed down considerably. Ben ordered the convoy over just west of Meridian, Mississippi with about three hours of light left, at a small deserted town. Scouts had checked out the town and found certain areas of it functioning—in a manner of speaking. The town had been one of the outposts, but those there had not been able to effectively combat the roaming gangs of thugs and could not bring themselves to adopt the harsh law of the Rebels. So they had left—no one knew where—and the town, at least parts of it, had turned into a squatter's camp.

"They're heavily armed," Ben was told. "And not at all friendly."

"Before you tell me," Ben said, "I can guess. They have hordes of half-naked kids running around, most of them with runny noses and rashes, and dirty diapers, or no diapers at all. They have no schools, no proper sanitation facilities, no doctors. The men all consider themselves to be 'rough, tough, rugged individualists,' who hunt and fish while their wives work the gardens, keep house, and bear children. All of whom are illiterate."

The Scout laughed. "It never changes, does it, General?"

"Unfortunately, no. It does not. Damnit!" Ben kicked at a rock and succeeded only in scuffing the toe of his boot. "We had this place all set up and fully functioning. We spent a lot of time and effort in this place. Why in the hell did the good people turn tail and run?"

No one answered him because they knew he didn't expect any reply.

"Maybe," Ben said softly, "it was because they were good people. Maybe we've been the bad guys all these years."

"Sure we are, to an extent," a company commander said. "You said yourself that a nice guy could never be President of the United States, or Prime Minister of En-

gland, or the leader of any large country. It takes someone who is part son of a bitch."

Ben smiled. "Did I say that? Yeah. I guess I did, at
that. Well, I was right. What does Meridian up the road
look like, as if I didn't know."

"Burned out, looted, picked over five thousand
times," the Scout replied. "Some pretty sorry outlaw-
looking types in there, General."

"Any sorrier than the ones now occupying what used
to be our outpost?"

"No, sir. Just about the same."

"Company coming," Corrie said. "Be here in about
five minutes. Fifty or so men, all heavily armed. And all
in need of a bath. Badly in need, according to the patrol."

"That figures," Ben said. "The easiest thing in the
world to make is soap. But will these bastards do it? No.
Come on. Let's get this over with."

The men, all bearded and blue-jeaned and booted,
carried a wide variety of weapons, but carried them like
men who understood guns. And Ben had no doubt but
what they did.

Ben halted them about twenty-five feet from where he
stood in the room. "That's far enough, boys! I can smell
you from here."

"I always knowed we'd meet up someday, Mr. Big
Shot General Raines. Yeah, I knows who you is. I seen
your pitcher. You just as ugly as your pitcher made you
out to be. I reckon you come here to tell what to do,
right?"

"Judging from your appearance and body odor, I
doubt that even your mother could tell you what to do
. . . or if she tried you didn't listen."

The man flushed under the grime on his face and cocked his head to one side. He narrowed his eyes. "You got a rale smart mouth on you, Raines."

"Why thank you. I take that as a compliment."

"I din mean it thataways."

"I'm sure. What do you men want?"

"To tell you to git, that's what. W'un's run this area around here."

"Oh, my!" Ben feigned great consternation. "He's ordering us to leave. Should we pack up, people?"

"He's just scaring me to death, General," the usually quiet Beth said, but she hated this type of men they were facing. If Beth could have her way, she'd line them all up and shoot them on the spot.

"Yeah, me, too," Jersey said, then quite unladylike spat on the broken asphalt. "Just about that much."

Corrie was leaning against the fender of a six-by, her CAR-15 pointed straight at the knot of men. There was a strange smile on her lips.

"You cunts got rale smart mouths, ain't you?" the spokesman said.

"If you don't back off and apologize for that remark," Ben told the man. "You're going to be in serious trouble."

"Oh, yeah? How's that?"

"Because I might be forced to turn these ladies loose. And believe me, boys, you don't want that."

"Shit!" one of the men said.

A slim but very shapely oriental Rebel stepped forward. Kim filled out her BDU's very nicely. She was one of the highly motivated and trained-to-the-edge Scouts, and she was lethal. At her side, in a pouch, she carried throwing stars, and was extremely accurate with them. She could also kill with her bare hands, and did, often, working behind enemy lines.

"What's that goddamn gook want?" the spokesman asked.

A whole gaggle of women and malnourished kids had appeared behind the knot of rednecks. The women were not much better to look upon than their men. Ben felt sorry for the kids, for he knew they did not have a chance in life. They would, in all probability, grow up to be just like their parents. Worthless. There would be the exception among them, of course. The occasional kid who would defy their parents' self-imposed ignorance and cruelty and learn to enjoy reading and expanding his or her mind; who would break away and better themselves. But those break-aways would be rare.

"Get your kids out of here," Ben told the group of men. "I don't want them to see this."

"You don't tell me to do nothin' wif' my younguns, Raines," the man responded.

"Back off, Kim," Ben told the young woman, quickly sizing up the situation. "These kids have had a tough enough time of it without seeing more violence."

"I knowed all the time that you was yeller, Raines!" the man said with a grin. His teeth were rotted and blackened.

Ben's eyes turned cold. "You ignorant son of a bitch!" Ben lashed out at the man. "I see it daily but I still have a hard time believing just how goddamn stupid some people can be. Look at us, you fool. You're looking at over a thousand troops. The finest weapons known to exist in the world today. One of those main battle tanks parked over there could wipe out your whole little gathering of stupidity. Look at these troops around me. Look at their weapons. In five seconds you could all be lying on the road, dead or dying. And you dare to get all up in my face with threats? Turn around and return to your stinking hovels. Go on, continue your lives of ignorance and bigotry. Raise a new generation of fools. We'll just come back here at a later date and wipe them out, just like we should do with you, right this minute!" Ben pointed a finger at the man. "Don't open your mouth again to me. Don't say another word. Because if you do, I will kill you on the spot!"

The man raised a hand to his face. The hand trembled slightly.

"We got a right to live decent lak and you cain't come in here and tell us what to do," a woman uttered one of the whining statements that most Rebels had learned to despise over the long warring years.

"Shut up!" Ben roared at her. "I'll tell you your rights. You have the right to work and to better yourself. You have the right to respect the land you squat on. You have the right to expect the same treatment you offer others. And under the present conditions, that is just about it. What do you want from us, lady? Tell me. Go on, tell me. Because you are looking at the only government that now exists in this battered nation."

The woman said nothing. But her eyes glared hate at Ben and the healthy and well-fed Rebels gathered all around him. Ben knew the look only too well. And the unspoken words that lie behind those eyes: Give me. You owe me. I demand. I got a right. I can fuck whenever I wants to and you gots to feed my bastard children. You gots to give me money for doing nothing. You cain't make me work ifn I don't wants to. You gots something and I ain't got nothin' so you gots to give me half of what you got. Whenever I wants to.

Words that helped to bring down what was once the most powerful nation in all the world.

"Hit's been a rale hard winter, General," another woman said. "And we din have no good crop last season."

"And that is my fault, I suppose," Ben said sarcastically. He knew he should just turn around and walk away. Knew he would never get through to these people. No one had been able to get through to them for decades. The government—when there had been a government—had wasted trillions of taxpayer dollars on people such as these. And gained nothing. The Rebels had learned that the only way to combat ignorance and bigotry was to go into the home and catch the young during their formative years, and if necessary, take the young from their parents and put them in caring foster homes. But those homes were now filled to overflowing. The Rebels were now taking few young as they traveled. There simply was no more room.

"Well," the woman said, "y'all seem to have a-plenty and we ain't got nothin'. You could share wif' us."

Ben shook his head in disgust. Same old story. "And when what we give you runs out. . .?"

She shrugged, as Ben had expected she would. Nothing ever changes.

"I bet you share with niggers all the time, don't you, Raines?" another man said with a sneer.

This stupid bunch was really beginning to annoy Ben.

"You damn shore got enough of 'em with you," the ignoramus added, looking at the growing ranks of Rebels.

Less than eight percent of his battalion was black.

"What is your name?" Ben asked.

"Carl Ray. Folks call me Jigger. Been called that near'bouts all my life." He narrowed his eyes. "Why for you want to know 'at?"

"I'm sure I'm not in the least interested in finding out why folks call you that."

"Is you gonna hep us, or not?" Jigger asked.

"We help those whom we know will try to help themselves," Ben told the man, trying to hold on to his temper. It was beginning to be a losing proposition. "That does not include your group. Now why don't you just leave us alone and we'll be more than happy to do the same for your, ah, group."

"We ain't a-gonna beg y'all for hep, Raines," Jigger said.

"Good. Now why don't you go away?"

"And we ain't takin' no orders from you, neither."

Ben turned around and looked at his troops. They were sitting on fenders, squatting on the ground, standing around him, all grinning at him, and all thoroughly enjoying this exchange.

"You think this is funny?" he asked.

They all nodded their heads.

"Except for their kids," Cooper put a damper on it, standing off to one side. "But what can we do?"

"Nothing," Beth said. "And it'll break your heart if you let it. Maybe we could take the very youngest. . .?" She trailed that off, knowing they could not. The Rebel adoption and foster home placement people were overloaded and terribly overcrowded. They simply could not do any more.

Cooper snapped his fingers. "Corrie. I got an idea."

"Wonderful," Jersey said. "All this time I thought you were brain-dead."

"What is it, Coop?" Ben said, overhearing much of the exchange.

"General Jahn and his people."

"What about them? Oh! Hey," Ben said. "That's right, Coop. Von Hanstein said that Jahn and his troops were always getting into trouble with the field marshal for taking in kids and being careful not to harm any . . . if at all possible. Corrie, find out where Jahn and company are located and give them a shout. Jahn said many of his men were married and they were going to try to get their wives up here, one way or the other. I . . ."

"Hey!" Jigger shouted, interrupting Ben. "Whut's all that damn whisperin' 'bout over thar?"

Ben glanced at him. "Shut up, Jugger . . ."

"Jigger!" Carl Ray hollered.

"Whatever. Just be quiet. Everytime you exhale you pollute the air."

Jigger looked at a friend. "Did that son of a bitch insult me, Flapper?"

"I do believe he did, Jigger. But I ain't rat shore, since I can't catch the jist of all them words he spouts. Whut do you say, Billy Joe?"

Billy Joe ruminated on the question "Ah personal thank he's been in-sultin' us ever' since we got up here."

Jigger thought about that for a moment. Then he grunted. "Ah thank I'll just, by gawd, walk up yonder and whup his uppity ass," Jigger said. He pulled at the waist of his jeans in a futile attempt to get them over his enormous gut.

"Ah'll be yore second, Jigger," Flapper said. " 'At's the way them folks in the olden times done 'er."

"My second what?" Jigger asked.

"Never mind, I know what to do. Come on."

The three men walked up to Ben, who had his back to them, talking with his personal team.

"Three locals coming up," Cooper said.

"Ignore them," Ben replied.

"Hey, you!" Flapper said to Ben's back.

Ben continued talking to Beth while Corrie set up a communications patch to Ike.

"I'm a-talkin' to you, boy!" Flapper raised his voice.

Dozens of Rebels watched the three men carefully as Ben continued to speak to Beth, ignoring the trashy trio.

That Jersey had taken a few steps away from Ben and had her M-16 leveled at the three men did not escape the notice of Jigger and Billy Joe. Both of them got a little nervous. Jersey's dark eyes held a menace that they both picked up on. Billy Joe and Jigger looked very carefully all around them. There were something like a hundred guns pointed at them. A little nervous turned into a whole lot nervous.

"Ah, Flapper?" Jigger said, suddenly breaking out in a very cold sweat.

"Hush up, boy. I'm a-talkin' to the general here."

"You bes' look around you, Flapper," Billy Joe said. " 'Fore you git any more hoss-tile."

The ignorant lout who had started this conversation, and who had not opened his mouth since being ordered by Ben to close it, suddenly had a nearly overwhelming urge to pee. But he was afraid to move for fear of getting shot.

The kids had been quickly taken away by their mothers. The women were showing a great deal more sense than the men.

"Goddamnit, boy!" Flapper hollered. "Is you deef?"

Then Flapper made a terrible mistake. He shoved Ben. Hard.

"Oh, shit!" Billy Joe whispered.

NINE

Ben recovered his balance and threw a short hard right fist that landed dead center on Flapper's big red nose. Flapper's big red nose suddenly got bigger and redder as he stumbled backward and fell hard to the asphalt, landing on his butt.

Billy Joe and Jigger raised their hands high into the air as a hundred rifles took steady aim at them.

"We's out of this!" Jigger squealed. "Lord God, folks. Don't shoot us!"

"I'm with him!" Billy Joe hollered. "What he just said, I mean."

Flapper crawled to his feet, his nose streaming blood and his eyes killing mean. "You gawddamn uppity son of a bitch!" he said. "I'm a-gonna stomp your guts out."

"Come on, then," Ben told him.

Flapper rushed Ben, swinging both fists, and Ben tripped him, once more sending the man hollering and flapping his arms for balance, and finally sprawling on the blacktop. This time Flapper landed on his face, skinned it up something fierce, and the man commenced bellowing like a mad bull as he fought to once more climb to his feet.

"I really wish you'd stop all this nonsense," Ben told him, pulling on a pair of leather gloves that Cooper tossed him. "Before I lose my temper and hurt you."

"Son of a bitch!" Flapper yelled, blood from half a dozen cuts and scrapes running down his face. "Stand still and fight lak a man, damn you!"

"How is a man supposed to fight?" Ben questioned.

"Wif' his fists!" Flapper hollered. He shook his head and the blood flew.

"Oh!" Ben said, stepping closer. "I guess I can perhaps manage to do that. Do you mean something like this?" He suddenly hit the surprised Flapper with a haymaker right that crossed Flapper's eyes and buckled his knees. "Or like this?" Ben asked, driving in a left that pulped Flapper's lips and knocked him up against the front of a truck. "Perhaps this?" Ben questioned, and hit Flapper in the belly so hard his fist was momentarily lost in the flab.

Flapper's face turned chalk white and he seemed to sigh as he slowly sank to his knees. He remained that way for a moment, and then toppled over, once more landing on his face in the center of the cracked old highway.

Ben looked down at the semiconscious Flapper. "Not bad for a middle-aged man," he muttered. He turned to Billy Joe and Jigger. "Either of you two have anything else you'd care to discuss with me?"

"No, sir!" they hollered, their hands still in the air.

"Are you both certain of that?"

"Yes, sir!"

"Will you please carry your friend away from here and leave us alone for the remainder of our stay?"

"Yes, sir!"

"Ike says Jahn's with him and they've started sending planes down to get their wives. General Jahn says to bring the kids on," Corrie called.

"Good, Corrie, thank you. I thought that would be Jahn's reaction. But before we do that, let's inspect the town and see if there is any hope for these people."

"Any hope?" Jigger hollered. "What do that mean? What is y'all gonna do—shoot us?"

"That's not a bad idea," Ben told him.

Jigger peed his pants.

"Oh, Lard!" Billy Joe yelled.

Ben sent teams in to inspect the living quarters of the tiny town's inhabitants. He had seen more than his share over the long years of how trash chose to live. Why they did so was something that had eluded him all his life.

Ben soaked his right hand in salted water while the teams were in town. He concluded that he was getting just too damned old for fistfighting.

He had just dried off his slightly swollen hand when the teams reported back in.

"Report," Ben told them, already reading the news in their eyes.

"Kids are filthy, suffering from malnourishment, and of course have never been vaccinated for anything," a doctor said. "Pisses me off," he added.

"Take those young enough to be rehabed," Ben ordered. "Corrie, have Cecil start sending planes in at noon tomorrow to transport them back. We'll have that old air strip cleaned up by then."

No one had to ask what to do if the parents objected. In truth, damn few of them would object. Most would be happy to get rid of the brats. The Rebels had seen that very thing happen, time and time again, coast to coast, border to border. And it never failed to astonish and disgust them.

No groups of people came out to the Rebel encampment from the shacks and hovels to protest the taking of their kids, although some did stand well back from the grass landing strip when the planes came in the next morning and watch the kids being loaded into the cargo planes for the flight back to Base Camp One. There, the children would be given medical attention, vaccinations, and first of all, treated for head lice. They would be housed—properly, for the first time in their lives—with Rebel families until Jahn and his people were settled and ready to take them. Ben sat and stared at the rabble, open contempt in his eyes.

A courier handed Ben a pouch and Ben sat on the ground, beneath the shady branches of a huge old tree, and read the dispatches.

Intelligence felt that most of what was left of Hoffman's army—with the exception of the SS troops—was nearing total collapse. Their supply lines severed, they were running out of ammo and food, and those who surrendered told tales of eating rats to survive.

Hoffman had vanished. Intelligence believed he had slipped through the lines and headed north. They also believed Brodermann was with him, as were many of Hoffman's staff officers. Their defenders were hard-core SS troops. What was happening in most places west of the Mississippi River now was tedious and dangerous digging out and mopping up.

Ben and battalion watched the last plane leave and then mounted up and headed out, following I-20 northeast. In their command posts in North Alabama, Moi Sambura and Wink Payne braced for what they knew was going to be the fight of their lives.

Wink Payne felt Ben Raines to be a nigger-loving, no good son of a bitch. Moi Sambura felt Ben Raines to be a black-hating, racist son of a bitch.

"But he's got African Americans in his army," a few of the more moderate members of Moi's movement pointed out.

"Uncle Toms," Moi would always reply. "Chocolate covered vanilla ice creams. Black on the surface, white in the middle. They're just as bad, or worse, than Raines."

What neither side could see was that all Rebels were, first, last, and always, Americans. People from every state in what used to be called the Union were represented in the Rebel army. Every creed, every color, every nationality and religion.

"Fight to the death!" Wink told his people.

"Fight to the death!" Moi told his people.

"I wish to hell I could figure out some way to get those two to turn on each other," Ben mused aloud over the evening meal. "That sure would save us a lot of time and bother."

Under the light from a gas lantern, Ben studied maps of the state. "From Birmingham north to the state line, everything east of I-65 to the Georgia line is claimed by Wink. Everything west of I-65 over to Mississippi Highway 45 is claimed by Moi." Ben put aside the maps and smiled, and with that, his team knew he'd come up with some plan; probably a very perverse one.

"We attack tomorrow?" Corrie asked.

"No," Ben replied. "We'll stay on I-20 over into Georgia. When we reach Georgia Highway 27, we'll split up into company sized units, with each company having armor and artillery. Then we'll start shoving Wink and his nuts and fruitcakes west." He laughed. "Right into Moi's territory. The results should be quite interesting. Wink's people might decide to run north or south, and if they do, that's all right. We'll be ready for that, too. Corrie, bump Base Camp One and have gunships standing by ready to fly. I want gunships flying search and destroy along the northern, southern and eastern perimeters of our TO. Get the PUFFs ready to go as well. Might as well do this right."

"It's a hundred and sixty six miles to Georgia Highway 27," Beth told him.

"We'll figure two days total to reach it and spread out south to north," Ben said.

"Soften it up with artillery first?" one of the company commanders in attendance asked.

Ben shook his head. "Not until we give the noncombatants time to get out of the area. I don't like the idea of a lot of collateral damage if it can be avoided."

"And if they refuse to come out?" he was asked.

"A lot of people are going to get hurt," was Ben's reply.

It was a confusing and sometimes chaotic time in Texas. The Rebels and the multinational forces were very nearly overwhelmed by surrendering and very hungry Blackshirts. General Payon helped the situation immensely by clearing a way south through Mexico for the

265

prisoners. The Blackshirts were disarmed and using their own captured vehicles, with the prisoners driving, were sent south, back to their own countries and to a very uncertain fate once they arrived. If they arrived. For the citizens of the Blackshirts' home countries, once the bulk of Hoffman's people had left for the north, had risen up and overwhelmed the dictatorial government in place.

Cecil appointed Ned Hawkins and his force of New Texas Rangers to be the law in Texas and to clean it up. Hoffman, Brodermann, their staff officers, and at least several thousand of their SS followers, had disappeared without a trace.

"We've won some battles but not the war," Ben said, upon hearing that news. "They'll stay down and quietly rebuild. For there are still thousands of people across this country who subscribe to Hoffman's ideas. We haven't heard the last of Hoffman. Not by a long shot. You've got to cut the head off before the poisonous snake is dead. And be damn careful when you handle the dead part, it can still kill you. Corrie, have Ike assign as many people as he thinks necessary to start scouring the land, looking for Hoffman. How about the plans of the multinationals?"

"They agreed unanimously that they'll stay until things are secure."

"Good enough. What about those that we learned were coming over?"

"Cecil told them many thanks and to head on back home. And that anytime they might need help, to give us a shout. They said they would and wished us good luck."

"Any word from Moi or Wink?"

"Yes." She hesitated. "Moi says for you to take your offer and stick it up your honky racist ass. Wink says to take your offer and stick it up your nigger-lovin' ass."

"Being misunderstood," Ben said with a smile. "That's the story of my life."

His team all groaned at that.

"And no respect either," Ben added. That got him another series of groans.

"Gunships up?" Ben asked, when the groaning had died down.

"Up," Corrie said. "No signs of anyone trying to bug out."

"Fools," Ben muttered. "The arrogant fools. Well, you can bet one thing, when the shells start dropping in on them, there will be some quick rethinking on our offer."

"But it'll be too late then, won't it, General," the CO of Dog Company asked.

"Yes," Ben said slowly. "It will."

Jesus Hoffman had split up his remaining forces, disseminating them among the population and countryside. Hoffman could wait. He would choose his new people very carefully and proceed ever so slowly. And he now knew just the type of person who would jump at the chance to join his forces. The rabble of Paris had helped defeat Burgundy—so he had been taught in school—so too could the rabble of America help bring down Ben Raines. They all despised him with a burning passion that bordered on fanaticism. Hoffman knew that. So why not use them? The more he thought about it, the better he liked it. He had broached the plan to Brodermann, who had agreed to the genius of it.

"Yes," Hoffman said, leaning back in his chair and smiling. "It will work."

They had all carefully packed away and hidden their uniforms, and were now dressed in civilian clothing. They spoke only English. Any other language was forbidden. The men had all grown moustaches and many had grown full beards. They hunted and fished and scratched out gardens. All had plans to take American women as wives; those with children preferable.

"One year, Ben Raines," Hoffman spoke to the silent room. "Give me one year, and I will smash you into the ground. I learned from you, Raines. I learned much from you. I learned that you are not a gentleman. I learned that you are no more than a cut above a very cunning savage. Yes, I learned much. And for that, I will thank you just before I kill you."

Moi Sambura could not understand what was happening. He had sent scouts out north and south of his seized territory, but they could find no sign of the Rebels. But lots and lots of attack helicopters. And some strange-looking old slow prop planes, that fairly bristled with guns. Moi was the furthest thing from a fool. He knew from the description what his scouts had seen. PUFFs. One PUFF could effectively clear an area about the size of two or three football fields . . . of all living things. And do it very quickly.

What the hell was that damnable Ben Raines up to?

* * *

"We got to get the wimmen and the chil'ren out of here, Wink!" one of Payne's men said, panic in his voice. "They's thousands and thousands of Rebels gathered over yonder to the west."

"Sit down, Ed," Wink told him. "Calm yourself. There are not thousands and thousands of Rebels. There is one, maybe two battalions of Rebels. That's it. That's a total of no more than two thousand Rebels. And some of them is women. And we all know the only thing women is good for. So they're probably along to screw the troops, is all. The crap we been hearin' about women Rebels bein' tigers in battle is just that, Ed. Crap. We got machines guns, mortars, and the bes' automatic assault rifles anywhere in the world. Hell, Ed, we been coon-killin' Moi's people for years, ain't we? Don't that tell you nothin' 'bout how tough we is, boy?"

"I reckon you be right, Wink," Ed said, sitting down. "But you better talk to the men. Some of them is gettin' spooked about the rumors of thousands of Rebels."

"I'll settle 'em down, Ed. You just leave that to me."

After the calmed down Ed had left, Wink sat in the study of his home and pondered what faced him. Unlike many, if not most, of his followers, Wink Payne was not an ignorant man. It was his radical views that drew the ignorant to him like steel shavings to a magnet. He would have been highly insulted had anyone suggested that he and Moi Sambura were so much alike in their thinking they could pass for mental twins. But it was true. The main difference between them was their color. Wink hated black people, Moi hated white people.

Both were highly intelligent men, well-read and well-versed, but both were so blind in their individual hatred they could not see that even if they could somehow miraculously combine their forces, they would still be unable to defeat the Rebels.

They didn't know this, but Ben Raines did.

The sadness of it all, Ben thought, as he leaned against the fender of his Hummer and stared at what used to be the Alabama-Georgia state line, is that both Wink and Moi are correct to a small degree in their thinking. Back when we had a central government in Washington, D.C. the nation's leaders overreacted in an attempt to try to make up for two hundred years of injustice toward the blacks. Some white toes got stepped on; in many cases, trod on hard.

Ben didn't believe that standards should have been lowered to help the blacks, and neither did any intelligent black that he had ever met . . . once confidence was gained and both sides could speak freely.

Cecil Jefferys had once said, "Toss them all into society with the same standards for everybody, no matter what color. It will be brutal, but the best and the brightest and the mentally toughest will make it."

But that didn't happen until men like Ben Raines and Cecil Jefferys came into power. And Cecil's words were proving to be correct.

Ben had often written to and said to government leaders, back when the government was whole: "This nation cannot be all things to all people, all the time. To attempt to do that is not only physically impossible, but economically unreasonable and grossly unfair to the hard working taxpayers who are being forced, in most cases against their will, to foot the bill."

But the elected officials would not listen to men like

Ben Raines and Cecil Jefferys. The best of friends. A black man and a white man of like mind. Hard men.

"Wink," Ben muttered, as he stared toward the west. "And Moi, too. You'd better get your acts together. And you damn well better do it quickly. 'Cause in about five minutes, I'm coming after you."

Ben walked back to where Corrie sat with her radio equipment. "Any word from either of them, Corrie?"

"Not a peep directed at us, sir. But Beth has been listening to Wink's people talk back and forth."

Ben cut his eyes. "What are they saying, Beth?"

"That they're going to kick our asses."

Jersey slapped a full clip of .223 ammo into the belly of her M-16. "I wonder if anyone over there would like to bet on that?" She stood up and looked at Ben. "Kick-ass time, General?"

Ben nodded. "Kick-ass time, Jersey."

TEN

In slightly less than fifteen minutes, eight towns that once bordered the Georgia line were reduced to blazing rubble and thick, swirling, choking smoke from the artillery barrage. Wink had finally used some common sense and moved women and children back to the center of his controlled territory, momentarily out of harm's way. But when the barrage ended, not quite half of those men he had assigned to the eastern front lines made it out of the savage barrage of HE, WP, and antipersonnel rounds that rained down on their heads from miles away.

Wink's men had been told the Rebels would be easy to stop. And his ignorant followers had believed that. They had believed that right up until the shelling. They fired their mortars toward the east. But the rounds fell miles short of the Rebel artillery.

Wink ordered his followers to fall back. "Blow the bridges on the Tennessee," he ordered. He thought that might buy him some time. It wouldn't. He thought that would show the Rebels how determined Wink Payne and his followers really were. It didn't. He thought he would be able to rally his men and stop the Rebel advance. He was wrong.

Ben, at the top of the state near the Tennessee line, simply drove straight down a secondary road, on the east side of the river and Guntersville Lake, blocked off the southern escape route, helped Baker Company put any of Wink's stragglers into a box, and systematically set about mopping up.

"We have one of Payne's senior officers," a scout reported, just as Ben was finishing the evening meal.

It was pleasant in this part of the state, with thick forests, the foliage lush, and flowers at high bloom. The air was softly scented with dozens of fragrances, and the evening was cool for this time of the year.

"Bring him in," Ben said.

The man was scared, and tried not to show it. But Ben and his team could smell it. They'd smelled it many times before. The man looked to be in his mid- to late forties, and was clean-shaven. Ben, knowing the man had been thoroughly searched, waved him to a chair.

"Coffee?" he asked. "Mr. . . . ?"

The prisoner looked startled. "Jeb Brown. Yeah, might as well," he said. "I haven't had real coffee in years." He smiled thinly. "You give me a cup of coffee and then you shoot me, is that it, General?"

Ben smiled and tasted his own just-poured cup. "No one is going to shoot you, Mr. Brown. You're a prisoner. As soon as Wink is put out of business, you can go back to farming, or whatever it is you do. As for the coffee, our friends from South America just sent us tons of fresh beans. And we, ah, liberated more tonnage from General Jesus Hoffman and his Blackshirt army."

The man took the cup of fresh coffee, sniffed it several times and smiled. "That does smell good. Thank you, General."

"*Por nada*," Ben said, his eyes hooded.

"I don't speak no greaser language."

"They are not 'greasers,' Mr. Brown. They are Mexicans, South Americans, Latinos. They might be Peruvian, Chilean, or whatever. But they are not greasers."

"They ain't as good as no white man." Brown took a gulp of coffee, holding the mug as if fearful it might be snatched away from him at any moment.

"You are right about that, Mr. Brown. They are much better than you and your cohorts."

"Well, it figures you'd say that. You bein' a nigger-lover an' all."

"Wrong again, Mr. Brown. I don't judge people by the color of their skin, but by their actions and deeds and how they treat other people. There are a great many black people I cannot abide. Just as there are people of all colors I personally have no use for. Including whites."

"Like Wink Payne."

"He's one."

"Moi Sambura?"

"He's another."

"Can I have another cup of coffee?"

"Sure."

Jeb gulped at the fresh cup of brew and said, "I'll make a deal with you."

"What kind of deal?"

"Well, I'll tell you everything I know and you turn me a-loose."

"We already know everything you know."

"Huh! The hell you say! How would you know that?"

"We infiltrated Wink and Moi's groups years ago, Mr. Brown. We didn't consider either of you important enough to waste much time on back then. You could wait. We had other, more pressing battles to fight. We know what you have in the way of weapons, and the battle plans of both groups. So you see, Mr. Brown, you have nothing to barter."

"I'll be damned. You ain't got no smokin' tobacco on you, has you?"

Ben tossed him the makin's.

Brown rolled and licked and lit. He tossed the bag and paper onto the desk.

"Keep them, Mr. Brown," Ben told him. "I doubt you'll have the bag smoked by the time this little exercise in futility is concluded."

"Huh?"

"It's going to be a very short war."

"Can I speak frank with you, General?"

"Go right ahead."

"Where do you come off roarin' in here and stickin' your nose into our business?"

Ben smiled. "Brown, I could talk for the rest of the night, but I don't know if you would ever understand. We don't care if you don't subscribe to our way of life. We really don't care. But when you start killing innocent people, children in many cases, simply because they wouldn't get off the sidewalk and let you walk by. When you horsewhip and lynch black men and boys for daring to speak to a white woman, and all the other atrocities you people have committed . . . well, Mr. Brown, that offends me. I feel obliged to come to you and read to you from the scriptures, so to speak. Do you understand what I'm saying?"

"You don't think Moi Sambura done the same thing to white folks? Hell's far, man, that nigger come in over yonder and run off or kilt hun'erds of good decent white people!"

"We are going to deal with Moi, Mr. Brown. Rest assured of that."

"You gonna kill him?"

"In all likelihood."

"Good."

"And Wink Payne too."

"But Wink's a lay preacher. He's a good Baptist. He's a religious man. He can show you right in the Bible where it says plain as day that niggers ain't as good as white folks."

Ben reached into his rucksack and tossed a Bible on the desk. "Show me, Brown."

"Well, now, I can't personal show you. But Wink can."

"And you believe that?"

"Shore." Brown looked at Ben for a few seconds. "You really read the Bible, General?"

Ben thought of the remark attributed to General George Patton when a reporter asked him that same question. "I sure do, Brown. Every goddamn day."

Jeb Brown blinked at that.

"Get him out of here and feed him," Ben said. "Then lock him up."

Wink Payne was a good speaker. He could motivate a crowd to do just about anything. But as a soldier, he had a lot to learn. The Rebels were kicking the butts of his people at every report. Wink kept backing up until he found, much to his surprise, he could back no further. I-65 was the separation line between Wink's little nation and Moi's claimed territory.

"That dirty, no-good, rotten, honky son of a bitch!" Moi cussed Ben.

His aides stood quietly. Moi and his people all wore flowing robes and cute little Muslim caps. They would soon discover the outfits, while quite African, were very impractical as combat uniforms.

"Be sure and get me one of those hats," Ben said, after interrogating one of Moi's scouts. "I want to give it to Cecil."

"And do you have any idea what General Jefferys will tell you to do with that hat?" Jersey asked.

"Oh, yes. With complete verbal instructions on where to shove it. What is Wink's position now?"

"Backed up to the north-south Interstate," Beth said. "With Moi's people taking shots at his men."

Ben chuckled. "Worked out just like I thought it would."

"You goddamn stupid African bastard!" Wink yelled into a microphone. "What the hell are your apes shootin' at my people for? We're all in this together now. Ben Raines is after *both* our asses, you idiot!"

"Give me that microphone!" Moi said, grabbing frantically at the mic. "And will somebody please get that goddamn goat out of my office!"

"Do you hear me, you burr-head?" Wink shouted.

Ben and his team were gathered in the shade of a lovely old tree, having lunch, drinking coffee, and monitoring the conversation. And immensely enjoying every word of it.

Moi got his volatile temper under control and keyed the mic. "Are you suggesting that I actually link up with you and that pack of morons you command?"

"I damn sure ain't whistlin' Dixie!" He turned to an aide. "That is one dumb nigger over there."

"Praise Allah for small favors," Moi muttered. "And then what, Wink?"

"Well, hell, you dumb gorilla—we fight Ben Raines and whip the bastard. Then when it's over you stay on your side of the line and we'll stay on ours."

Moi then knew he was attempting to converse with a lunatic. Raines' Rebels had just proven themselves over an army of about one hundred and fifty thousand, seasoned combat veterans. And now Wink Payne, self-proclaimed preacher and all around flake, actually thought he could defeat Ben Raines' personal battalion of Rebels. Moi knew from months of monitoring open Rebel frequencies, that the First Battalion of the Rebel Army was comprised of the toughest, hardest, and meanest men and women who ever wore the black beret of the Rebels.

"Well, are you gonna answer me, or not, you ape?" Wink yelled.

Moi keyed the mic. "Are you listening, Ben Raines?"

Corrie handed Ben the mic. "Oh, yes, Charles," Ben said. "I'm listening."

Wink Payne was sudden rendered speechless, something quite novel for the man.

"My name is Moi Sambura!" Charles/Moi yelled.

"Your name is Charles Washington," Ben replied. "Your father was a well known and highly respected sci-

278

entist and your mother an educator at a very prestigious university in New York State. You hold a PhD. You founded the Back to Africa movement just before the great war. The way you, and your people, choose to live, peacefully, is of no concern to me, Charles. But peacefully is the key word. I won't tolerate closed borders in this country. Not for me, not for you, not for any group. How you dress, how you worship, is strictly your business. None of mine. You open your borders and stop hassling whites, and we're out of here. That's a stone cold promise."

Moi looked at the speaker for a moment. "Brothers and Sisters in the Rebel Army. Arise and kill the white devils around you!" Moi screamed the words.

A black Rebel squad leader, who was resting on the ground, opened his eyes. "That is sure one loud-mouthed motherfucker."

"Is that your answer?" Ben asked.

Silence greeted his words.

"Moi," Ben said. "Listen to me. Neither you nor Payne has a chance. But it doesn't have to be this way. The killing can stop right now. Keep your weapons, you know how I feel about Americans having the right to be armed. Keep your nation intact. Call it what you wish. Let's just stop the hostilities."

"I hate that son of a bitch!" Moi said, after Ben's words sank in.

An older man on Moi's staff asked, "Why, Moi? What has Ben Raines ever done to you? He's certainly never done anything to me."

Moi stood silently, trembling with rage. He didn't just hate Ben Raines. He hated all white people just as deeply as Wink Payne hated all black people. Neither

Moi nor Wink had ever learned that there are good and bad among all people, and that color has nothing to do with what is in a person's heart.

"How 'bout me and my people, Raines?" Wink screamed into his mic. "You goin' to give us the same offer you just give to that nigger?"

Ben sat in his camp chair for a long, silent moment. Then he sighed and lifted the mic. "Yes, Wink. I am. Can you and your followers live in peace with people of color?"

"That depends on the people of color, Raines."

"Interesting answer," Ben said to his team. "I wonder if he realizes just how profound it was?"

"You expect me to live side by side with that ignorant Cracker, Raines?" Moi shouted the words.

Ben recalled Cecil Jefferys' words: "Only the best and the brightest and the mentally toughest will survive, Ben. Sooner or later we'll have to deal with the stragglers and the outcasts and the ones who hate for no good reason."

Ben slowly lifted the mic and spoke calmly and carefully. "Yeah, Moi, I do. And the same goes for you, Wink. I'm going to call a cease-fire for the rest of the day. It'll stay in effect until 0600 tomorrow. You two get together and talk this over. See if you can find some common ground. Canvas your people; see what they have to say about it. If the two of you can't work something out, at one minute past six in the morning, I'll blow you all right straight to hell."

"How about our women and kids?" Wink asked.

"They can leave anytime they choose. They will not be harmed."

Moi tossed the mic to the table and stalked out of the room.

Wink handed the mic to his operator and sat down, his face mirroring the man's inner fury.

"Too much hate between those two," Jersey said. "It isn't going to work, General."

"I don't think it will either," Ben replied. "But at least we can say we tried."

ELEVEN

By the middle of the afternoon, women and kids began leaving the contested areas, a few elderly people with them.

"Corrie, tell our medical people to treat the very young and the very old," Ben said. "The rest of them can go to hell."

"One of Moi's people to see you," Cooper said.

"Show him in."

"Moi will never agree to your terms, General," the white-haired black man told Ben.

"Then he's got a problem."

"Black and white will never get along, is that it, General?" the elderly man asked.

"No, that isn't it. That is probably true with Moi and Wink, but the rest of us can, if we work at it."

"Suppose we just want to live alone?"

"Fine," Ben told him. "Just do so in peace with open borders. But if you want any help from us, you'll have to abide by Rebel law. And don't tell me that I owe you anything. I don't owe you a damn thing."

The old man chuckled. "I can remember when my people weren't allowed to vote."

"I guess we've come full circle then. Because none of us are voting now. And probably won't for a long time."

The man held out a part of his robe. "You should try one of these. They're really quite comfortable."

"It is your right to wear it, and my right to think they look silly as hell. But I don't have the right to taunt you for wearing it. Do we understand each other?"

"Quite," the elderly man said. "I am free to go?"

"Mister, you are probably the most free you have ever been in your life." Ben paused. "Most free?" he muttered. He shrugged. "It'll do."

The old black man stared hard at him for a moment. "You must realize that Moi and his hardcore followers will fight to the death."

"It won't be a very long fight," Ben assured him.

"And his death won't bother you?"

"Not in the least."

"You have to be the hardest man I have ever met, General Raines."

"You might be surprised just how much compassion I have in me, Mr. Whatever Your Name Is. But since I'm the one who can give it or withhold it, it's up to me to decide who gets it. And Wink Payne and Moi Sambura, I assure you, are not on the list." Ben pointed to a chair. "Sit down. You want some coffee?"

"Real coffee?"

"Yes. What is your name?"

"Franklin Sharp. And yes, I would like some coffee. It's been years."

Ben hollered for a fresh pot of coffee and it was there in half a minute.

The elderly man sighed contentedly after the first sip. "That is so good. I had forgotten how good." He smiled at Ben. "Are you surprised I did not take a Muslim name?"

"Damn little surprises me anymore, Mr. Sharp."

"Mr. Sharp? How odd to hear a white man say that."

"You're my elder and you're polite to me. Why shouldn't I be polite to you?"

Franklin smiled and sipped. "Moi had us believing you were a Negro-hating devil."

"Moi is as much a racist as is Wink. Negro?" Ben asked. "Not black or African-American."

"After years of being called boy and nigger, when it got to Negro, that was quite good enough for me. Not all of us are black, I'm certainly not, so I don't care to be called black, although it doesn't offend me in the least. As for African-American, that's rather a mouthful when faced with a long day of conversation."

Ben laughed. "Next thing you're going to tell me is that you're a Baptist."

"Actually, I'm Episcopalian, and have been for many, many years."

"You look tired, Mr. Sharp. Have you eaten today?"

"Ah . . . not since breakfast."

"Well, drink your coffee and I'll have some food sent in. Then we'll let the doctors check you over."

"That's kind of you. But might I trouble you for one more little item?"

"Sure."

Franklin Sharp smiled and said, "You wouldn't happen to have a couple of pairs of Levis that would fit me, would you?"

"That old man is really something," Cooper said. It was late and the camp was quiet.

"Which old man, Coop?" Ben asked, turning down the lantern on his desk and closing a journal.

"Mr. Sharp. He was a college professor when the war came. He's just full of stories. He asked if the Rebels would accept a Negro as a teacher?"

"Well, of course, we do. You told him that, didn't you?"

"Yes, sir. He was sure surprised. You know, General, we have a really bad reputation. There are a lot of damn lies being spread about us."

"For sure, Coop. Mr. Sharp wants to come live with us at Base Camp One, huh?"

"Yes, sir."

"He's sure welcome."

"I like him," Jersey said. And Jersey didn't have many kind words for a lot of people. "I think he's a nice old man who ought to be able to live and work in peace. And he probably knows a lot, too."

"He might not be so friendly to us after we start killing Moi's followers," Ben put a damper on their spirits. "You all had better think about that."

"He's kind of sad about that," Cooper said. "But he told me Moi was wrong in doing what he did and should have taken your offer of peace."

Ben looked at his watch. "He's got eight hours to reach a decision. After that I'll make up his mind for him."

* * *

Ben gave Moi and Wink the benefit of the doubt and waited until 0605. Then he turned to Corrie, standing to his left. "Drop them in, Corrie."

From miles away, the big guns of the Rebels boomed. When the first of the almost one-hundred-pound shells struck, Wink and Moi knew that enormous blast signaled the beginning of the end of their twin racist dreams.

Ammunition was no problem for the Rebels. With thousands of rounds already stockpiled all over the nation, they had, in addition, thousands of rounds seized from the Blackshirt army. And Ben really walloped the positions of Moi and Wink. He kept up the barrage for six hours, with no let-up, turning the land in front of him into a smoking, hellish, no-man's-land of pock-marked earth and burning buildings.

The gun crews would stagger fire for half an hour, then the crews would stand down, hook up, and move forward a mile or so, and repeat their performance. At noon they had advanced to within sight of the eastern side of I-65. Ben called a halt to the artillery barrage.

When the 105s and 155s ceased their booming, and the area had turned eerily silent, Ben ordered helicopter gunships and PUFFs to go in and strafe and rocket anything that moved.

Ben was determined to keep his own casualties down to a bare bones minimum. The lives of ten thousand Moi Samburas and Wink Paynes were not worth one Rebel loss.

At two o'clock that afternoon, Ben ordered the choppers and the PUFFs back to their temporary bases and told his people to mount up and advance.

Not one shot was fired at them as they crossed the interstate into Moi's claimed land. That land was now a smoking ruin, with a mangled body, or part of a body, littering the ground every few hundred yards. Wink and his people had scrambled across the interstate, fleeing from the crashing artillery rounds, and had run straight into the guns of Moi's front line defenders. While the explosions boomed all around them, raining down fire and death, the two groups fought each other in hand to hand combat, with pistols and rifles and shotguns and knives and hatchets.

"Idiots," Ben said, standing in the midst of the body-strewn carnage.

"They sure hated each other, didn't they?" Coop remarked, looking down at a dead black hand still gripping a white neck, and a white hand still closed around a black throat. Both hands were stiff in death.

"Maybe this was the only way it could end," Beth said.

"But if Moi and Wink made it out," Jersey added, "it isn't over."

"All right," Ben said, adjusting the chin strap to his helmet. "Let's end it."

The Rebels broke into squad-sized units and stretched out from the deserted towns of Lester in the north to Flat Creek in the south and slowly began working their way west, in the tedious and dangerous job of house to house searching and mopping up.

Ben and his team found two black males and two white males huddled together in the basement of a country home. They were tired, dirty, hungry, scared, and weaponless.

"For folks who claim they don't like each other," Jersey said, prodding them to their feet with the muzzle of her M-16, "you're sure sitting mighty close. Move!"

Outside, the quartet squinted and blinked in the light of the sun. "I think they're suffering from battle fatigue," she told Ben.

"How could they be suffering from that?" Beth asked. "They didn't fight!"

"That one's covered with dried blood," Ben said, pointing to one of Moi's men. "Have the medics check him out."

"It isn't my blood," the man stated. "The building I was in took a hit from one of your artillery rounds. I'm the only survivor. I was literally splattered with the blood of my brothers." He stared defiantly at Ben. "Now their blood is on your hands."

"I can live with it," Ben told him. He looked at Wink's men. "What's your story?"

"You had no right," one said.

"I'm trying to put this nation back together, pal," Ben replied. "And if I have to kill every sorry son of a bitch like you four to do that, I will. And I'll have no regrets about it. Get them out of here."

It took over a thousand people two weeks of hard searching to cover the area. There was no sign of Moi or Wink. Of course, that didn't mean anything. Many of the dead had been ripped apart by the hundreds and hundreds of artillery rounds, burned to unrecognizable char in blazing buildings, or buried forever under tons of crushing rubble.

"I'd bet they made it out," Ben said. "Their kind is hard to kill. They'll pop up somewhere, spewing their venomous hate. We'll see them again."

The survivors of the attack, black and white, mostly women and kids, had elected spokespeople. They came to see Ben, asking about their future.

"That's up to you," he told them. "If you want to stay here and work together, rebuilding, we'll help you all we can. If you want to go on hating each other, well, I can't stop you from doing that, either. But if you choose that route, I can tell you what you'll get from us. Nothing. Zero. You will get not one aspirin or antibiotic from my medical people. You will be totally alone. You will not receive food, protection, or any other type of assistance from us. And we'll take the younger kids with us right now. Before any of you have the time to poison their minds with bigotry. Think about that. Give it a lot of thought before you reach any decision."

About half of them, nearly an equal number of black and white, agreed to stay and rebuild. Franklin Sharp and several dozen other men, black and white, ranging in age from twenty to eighty, had already agreed to stay. The other men and women, both black and white, sullen and with hate-filled eyes, told those remaining to go to hell. They left, the blacks in one group, the whites in another, each looking for their own peculiar version of utopia on earth.

"What do you suppose will happen to them, Ben Raines?" Franklin Sharp asked.

"Oh, they'll seek some isolated spot and squat, and there they'll fester in their own hatred. Others like them will find them and they'll grow. In numbers, not in mentality. Someday in the future the Rebels, or the organized law of that time will have to go in and fight them. Some people change, others don't. Those that don't take their hate to the grave."

"You should teach, Ben Raines," the old man said.

"I'm too much of an arch-conservative to teach, Franklin."

"Oh, I don't think so, Ben Raines. You are somewhat of an enigma, to be sure. But I have doubts that you even know exactly what you are. Except for being the man who rose out of the ashes of destruction and is attempting to pull a nation back together. You are most definitely that."

"But am I right or wrong, Franklin?" Ben asked.

"Only the writers of history can be the judge of that, Ben Raines. We will be no more than dust in a lonely and forgotten grave when that question shall be answered." He held out his hand. "Good luck to you, Ben Raines."

White hand shook black hand. "And good luck to you, Franklin Sharp."

The Rebels mounted up and pulled out as engineers and doctors and road-builders and others from Base Camp One pulled in.

Ike had radioed in. All resistance in Texas had been crushed by the Rebels and their multinational allies. Hoffman and Brodermann had slipped out, that had been confirmed.

"We'll have to fight them again," Ben said, as the convoy rolled westward toward Arkansas and Thermopolis's command, dug in deep in a mountain.

None of Ben's team had to ask where Hoffman would recruit his army. They knew. From the hundreds of thousands of malcontents scattered all over the nation. People of all races who hated Ben Raines and his Rebels and the authority they represented.

"When we get set up tonight, Corrie," Ben said. "Have Ike send out teams all over the nation. We've got to start rebuilding outposts, and this time we'll make them stronger and with more people per post."

"Yes, sir."

"We'll use Jahn's people to start new outposts all over the nation, Beth," Ben added. "And that will keep them widely separated until we can weed out any Nazi's who have infiltrated his bunch," Ben added, knowing, as Jahn had confided in him, that there were hard-core SS people in his group, put there deliberately by Hoffman and Brodermann. Jahn just didn't know who they were. But he had suspicions.

"Jahn might not like that," Jersey said.

"It was his idea," Ben said with a smile. "Jahn wants to live in a free society, where he can enjoy the books he wants to read, newspapers that don't carry the party line, and where he can engage in open, spirited debate. And the man wants to farm his own piece of ground. Some of his staff officers told me Jahn had one of the most beautiful flower gardens they'd ever seen. You just never know about a person."

"Yeah," Cooper said. "Hitler played the harmonica."

"Cooper!" Jersey said.

"It's true! I read it in a book."

"General!" Corrie said, and the urgency in her voice stopped the bantering. "Thermopolis is under heavy attack. He's holding, but says he can only hold out for another twenty-four hours at most."

Ben lifted a map. "We roll all night, change drivers every two hours. Corrie, tell the trucks pulling the artillery to catch up when they can. Who is attacking Therm?"

"Therm says he doesn't have the faintest idea. But they're throwing everything but the mop bucket at him."

"Tell him to hang on. We're on the way."

TWELVE

The convoy bulled their way through the night until about midnight, when the skies opened up and began a torrential rain on them; a hard rain that slowed the convoy down to a careful creep. The roads were in horrible shape anyway. After years of neglect, they were full of ruts and holes and places where entire sections had been washed out by flooding. Scouts had gone racing ahead, bouncing over, around and through the holes and sometimes leaving the road altogether, driving in the ditches and in fields, doing their best to stay ahead of the convoy.

Just about the time the rain slacked, the drivers pulled over for a shift change and Ben took the wheel.

"Oh, shit!" Jersey muttered. "Here we go. Hang on, people."

"I heard that," Ben said, and roared ahead.

"I've lost contact with Therm," Corrie said.

"We don't have far to go now," Ben spoke over the roar of the engine.

The Hummer Ben was driving soon overtook the Scouts, and Ben pushed the advance party hard, staying right on the bumper of the last Scout vehicle. Finally, Ben spun the wheel, raced around the Scouts, and took the lead. Behind him, the convoy picked up speed, staying with Ben.

After an hour of sliding around hilly curves on the rain-slick old highway, with Ben's team holding on to anything they could grab, they sped past the old county line sign and were within a few miles of Therm's HQ. Ben slowed, then pulled over to the side of the road. Ben and team got out.

"Try it now, Corrie," Ben said.

"I have them, General."

"Give me the mic. Therm! This is Eagle. What's your status?"

"Grim." The sound of gunfire was sharp. "Where are you?"

"Within spitting distance. What are we looking at?"

"Several thousand. We now believe they're a combination of Hoffman's Blackshirt troops, right-wing survivalist groups who've kept their heads down until now, and what's left of Hoffman's terrorist groups. They have exhausted their mortar rounds and are attacking with small arms only. We are completely surrounded, Eagle. You ten-four that?"

"I copy, Therm."

Therm was telling Ben that it didn't make any difference which direction he chose to attack from. Just come on.

The COs had run up to Ben's position. "My company will attack from the north," he told them. "Baker will take the south. Charlie take the east. Dog Company swing around and take the west side. When Dog is in position, we attack. Corrie, any word from the Scouts?"

"Coming in now, sir." She listened through her earphones for a moment. "Everything is clear around the attack zone. No surprises for us."

"Let's go 4-F, people," Ben ordered.

Find 'em, fix 'em, fight 'em, and finish 'em.

The Rebels, running without lights, quickly swung into position. The sounds of battle were sharp in the damp night. The rain had ceased and a few stars were beginning to poke through the cloud cover. The storm was moving rapidly off to the east.

"All units in position, sir," Corrie reported.

"Let's do it," Ben replied, and the Rebels moved out on foot.

The terrain was hilly, thick with brush and timber, and the going was gradual uphill, and slow and hard.

"Dog attacking from the west," Corrie said. "Enemy is swinging units around to meet them. They believe our main force is Dog."

"Did Dog encounter any mines, trip-wires, or any other impediments on the way?"

"Negative."

"Tell our people the password word is *Jerry,* response is *Lee.*" When that was done, Ben said, "Put it in gear, people." Then took off at a trot through the timber.

The Rebels crashed into the Blackshirts, right-wingers, and terrorists from the north, south, and east at just about the same time, catching them completely off guard. For a full ten minutes, it was hand to hand combat in the damp and treacherous footing in the darkness of the timber.

Ben slammed the butt of his Thompson into the pale face of a man and then shot him in the chest. Jersey jumped onto the back of a dark shape coming up fast behind Ben and rode the man to his knees. He threw her off and Cooper shot him in the face. Corrie's CAR-15 spat fire and lead and two dark shapes went down screaming in pain. Beth had slung her M-16 and had both hands filled with 9 mm pistols for the close-in work.

Ben saw dark shapes come running through the timber and leveled his old Thompson. The Chicago Piano roared and bucked in his hands. The heavy .45-caliber slugs tore into flesh and splintered bone and knocked the running shapes spinning to the ground.

A man leaped out of the darkness and onto Ben's back. Ben twisted and slung the man off, then kicked him on the side of the jaw with a boot. The man screamed as his jaw splintered and he rolled away, coming up fast to his knees, a pistol in one hand. Ben pulled the trigger on the Thompson and the slugs turned the man's face into a bloody, unrecognizable mess. If the man ever had any real thought processes, they were now spattered on the trunk of a tree.

Ben and team quickly and effectively finished what remained of the counterattack and knelt down on the damp earth to catch their breath.

"Therm says the situation has eased on his position," Corrie panted the words. She caught her breath and then smiled in the night, white teeth flashing against the tan of her face. "Smoot is all right. She crawled behind a foot locker and is still there."

"Dog's smarter than we are," Ben said, snapping a fresh drum into place. "Let's go."

It took the Rebels only a few minutes to break through on all sides and Therm's command poured out of the underground bunkers to join them. The attacking forces faded into the night, leaving behind their dead and wounded.

Ben did not have to order his medical people to see to the Rebel wounded first. They did that automatically, ignoring the pleas from the enemy wounded.

It took Ben a few moments to find Thermopolis. All of Therm's command had returned to their usual manner of dress. Jeans, sweatshirts or T-shirts, headbands, and tennis shoes.

"Are we going to have a love-in?" Cooper asked, casting hopeful eyes toward Jersey.

"Forget it," she told him.

"You're breaking my heart, Jersey."

"You'll get over it."

"Ben!" the voice of Thermopolis reached him.

The two men found each other, shook hands and smiled at one another.

"Good to see you, Thermopolis," Ben said.

"Bastards seemed to come out of nowhere," Therm said. "Those right-wing survivalist types must have been very familiar with this part of the country and linked up with Hoffman's Blackshirts. Then they slipped in small groups at a time."

"Probably part of those we chased out of southern Missouri a while back," Ben replied. "We knew we didn't get them all. Let's get a body count."

If Therm's estimate that he had been under attack by several thousand men was correct, and Ben had no reason to doubt it, the Rebels had broken the backs of that particular bunch. By dawn they had counted more than fifteen hundred dead and wounded. Most of the wounded critically hurt.

One slight confrontation stuck in Ben's mind. Shortly

after the sounds of battle had faded, Therm and Ben had been standing and chatting.

"How about the enemy wounded, Ben?" Therm suddenly asked, after a civilian had walked up, carrying a medical bag and with unspoken questions in his eyes.

"Who is this?" Ben asked.

"Dr. Sessions," Therm said. "He and his wife, who is also a doctor, joined up shortly after we got here. We have the makings of quite a community here."

"I'm glad to hear it," Ben said.

"The wounded, General?" the doctor pressed him. "They are suffering."

"That's their goddamn problem," Ben told the man. "You make sure that my people are taken care of, any civilians who might have been in the area, and then, and *only* then, do you jack around with the enemy. And if they're going to die, you give them a shot to kill the pain and leave them alone. Now, did you hear all that loud and clear, doctor?"

Therm was inspecting the stars. They were quite lovely this night, since the storm had blown clear.

"Help me, Doc!" a man called out. "I took one in the legs."

Cooper walked over to the cammie-clad man. "How'd you like to take one in the head?"

"You got to be kidding!" the fallen man blurted.

"Trust me when I say he isn't," Beth told him. "Shut your damn mouth. You get treated after everyone else."

The doctor's wife had joined the group. Sessions looked first at Ben, then at Thermopolis. "I thought surely you were kidding when you told me about Ben Raines. My wife and I had a good laugh about it."

"You're not laughing now," Therm replied.

297

Sessions looked at Ben. "I don't think I like you very much, General."

"I don't give a damn whether you like me or not. You just treat my people and do it right the first time. Get to it, Doctor."

Doctor and wife left in a huff. Ben looked at Therm. "He'd better learn how we operate, Therm. If he stays here, and if he ever leaves a Rebel unattended to work on an enemy, and that Rebel dies, I'll kill that bastard. Personally."

"I tried to tell him, Ben. I thought I got through. But I shall pass along your latest words."

"Good," Ben said with a smile. "Now let's go get some coffee."

Therm had lost ten of the people who had been with him for years, and eight more had been badly wounded. Fourteen regular Rebels had been killed, and more than twenty wounded.

"I take the blame for this, Ben," Therm said, after they both had slept for a few hours and were now sitting, having a late breakfast.

"Don't," Ben told him. "That would be nonsense. It wasn't your fault. I've read your logs. You had patrols out, Scouts out. You did exactly what any other commander would have done. These things happen. I know you feel bad. So do I. I have a thousand times over the years. And you never get used to it. You just have to learn to live with it." Ben looked around. "Say! Where is Emil?"

Therm laughed. "Leading a recon patrol up in Iowa. You lucked out."

"Regular Rebels are taking orders from Emil?" Ben asked, astonishment in his words. Emil, the little ex-con artist, was liked by everyone. But a leader of men?

"Well . . ." Therm again laughed. "They pretend they take orders from him. Sergeant Mack is with him."

Ben relaxed. Mack would see to it that Emil didn't get in much trouble. "You've got it looking good around here."

"Yeah, I'll have to agree with you. A few of the folks from Mountain Home and surrounding towns came here to settle with us. We're going to have a good place to live here . . . someday," he added.

"Keep the faith, brother," Ben said. "Power to the people and all that."

That really set Therm off in a burst of laughter. He wiped his eyes and said, "Way to go, Ben. Dylan and Baez would love you for that."

"Yeah. I'm sure the three of us would get along famously. Did you know I used to sing a lot of Dylan's songs?"

Therm suddenly stopped smiling. He frowned. "That's not funny."

"I didn't mean it to be funny. I used to be able to cord a guitar pretty damn well."

"You never told me that!"

"Yes, I did."

"You did not! *You* sang protest songs?"

"I didn't consider them protest songs. I just liked them."

"That's incredible!"

"No, it isn't. Where is your guitar?"

"You wait right there. Don't move. I'll get it. This I have to hear personally."

"Fine. I'll be right here." He hurried off.

"I'm leaving," Cooper said.

Jersey lifted her M-16. "If I gotta hear this, so do you. Sit down, Coop."

Coop sat.

"You two are hurting my feelings," Ben told them.

"Has anybody got any ear-plugs?" Jersey said.

Therm returned with a Martin guitar and handed it to Ben. Ben flexed the fingers of his left hand a few times. "You have to realize that I haven't played in years. The tips of my fingers are going to get very sore, very quickly."

"Just a few chords and a few lines will convince me that you're not bullshitting me," Therm replied.

"Oh, ye of little faith," Ben said.

"I'll believe it when I hear it," Therm said.

Ben selected a big triangle pick from the case, hit a few practice chords, cleared his throat a couple of times, and then launched into Dylan's "Subterranean Home-sick Blues."

Ben's voice was deep and husky, but he could carry a true tune and his singing wasn't all that bad. He did a few lines and then went into "It's All Over Now, Baby Blue," and did a respectable job of it.

The look on Therm's face was priceless.

Ben sang a few lines of a dozen songs from the protest days, hitting all the right chords. Then the tips of his fingers started hurting. Ben smiled and handed the guitar back to Therm. "Nice axe, Therm."

Thermopolis said, "Well, I'll be goddamned! You really can pick."

Ben smiled. "Yeah. Thanks. That was fun. Took me back years."

Therm's eyes narrowed and he was thoughtful. "Yeah. Probably back to when you worked for the damned CIA and infiltrated student dissident groups. I'll make a bet that's why you know all those songs."

"You never heard me say that, Therm."

"Oh, well," Therm said with a shrug of his shoulders. "At least you're continuing your habit of constantly amazing me."

"Ike and Dr. Chase are on the way here," Corrie informed them.

"Why?" Ben asked.

"They didn't say."

"ETA?"

"One hour."

Ben looked at Therm. "Did the good Dr. Sessions get over his huff at me?"

"Not really," Therm leveled with him. "But I told him if he wanted to practice medicine, and have drugs available to him, that's the way it had to be."

"And he didn't like that very much, did he?"

"Not at all."

"His wife of like mind?"

"Absolutely."

"You're going to have trouble with them, Therm. I sense it and I'm pretty good at picking out troublemakers. But that's your worry. I'm sure they're both good people. But they've got to be made to understand about the time and place and the hundreds of thousands of people out there who would like to destroy this movement. If you can't get through to them, then whether they stay or go is a judgement call you're going to have to make. And you'll make the right one."

Therm shook his head. "Just think. A few years ago I

301

was a contented hippie, living as one with the land, in my own little commune, and enjoying life."

"And singing protest songs about me," Ben said with a smile.

Therm's eyes twinkled. "You do get right to the truth, don't you, Ben?"

THIRTEEN

Dr. Chase took an immediate dislike to both Dr. Sessions and his wife. He said to Ben: "You would think, after more than a decade of this world being turned upside down, the idealistic views of those two would have been knocked out of them."

"Perhaps that is precisely why they still cling to those views, Lamar," Ben replied. "Forget about them. They'll make it or they won't." He looked at Ike. "Why this trip, Ike?"

"We think Hoffman and Brodermann are holed up somewhere in the northwest. Intell has narrowed it down to that location. They believe that the troops have spread out over a couple or three states, taken wives, probably with children, and settled in while their leaders recruit new members. There has been quite an exodus of sorry-assed people from all over the nation. All heading west."

"What states?" Beth asked, sitting at the table with her notepad.

"Washington, Oregon, Wyoming, Montana," Ike said, looking over at her.

She nodded. "That's almost half a million square miles."

"Did you just add all that up or do you keep those facts in that head of yours?" Ike asked.

Beth smiled sweetly at him.

"And you have a plan on how we might ferret them out?" Ben asked.

"No," the ex-Navy SEAL admitted. "Intell thinks they speak nothing but English, have become solid citizen types, helping all others around them, thereby making themselves a valuable part of a hundred or more communities. And there is not a way in hell we could prove they aren't what they claim to be. And here is something else: Some senior general, a Frederick Rasbach, an uncle or great uncle to Hoffman, apparently slipped out of Texas weeks ago and returned to South America. There, he and his people destroyed all records of the NAL. Right down to the last scrap of paper. Our allies down there report there is nothing left to link anybody with the NAL."

"This General Rasbach?"

"Vanished. He'll probably live out the remainder of his years in some remote part of South America."

"Well, you can bet your boots on one thing: If Wink Payne and Moi Sambura made it clear of Alabama, they're heading that way to join the new movement. Shit!" Ben added.

"One conflict after another," Therm said softly. "It just never ends. I swear to God, I don't see how you people have kept your sanity all these years."

Ben looked at him. "By not just believing that we're in the right, Therm. But *knowing* we're right."

"I could argue that, Ben, but I don't feel like it right now. So what are you going to do?"

"Try to stop the flood of crud and crap from joining up with Hoffman."

"And how do you propose to do that, Raines?" Lamar Chase asked.

Ben smiled broadly and winked at Jersey, sitting across the room. She knew immediately something big was in the works, and muttered under her breath, "Oh, shit!"

"Why, Lamar," Ben said. "By doing what I do best. Going out and getting into an argument."

Knowing that Ben would not be dissuaded, Ike offered only a token verbal resistance, and quickly gave that up. Chase just cussed for a few minutes, then set about adding to the medical personnel going with Ben.

Then he said he was going with Ben.

"What?" Ben shouted.

"You heard me. And don't shout. There is nothing wrong with my hearing."

"Why, you old fart! You'd get in the way."

Lamar smiled sweetly. Very sweetly. Ben braced himself. "I don't go," the chief of medicine said. "You don't go. It's just that simple."

"That's blackmail, Lamar!"

"You damn right it is. Pure and simple. Now what is your answer?"

"Oh, all right. But I don't want to hear a lot of bitching from you about the field."

"Me? Complain?" Chase attempted to put a very innocent look on his face. He managed to look like a satyr trying to slip into the back of a church with screwing the organist on his mind. "I never complain, Raines."

"Everybody make sure your boots are laced up tight," Ben called. "The shit is getting deep around here."

"I resent that," Chase said.

"Get your duffle packed, Lamar," Ben told him. "We pull out in the morning. Early."

Lamar started to say that he'd be up before Ben. But he checked that. Nobody got up before Ben Raines.

"Therm," Ben called. "You're sure Emil is still up in Iowa?"

"Right. The extreme eastern part. I spoke with him last night."

"Good. Keep him up there and out of trouble. We'll head for the Kansas-Colorado line and start stretching out. Corrie, have our people in Texas and Oklahoma stop any westward movement. They know the types to stop and turn around. Have Buddy, Dan, and Jackie start moving their battalions north. We'll all intersect . . . here," he pointed to the map. "And I want full battalion strength. Make sure they double the artillery that normally travels with each battalion. We don't have any way of knowing how many of the crud and crap have migrated west to join Hoffman—probably thousands, the way those bastards network—but we can damn sure put a stopper in the bottle. We're out of here in the morning. 0500 hours."

"How does he know which types will join with this Hoffman," Dr. Sessions asked Therm. "Does he think he possesses some magical powers?"

Therm ignored the sarcasm. "He knows. Believe me, he does."

"That's impossible!" the doctor snorted.

"I thought so too. Until I spent some time with him. He's a very unusual man."

"I'm sorry, Thermopolis. But I have to disagree. He's a right-wing savage. My wife can't stand to be around him and quite frankly, neither can I. As gentle a man as you are, I find it incredible that you are a willing part of the Rebel movement."

Therm smiled. "Ben Raines is a walking contradiction, Doctor. That's what he is. And hard-headed as a goat. But if this nation is ever to be whole, he's the man who'll do it. Five years ago, you would have had a most difficult time convincing me of that. But I believe it now."

"If he doesn't kill half the population first."

Therm looked at him and then shocked the doctor and astonished himself when he said, "Did you ever consider that perhaps half the population might need killing?"

Therm walked out to the long lines of vehicles grumbling and snorting and farting in the predawn darkness. He knew he'd find Ben at the head of the column.

The two men stood shoulder to shoulder for a silent moment. "Dr. Sessions and wife are considering leaving us," Therm broke the silence.

"His option." Ben didn't give a good goddamn what the doctor and wife did.

Thermopolis smiled in the darkness. He knew how Ben felt and he pretty much felt the same way. At first, he and Dr. Sessions and wife had gotten along well. But Thermopolis had been too long with the Rebels. He had learned that the Rebels did not crave war; they were not bloodthirsty savages, but rather just flesh and blood and caring and feeling men and women who had a very ugly job to do, knew that there was no one else around to do it, and so were doing it. Every army throughout history has drawn its share of homicidal maniacs, and the Rebels were no exception. But they were always quickly discovered and booted out. Many of the Rebels were family men and women, whose spouses were the home guard back at Base Camp One. To a person they longed for the war-days to be over. But until that day, they would fight.

As for the new doctors, to put it bluntly, they were getting on Thermopolis' nerves.

Standing by Ben, he said as much.

"Run them off," Ben told him. "It's your command."

"We need them."

"Then put up with them, Therm."

"Goddamn it, Ben! Everything is black and white to you. Life isn't that way."

"It is if that's the way one chooses to see it," Ben replied, hiding his smile.

"Shit!" Therm said, and stalked off. He stopped and turned around and yelled, "You are a very exasperating man, Ben."

"Right," Ben called.

"You be careful out there."

"Will do."

Ben made his slow walking tour of the column. Heavy weapons had been beefed up, with the battalion carrying nearly twice the artillery they normally carried. Each squad carried an additional heavy machine gun and mortar. More M249s had been assigned to each squad, giving each squad awesome firepower. Any band of outlaws or malcontents who attacked this unit would be in for a very unpleasant surprise.

"Let's roll," Ben said, climbing into his Hummer. "Head west, Coop."

Ben and battalion left Therm's HQ and headed west, toward the Oklahoma state line. Long before they reached the Arkansas' western border, they cut north, up toward Missouri. For the first several hours, their journey was uneventful. They saw many people; more than most felt they would. But the people showed no more than a passing interest in the long Rebel column. Ragged kids watched with more interest than the adults, looking at the towed artillery and the tanks that rumbled along the old roads. The kids grinned and waved at the Rebels. Most of the adults did not. Soon, the Rebels contented themselves matching the civilians' unfriendly looks stare for stare.

"What the hell's wrong with these people?" Jersey asked. "They act like . . . well, I don't know what the hell they're acting like. Stuck up, I guess."

"They don't need us," Ben replied. "So they think. They've lived isolated for years and like it that way. Intell said there were a large number of religious fanatics beginning to surface all over the country. Many of them accepting what has happened as God's will. Let them think what they want. I don't give a damn about the adults. It's the kids that bother me. They're being denied medical care because of the beliefs of their parents and that's wrong."

Ben stopped it there. He just didn't know what to do about the kids. General Jahn and his people would take as many as they could. When they could handle no more . . . ? Well, Ben didn't like to think about that. Ben knew there would be thousands more kids, just like these, in the years to come. The Rebels would try to help the little ones. But the Rebel homes were already very nearly overwhelmed.

The Rebel column hit a stretch of country where they saw no humans. No signs of life except for plumes of smoke, coming from homes or camps set well back off the road.

"They don't want any part of us," Cooper said, gesturing toward the smoke. "It's gonna be like I read in books written before the Great War. The haves and the have nots. Many of those people will begin to see what we have, and then look at what they don't have, and they'll revolt."

"Yeah," Jersey said. "And what makes me mad is they'll blame us for what they don't have. I read those books too, Coop. They don't want to work for anything. They want someone—meaning us—to hand everything to them. Piss on them."

Ben smiled secretly, letting them talk. There were no free rides in the Rebel society. Everybody who could work, did so. Refuse, and you were kicked out and nobody gave a damn what happened to you. Those people who lived in the camps and houses where the smoke was originating could step forward and join the Rebel movement, and they would be welcomed. But if they expected a free handout, they were sorely wrong. And if any group tried to take by force what the Rebels had, they would die. There were no pseudosociological excuses here. The Rebels did not give a damn for color or how a person was raised. One was either a part of the Rebel movement, or one was out in the cold. As Therm had pointed out: the Rebel philosophy was black and white, with no gray in the center. And until conditions returned to some sort of normalcy, that was the way it had to be.

"Order everybody to button up and make certain all body armor is on," Ben told Corrie. "This is sniper country. And we are not the best-loved group of people in the world."

"Putting it mildly," Beth said drily.

"Scouts report a large number of people, men, women, and children, moving west on Highway 160," Corrie said. "Estimated six or seven hundred of them, four or five to a vehicle. Too many for the Scouts to stop."

Ben lifted a map. "We're almost at an intercept point. Tell the Scouts to keep them in sight and us informed. As soon as we're in position, have the Scouts fall back and join us. Step on it, Coop. Corrie, tell the tankers and supply vehicles to catch up with us."

The column reached the intercept point and set up roadblocks. The Scouts joined the main body and reported verbally. After the report, Ben stood in the center of the highway, cradling his Thompson. He waited for the first forward units of the civilian column. He felt he knew what he would initially see, and he was not disappointed.

Main battle tanks, Dusters, and APCs were behind him and on both sides of him, forming a U-shape, vehicles staggered, with all guns pointing toward the east. Rebel units had taken up defensive positions all around Ben and his personal team. It was quite an impressive sight. And the sight was not lost on the rattletrap cars and trucks that soon came chugging and rattling up the road, many of them belching smoke. Ben could see that only about one out of every three vehicles was in fairly good shape.

From hidden vantage points, Scouts reported in. "Kids are all at the rear of the column. Only armed men and women at the front half of the column."

"Millions and millions of spare parts all over the nation," Jersey said, disgust in her voice. "New cars and trucks everywhere, and these clowns show up driving this crap."

"Dr. Sessions and his kind say we should pity these people, Jersey," Ben said with a smile.

"Sessions and his kind haven't been out here fighting these sorry types for years," she retorted. "He'll get a bullet up his butt one of these days and that might change his mind."

"You really believe that?" Cooper called from the other side of the road.

"Hell, no," she said. "It hasn't proved true very often in the past."

The convoy of movers stopped several hundred yards from the roadblock.

"Give me that bullhorn," Ben said.

A man wearing two pistols got out and stood on the cracked old highway. "What's the trouble here? We're not lookin' for no fight, mister."

"You won't have a fight if you just turn those jalopies around and head on back where you came from."

"You just ain't got the right to tell us where we can or can't go."

"I've got over twelve hundred heavily armed Rebels that says I can," Ben's voice boomed over the yards between them. "You people just turn around and head on back where you came from and there won't be any trouble. But I can assure you of this: you are not going to go west to join Hoffman and his Nazis."

The man waited just a couple of heartbeats too long before he replied. "What's that you say? Hell, I ain't never heard of nobody called Hoffman."

"His face is flushing," Beth said, looking at him through binoculars.

"Mister," Ben said flatly. "You're a liar."

The man opened his mouth to return an angry protest. He bit off the protest as his eyes swept the hundreds of rifles pointing at him. "We got a right to choose the type of government we want to live under, Ben Raines. And yeah, General, I know who you are."

"The Nazi movement will not flourish in this country, mister," Ben told him. "Not now, not ever."

"We got a right to live decent!" the man shouted, his anger boiling over.

"Who is stopping you from doing that?"

"You are, you son of a bitch!"

"How?"

"By forcin' us to live under rules that we don't want to live under. That's how."

"And you think Hoffman will be an improvement, right?"

"It'll damn sure be better than the rules you people enforce, that's for sure."

"Boy, has somebody fed him a line of crap," Jersey said.

"Teams are attempting to flank us," Corrie said. "Left and right."

"This guy's going to open the dance any second now," Ben replied. "Get ready to roll for the ditches."

He lifted the bullhorn. "Nobody is forcing any of you to live under Rebel law, mister."

"That's shit!" The man started to lift a hand.

"Don't do this, Roy!" a man's voice called out from among the movers' vehicles. "Hear him out."

"Shut up, Tom!" the spokesman said, turning his head. "How come you and your people want to argue with me every step of the way?"

"Because you're wrong!"

"Mister," Ben spoke through the bullhorn. "Call back your teams trying to flank us. They haven't got a chance."

The man's hand shot up into the air. "Now!" he screamed. "Kill the bastards. All of them."

Ben and his teams dropped to the old road and rolled to the shoulders, then behind APCs. The Rebels opened fire. They just got out of the line of fire as the main battle tanks and Dusters opened fire with cannon and heavy machine guns. For several hundred yards eastward, the lines of cars and trucks erupted in a seemingly endless wall of flame as the gas tanks exploded. Parts of vehicles and pieces of humans were sky-rocketed into the air by the thunderous explosions.

Ben came to his knees, lifting his Thompson to fire, but lowered it when he saw there was nothing to fire at. The Rebels had kept their fire away from the last half of the column, in order to spare the women and kids. Those women had now grabbed up their kids and were running for the safety of the fields, left and right of the road and the inferno. Bodies and pieces of bodies were sprawled in death on both sides of the old highway. Only a few were moving and moaning in pain.

"Cease fire," Ben called. "Shut it down. It's over."

The movers had been able to fire only a few rounds before the Rebel wall of death collapsed on them. Ben lifted the bullhorn to his lips. "Stand up with your hands empty. Do it, people."

Slowly those movers still alive—most of them to the rear of the column—began getting to their feet. All were careful to keep their hands in plain sight, without weapons. Many held their hands over their heads.

Cooper lowered binoculars. "They're complying, General. All up and down the line."

Ben lifted his own binoculars. He could see plainly the shock on some faces and the open anger on others.

"How's it feel to be the most hated man in all America, Ben Raines?" a woman screamed out of the thick smoke.

"Hate me all you like, lady," Ben muttered. "You're at the end of a long line."

FOURTEEN

The badly shaken survivors of the attack were gathered up and placed under guard. A man was brought to see Ben. Ben sat on a camp stool on the front lawn of an old home, under the shade of a huge tree. The home had been a nice one, made of native stone. Ben looked at the man with a bloody bandage around his head.

"What in the hell is the matter with you people?" Ben asked. "Why would anybody in their right mind want to join the Nazi party?"

"I really didn't. Believe that, or not. It's the truth. Roy and his bunch convinced us to come along. That was me you heard holler for Roy to hear you out."

"But you went along with him."

"Yes, I did. We did. I wanted to see this Hoffman. See if he was as bad as you people made him out to be."

"He is," Ben said. "Believe me. Ask some of the Spanish people I have in my battalion. Ask them what he did to their people. That is, if you have no objection to speaking with people of different backgrounds."

"I'm not a racist, General. Never have been. But I'm

old enough to remember quotas and giveaway programs for minorities, and I'm dead set against them."

"So am I. So why are you opposed to joining us?"

"I don't like what you teach in your Rebel schools and your laws are too damn harsh. You have too many rules and regulations for a man to have to follow."

Ben studied the man. "What is your name?"

"Tom Riley. I was born in Kentucky, thirty years ago. I have never been in trouble with the law in my life. I was raised to respect the law."

"The law is what we represent, Tom. Yet you refuse to join us. Tell me, why are you so afraid of your children being educated?"

Tom Riley looked around him. He saw Rebel doctors and medics taking care of the wounded. Other medical personnel were seeing to the needs of the mover children. "Nice of y'all," he said, a wistful note in his voice. "We had us a doctor once. Outlaws came and took him to care for some wounded they had. Then they killed him. I found the body. He'd been tortured. You folks are well-organized," he added, almost as an afterthought.

"You're welcome to join the movement, Tom."

Tom Riley sighed heavily. "Maybe it's time. I guess it is. We've been on our own for years. Me, and those seventy odd families who sort of follow my direction. Even though we don't agree with a lot of what you do, General Raines, you folks put others in a hard bind." He tried a smile. "Sure, you'll leave us alone to live the way we choose. But when you say alone, you really mean alone. No help of any kind. Our kids subject to being taken from us. That's blackmail, General."

"It sure is," Ben agreed cheerfully. "Tom, let me try

to explain something to you: this old planet has taken quite a beating over the last few centuries. Now, what is left of the population has a chance to give something back. You can either be a part of that, or you can sit back and do nothing except complain. The Rebels have set aside hundreds of thousands of acres for the animals to live free and wild, as God intended them to do. We will never cut timber or build homes in those areas. We will allow no hunting in those areas.

"We still don't have a clear idea how much of the population we've lost. We're constantly having to revise figures. But we believe there is room for all of God's creatures. There was before the Great War, but Americans were just too shallow and greedy to give much thought to God's lesser creatures—and there is still a lot of spirited debate among the Rebels as to just who is the lesser of the creatures—us or the animals.

"You say you don't like what we teach in our schools. Do you even know what we teach? Probably not. So I'll tell you. We teach reading, writing, math, and keeping one's body in good shape. Every child who is capable of engaging in physical training gets eight to ten hours of that per week. But we really don't give a damn who can throw a baseball or football the farthest, or dribble a basketball better than others. What is put into a child's mind is what we're concerned about. It's senseless and useless to have a highly motivated teacher put something in a child's head during the day only to have it removed by stupid parents when the child gets home. Our children are taught respect for the land, the animals on it, and the people who are trying to rise out of the ashes of war. For those who choose not to take part in the rebuilding, they can, quite frankly, go straight to hell. Do I make myself clear, Mr. Riley?"

Tom Riley looked back at the twisted carnage on the highway, still burning and smoking. He looked at the rows of dead laid out in the fields, ready for mass burial. He looked at the Rebels, tough and capable and well-fed and in the peak of physical conditioning. He nodded his head. "Oh, yes, General. You're quite clear on that matter."

"Fine, Tom. You and your people can join us and be a part of that rebuilding, or you can fight us, and most of you will die. It's all up to you."

"Can I take your offer up with those who sort of look to me as their leader?"

"Certainly. I want you to do that."

Tom Riley and his people agreed to return to Kentucky, and after being resupplied by the Rebels, they pulled out. Teams of Rebels would meet them back east, to assist in the setting up of an outpost. Most of the outposts of the Rebels had been destroyed by Hoffman's terrorist teams, with all of the Rebels having lost good friends to Hoffman's vicious and twisted philosophy, so it was all back to square one for Ben and the Rebels. Nearly everything they had physically accomplished over the long bloody years, Hoffman and his people had destroyed.

But starting over was nothing new for the Rebels. They'd been doing that for years. The Rebels just resigned themselves to do it and did it.

The Rebels pulled out the following morning and linked up with the battalions of Buddy, Dan Gray, and Jackie Malone. The Rebels began stretching out, south to north, and setting up roadblocks on every highway leading west. They were fully aware that they could not possibly stop all western movement, but they could block a large percentage of it. Ben ordered helicopter gunships to join them and had light fixed-wing aircraft up as eyes in the skies.

Recon was reporting a massive movement from the east, many of the groups well-armed and spoiling for a fight with anybody who stood in their way of joining the new Nazi movement.

"I guess we now know what all the people we couldn't account for were doing all these years," Dr. Chase said to Ben at a staff meeting. "Practicing Nazism."

"And now their great savior is calling on them to rise up and fight," Dan Gray added. "Hoffman," he spat out the last.

"Yes," Ben agreed, and then smiled. "But they've got one hell of a mountain to climb before they can join Field Marshal Hoffman. And that mountain is us."